DARIA LAVELLE is a speculative-fiction writer. Born in Kyiv, Ukraine, and raised in the New York metro area, her work explores themes of identity and belonging through magic and the uncanny. Her short stories have appeared in *The Deadlands, Dread Machine* and elsewhere, and she holds degrees in writing from Princeton University and Sarah Lawrence College. She lives in New Jersey with her husband, children and goldendoodle, all of whom love a great meal almost as much as she does. *Aftertaste* is her first novel.

darialavelle.com

Praise for *Aftertaste*

'A fun romp through New York's restaurant scene and the world of the undead' *Sunday Times*

'A masterful debut with a highly original concept that will pull you in and keep you hooked until the very last page . . . an exceptional novel about hunger, grief, love and learning to let go' *Woman & Home*

'Food, memory and a quest for closure drive this piquantly inventive debut . . . part ghost story, part gastro romance . . . a Russian gangster, a psychic and lashings of bittersweet humour complete Lavelle's moreish recipe' *Mail on Sunday*

'An amalgamation of hypermodern satire, slushy romance and savvy cultural allusion that is as vigorously brought together as its lead character's recipes . . . the novel is seasoned with plenty of imagination, pathos and novelty; it pulls together familiar elements of romance and the supernatural, adding a dash of Anthony Bourdain-style bullishness and a pinch of Lavelle's own authorial smarts' *Guardian*

'The much anticipated darkly comic debut about food, ghosts and the New York culinary scene' *Vogue*

'*Aftertaste* is simply one of those books everyone's going to be talking about' *Radio Times*

'There's Stephen King in this novel's ancestry, in style as well as scares . . . Lavelle's writing pounds with bada-boom dialogue and the kind of adrenaline found in an over-heated kitchen during service' *Irish Times*

'Brilliantly constructed and wholly original, *Aftertaste* is like no novel you've ever tried before. It's much more than your usual dish – it's a whole literary tasting menu. Packed with ghosts, romance, fine dining and the mob, it will leave you stunned, thrilled and totally satiated' Julia Phillips

'*Aftertaste* is a wondrous work where the culinary transcends the ordinary. Lavelle's debut of grief, memory and loss is deftly and satisfyingly layered' Kevin Jared Hosein

'A decadent debut that marks the arrival of a sparkling new voice. Dark and delicious, sincerely moving and at times laugh out loud funny, a heady, bittersweet, beautiful novel about life and death, grief and closure, passion and hunger. A must-read' Rachel Harrison

'*Aftertaste* is a breathtaking novel. Combining the grit of the restaurant world with the magic of the afterlife, Daria Lavelle perfectly blends unexpected ingredients into a book you'll want to savor. It's a story about grief that's filled with humor, warmth and astounding creativity, and I already can't wait to read it again' Laura Hankin

'This is a terrific book. *Aftertaste* offers the glories of food and cooking – all the yes-chef details we now love – in a cool, brilliant and suspenseful novel whose spec-fic plot wants to talk about the mysteries of sense-memory and death. I could not put it down' Joan Silber

'A raucously witty and entertaining novel. This expertly crafted, suspenseful tale is seasoned with a perfectly judged amount of the supernatural. The genuinely heartfelt, touching moments elevate Lavelle's writing to a level that is nigh on impossible to put down. Meanwhile, the lavish culinary descriptions are a real danger – do not read on an empty stomach!' Leo Vardiashvili

'Food lovers will find a huge amount to enjoy here, as will anyone who enjoys ghost stories with a twist' *Crack*

'Debut author Daria Lavelle has distilled the tension of "The Bear" with the descriptive floweriness of *Perfume: The Story Of A Murderer*, then played with snappy, pacy prose and fascinating psychology . . . a fun, thoughtful exploration of grief, love and the nature of hunger. Feast upon its pages' *SFX*

Aftertaste

DARIA LAVELLE

BLOOMSBURY PUBLISHING

LONDON · OXFORD · NEW YORK · NEW DELHI · SYDNEY

BLOOMSBURY PUBLISHING
Bloomsbury Publishing Plc
50 Bedford Square, London, WC1B 3DP, UK
Bloomsbury Publishing Ireland Limited,
29 Earlsfort Terrace, Dublin 2, D02 AY28, Ireland

BLOOMSBURY, BLOOMSBURY PUBLISHING and the Diana logo are
trademarks of Bloomsbury Publishing Plc

First published in 2025 in the United States by Simon & Schuster
First published in Great Britain 2025
This edition published 2026

A catalogue record for this book is available from the British Library

ISBN: HB: 978-1-5266-8394-6; TPB: 978-1-5266-8398-4; PB: 978-1-5266-8399-1;
EBOOK: 978-1-5266-8397-7; EPDF: 978-1-5266-8396-0

2 4 6 8 10 9 7 5 3 1

Typeset by Integra Software Services Pvt. Ltd.
Printed and bound in Great Britain by Clays Ltd, Elcograf S.p.A.

To find out more about our authors and books visit www.bloomsbury.com
and sign up for our newsletters
For product-safety-related questions contact productsafety@bloomsbury.com

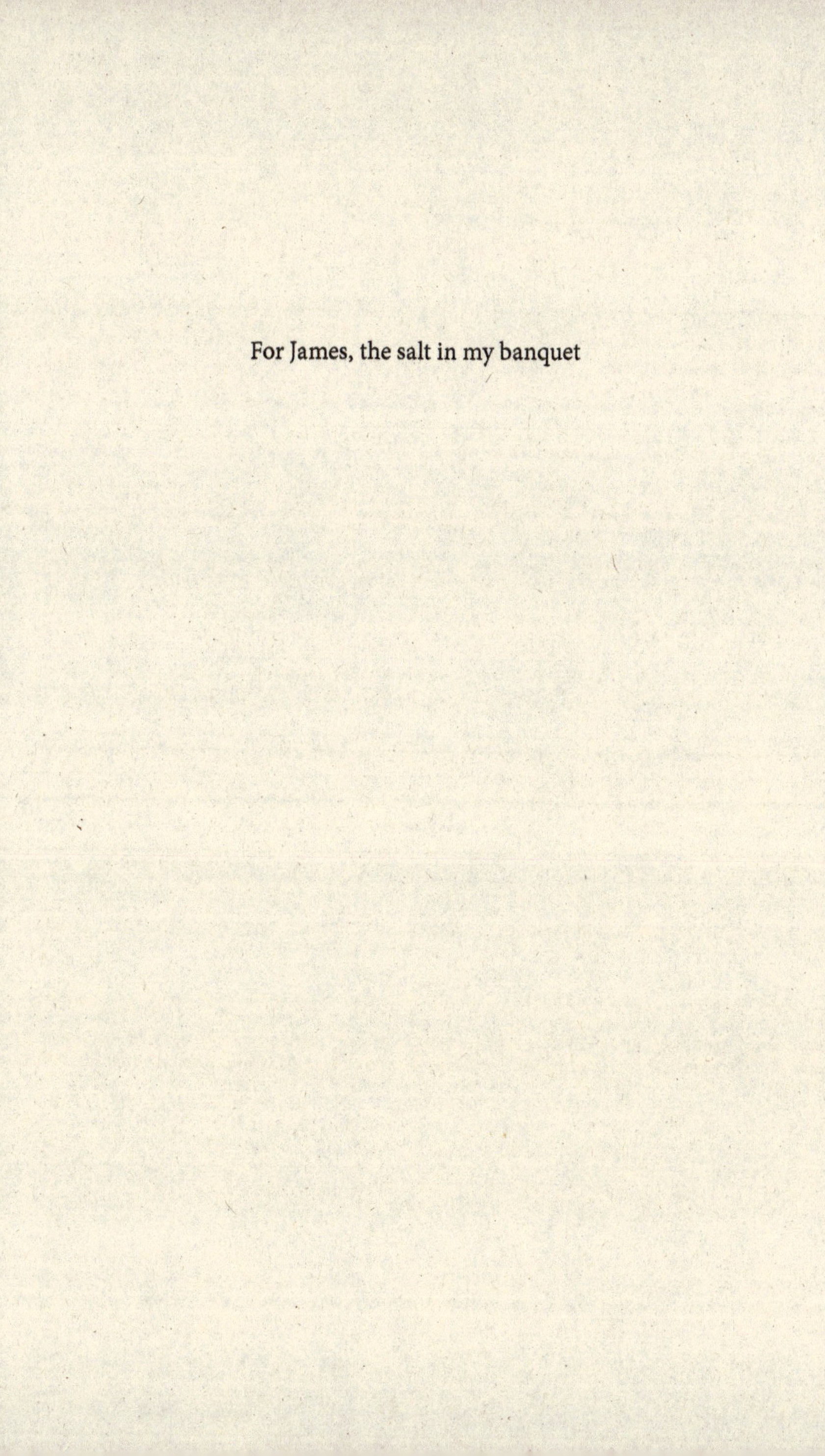

For James, the salt in my banquet

Mouthfeels

My father died when I was young.
That is the central tragedy of my life.
But his spirit never left me, and that may
be the defining miracle of my life.

Eric Ripert
32 Yolks

Bitter

THE FIRST TIME Konstantin Duhovny tasted something he hadn't actually eaten he was eleven, seated on the edge of the public pool in Brighton Beach, his heels churning grey water into foam.

He was watching the backs of the other boys—the ones he was supposed to be swimming with, but who never invited him, even out of politeness, into their circle—as they splashed about, showing off handstands and lung capacities, spouting chlorinated water a foot into the air like porpoises.

He watched them all afternoon—Mitya and Sasha and Misha K. and Misha B. (whom they kept calling Bear because of the thick, black hair up and down his back)—until, one by one, their fathers finished their waterlogged *Russkaya Reklamas*, scratched their nipples through threadbare white undershirts, and peeled their pasty bodies from the rubber loungers, signaling quitting time.

Kostya had come chaperoned by his cousin Valerik—not his real cousin, but the teenage son of Tetya Natasha, not his real aunt but an acquaintance of his mother's—who had promptly dumped him when his girlfriend whispered something about a kissing booth at the boardwalk nearby.

Don't you move, Valerik had hissed at Kostya. *I'll be back.*

That had been two hours ago.

As the last boy, Mitya, raised the handle of the chain-link fence, Kostya felt himself blister with jealousy. There was no one to ferry him home, just like there had been no one to slather sunblock onto his back—which he could already feel was red and tight and burnt—and just like there would be no one to teach him how to talk to these boys in a way that made it clear that he was one of them.

But then, of course, he wasn't one of them. *Their* fathers were alive.

He kicked faster at the water, kicked violently, kicked at the fathers and sons, kicked at the great cavity of longing inside himself, this way of missing someone, missing them desperately, missing every part including those he'd never known, a pocket so deep he thought that if he could only reach inside of it, worry its lining long enough, break through it to the other side, to where empty could grow full as a belly round with food, he might just find what he was looking for.

Right then, something traveled across his tongue, and Kostya stopped kicking. It coated the inside of his mouth, thick as paste, the taste—the uneaten taste—overpowering. It was savory, salty, the texture mealy, slightly sweet and fatty, something tart, barely, and then, at the tail, in the back of his throat, bitter, *bitter*, blooming like a bruise. Good, but also bad, just a little bit like shit. He wondered briefly whether one of the boys had found a way to make him ingest a turd—it seemed the sort of thing that boys with fathers could do to a boy without one—but just as quickly, the sensation vanished. Kostya smacked his lips, trying to call it back, but there was nothing left now, only a warmth spreading slowly across his tongue as he choked back tears.

It was only in the absence of the taste that he suddenly recognized what it had been.

Chicken liver, sautéed onions, fresh dill garnish, squeeze of lemon. Pechonka.

His father's favorite dish, according to his mother, who invoked it infrequently and had stopped making it after he died. Kostya had never tasted *pechonka*. He just knew, like an instinct, like another sense he'd only now become conscious of, that the ghost of that dish—not its taste, but its aftertaste—had just been inside of his mouth, spirited there by the person who most longed to taste it again.

Salty

BEFORE THAT, TWELVE months prior.

A Tuesday. Hot. Summer, simmering.

Kostya's dad tying a revolting tie, standard issue from the Metropolitan Transit Authority.

Kostya glanced over at him from the kitchen—he was always in the kitchen then—standing in one sock before the refrigerator, the door agape. He'd been there long enough to make the kefir sweat, beads dribbling down the side of the carton, the motor gasping as the temperature rose. He was studying the contents; his dad had stumped him last time, but not today.

"Close icebox," his father tsked. "You break like this. Spoil produce. Expensive to fix."

"Sorry," Kostya muttered, and swung the door shut with no urgency at all, stealing a last long look at the chilled jars and tins and plastic containers marked in Cyrillic.

Kostya couldn't really read Russian (he was ten, and smart enough, but this was America, not Soviet Ukraine) so he'd memorized how the Russian grocery stores packed their wares, that the *lyulya-kebab* and rice were scooped into Styrofoam boxes; that the pickles—half-sour, full sour, pickled cabbage, brined tomatoes—bobbed gently in opaque plastic quarts;

that the salads—spicy carrot slaw, mayonnaise-thick *olivié*, earth-sweet beet *vinegret*—were contained in small, clear pints with rectangular labels; that the white paper bags growing steadily transparent with grease held meat or sour cherry or sauerkraut or poppy seed *piroshky*, and he peered around the refrigerator shelves, taking inventory. Then he sat down at the small dinette, his hands folded businesslike on the sticky plastic tablecloth.

"I'm ready," Kostya announced.

His father was fussing with the tie and didn't look up.

"*Papa*," he whined, switching to Russian, "*do the game! Give me a taste!*"

Kostya hoped the effort at his native tongue might tip the scales; his dad had spent the last few weeks battling Kostya's aversion to Russian, the language beginning to feel foreign, mealy on his tongue. Kostya just wanted to be like the cool kids in school—American, English-speaking, *normal*—and to fit in, be seen instead of ignored.

Kostya's dad gazed with weary longing at the fridge, then up at the clock over the stove, a frown replacing his momentary consideration.

"Can't today, Kostochka." He sounded truly sorry. "I have new route. Can't be late."

"But, but!" Back to English. "Just *one* time. It'll be quick."

The last time they played their tasting game—his father slipping morsels into Kostya's mouth for him to identify (eyes closed, no peeking)—Kostya had gotten four in a row right (*doktorskaya* bologna, apricot preserves, a buttered radish, a halva cube) and was on the high of a winning streak when his dad fed him an oily piece of fish on the tines of a fork.

"Easy! Sardine!" he'd yelled, triumphant, before he even finished chewing.

"*Nyet!*" his father yelled back, smacking the table with delight, and Kostya opened his eyes in stunned surprise. "Sprats!"

But that had been weeks ago.

"Just *one* time," Kostya repeated now, his voice a donut, glazed.

His dad smiled and kissed him on the head.

"With you is never one time."

They started the game years ago, when Kostya was eight, in the early days of emigration. A way to remind him where he'd come from. To hold heritage in his mouth. To taste their past, an ocean away. It was Kostya's favorite thing, the bright memory he clung to when other kids, American ones, laughed at his ill-fitting clothes, his unfamiliar food, his poor grammar.

"I swear!"

"Kostochka, I must get bus."

Kostya stalked his dad back down the hall and into his parents' bedroom, where he watched him hunt on the nightstand for his name pin—*Sergei Duhovny (Driver #0727)* etched in chintzy gold lamé.

"But Papa—"

His dad sidestepped into the cramped corridor, back toward the kitchen. Kostya tailed him, relentless. He needed this now, needed it badly, needed something good. The day before, on Riegelmann Boardwalk, two boys had walked by the bench where Kostya was eating lunch, not bothering to lower their voices as they appraised his meal, the leftover *zharkoye*—soft-stewed beef in thick brown sauce—in its mismatched Tupperware an affront to the all-American beef franks in their hands. *What a weirdo*, one said to the other. *Can you hear us, weirdo? What's he eating? Looks like diarrhea.*

"*Later*, Kostya. When I come back."

"No," Kostya whined, a petulant pout materializing on his lower lip. "Now."

"*Nyet*," his father repeated firmly. "*Later*."

"There's never a later!"

His father sighed, equal parts exhaustion and apology.

"I must run. I kiss you."

"All you do is work. This is our one thing!"

"Go in your room, Kostya," his father whispered.

But Kostya didn't budge. He was toeing an edge, deciding to leap.

"Mama's right," he spat out. "We should have stayed in Kyiv!"

He'd overheard his mother talking once, in a hushed voice to her sister on the phone. A whole-pack-of-cigarettes conversation.

"Mama? What does she—"

"You'd cook! You'd own a restaurant instead of driving a stupid bus!" Kostya shouted over him. "And I wouldn't be so ashamed."

"Go in your room," his father said, louder, a crackle to his voice like onion skin. "You understand nothing."

He reached for the doorknob.

Kostya's hands formed fists, his nails making crescents in his palm. There was a bad taste in his mouth, a morning mash of unbrushed teeth and anger.

"You brought us to America," he spat out, repeating things he'd never been meant to hear. "Because you wanted to come. Because you only thought about yourself. You didn't think how it would be for me. So go, then; I don't care. *Go to the Devil!*"

It sounded different in English. Better. The way the popular kids said it as they slammed their lockers shut. *Go to Hell.* Still, Kostya felt the power of it course through him, thunder in his chest, a sudden stillness in the room.

His father stopped, his back to Kostya.

"As you say," he said quietly, and slipped through the door, his shoulders sagging with defeat.

If his father had yelled, had punished him, had retaliated in any way, it might have turned out differently, made it easier for Kostya to tell himself, days and months and years later, that his dad had known he hadn't meant it. But the resignation in his father's voice, the obvious pain that Kostya had inflicted on the person he loved most in the world, lanced him like a barb.

Even in the immediate hangover of the moment, he couldn't take his eyes off the door, kept waiting for his dad to come back and forgive him. To fix what Kostya had broken. He told himself not to cry as he tasted the salt of his own tears, like drinking in a sea. It was as if Kostya already knew—the way his father's farewell echoed in his head, the catch in his voice like a tear in time—that it would be the last thing he'd ever hear him say.

Sweet

THREE MONTHS AFTER his dad's death. Konstantin's birthday. Terrible timing.

It was fall, the leaves beginning to bronze, the air to cool, their lives to set into the strange new shape they would mold to now, Jell-O, without him.

There was a knock on the door, which was impossible, because they hadn't had a single caller since the funeral and no one cared that Kostya had turned a year older, or that his mother hadn't risen from her bed in days, or that there was no food in the fridge and precious little in the cabinets.

It was a delivery guy.

Flowers in his hand. A note.

His father had ordered the bouquet in advance, had settled it with the florist, had written out the card just like always, never expecting that he wouldn't be at the door to receive it, to present it to Kostya's mother himself.

The arrangement filled the room with thick, sweet musk. The flowers of his mother's perfume: patchouli, lily of the valley, tuberose. The same blooms his father had given her every year since Kostya was born.

Their scent seeped through the apartment; it marinated the walls. Mama smelled it from her bed and stumbled, disbelieving, into the living room.

When she saw the vase on the table, the small card stapled to it, the handwriting Sergei's—her Sergei's!—she gave a cry.

Kostya had been trying to read the note, struggling to decipher the slanted Cyrillic dashed across the square of card stock. He'd been lured by the recognition of his name—*Костя*—amid the squiggles rendered in his father's hand. But his mother snatched it away and read it and wept like she was losing him all over again, this gift from his ghost a cruel crumb.

She hurled everything into the trash—the card, the flowers, the vase cracking in two against the bottom of the bin. But Kostya couldn't bring himself to lug the can to the curb. It would stay there for weeks, the flowers rotting inside, their stems dissolving into mush, their petals withering brown, the odor indolent, more like death each day.

THAT NIGHT, AFTER he stole the card out of the trash, Kostya also stole a cake.

A Kyiv Torte, hazelnut meringue and thick, chocolate buttercream, from a bakery on Avenue U. He sat on a park bench in the dark and gorged himself on rich frosting, on the crispy crumble of stiff-peaked egg whites, on the way they ground to sweet, white dust between his teeth. He ate with his fingers, the sugar sticking to his skin, chocolate staining the palms of his hands.

It was too sweet after the first few bites, difficult to swallow, but he shoveled scoop after scoop into his mouth anyway, trying to fill something inside. He ate even as his body warned him to stop, and then he ate more, *more*, every morsel in that blue bakery box, everything, *everything*, all at once.

My Sweet, My Vera! the card in his pocket read. *When Kostya was born, my greatest gift, I did not think I could love you more, but like always, you have proven me wrong. Today is Kostochka's celebration, but I celebrate you.*

Thank you for our perfect son, and for your love, and for our lives. More than life itself, S.

Kostya had sounded it out one slippery letter at a time, the words like sugar to a cavity. *My greatest gift. Our perfect son.* He'd never forgive himself for how profoundly he had failed to earn that praise.

Savory

IN THE WEEKS after the *pechonka* at the pool, it happened again.

And again.

Aftertastes appeared in Konstantin's mouth like messages. Different foods each time. More frequent. More intense. The flavors uninvited, haunting the back of his throat.

These hadn't come from his father; they were too different, too foreign. They wouldn't leave him alone.

When he finally grew unsettled enough to tell his mother, to confess how he'd tasted *pechonka* and thought—*known*—that it had come from his dad, he'd been hoping that she might understand. Might reassure him. Part of him was even hoping that this might resurrect her, snap her out of her distant stares and frequent sighs, give her a reason to leave her bed. A year had passed, and she still wore the weight of loss around her shoulders like a stone. Kostya thought that maybe, if he needed her, a *real* need, the kind only she could fill, she might finally decide to set down her load.

Plus, she was uniquely qualified.

Vera Duhovny was the most superstitious person he had ever met. She had talismans and taboos and countless compulsions that she employed to navigate around and over and through life's many wrong turns. She knew never to sweep while a loved one was traveling, how to dispel an evil eye, that you should never gift knives. She greeted guests with bread and salt. She welcomed good spirits and warded off bad. And if she had been unfazed by Kostya's revelation, had heard of this sort of thing, it would have diffused the growing uncertainty that accompanied each new sensation in his mouth.

Instead, when he told her, her face curdled.

He could see it in her eyes—fear, doubt, dismay. She didn't believe him.

She asked him, again and again, to repeat it. To explain.

Only, he couldn't explain. Not what these flavors were, or how he managed to taste them. Not the ease with which he identified their ingredients, like reciting a recipe. Not how he knew—like an expression of terroir on his tongue—that they had come from the Dead.

Instead, he tried again to explain the pool. The boys and their dads. *Pechonka.*

His mother nodded slowly, twice, and sent him to his room to lie down.

Then she called an ambulance.

No one else believed him either. Not the EMT who insisted they bring him in for a psych eval. Not the skinny intake nurse who popped her gum. Not the staff psychiatrist in the children's ward of the Gravesend Psychiatric Center, her pen clicking as she took down notes.

Two weeks, he slept on a white cot with itchy sheets, naked beneath a hospital gown. No socks.

They fed him tablets three times a day, anonymous white tranquilizers in paper cups, the kind kids filled with ketchup in the school cafeteria.

He'd never learned to swallow pills, gagged as he tried, so they watched as he dissolved them beneath his tongue instead. They melted into chalky chunks—bitter, foul—awful enough that he would have thrown them up if they hadn't made him so numb he could barely feel.

The next time the doctor evaluated him, in an office that reeked of Cup Noodles (Beef Flavor), he lied his way out of it. Said that he'd never actually tasted the *pechonka.* That he knew his dad wasn't haunting him. That ghosts weren't even real. That he'd made the whole thing up because his mother had ignored him after his dad died, and he'd been angry, and wanted to scare her. That he took it too far. That he was sorry.

There was a thick satisfaction to the way she believed him, to the way his distortions put her at ease, to the way fiction protected him from the repercussions of the truth. Lying was carving into a roast, and he savored it, sank his teeth into each bite.

He maintained his deception even as another aftertaste spread over his tongue, right there in her lifeless office—her photographs sepia, her plants artificial, her smile placating, never reaching her eyes.

A thick, chargrilled patty—medium-rare, oozing juice. Smear of special sauce. Butter lettuce; beefsteak tomato; white onion, lightly fried. Crinkle-cut pickle chips, Kosher dill. Toasted sesame seed bun.

The air went still around him as he tasted, the edges of the world softening away, the flavors of the Dead more real and alive than anything else in the room.

Sour

YEARS TRICKLED BY, his life fermenting.

HE WAS FIFTEEN, walking home. Fat textbooks slung across his shoulder, pounding into his hip. His stomach clenched and unclenched, a fist. Empty.

His mom had blown the grocery money, traded their neighbor the food stamps Kostya had painstakingly applied for—hours of bureaucratic paperwork—in exchange for six cartons of Virginia Slims. He should have smoked them himself out of spite, or resold them cheap in the school parking lot, but he didn't like the taste, and didn't need any more help becoming a social pariah, thank you very much.

His abdomen moaned as he passed the Russian store—the smell of Rizhsky rye and loops of dry salami such exquisite torture—and the McDonald's—oh God, fries—and stopped at a traffic light on the corner, beneath the awning for the Olympia Greek Diner.

Kostya peered inside long enough to confirm that it was busy, most of the tables occupied, waitresses whizzing in and out of the kitchen. He pushed through the door and beelined to the coffee station, a table between the bar and bathroom that housed pots of coffee and sugar and sweetener and single-serve pods of half-and-half.

He shoved the creamers into his bag, followed by Dominos packets, and—his lucky day—a stack of individually wrapped saltines. Breakfast of Champions.

When he got home, he was so hungry that he dumped it all into a mug, mashed the saltines and sugar and creamer together before he realized that—no! *no!*—the half-and-halfs had turned.

He stared at the concoction, at the white chunks dotting the crackers, at the thin, sour whey pooling in the bottom of the glass.

He was so hungry he ate it anyway.

HE WAS EIGHTEEN.

An adult, technically. He had a job, stocking shelves in a bodega. Had a license, though there was no car to speak of. He could buy porn and fight a war and sign a lease if he wanted. But he still missed his dad like a little kid.

Kostya had always assumed it would get better, but it only got different. His pangs of loss had receded into a numb, ever-present ache, yet every new experience—each minor tragedy or major milestone he wished he could share with his father—soured him, made him feel as if his dad had just died, was dying all over again, like he always would be.

When the kids from school fucked with him at that party, it happened. When he had to convince the social worker that his mom was fine, it happened. When he walked across the stage at graduation, the superintendent mispronouncing his name, it happened. When he had his first drink, cashed his first paycheck, first kissed a girl, it happened. When he nursed his first heartbreak, his first hangover, his string of rejections from colleges and jobs and relationships, it happened, and happened, and happened again.

But that afternoon, when Kostya opened the door to find their landlord, to learn that he had sold their apartment—the last place Kostya had seen his dad alive, had heard his voice, had hugged him—sold it to some new guy who was raising the rent so high they couldn't possibly stay, Kostya had wept, wept unabashedly, ugly-cried. The landlord apologized, said it was nothing personal, said his dad had been a good guy, reminded him of his own father. Kostya had been about to tell him where to shove his platitudes when he felt the puff of air, the flavor materializing in his mouth—*delicate flakes of frozen limoncello, scraped with a fork, spooned into a hollowed-out rind*—and felt, without really knowing how, that the landlord was being sincere. That he really was sorry. That he'd lost someone once and remembered how it ached.

HE WAS THIRTY.

Two decades fatherless, peeled back a year at a time, the segments of a lime. He had another job now—two in fact, both of which sucked. A shitty apartment, and a Craigslist roommate who'd become his best friend. A life, or something like one.

But too often, instead of looking forward, Konstantin found himself looking back.

To when he was ten, waiting at the kitchen table.

Or nine, walking through the neighborhood at dusk, sucking the wet wooden stick of a Popsicle.

Eight, holding both his parents' hands, the thrill in his stomach as they swung him high in the air, Coney Island Cracker Jack lodged in his teeth.

Seven, lying on a patch of green grass, his dad picking wild mushrooms, peeling open their caps to show him inside.

Six. *Six.* The one he always came back to.

A Kyiv park, sunlight overhead, a pouch folded from newsprint weighted on his lap. Full of soft, overripe fruit. Sour cherries, their skin so thin, their flesh the bright red of a bleed.

"*Chereshnya*," Kostya said, placing one into his mouth, the juice squirting down his throat, wonderfully tart.

"*Nyet*." His father shook his head. Smiled. "*Vishnya*."

They came from different trees, he explained. Had different fruit, different pits. His father's grandmother had grown *vishnya* in the countryside of Ukraine, the mottled bush spilling fruit everywhere, smearing the ground with red come summer. Konstantin had never met his great-grandmother, couldn't now that she was dead, but he could almost taste her in this bag, inside each sour cherry.

"One day," his dad told him, "I'll take you there. To see her village, her old dacha. To taste fruit from her tree." He spat a pit into his hand, perfectly beige, sucked clean of flesh. "*Kostochka*," he told Kostya, "a cherrystone."

"Like me." Kostya had grinned.

"Like you," his dad agreed. "My cherrystone. So much waiting in so small a thing."

BUT THE PAST his father promised him was gone.

His future had soured, its possibilities curdled.

Now Kostya kept his secrets, his aftertastes, in the unremarkable present. In a bland, haunted loop. He'd stay that way awhile.

But not forever.

PART TWO

Bitters & Heat

*But when the past is gone, after
the people are dead, after their things are
destroyed . . . smell and taste still linger on,
like souls, ready to remind us. . . .*

Marcel Proust
Swann's Way

Aperitifs

The Konstantin Duhovny Culinary Experience

ALRIGHT, ALRIGHT! Can everybody hear me? Can y'all see me?

Let's just do a little mic check. If you're here for the Konstantin Duhovny Culinary Experience, you're in the right place. Anyone in the wrong place?

. . . .

Okay, nah. That's Food & Spirits, down the block. If you hurry you can make it!

. . . .

Everyone else, we good? Last chance to bail; we got a tight schedule. Let's kick it!

My name's Frankie, but I'll answer to Kosh, Shaun, Shaunessey, Key, Shy, and, of course, Tall, Dark, and Handsome—I see you, ladies!—and I'll be your guide today. Like the name implies, this here's all about the culinary stylings of Mr. Konstantin Duhovny—Kostya to his mom, Bones to his buddies, KD for short.

Now if you're on this tour, I'm guessing you know a little something about what our guy's food can do, and you're itching to try it for yourself, see if all the rumors are true. Well, I'll tell you right now: they're just the tip.

Bones is the real deal—feeds folks body and soul!—and we'll be making our way through his past together, retracing some footsteps, watching his evolution as a chef before we head on over to our grand finale—opening night at his brand-new digs downtown, reservations im-poss-i-ble to get. 'Less you're with me.

Now, I used to work in the restaurant biz—not just in the dining room, but in the actual kitchens, right where the fire is—so I'll get you real up close and personal with what goes down on the line. Matter of fact, I did a stint at Bones's own spot in Hell's Kitchen—we'll hop on over there in just a bit—and that means you're gonna get to hear some stories not one other food tour's got on the menu.

We're about a block away now—anybody got a guess where we're headed?

. . . .

Alright! Get it, girl! Somebody's been doing her homework.

Here's a little history for the rest of you. The Library of Spirits's been around since '02; started out as a mixology school, training up bartenders for the city's best watering holes. Really raising the bar. (Sorry, man. I had to!) It's a tiny little spot—six, maybe seven stools—and it's a speakeasy, so don't wake the neighbors. We get in through this indie bookstore right here. They got one of them trick shelves in back; I'll give y'all a chance to see if you can figure out which book gets you in.

Now our guy didn't make it to The Library till 2016, and he wasn't here to shake or stir. He was up in the back dishwashing, going nowhere fast till this one night, when he mixed a drink that changed everything.

Y'all ready? Get excited. Let's head on in.

Champagne Problems

THE BOOKSTORE IS called Bibliomecca and the book *Fantasmagoriana, ou Recueil d'histoires d'apparitions de spectres, revenans, fantômes, etc.* The book is old and French and horrible, all of which makes it somewhat conspicuous on the shelf of brightly colored, contemporary American fiction. When you compound this with its cracking spine, grubby dust jacket, and the fact that it sticks a solid four inches past the lip of the ledge, it seems rather miraculous that more people don't stumble into The Library of Spirits by mistake.

But then, New Yorkers can be remarkably myopic.

The douchey weekend manager, Kevin, once told Konstantin that Mary Shelley had borrowed liberally from *Fantasmagoriana* when writing *Frankenstein*, but he had never cared enough to confirm that fact. Kostya had no head for fiction, and no stomach at all for ghost stories. He had tasted enough phantom food over the years to hold the conviction that ghost stories had nothing in common with actual ghosts. Their writers had clearly never come in contact with a spirit; if they had, they wouldn't make every ghost into a haunt, some creepy ghoulie come back from the Dead to wreak havoc and incite fear. That was baloney. The ghosts he encountered (if you could call it that) seemed mild mannered, even sentimental.

At least, that's what Kostya inferred from the flavors they left in his mouth:

Poppy-seed piroshky laced with boozy rum raisins, scoop of melting vanilla soft serve, mouthful of watered-down blackcurrant tea. Late April, walking past a funeral home in Sheepshead Bay.

Deep-dish pizza, crust crispy and layered as a croissant, pepperoni and pineapple topping, so hot it burns the roof of your mouth. Two weeks back, riding the northbound Q past Times Square.

Pork dumplings, the wontons deep-fried but eaten refrigerator cold, hint of chive, hoisin, and rice wine vinegar, kick of spicy mustard. Just that morning, stuck in Holland Tunnel traffic on his way to drop off a pallet of cheap vodka for Uncle (not his real uncle) Vanya.

These didn't taste like the throats of people looking for blood. They struck Kostya as nostalgic. Maybe they were hungry, the restaurant options in the Afterlife not quite hitting the spot. Or maybe they just communicated with whatever receiver they had available and his happened to be a tongue. He wished there were a way to ask them, to discover what they wanted him to do with these flavors they kept pushing on him, but the moments were so brief, the tastes so fleeting, that often he barely had time to register what he had been tasting before it vanished without a trace.

Most of the time, the flavors were typical—more dead people than you'd think crave some variety of sandwich—but sometimes they were entirely foreign, hailing from cuisines Kostya hadn't known existed, spices he couldn't have imagined. Even the obscurest tastes would somehow disclose themselves to him, a metaphysical-ethereal-neural miracle that let him intuit the component parts of everything he tasted.

Like the chicken wings smeared with *sambal oelek*, which scorched his throat one night as he traversed Bryant Park by Citi Bike.

Or the warm, heady *ras el hanout*, smothering the beef tagine he got as he handed the rent check to his frowning landlord on the third of the month.

Or the mouth-puckering *amchur* in the *kati* roll that visited him at the Urgent Care clinic, awaiting the results of a strep test (negative).

He'd known the names of those flavors though he didn't know how. He had never tasted them before, had never even seen them on a menu; they were just *there*, identified, companions to the aftertastes, escort ingredients simmering beneath the surface of his consciousness, waiting to be invoked. The bubbling answers to a question.

Too bad it was the wrong question.

Sure, it was nice to know what he was eating, but he'd much rather know why, or who had sent it. What he was supposed to do with it. Without all that, it was just an odd, abnormal quirk, something he'd spent the better part of two decades hiding from people who, once they got a whiff of this thing, would almost certainly insist he be committed (his own mother included).

Not that an institution—or heavy sedation—could stop the aftertastes from coming. Sometimes just hearing about dead people triggered them. Listening to some deceased's name pronounced in reverent tones on the late-night news. Catching an overheard snippet of mournful conversation on the sidewalk. And there it would be: a message from beyond, unfurling on his tongue. Other times, there would be no prompt at all, like that morning: driving bumper-to-bumper and the idiot behind him leaning on his horn and Nirvana screeching on the radio and—*voilà!*—pork dumplings, dead ahead.

Kostya hadn't stopped thinking about them. They'd been good. Like, *really* good. The kind of thing he wished he could taste again. He thought about the filling—it had just a touch of sweetness—across three boroughs as he delivered bottom-shelf booze. He thought about who would have eaten them cold, the wonton skins soggy, as he parked the truck in Uncle Vanya's warehouse in Jersey City (*Vanya's Victuals: Proud Purveyors of Fine Food and Spirits since 1992. Cash Only!*). He contemplated the hoisin and the rice wine vinegar as he rode the PATH back into Manhattan, as he wove through the tourists overrunning Times Square, as he trudged up the steps to his minuscule apartment in Hell's Kitchen. He thought about the banality of the situation—cars, horns, traffic—and about the mad magic—ghosts, real actual fucking ghosts—as he showered, changed, and went back out to work his night shift dishwashing at The Library of Spirits.

And he was thinking about it now as he wiped another glass dry. There were a dozen clean, wet glasses lined up on the bar in front of him, dripping onto the heirloom oak. Probably making water stains.

Kostya selected another and smiled smugly to himself.

He wasn't supposed to be in the front-of-house, and he liked sticking it to Kevin, who was absurdly easy to hate. Kevin wanted Kostya and his stained T-shirts in the back, where he wouldn't interrupt the high-end gentlemen's club vibe he'd crafted, right down to the self-congratulatory cocktail napkins (*Bravo, Old Chap!* in Edwardian Script, without any hint of irony). When Kostya complained about having to wait until the bartenders had a break in service to haul the dirty glasses back to him (which sometimes wasn't until the very end of his shift), Kevin smiled with all his teeth and said he'd be happy to let him out front if he'd look the part, which in Kevin's world meant spending more on a tailored shirt than Kostya made in a week. Kevin was a real piece of New York shit.

Duncan, the Tuesday night bartender, may have been an *SNL* sketch of a Park Slope hipster—tailored vests, Dublin accent, well-oiled beard—but that also made him look like a guy you could trust to pour your twenty-four-dollar apothecary cocktail. But Duncan had bailed when his girlfriend's water broke, so Kostya got upgraded to the bar—*Kostya*, who, in stark contrast to Duncan, looked like he could only be trusted with the kind of schlock you'd pay a buck fifty for from a Port Authority vending machine, and no promises he wouldn't keep your change.

It hadn't always been like that.

Not that he could ever have driven home handsome, but he used to be able to at least idle in the vicinity of serviceable. There was a certain appeal (boyish face; bright eyes; good teeth; dark hair) that had gotten him by in the past, and he'd always felt (even if he never acted on it) that if he just lost the extra weight in his jowls and gut (twenty years and fifteenish pounds' worth of eating his feelings), he'd be a solid six (seven in dim lighting).

But the last few months had been rough, so rough that he really wasn't fit for public consumption: dumped (*yet* again), moping (continuously), ungroomed and unmotivated and seriously unhappy, the weight the least of his issues. His wardrobe (like the T-shirt he wore now—phlegm colored, with Uncle Vanya's sickle-and-shot-glass branding on the chest) had suffered considerably when Alexis, his ex, left him. And his body, grown soft on beer and burgers, had never done well in the standard-issue humidity of Manhattan summers, but had rebelled spectacularly since he'd stopped exercising altogether (coinciding with Alexis's departure and her custody of their dog, Freddie Mercury, whose walks had wholly comprised Kostya's calisthenics). Just now, there were dark rings of sweat migrating down from his armpits, where even the antiest of perspirants couldn't penetrate.

If Kevin were there, he would have murdered Konstantin on the spot, wrung him out with his own dishrag. But Kevin was probably doing lines of coke off somebody's bikini wax in the Hamptons, so fuck him and fuck his rules. Kostya would dry all this right on the bar, in plain sight of anyone with the balls to stroll in and order five minutes before The Library closed, fuck you very much.

OUTSIDE THE BAR, in the stacks of Bibliomecca, a man paced back and forth, casing the spine of *Fantasmagoriana*. He passed its shelf four and a half times before his itchy fingers finally gave in and tugged the book forward. As he watched the bookcase shimmy away from the wall, revealing the dim staircase down to a chamber that smelled like old money and privilege and Scotch—weren't those all the same things?—a wave of relief broke over him.

He'd promised a half-dozen people that he wouldn't drink tonight, and he'd really meant it then, but he didn't mean it now. They must have known, he told himself, that he wasn't good for his word, not on this. Not on the anniversary. So there he was, minutes to midnight, scurrying down the steps to The Library of Spirits, three hundred and five days sober. Or was it three hundred and four?

Didn't matter. He'd have to start the count over again in the morning. If he woke up.

WHEN KONSTANTIN HEARD the click-latch of shelving, his eyes darted up from the highball he was drying, barely believing his ears.

In the six months he'd been doing this job, not one person had shown up past eleven thirty. It was an unspoken rule. Speakeasies weren't like the sleazy sports bars or collegiate watering holes where you could pop in for a single shot of Fireball on your way to your hairdresser's Uber driver's house party in Alphabet City. They were intimate spaces with exorbitant prices and cocktails that begged to be sipped, savored. He was dying to see what kind of person—money to burn, surely—would roll in at five-of only to lay down thirty bucks for a drink they'd barely get to taste. So imagine Kostya's surprise when down the steps came a guy who looked—was it possible?—rougher even than he did.

The man was a rail. Tall. With dishwater eyes shining beneath a ball cap, and a huge, sad Steven Tyler mouth.

"Uh, hey?" he said.

"Hey." It took Konstantin a second to catch himself. "I mean, hi! Hello! Welcome to The Library. Of Spirits."

Steven Tyler's long-lost twin blinked uncertainly at him. "You still open?"

He nodded at the pile of glasses.

"Yup. For the next"—Kostya consulted his watch—"three minutes."

"Cool." He slid a stool from beneath the bar and settled onto it, sniffing once, loudly. Kostya hoped he wasn't getting comfortable; what he needed was some extra sleep before his delivery shift, not a late close because this dulcet brosky wanted a nightcap. "Uh, can I get a Manhattan?"

Oh, here we go.

"Yeah, so . . . I'm not actually a bartender. He had to take off. Family thing. I'm just the dishwasher."

"But you can still make a drink, right?" There was an edge of desperation to his voice.

"I mean, I don't technically have a bartending license—"

"So I didn't get it from you."

"And it might not taste right."

"A risk I'm willing to take! Just hit me. Whatever's easy."

"Okay . . . but I still gotta charge you full price."

The edges of Steven Tyler's enormous mouth twitched. His eyes were fixed on Kostya's hand—the highball glass he was polishing held midair—as if he was willing its movements telepathically toward the booze.

"You okay, man? You don't look so—"

"Just get me a goddamn drink!" He was suddenly shouting, his eyes darting and frantic.

"Chill out, okay? I was just—"

"Now. Now! Before your fucking bar fucking closes and I can't fucking toast to my poor, dead, beautiful wife!"

In the silence that followed, it felt like all the hot air had left the room. Particles of dust danced slowly in the space between them as Kostya and this sad, strange, large-lipped man gazed across the bar at each other, their stares combusting, gunpowder in a long, still moment before everything sparked.

Steven Tyler snatched a wet glass from Kostya's lineup and smashed it on the floor. He shattered another and another, smithereens flashing like lightning. Kostya made a lunge for him, but a familiar puff of air hit the back of his throat, an aftertaste coming on. It happened so quickly, so clearly—like it was as desperate to make it into his mouth as this guy was for a drink—that Kostya froze in concentration.

It was a cocktail.

Light effervescence, slight tang. Champagne? Or, no. Drier. Cava. And gin. Lemon juice. Sweeter than sour. Meyers, maybe. And something floral. Elderberry and . . . and lavender? With mint? Not quite. Something that tasted like this candle his ex used to burn. Patchouli Dreams. Yes, patchouli. Did people even eat that? There was a smear of syrup, too, thick and sweet and tart. A cherry. A Luxardo cherry.

It seemed almost contrived that here they were, in a bar stocked with obscure tinctures and infusions, when someone—this guy's dead wife, surely?—sent through an obscure cocktail made of just such tinctures and infusions.

Kostya could feel an electric tingle in his fingers. He had never before tried making the dishes he tasted. For one thing, though he was a championship eater, he rarely cooked, and for another, it had always seemed taboo, like chanting *Bloody Mary* into a mirror by moonlight. But this aftertaste—this drink, here, in this place—was a provocation as much as a libation. A dare.

Steven Tyler broke another glass.

"Quit it!" Kostya whined, and as the guy wound up to smash another snifter, he blurted out, "She liked Cava, right? Your wife?"

He set the snifter down so slowly it seemed like it might never arrive.

"How did you know that?" he asked, his enormous mouth a thin white line.

"I'm going to make you something," Kostya answered instead. "Sit."

He turned toward the illuminated shelves behind him and selected a number of jars and eyedropper vials. He gathered ice and a shaker. A jigger. A glass. A bottle of Bombay, but then, thinking it over, smacking his lips together although the aftertaste was gone, swapped for Hendrick's. There was an open bottle of Cava in the wine fridge behind the bar, and—Kostya nipped a little taste—it was exactly right.

"I thought you weren't a bartender?"

"I'm improvising," Kostya answered.

Though that wasn't entirely true. Something—someone—was guiding him. He'd always been able to pinpoint the ingredients, but now someone was illuminating the pale memories of the aftertaste for him, showing him exactly what he had to do with them, each step apparent. He layered the ingredients together, concocting the drink from the way it had danced around his mouth: the Luxardo cherry and a half teaspoon of its juice was drizzled directly into the bottom of the glass; the Cava and gin went into the shaker with a single drop of patchouli oil, a splash of St-Germain, and a healthy squeeze from the pipette of the preserved Meyer lemon jar. Konstantin added ice, and shook like he was James Bond.

"A Jack and Diet would've done the trick."

"Shut up," Kostya snapped, struggling to concentrate.

He strained the cocktail into a frosted Collins glass and used a drink stirrer to taste. Nearly there. He pinched a few grains of salt from the well behind the bar and sprinkled them on the drink's surface. He didn't even need to taste it again. His stomach gave a lurch, like a leap over a hill, and he just knew.

Kostya slid the glass across the bar.

Steven Tyler lifted it slowly to his lips, hand trembling, and closed his eyes.

"What's it called?" he asked.

Kostya thought a moment. "A Spectral Sour."

EYES STILL CLOSED, Charlie Katzowsky—no relation to Steven Tyler—took his first sip of alcohol in nearly a year. Tears streaked his face as he did it, making two straight paths to his chin. It wasn't the alcohol—though his body did feel like it was unfolding, the tension melting away at the removal of the prohibition—but the drink itself, its flavors and notes and highs and lows. He hadn't had much hope for this guy beyond being able to pour him a few fingers' worth of whiskey, but *this* drink—it was poetry.

It tasted like Anna's last year: sweet and bright and bubbling with life at the start, and then complicated, striated, serious and earthy and saline in drips, and then, at the tail, bitter and nauseous, bilious, whatever floral he'd put in there the exact same scent as her hospital room when things got bad, when she stopped responding to treatment and all the flowers people had sent started rotting at the same time, the air thick with waterlogged stems, suffocating, that awful smell. He took another sip, and he was back with his wife, alive, with her smile and the gap between her teeth, her ringing laugh, her short, sunshine hair dappled with light in his lap in the park, the blanket beneath them damp with dew, and he was reading something aloud, a *New Yorker* review, but then no! The salt! The way they'd both cried when she said goodbye, the stale wreaths and floral crosses overwhelming the funeral parlor, their petals curling as he wept. He'd taken a third sip when he heard the shlumpy mock-bartender yelp—*Holy fucking fuckballs!*—and opened his eyes in time to see it happening.

Anna was materializing on the edge of the bar.

She arrived in a million pinpricks of light, each one glowing and fading and glowing again like a field of atomic fireflies. Her hair and face and smile illuminated in ghostly green, beaming at him, all of her exactly how she'd looked at the very end—thin, pale, ready to let go—only absolutely transparent, so clear he could still see the dishwasher's disbelieving face through hers, the rows of liquors and infusions and syrups behind where her neck and shoulders and breasts were coming into being. She was sitting on the bar, laughing—could he bottle the sound?—with her long, lanky legs dangling down, kicking with life, and when they bumped his knee he gave an anticipatory jump even though they passed right through.

He looked back down at the Spectral Sour, then through Anna's slender arm at the wannabe mixologist, who was inching his way back into the kitchen.

"Hey!" he called. "What the hell was in this?"

But the coward retreated through the swinging door and was gone.

"Hey, loser," Anna said then, and the familiar rasp of her voice—a voice he'd have paid anything to hear just one more time—snagged something in his chest.

He opened his mouth, but nothing came out.

She leaned toward him and whispered, "Your line is 'Hey, bitch.'"

IN THE SANCTUARY of The Library's supply room, Konstantin was trying to wrestle his heart back down his throat. There was a lady ghost on the bar. A *lady ghost* on the bar. A lady ghost! On the bar!

Shit.

He took several deep breaths and then a swig of Tito's from the family bottle.

Okay. Okay okay.

He'd made a drink. And his drink had brought someone back from the Dead. No need to panic. Nothing to see here.

No. Big. Deal.

He took another swig of vodka.

In a weird-ass twist of fate, the kind of bullshit plotline only a novelist could devise, he had somehow managed to prop open a portal, all *I-see-dead-people* style, only without the crazy color-coding. Was *this* what the ghosts had been waiting for all these years? A fucking snack?

Kostya clambered onto a step stool and peered through the smeared window of the swinging door. There she was, firework bright, gesticulating, sending sparks. He nudged the door open, just enough to hear.

They were arguing. About celebrities.

" . . . and I was just kind of expecting you to look more like Bradley Cooper by now."

"You're impossible, you know that? It's not like you came back as Zoë Kravitz!"

"You still into her? You know there's, like, no chance, right?"

He grinned. "Screw you."

"I'd love to, babe, but I'm not exactly corporeal. Though I guess we cou-ld-d—" She suddenly jittered, her spangled image blinking in and out like a bad connection.

"Anna?" He gasped as she blipped out of sight. "*Anna!* No!"

He was shouting, his hand trying to grab hold of hers, closing in on itself.

"No-no-*no*. Come back!"

"Drink!" her voice instructed, disembodied somewhere.

He fumbled for his glass—spilling half in the process—and took a big gulp.

A moment later, there she was again, all chartreuse and sparkles, a movieland extra from the Emerald City.

"Sorry!" she gasped. "You have to keep drinking. The taste of that thing—I think that's what's keeping me here."

He frowned at her, dubious.

"Really? *This?*"

"Don't you remember it?" She gave him a meaningful look. "From Santorini? That place with the boats?"

His eyes lit up. "Oh. *Oh.* Really? That was *this?*"

"Down to the garnish."

"That was a good night."

"The best."

Something passed in the air between them, both breathlessly happy and devastatingly sad.

"But, okay? So we'll make more." (Backstage, Kostya was nodding. Yup. Game the system.) "That guy's just hiding in the kitchen; I can see him spyi—"

But she shook her head. "I think it's a one-shot deal."

"What? Why?"

"Just a feeling. Like this is kind of a swan song. A final bow."

"I don't understand."

She glanced at his glass. "It doesn't matter. We don't have much time."

"For what?"

"To make peace."

He went pale. "Peace? Oh God, Anna—have you been haunted? All this time? I fucking *knew* we shouldn't have scattered your ashes on the Belt Parkway!"

She shook her head.

"Oh, honey." She was gentle as she said it. "I made peace with my death a long time ago. I came back for *you*. Because you would have taken those pills in your pocket if I hadn't. Because you're still holding on to us, and it's ruining your life."

He went pink. "I wasn't actually going to do it."

"Yeah, you were. And when you did—oh, Charlie. You'd miss so much more that's waiting for you. Good stuff. Great stuff. Worth sticking around for."

He blinked rapidly, fighting tears. "What kind of stuff?"

She gave him a smile. "You'll have to wait here to find out."

"I hate waiting."

"I know. You couldn't be patient to save your life. It's why I came back." She gave a little laugh, but when she blinked, a streak of molten emeralds cascaded down her face, beautiful tears. "To tell you to live. To let go. Because when you do, you'll get to move on. And so will I."

Her light dimmed again, a bulb dying, and Charlie lifted the glass and took a tiny sip. Konstantin could see its perfect synchrony, the way her skin lit up in time with the dip of the drink. She glanced, nervous, at his near-empty lowball, and spoke very quickly.

"Please. I have to get this out. What I said at the end, about never loving anyone else, about expecting the same from you—it was selfish. It was cruel. I was in a bad place, and I thought you'd figure that out once I was gone; I hoped you'd know me well enough to know that I didn't mean it. That I wanted you to be happy." She reached for his hand, but her fingers went right through. "But it's been years and you haven't even tried to meet anybody. And I know it's because of me. I can feel the way you hold on, like we're chained together. And you're still young now, but if you don't let me go you're going to die young and alone. Or worse. You'll die old and alone and you'll have lived a miserable, empty life."

He looked at her for a long moment, fine as crystal, something shattering in him.

"I really fucking miss you."

"I miss you, too."

He stared into the bottom of his glass. "I don't want to let you go."

"I know." Anna sighed, in a way that really did feel like she knew it. "But letting go doesn't mean that you forget me. Just that you don't let the memories hurt you anymore."

"That sounds healthy. I hate it."

"Remember that green drink? From the health food place?"

He cracked a smile, a faraway memory flickering over his face. "Friggin' kale."

"Friggin' kale," she agreed.

"But I—"

"No buts," she said firmly. "Not unless they're—"

"—yeah, yeah, a Kardashian's, I know—"

"I would've gone with J.Lo."

"Well, you've been dead a while, so."

They smiled at one another, something unspoken passing between them as her light dimmed again, and he took another precious sip.

Kostya watched through the door, a gnaw in his chest. It was saccharine, sure, and he barely knew them, but still. The way this guy looked at her, even dead, you couldn't help but feel for him. It was love like starving.

"It's time," she whispered.

"I don't know how," he whispered back.

"You just live. Like I'm not here. Like nothing you do can hurt me. Just let go," she said, and reached a glittering jade hand out to him, cupped his face.

Charlie's eyes fluttered closed, his chin buckling. Kostya could see him shiver, the sensation of her touch both real and imagined.

"It isn't fair," he gasped. "That you got sick. That I got to live."

"You don't have to feel guilty," she told him, "for wanting your life. My death—none of it was your fault. I died, babe. I just . . . died. You didn't kill me."

Kostya felt something inside of him blister. He would have given anything, *anything*, to hear his dad tell him that.

Anna's light dimmed again, but Charlie's eyes were still closed, and he didn't budge this time, didn't reach for the glass.

"Char—" she began, but her final thought was cut short, her burst of light going dark right in the middle of his name.

Charlie opened his eyes. He blinked at the afterglow of where his wife's spirit had just been, the retinal burn of her brilliant outline its own sort of ghost. His fingers fumbled with an orange pill bottle in his pocket. He flipped it open, stared long and hard at the contents, then spilled the tablets across the lacquered wood of the bar.

Kostya wondered what was going through his head. Whether Charlie believed what he'd just been told about his future. Whether he was mourning his wife, or his marriage, or the arrested possibilities of his own life. Whether he thought he'd hallucinated the whole thing. Whether he was still planning, after all that, to take those pills. The only thing Kostya knew for sure was that if this guy started popping painkillers, he'd have to step in, call an ambulance, save his life, et cetera. And that meant another late shift and a ton of questions, none of which he felt like fielding.

But instead of ingesting anything, Charlie just kept staring. When it felt like he couldn't possibly sit in limbo anymore, like he'd been in that bar all his life, had been born on that obnoxious barstool, swaddled in those asinine cocktail napkins, Charlie picked up his Spectral Sour, and tipped its cherry back into his mouth.

He chewed. Tasted. Licked his lip.

And Anna blipped back into existence, her face streaked with phosphorescent tears, like someone had broken a glow stick. She looked surprised to be there.

"Charlie?" she whispered.

"How did you know?" he asked, voice reverberating with pain. "How'd you know I was really going to do it? *I* didn't even know."

"I know you like a book, babe."

"You always did." He nodded, sniffing. "Guess it's time for a new chapter."

They gazed at one another with the electric intensity of an imminent goodbye.

"Have an incredible life, Charlie. And when you're done, find me in the next one, okay?"

She pressed her radiant mouth to his, fighting all the boundaries between them, time and space and life and death, to try to make him feel her there, the ghost of their love story, its arc complete.

When she pulled away, he lifted his empty glass.

"Here's to you, bitch."

"See you on the other side, loser."

And he smashed the tumbler onto the floor, shattering the glass and spraying the minute particles of Spectral Sour across the speakeasy, releasing Anna along with them.

KOSTYA FELT LIGHT-HEADED. He had to grip the wall to steady himself. He waited until he stopped shaking (mostly) and then an extra couple minutes out of respect for the Dead before forcing himself to shuffle back out to the front-of-house.

He wanted to get Charlie's hot take, to compare notes about what they had heard Anna say, to discuss the mechanics of the drink and the taste and how it had all worked because, hell, who else (except maybe Frankie; he lived for this supernatural shit) would believe this if he told them? He was exploding inside, aching to understand if he could do it again, if maybe, *maybe*, he could bring someone else back, just for a drink, a last conversation, an apology.

His father felt so close, suddenly. Manifest. *Reachable.*

But as Charlie began thanking him up and down—*Look, I don't know what that was or how you pulled it off, but you just saved my life. Thank you, man.* Thank you. *How can I repay you?*—Kostya lost his nerve.

This—what had just happened—he'd done it, sure, but it wasn't about him. It was bigger. Much bigger. Perilously large. And he'd have to uncover it on his own.

"It's on me," he told the Charlie formerly known as Steven Tyler. "Just, um—do me a solid? Don't tell your friends."

But in that case [illegible] he had by any [illegible] now where [illegible] which was the [illegible] house of [illegible] 1920 [illegible] was the American [illegible] Thank you, Mr. [illegible] pp. [illegible] exhibitions he there [illegible] had the [illegible] meeting [illegible] in his [illegible] parliament [illegible] a moral power to act in Parliament.

[illegible] Lord for Devils [illegible] through [illegible] as though [illegible] justified [illegible] Afrikaan [illegible]

Amuse-bouche

The Konstantin Duhovny Culinary Experience

SO? SICK STORY, RIGHT? We got love. We got loss. We got glow-in-the-dark ghosts and some unexpected tasting notes! What y'all think? That enough to make believers outta you?

.　.　.　.

Dang, coming at it with some shade! That's alright; we got a lot more stops to make.

The Library's just a warm-up.

Still, that drink's important. It's our guy's gateway drug. Kicked off this entire culinary adventure. And hopefully it situates you just a little bit to where Bones was at the start. He could taste the flavors down to the component parts, which works fine for a drink, sure, but he had to get a clue about technique if he wanted to make food. Had to know whether to brown or boil or bake or braise, right? Take it from someone who spent a lifetime in kitchens—it's a ways from mixology to meal service.

.　.　.　.

Oh hell yeah, I miss it! Kitchen life's not for everybody, but if it's for you—nothing else like it.

. . . .

Me? Well, I hustled a long time. Worked my way in and out of restaurants. Had a whole path mapped to running my own place. But I lost my way a little bit. Got some talent, a little ambition, couple good reviews, and forgot what I was there to do. I stopped doing it for the food; started doing it for the fame. Just the status, you know? Thought I was hot shit, the next big thing. Put me up on the Food Network next to Ina. But life's got a way of making you humble real quick. I was this close to my own spot when things went south. Wound up here instead.

. . . .

Honestly? Bones is my boy. Helped me through it when my dad died. When my first restaurant failed. Those times half the people I knew were conveniently busy, he had my back. And now I got his.

Besides, I saw firsthand what he was doing in the kitchen. What his food meant to people. Reminded me why I loved cooking. Way it connects people. Like being in my mama's house, watching her make my 'lita's old recipes, the ones her mama taught her. Food's history. It's tradition. It's gotta mean something to be worth anything, you know? And his did. Does. It's why we're all here, right?

This tour's my little way of giving back. Of helping out my boy while getting me some of that good restaurant karma. But enough about me!

We got another stop to get to.

On the way, lemme tell you how Bones almost quit before he started. Psychic damn near talked him out of it. Happened down at this big warehouse party in Vinegar Hill. Hipsters for days—think Brooklyn Burning Man. Maybe some of y'all got over that way in a past life?

Mixers & Chasers

IN VIEW OF the Williamsburg Bridge, where the Brooklyn Navy Yard French-kisses 3rd Street, in an old, abandoned, unremarkable waterfront warehouse—its brick crumbling in places, half the windows broken and the others smudged out with bars of Irish Spring—a group called Seyoncé hosts legendary parties.

There are elaborate art installations and neon signs and indoor fireworks and black-light body paint and edibles and whiskey drinks and fortune tellers and fire-eaters and avant-garde themes and people in costume and people in nothing at all and solid beats and piss-warm beer and gold glitter and dance floor sweat. On a party night, the whole place smells like sex and Fun Dip and curly fries. To get in, you need code words and private invitations and someone with you who knows where the door—obscured by design—is hidden.

As the private Listserv never hesitates to inform Seyoncé subscribers, these were so much more than parties. These were events. Experiences. Life-altering encounters bestowed upon few but desired by all.

And they were also absolutely, in no way, not even a little, what Konstantin thought of as a good time.

He was wedged in the corner of a crowded room in the warehouse's sprawling basement, its walls entirely covered with life-sized papier-mâché eels, strips of glow sticks illuminating their backs and bellies, their rows of sharp, X-Acto-knife teeth flashing in the strobing light. Tonight's theme was Water Worlds, and a raving horde of sweaty bodies—dressed as sea creatures with their arms, legs, and PVC appendages flailing—kept bumping into Kostya as he nursed a watered-down cocktail that tasted undeniably like lemon Pine-Sol.

He swallowed. Frowned. Gagged.

He knew all about the taste of lemon Pine-Sol, had been tricked into ingesting it once at another ill-fated party, the single time in his entire high school career he'd been invited anywhere.

When Kostya arrived at Anthony Russo's house, the in-crowd had made a big deal of noticing him. They said they couldn't believe that he came, that they didn't think he'd show, that they'd been waiting for him—the VIP of the night!—and then they'd laughed at one another, exchanged coded glances, and shoved Kostya down into a club chair. They mixed him an enormous glass of the House Special—Popov, Pine-Sol, and Sprite, he'd later learn—an entire room of people chanting—*Drink it down down down down! Down down down down!*—as he struggled to chug the whole thing.

He spent the subway ride home vomiting shades of green all over the floor, the taste of lemon solvent so caustic he could feel it in his throat for days. Every aftertaste he got that month had an acid wash to it, the cleanser overpowering everything like too much salt. Each time he belched, it smelled like a mop.

Kostya took another sip of Seyoncé's sad excuse for a sidecar, ran his tongue over his teeth, and abandoned it on a nearby octopus tentacle. No buzz was worth reliving the smug looks from Jack Stenger and Paul Rabinowitz as they deposited him onto the sidewalk, saliva pooling in his mouth as his body prepared to eject the offending contaminants.

"Thanks for coming!" Stenger had grinned at him. "You really made our night. Paul and I got a hundred bucks each for reeling you in. Bigger the loser, bigger the payoff."

Kostya left the safety of his corner to negotiate the gyrating throng, his eyes peeled, scanning the crowd for Frankie.

Frankie was his roommate. His best friend. The only person who could have convinced Kostya to brave this godforsaken ring of Dante's Inferno. They'd met through a Craigslist ad Frankie had posted—SPLIT THE RENT, MIDTOWN—and had spent nearly six years together in their cramped Hell's Kitchen apartment, the experience of navigating the highs and lows of their twenties basically bonding them for life.

Which was lucky, because if Kostya didn't love Frankie so much, he would have totally hated the fucker.

All the things Kostya could only achieve through outlandish fantasy— good looks, social graces, copious copulation opportunities, a job he didn't hate—Frankie possessed in excess. He was handsome, almost absurdly good-looking, half-Dominican and half-Irish, with the kind of body type that never put on weight no matter how much garbage he shoveled into it (for the record: lots). He had friends to burn, and made new ones all the time, everywhere. He was so damn affable—quick with a joke or a story so crazy it couldn't possibly be true (but always was). People orbited him. Women loved him. So much so that most of them stayed friends long after the inevitable—since Frankie was too married to his job to commit to anything else—breakup. He worked as a sous-chef in a Michelin-starred restaurant uptown. He was a culinary juggernaut, if his own drunken boasts were to be believed, or at least someone to watch, if *Time Out New York*'s restaurant column was.

Frankie had gotten Kostya through the Seyoncé door ("It's like SeaWorld on acid, bro." "Why would I want to be at SeaWorld on acid?" "Why you getting salty on me?") and then abandoned him for a redhead he'd met in the entry line.

She'd come dressed as the Little Mermaid—long, poppy hair dripping with strings of pearls, legs bound by an elaborate, iridescent skirt, naked on top except for two large shells that Kostya could only assume had been crazy-glued there. As they crawled toward the door, Frankie zeroed in and made his move, interrupting her conversation with a friend who was either a sexy tortoise or a sexy Bowser (or both).

"Ladies, I hope you can excuse the interruption, but I just gotta know—those clamshells real?"

It even sounded like a line coming out of his mouth, but Ariel turned around, took one look at him—six-two, brown-skinned, dreamy as a soap star—and giggled.

"I made them at my studio. They're silicone," she said, a coy smile teasing the edge of her mouth. "But they feel real."

"That so? You an artist?"

"A sculptor."

"I like a girl who's good with her hands. And"—Frankie took her hand and lifted her arm to ogle from another angle—"by the look of it, you got talent." He twirled her around. "They legit look like abalone. Last time I saw one of them was at the CIA."

Kostya smirked, watching him work. The secret, Frankie had once told him, is to make them think they're the most interesting person in the room, and then show them that, actually, you are.

The mermaid grinned. "Are you a secret agent?"

"Hell no." Frankie laughed. "I'm slicker'n that. I'm a chef."

The next thing Kostya knew, Frankie had his hand on the small of her back and was guiding her toward the bar, mouthing over his shoulder that he'd see Kostya later.

It wasn't the first time Frankie had ditched him for a shot at lust, and it probably wouldn't even be the last time tonight, so Kostya was debating whether or not to just bail on the whole thing and slum his way back to their apartment in Hell's Kitchen when he realized that Frankie had the only working set of keys between them.

After his misadventure in bartending, Kostya had been so busy fleeing the repercussions of his actions that he'd left his keys at The Library, which wouldn't have been a big deal, except that Kevin (Manager of the Year) came in the next morning, took one look at the sorry state of the place (broken glasses; dishes stacked in the front-of-house; his beautiful cocktail napkins ruined), and left an irate voicemail on Kostya's cell telling him not to bother showing up to work anymore.

Kostya told himself to let it go, that there would be plenty more dish-washing jobs, that Frankie might even be able to hook him up at Wolfpup, but the more he tried *not* to think about it, the more it pinned itself to the top of his mind. Not the job, exactly, but how he'd lost it.

He couldn't stop thinking about the ghost. About the drink that brought her back. About what he'd done. At first, he'd been afraid, horrified by this unexpected punch line to decades of aftertasting. But once the fear subsided—once Kostya grew used to the idea that he had, in fact, summoned the Dead—what remained was a frenzied itch to understand *how*.

Were his aftertastes shortcuts to another dimension? Could any one of them summon a ghost, or was it a Goldilocks thing, where the conditions had to be just right? Could he bring back anybody, anytime? Or were there expiration dates? Statutes of limitations? And what about Charlie? If he hadn't been there to see it, Kostya might have believed he'd snapped, that years of ghost tasting had finally rotted his brain. But with a witness—an *accomplice*—the only things he questioned were the rules. Charlie had been the one to drink Anna's cocktail, but did every aftertaste need an eater? Could Kostya step in as pinch hitter? And if it was his own Dead he was trying to bring back—he barely let himself consider the possibility—if he ate the right thing, could he bring back his dad?

Kostya squeezed his eyes shut, trying to will the taste of cheap gin and imitation lemon off of his palate in lieu of a memory: *thick, rich chicken liver; onions on the edge of caramelization; the faintest hint of dill.* There had been an acid, too, something citrusy. He'd just started to recollect it when a new aftertaste kicked him in the mouth, pushing every other sensation away.

It was so simple—so *basic*—that Kostya wondered whether it was for real.

Soft milk chocolate. Peanut butter, whipped with powdered sugar and a hint of vanilla. The slightest trace of residue from the wax-paper wrapper. A Reese's Peanut Butter Cup.

He barely had time to consider it when Frankie appeared in the crowd, his captain's hat missing, sailor shirt untucked, a get-some grin on his face.

"Lemme tell you something, Bones." He wrapped a muscular, tattooed arm around Kostya's neck. "We oughta get down on our knees right now and pray to the God of Bathroom Sex, 'cause he just did me a solid party favor!"

Kostya smiled weakly and disentangled himself.

"Hey, man, you think I can get your keys? This isn't really my scene."

"Nah. Nah nah nah. No more moping." Frankie frowned at him. "Listen to me, my guy. DJ Skull's about to spin downstairs. The rooftop's got this foam toga thing going on. Let's get you shit-faced—feeling so good you forget all about Alexis. It's been months, man! I hate to see you all wrung out. And who knows? Maybe you'll meet someone tonight. My Little Seahorse by the stage is looking fly. Or how about Octopussy, over at the bar? Or—*yes*. Upstairs! There's this dime psychic, doing readings. Go turn on the charm, ask her what's up."

"I'd rather take my chances with Octopussy."

"You don't even know what she does! She's like straight-up mystic."

"Lemme guess," Kostya said dryly. "She already knew I was coming?"

"Always the cynic." Frankie nudged his shoulder. "You're not even a little curious what she can tell you? This is Seyoncé, bro. Shit's authentic."

Something shivered inside Kostya at the thought, a seed planted. He had never seriously considered consulting a psychic. He'd always waved them off as money-grubbing phonies, had never even entertained the possibility that there might be someone genuine, someone who might understand what had happened that night at The Library of Spirits, what had, in fact, been happening inside his mouth for nearly twenty years.

"You really think she's legit?"

"Only one way to find out."

Before he could change his mind, Frankie grabbed Kostya by the elbow and, his protests drowned out by the death metal band, dragged him through a bloom of human jellyfish, past an indoor hedge maze, and up a staircase that looked like the Cheshire cat's throat—enormous candy-striped canines baring down from the ceiling and floor, framing a sticky red carpet that led up, up, up to an enormous, sequined uvula dangling in the doorway.

Feeling as if he'd actually been swallowed, Kostya ducked past the uvula (a bedazzled boxing bag), and into a room that felt like the first sip of bourbon after a long day. It was smaller, dimly lit, the walls covered in deep, mossy velvet and lined with bookcases full of crumbling old books. Frankie hustled him toward a striped tent in the corner, an ornate sign out front announcing:

THE SPIRITUAL ARTS BY MADAME EVERLEIGH
Tarot Readings $15 | Palmistry $25

NO Ouija, NO Seances, NO Refunds

"On second thought, *no* thanks."

Kostya turned to retreat, but Frankie halted him.

"Get in there, Bones. You're gonna have some fun if it kills me."

"Not if it kills me first."

"Hey, you guys coming or going?" a voice from inside the tent asked.

"*Go!*" Frankie breathed, giving him a push. "All else fails, at least try to get laid."

Kostya flipped him the bird, pulled the flap of the circus tent open, and stepped inside.

THE SPIRITUAL ARTIST, Madame Everleigh, reclined on a cheap, peeling love seat, an issue of *Game Informer* propped open on her knees. She had flickering, wide-set eyes and sharp, intelligent features. Elaborate hair—long, wavy, dyed violet at the ends and silver at her roots and lavender in-between. A slender frame made slighter by so many shades of black—black Converse and black jeans and a black hoodie (in this heat?!) that read: *More Freddie, Less Retrograde.* A careless hand held up a finger—one sec—then turned the page of the article she was reading.

Frankie hadn't lied. She *was* a dime. The most beautiful woman Kostya had ever seen. So far out of his league that he wasn't sure they were playing the same sport.

He cleared his throat and Madame Everleigh lowered her magazine just enough to peer over it at him. She registered his presence and gestured to a table and a couple of folding chairs to his right, and then lifted the magazine back up, her gum snapping noisily at him from behind the cover. Kostya nodded and sat down, deeply regretting the shirt he'd worn—a too-snug aquamarine number to which he'd taped some badly cut construction-paper fish—as it stretched across his gut. He sat up taller and sucked in.

"You seem tense," Madame Everleigh noted from behind the magazine. "Try and clear your mind before the reading or you might get mixed messages."

Kostya frowned. It wasn't his mind that needed clearing, he thought mutinously, but his mouth, his tongue, the taste buds that seemed to tingle, even now, with restless energy. He was having second (third?) thoughts about coming in here, and shifted in his seat, about to stand up and abandon the enterprise, when she suddenly lowered the magazine.

"And . . . done!" she announced. "Sorry. There was a piece on the new Zelda, and I couldn't stop once I started. Like Pringles. You ever get that?"

Kostya nodded, gaping at her and trying to remember to breathe and swallow. Holy smokeshow. It almost hurt to look.

She rose and tossed her magazine onto the floor.

"So, you a virgin?" she asked, crossing the tent and taking the seat opposite him.

"Um, no?" Was she planning on sacrificing him to a demigod? "Why?"

"It's totally okay if you are."

"I," Kostya scoffed, "am no virgin. I'm *extremely* experienced. An expert."

"Oh." She looked surprised. "Okay. Cool! In that case, do you have a favorite way in? Or should we just start slow? Sometimes you can get deeper that way."

Kostya gulped. "Deeper?" Maybe he'd sacrifice himself.

"I mean, that's the whole point, isn't it? You'll never get an accurate reading otherwise."

Was she saying what he thought she was saying? Did this spiritual experience come with a little something else? This *was* Seyoncé; anything was possible.

A bead of sweat ran along the back of his horrible shirt.

"Are you . . . I mean, is this . . . ?" He lowered his voice. "Are we going to . . . because I didn't bring protection."

Her eyes grew wide. "Excuse me?"

"You just asked if I was—and I'm not!—but . . . *deeper*?"

"Oh my God." She threw her head back and laughed. "I meant was it your first reading!" She pulled a ragged deck of cards from her back pocket and set it between them. "You know, tarot? Like the sign out front says?"

"Oh! No! Yeah! *Obviously.*" (Sweet relief! But also . . . definite disappointment.) "My bad. Yes. In that sense—and that sense only—total virgin territory. Please be gentle."

"*Right.*" She laughed again, swiping a finger beneath one eye and smearing black liner. "Okay. Well. Here's how it works. I'm going to shuffle the cards, and you're going to think of the question you want answered. Meditate on it, put your energies into it, and just give me a nod when you're ready. Cool?"

She offered him the deck to cut and Konstantin watched as she manipulated the cards, her slender fingers pulling the past, present, and future into complicated bridge shuffles and mesmerizing flourishes. He wasn't thinking about the aftertastes at all now, or about any of the questions that normally plagued his thoughts. Kostya was busy feasting his eyes on Madame Everleigh—the curve of her face, the tilt of her shoulder, the tiny dots of lint caught on the collar of her sweatshirt, the freckles in her eyes like the jackets of bees, dusted with gold, the shade of lipstick she wore, the shape of her mouth—

"How you comin' on that question, champ?"

Kostya's eyes darted to the tabletop, his thoughts yanked back to what he was supposed to be doing there.

"Actually," he said, shifting slightly in his chair, "I'm not really here for a reading."

"Okay?" She placed the deck on the table between them. "So what *are* you here for?"

Your phone number. Your hand in marriage. Just one night, gimme just one night. . . .

"Information."

She leaned back and crossed her arms over her chest.

"Information?"

"Of a *mysterious* nature."

"Okay, Deep Throat. Think you can be a little more specific?"

Kostya exhaled. "I need to know if it's normal—or, I guess, I know it's not *normal* normal, but is it a *thing* to be able to taste the Dead?"

Whatever she had been expecting, it wasn't that. She uncrossed her arms.

"Taste them how? Like their body parts?"

"No! No. Ew. No. Their food. Like . . . like tasting something you haven't eaten. That's not in your mouth. But that you think—you know—is coming from someone who's died. I'm asking for a friend."

She sat up straighter, leaned closer, her whole body at attention.

"Uh-huh. Well, you can tell your *friend* that yeah, it's possible. Not very common, but it's definitely a thing. Taste is one of the Psychic Clairs."

"The who?"

She smiled. "It's shorthand for the psychic senses. Everyone's heard of clairvoyance, but that's just seeing. Some spiritualists can smell or touch or hear from the other side. Tasting's called clairgustance."

"Clairgustance," he repeated, trying it on.

"Mm-hmm. But, like I said, it's not typical." She hesitated for half a moment before adding, "What was your name again?"

"Konstantin."

"I'm Maura." She reached her hand out across the table and he took it. Her touch was like candy, a sugar rush.

"I thought you were Everleigh."

"Ev's been dead awhile."

"Funny."

"I wish I were kidding." Her mouth gave a slight twitch, which she recovered with a smile. "But hey, maybe *your friend* can taste her. How often does it happen? The clairgustance?"

He opened his mouth to answer and, right on cue, the familiar sensation burst over his tongue. He arranged his face into a blank stare that quickly turned to surprised confusion, followed by déjà vu.

The subtle grit of smooth, sweet peanut butter. Soft milk chocolate, so pliable it seemed half-melted. The texture of the ridged edge on the tip of his tongue, like the teeth of a comb, but with a sudden break, like it had been dented. No wrong way to eat one.

Kostya rarely tasted the same thing twice. There were many similar dishes, though there were always distinctions—Nonna's meatballs versus Great-Grammama's; a sprig of basil versus a handful of parsley. But this Reese's Cup was identical to the one from downstairs. A packaged good, not a prepared one. Too close in timing to be purely coincidental.

Someone was dying to break through. Throwing themselves at him, practically. All he had to do was get his hands on some candy, figure out who at this party had to eat it, and Trick-or-Treat.

"Hey, uh, you okay?"

"Is there a vending machine?" Kostya blurted out. "Or a bodega? I—I need a Reese's. Right now."

He started to push himself out of the chair, but what she said next made him sit back down.

"Over my dead body."

"Oh, um, sorry? You allergic or something?"

"Or something." She frowned at him. "What the hell, Konstantin?"

"That—the Reese's Cup—I just tasted—it *just happened*."

"You tasted *that*? Just now?" She cast around the tent as though trying to catch a ghost in the act, to witness a vanishing limb or a disembodied face.

"Yeah. But it was"—he shook his head—"weird."

"Weirder than when you normally taste the Dead?"

"No. I mean, yes? It's—I tasted the same thing just a few minutes ago. Downstairs. Someone's really trying to get my attention."

She blinked at him for a moment, her mouth going taut.

The aftertaste was already starting to fade. Maybe he could try again later. Maybe the ghost would hold on until he could get to a grocery store or a newsstand; he thought he'd seen one when they were pissing around in that interminable entry line, a couple blocks back, near an overpass—

"How come you wanted it?" Maura asked cautiously. "The candy?"

There was a strange tone to her voice, like she'd guessed the answer and didn't like it.

"I just—I wanted to try something."

"What happens when you make the stuff you taste? If you eat it?"

Well wasn't that the million-dollar question, the peanut-butter-cup-shaped elephant in the room?

"I don't really know."

She raised one incredulous brow. "You've never tried it?"

"Well, not *never*. I did it last week. With a drink."

"And?"

Kostya's head gave the tiniest shake, more reflex than response.

"Konstantin, look, you don't have to tell me—"

"It's going to sound crazy—"

"—but maybe if you do, I can help you. We can figure out what they want. And if I help you, maybe you can help—"

"Oh, I know what they want." He gave a desperate, manic, half laugh. "Isn't it obvious? They want to come back."

Somewhere inside, in that chasm he tried so hard to keep shut, to block out with binge-eating and heavy drinking and dead-end jobs and women he didn't love and parties he didn't want to go to, maybe he'd always known. If he didn't admit it to himself, maybe he could have unknown it, or convinced himself that there was nothing he could do but taste what they sent through and be on his way. But he'd proven that more was possible, hadn't he? He'd brought someone back, pulled a spirit through a loophole across a plane she was only supposed to have crossed once, in a one-way trip.

"What happened," Maura asked slowly, "when you made that drink?"

Kostya picked at a gash on the surface of the table.

"At first, nothing. It was just a cocktail. But when her husband drank it, she—the ghost it belonged to—she came back."

Maura's eyes grew round.

"Came *back*? Did she stay? Is she still here?"

The mood in the room was different now, colder, the air contaminated with something.

"No. When the drink was done, she disappeared."

Maura closed her eyes and released a breath.

"Thank fuck. Okay. Listen to me. You need to tread *very* carefully." She spoke softly, as if afraid someone would overhear, but her voice was serrated, dangerous. "You're dealing with hungry spirits and capital-*D* Death and the Hereafter. That's not stuff you just casually mess around with."

"I know that—"

"There are balances involved," she continued, "and systems that've spent eternities calibrating themselves. You got lucky once, but that was just dumb luck."

"It wasn't luck," he protested. "It was instinct."

"You got lucky," she repeated. "Because no one got hurt."

"How could anyone get hurt? The ghost was already dead, and raising the Dead isn't exactly—"

"You're not listening!" Madame Everleigh—Maura—shouted. "Let me be as idiot-proof as I possibly can here. Don't ever make their food again."

"Wait, *what*?"

"Quit while you're ahead."

"No way!" His voice rose now, too, his arms crossed over his chest like a petulant kid's. "A second ago you were all *Let me help*, and now, what, the kitchen got a little too hot for you?"

"I was offering to help you *stop* it. Because what you're doing? Screwing with ghosts? You have no idea what you're tasting."

"And you do?"

"I'd have to kill you to explain."

"You're a real treat, you know that?"

"And *you're* no match for the Afterlife."

He stared at her in disbelief, as if she'd just pushed him. A part of him that wanted to push back.

"You know what?" he said slowly. "Forget it. Forget *you*. *I'm* the one with the magic tongue. The one who's been tasting the Dead for twenty years. And it was *me*—not you—that brought one of them back. What've *you* ever done, Spiritual Artist? Burned some incense? Shuffled some cards? Made a snap judgment about someone and used it to give them bad advice?"

Maura glared at him for a deafening moment, something hot simmering behind her eyes.

"You have no idea the things I've done."

"Try me."

"Hard pass." She gave a small, mean smirk.

"Fine. Whatever." He slid his chair back, stood up.

"But if it'd been me," she added, "tasting those spirits? I sure as hell wouldn't wait *twenty years* to do something about it."

"That's not fair."

"No? You just said you didn't try anything till *last week*. And the result got you so spooked you're, what, consulting a party psychic? Well. You already got my advice, so here's a snap judgment. You're a coward, Konstantin. Afraid of your own potential. More interested in self-preservation than making any sort of meaningful connection. You're paralyzed by—oh, I dunno?—something in your past? Death of a loved one? Am I warm? Yeah. And now you think this ghost thing makes you special. That messing with the Afterlife can somehow undo all those shitty years you've chosen to have instead of just moving on. But it won't. It'll only make it worse. So you need to just stop."

Kostya stood there, dumbstruck.

Of all the things to happen at this seizure-inducing party, this felt the least like reality—not the Under the Sea flash mob or the salmon spawn dancers or the piranha piñata whose boxcutter teeth had drawn Kostya's blood—*this*. If someone had told him that a sideshow psychic would be the first person to see him clearly, to peer through his bullshit and call him out on it, he'd have asked for a dose of whatever they were on. And yet, here she was—barely ten minutes of conversation between them, not even a card reading to help her along—getting it so on the nose she may as well have been a whitehead, a giant pimple on the face of everything that had held Kostya back his entire life: fear and denial and self-doubt. The inertia that had plagued him since his dad died.

"I should go."

He found a twenty in his wallet, dropped it on the table. Then he took one last look at Madame Everleigh—painfully beautiful, emphasis on pain—and shoved his way back through the tent.

Kostya had miscalculated. It cost him twenty bucks (should have been fifteen, but there was no way he was asking for change), all of his pride, and more than a little dignity. In return, he'd gotten part of what he came for—clairgustance, the name like a small ray of light—though everything else she'd told him he'd have to work to compartmentalize, another dense box of himself to stack in front of that chasm inside.

MAURA ELIZABETH STRUK—Madame Everleigh—watched him go, her heart pounding. She felt badly about how it had gone, how cruel she'd been to make him leave. But she couldn't have him around her, not if he was tasting *that*, not if he was some sort of gateway, a conduit back to where she wasn't ready to go.

It wasn't like she didn't mean what she'd said; it was just that she'd done it so tactlessly, so full of pointed intention, that she was sure it would leave a bruise, if not a scar. Then again, she *had* tried, at first, to simply warn him. But he'd blown her off. So he deserved what he got.

It was a shame. Aside from haphazardly summoning a Hungry Ghost, he'd seemed nice. Endearing. Cute, kinda. Not her type exactly (not nearly enough tattoos), but passable if he took a little more care of himself. Still, he'd been playing with fire. Not a single match at a time, but more like setting a flamethrower off beside a gas pump.

What she couldn't understand was how he had gone beyond serving as a medium to bring an actual spirit back. From what Maura knew about clairgustance—which was, admittedly, more snackable summary than seven-course meal—most of the time, the tastings were just flavors associated with the Dead. Cigarettes if the deceased smoked. Chemical residue if they'd been poisoned. The taste of their lipstick, or the hot sauce they liked. More clues than cuisine, and certainly not bridges. But what Konstantin tasted—a specific drink with all its component parts; a specific candy, *that* candy—seemed different. Not something simply reminiscent of the Dead, but integral to them, to some experience or memory they still craved. And by making that food, it appeared he could lure the spirits in, bait the hook with their favorite chum.

Well, whatever.

This, at least, wasn't her problem. And hopefully what she'd said had gotten through to him. Hopefully, it was enough to keep him from making a bad mistake. The Hereafter was an intricate balance—of famine and feast; of hunger and satiety; of emptiness and fulfillment. Screw with that balance and, sooner or later, you'd regret it.

Just like Maura.

Her body trembled, suddenly ravenous. When had she last eaten? She pulled open her backpack, found a bag of Cheetos, and sat down at the table to inhale them when she noticed the tarot cards still there.

Her fingertips hovered over the deck, itching to read.

He'd already cut. It seemed like a waste not to divine when it was already primed. She flipped the top three cards over and studied them.

Oh, for fuck's sake.

She rushed out of the tent to see if she could catch Konstantin, but he'd already gone.

AROUND 4:00 AM, hunched over the peeling laminate counter in their cramped kitchen, Kostya and Frankie annihilated a plate of Disco fries and a platter of street meat without the use of a single utensil.

Konstantin shoved food into his mouth with his fingers, wolfing it down, swallowing so fast he barely tasted anything. It had been a long time since he'd gorged himself like this, but it came back like riding a bike.

This was comfortable; this was familiar.

Not raising glittering ghosts in some first-class a-hole speakeasy.

Not some unhinged party or vindictive psychic.

Not confessing his aftertastes for the first time since he'd been institutionalized for them, followed by having the most beautiful woman he'd ever laid eyes on blow it all up in his face.

This. Binge-eating his feelings in the form of a half-cold halal platter and its various accoutrements.

"Yo, uh, you good, man?" Frankie asked, watching him, a fry halfway to his mouth. "I seen that look before. Listen, I know Alexis meant a lot to you, but bro—"

Kostya shook his head, cramming more meat into his mouth.

"Not about Alexis," he said, still chewing.

Frankie put down his fry and pulled the Styrofoam box out of Kostya's reach.

"Well then what? 'Cause this ain't healthy."

Kostya swallowed and stared for a long time into Frankie's face, deciding.

"Actually," he said at last, "you wanna hear something crazy?"

FRANKIE TOOK HIM at his word.

It was how he was raised, to believe that the world was more mysterious and miraculous than most people ever saw. His Dominicana grandmother practiced Las 21 Divisiones and made daily sacrifices to the Loas for his protection. His Irish grandmother was as Catholic as they came and stronger than she looked, and had just about beaten the Lord into him as a kid. As a result, Frankie's own belief system fell somewhere between spiritual and superstitious, gospel and Vudú and Jesus and the Diablo Cojuelo all sitting around, having a beer, and there was a lot he believed in that most people wouldn't.

"That's fucked up," Frankie pronounced when he'd finished, handing Konstantin a beer. "I can't believe Madame E did you like that."

"She's probably right." Kostya took a long sip. Thinking. Wallowing. "I mean, I should just leave it alone, right? Let sleeping ghosts lie, or whatever."

"Nah, man. Listen to me. Way I see it, they chose *you*. They're all 'Help me, Obi-Wan Kenobi,' and you gon' be like, 'Sorry, no, I'm good'? You're their *dude*. Maybe their only shot at a happy afterlife. Fuck what she said! Think about *them*."

Kostya picked at the label on his bottle. Peeled it off.

"I only did it the one time. That's not enough to be sure of anything."

"All right, then. Come on. You're gonna pick another recipe and we're gonna hit it. We can use Wolfpup."

"I dunno."

"You really wanna spend your life standing still? Taking orders from people who don't know you from Sunday?"

Kostya wasn't sure what he wanted, but looking around their apartment—the mold-eaten brick, the watermarked ceiling, the pocked hardwood and saggy futon and greasy counter and ancient stove, the drafty bay window just threatening to glow with the first quivering rays of another new day of unemployment and self-loathing—it probably wasn't this.

"I guess not."

"Tell me something. How'd it feel when you mixed that drink? Before the ghost shit. Just the act of making it."

"Pretty amazing."

Frankie nodded knowingly. He talked all the time about how the kitchen called to him, about how he'd been applying to business schools until he picked up a chef's knife for the first time.

"Then you owe it to yourself to at least give it a shot. Nobody likes regret."

Kostya didn't like it, exactly, but regret was a sort of personal comfort zone. He'd spent years familiarizing himself with its terrain, its streets and alleyways and all the doors of Opportunity that populated them, locked and dead-bolted against some stupid whim he might one day have, to try to open them.

But maybe this wasn't like that.

He even knew what dish he'd try, the aftertaste that mattered more than any of the others.

"Okay." He nodded at Frankie. "What do you know about liver?"

Frankie grinned back. "Enough to be dangerous."

Hors d'oeuvres

The Konstantin Duhovny Culinary Experience

ALRIGHT, BOYS AND GIRLS. *Let's get serious. We're gonna see where Konstantin trained up.*

Our next stop's just over here. Up on the left.

Through that old door with the big brass latch.

Anyone know this gem? Crown jewel of New York dining, run by a living legend?

. . . .

No, man, that ain't Bobby Flay! Read a cookbook. Anybody else?

How 'bout a hint?

She's open for lunch and dinner, but don't even think about walking in—they're booked six months out, every seat taken. Those velvet curtains? They keep folks from peeping the set change between the communal tables at lunch and the dinner fine dine. And the stars in the window? That ain't Yelp. Kitchens bust their balls to get just one nod from Michelin, and this beaut's earned three.

Well? Any guesses?

Damn, you really make a guy work for it.

This here's Saveur Fare.

Mise en places

THE DINING ROOM at Saveur Fare dazzles diners for ten immaculate hours a day, six days a week.

The front-of-house is legendary for making guests feel like they never want to leave. Before service, the waitstaff are painstakingly briefed on that night's reservations, so that each of them can anticipate, like a modern-day haruspex in slinky black silk, their diners' aversions and allergies and gastronomic inclinations without ever having to be told. During service, they charm and delight. They tell stories; they are quick with jokes. Most of the staff are recruited from the New York theater scene, but even the ones who are not give Tony-worthy performances night after night.

Saveur Fare employs three sommeliers, two of them Masters, which means you can blindfold them, give them a sip of wine, and receive an identification of the varietal, the vintage, the region and vineyard, no matter how obscure—we're talking the difference between grapes grown on opposite sides of the same Burgundian hill here—just based on the characteristic qualities of that single taste. There's also an award-winning mixologist available for bespoke cocktail pairings. You know, if wine isn't your thing.

And that's just the beverage program.

The main event—the food—is a Chef's Tasting of twelve elaborate, palm-sized courses. The menu changes weekly to take greatest advantage of seasonal and micro-seasonal delicacies, and ingredients come from all over the world: sea urchin overnighted from Osaka, their spiny shells safeguarding briny, golden goo; black and white truffles from Provence and Piedmont, the smell of the cases like hay and Heaven; impossibly fine beads of beluga and sterlet, popping their tins like breathing the Caspian Sea. A partner farm in the Hudson Valley supplies local meat and produce; bread and pasta are made twice daily, in-house. The patisserie is on premises, with tarts and cakes and jams and petits fours changing daily to incorporate local produce—sour cherries from upstate New York; quince from a rare fruit-bearing tree in eastern Pennsylvania; winter cranberries hauled in, dripping wet, from New Jersey.

In the kitchen, a precise choreography is performed to support the curated dining experience that commands Michelin's highest honor—three stars, four years running. Recently, management etched this award onto the enormous front window as a dare to the chef, the sous-chef, the line cooks, the whole *brigade de cuisine*, a bastardly way of reminding them that the loss of so much as a star would ruin them—not to mention require the replacement of the entire vitrine.

But they're not worried. What they do is pristine.

Their executive chef, Michel Beauchêne, works them like demigods, producing magic and miracles from the swipe of their fingers across a finishing plate with a towel, or the flick of their wrists as they sear and sauté. The portions are small, each ratio of salt and fat and acid, heat and sugar, umami and bite, perfected in miniature. There's no room for excess or miscalculation. And it's all done at speed; hundreds of plates served every night, rapid-fire. Consequently, the men and women in this kitchen—from the tippity top to the runners and bussers—are exceptional.

What they make is fleeting—edible raptures that last only as long as it takes to consume them. But the recollection, the conversations about these morsels, the sweet nostalgia of the best things their clientele have ever eaten—*those* last forever.

Frankie told Kostya all this between huge bites of a street cart bagel and sips of burnt coffee as they made their way to the restaurant. There was a gleam in his eye, and he spoke with the kind of awestruck reverence normally reserved for places of God.

It was 6:00 AM (decidedly ungodly).

A Monday (Satan's day, if ever there was one).

The sun was shining (and hot as Hell).

And the more Frankie talked, the more Kostya wanted to crawl into a hole and forget the whole thing.

There was an opening at Saveur Fare for a dishwasher, and Frankie, who'd been a line cook beneath Michel Beauchêne right out of culinary, had put in a good word (and several lies) to get Kostya an interview. He'd done it partially out of self-interest—if Kostya didn't find work soon, they'd be short their next rent check—but also as a form of apology. The night they'd messed around at Wolfpup, trying to re-create Kostya's dad's liver, had been an unmitigated fuckfest—and all Frankie's idea.

He could still see the hope draining from Kostya's face each time he plated a new variation and handed him a fork—this one sautéed, this one flash-fried, this one with a squeeze of lemon, this one with pre-served lemon reduction, this one with Kosher salt, this one with flaky Maldon. Kostya had been so certain each time that they'd gotten it, and each time the disappointment had shone in his eyes when it was just another bite of liver, entirely off from what it was supposed to be. By the time they called it, Frankie felt like he'd just kicked the emotional shit out of him. And then he'd heard through the grapevine that his old mentor was hiring.

"You *know* that I don't know all that much about food, right?" Kostya protested.

Frankie waved him off, sending coffee crashing over the edge of his paper cup.

"No one's gonna give a shit if the *escuelerie* can't boil water. You got one job in there—spotless plates."

"It just seems . . . intense. Like, really high stakes."

"It *is* intense. It's at the best of the best! That's why the pay's so good." He took a long sip of his coffee. "I'd give my left nut to cook in that kitchen."

"So why don't you?"

"Man, Rio's been a fucking prince to me. What kinda piece of shit would I be to jump kitchens?"

Hilario Torres—Rio—was the executive chef at Wolfpup, and Frankie was his sous. Their relationship, Frankie liked to say, was like having a wife he'd never get to fuck or fuck over. Frankie was Rio's ultimate partner, his trustee, his gofer, his confidant. If Rio needed something—any time, day or night—an ingredient they'd run out of on Frankie's day off, a replacement part for the walk-in, a resolution to the beef between the grill guy and the bartender, Frankie found a way to work it out.

It got attention; chefs all over town tried constantly to woo him away. But Frankie was loyal, a real ride-or-die. Rio had mentored him, had helped him figure out what he wanted to say with food. They'd opened Wolfpup together and, so far, it was a smashing success.

"When I go, it'll be for my own place. Besides," Frankie added, "my act's not clean enough for these guys. I like the hustle. The ball-busting. That half-life we got going on at Wolfpup, just shit talking and bullshitting and dicking around. We charge forty bucks an entrée, and we're just a bunch of fuckers hanging out debating who's got the biggest man nuts." He took another bite of his bagel. "And it's me, by the way. In case you were wondering."

"I was *not* wondering, but thanks for that prize mental image."

"You ever see a durian, man? Just like that but *smooth*. I do that landscaping *perfect*—"

"Fuck, I am never going to be able to unsee that!"

"But got your mind off the interview, right?"

AT SAVEUR FARE, Frankie wished Kostya good luck, told him to call him after, and left him waiting in Michel's office while he went to say hey to some people he knew in the kitchen.

Kostya stared at the framed memorabilia on the wall—culinary school accolades, awards so prestigious even he had heard of them, clippings from big-name papers and magazines. Maybe, he thought, he could learn enough here to try his dad's dish again. Maybe he could get good enough that he could make any dish he tasted. And wasn't that what he was after? Control over his taste buds and his destiny?

He closed his eyes and told himself that he could do this.

The interview went horribly.

WHEN KOSTYA PICTURED Michel Beauchêne, he'd imagined a refined French gentleman in his early sixties, hair going slightly grey, belly round with years of buttering, a soft accent on the tongue, and kind, fatherly eyes that would see into Konstantin's soul and take pity on him.

The real Michel Beauchêne was not old, or fat, or even particularly French. He was young (an executive chef at just forty-two) and built lean and strong (body by Jivamukti) with cold, calculating eyes and a flat, New York edge to his voice. His parents were French expats, and he'd grown up in Manhattan, attended prep school in the city, and then slummed around Paris for a few years, living off his parents' dime and apprenticing in some formidable kitchens—this from his well-rehearsed opening spiel.

He wasn't interested in Kostya's familial connections to cuisine—Vanya's Victuals was nowhere near the stratosphere of Saveur Fare suppliers—and Beauchêne was decidedly unimpressed by Kostya's experience dishwashing at The Library of Spirits. ("But that's a bar, isn't it? So did you actually wash any *dishes*, like from food service? . . . I see.")

After about ten minutes of excruciating Q&A, Michel closed his notebook, the page empty except for Kostya's name, and steepled his fingers beneath his chin.

"Thank you for . . . all that," he said slowly.

Kostya felt a masochistic kind of relief. He'd failed, but the torture was over; he could slither back out to the curb where he belonged. But then Michel threw him this curveball:

"Okay, I'm going to need you to spell this one out for me." He leaned back in his chair. "Normally, the people that walk through *that* door and sit in *that* chair do so with a sense of wide-eyed wonder about what goes on here. They come in with a list of references *this long*, with notches in their culinary belts you wouldn't believe. And then there's you.

"*You* had a single dishwashing job at a bar—glassware only—and things went so swimmingly there that apparently I cannot call over for a reference. You have no experience in a professional kitchen." He gazed dubiously at Kostya's folded, unblemished hands. "And if I asked you to cook something for me right now, something you and Frank have been, uh, *practicing*, I'd get, what, a grilled cheese? Why are you even interested in working here? I'm dying to know. I really am. Is it the money? Because trust me, with the hours you'd be putting in, it would be less than minimum wage. The reason people come into my kitchen is because they want to be the best at something; they'll kill themselves to get there. And, forgive me for being blunt, but I don't really get that vibe from you, Mr. Duhovny. I mean, do you even like food?"

Kostya just blinked at him, which only seemed to prove his point.

"Seriously. What's the best thing you've ever eaten? And for the love of all that is good and holy do *not* tell me salad and breadsticks from the Olive Garden."

Kostya chewed his lip.

Should he tell him about the best things he'd ever eaten, the detail of their component parts? Or was that cheating? The best things, after all, weren't things that he had technically *eaten*. He'd only tasted them secondhand; they weren't animal or vegetable or mineral, but memory—comestible desires, the fantasy food porn of anonymous ghosts. To describe those to the chef would be a kind of lie.

The other option—the honest option—was to just let it go, to slink back and confirm this Wüsthof toolbag's cutting observations about his intentions, his experience, and his palate.

"What's the matter?" Beauchêne prompted. "Can't decide between a Big Mac and a Whopper?"

Something inside Kostya, deep in his gut, lunged. He could take the digs about being unqualified and a liar and even a bad cook—all those things were true—but he couldn't let this guy insult his taste buds. His tongue was special. It was maybe the only special thing about him.

"Nevermind. I can see that we're not going to—"

"Duck." Kostya spat it at him like another four-letter word. "Duck ragout. It had this thick sauce, cinnamon cognac. A demi-glace, I think."

Kostya closed his eyes, remembering where the aftertaste had happened, trying to reincarnate it. He'd been on the sidewalk outside his mother's apartment two New Years' ago, pacing around and nursing tea that had gone cold, delaying the inevitable argument about how he was living his life when it had hit him.

"The onions were sliced so thin they fell apart to almost nothing in the stew. And these dried fruits that reconstituted in the duck fat—peaches and apricots and plums and cherries—they exploded between my teeth like tapioca pearls."

Kostya's eyes were still closed, but the stony silence from Beauchêne invited him to keep going.

"And a couple years ago, there was this coconut curry and Kaffir lime fried chicken."

That one happened to him at a Gristedes. He'd been in the refrigerated section, his fingers closing around the handle of a gallon of milk.

"The skin was so crispy, paper-thin, covered in these tiny, burnt coconut shavings and desiccated slivers of zest, and underneath, the chicken was so moist. The juices dribbled down my chin."

He'd invented that last part for effect, and it seemed to be working. Kostya could feel the air change around him, sizzling. He thought he heard the chef swallow.

"I have to say, I wasn't expecting—"

"I once had young goat," Kostya cut him off, his eyes squeezing tight in focus. "The whole thing was fire-roasted, charred, the meat brined and rubbed with garlic, thyme, rosemary. Hand-crushed juniper."

This one had choked him awake one morning in bed a few months prior; he'd drooled so much he nearly drowned in his own spit.

"It fell apart in my mouth. Every bite, I got a little of the ash from the fire pit, the grit of the sand, the scent of pine from the dried needles on the lumber burned to cook the thing."

"Who *are* you?" the chef wondered aloud.

"But the *best* thing"—Kostya smiled triumphantly, the memory reigniting across his taste buds—"has gotta be the fish head."

Four summers ago, he'd been driving through Chinatown in Vanya's delivery truck, stopped at a light and staring into a storefront with a Lucky Cat on the counter and a flock of dead chickens dangling in the window. A teenage girl walked out of the store, twisting the white cord of her headphones through her fingers, and as he watched her unlock her bike, the taste had come exploding into his mouth.

"It was dorade. Just the head. Grilled over charcoal. The skin was so charred that it curled away from the flesh. It was insanely sweet inside. Delicate. Like shaved butter. It was finished with this flaked salt that just balanced every bite: the bitter skin, the sweet fish, the acid from a roasted lemon, and the brightness of this very herby chimichurri. The taste of the eye, all the jelly behind it, was just, *mmm*," he moaned, remembering, "like thick, gelatinous soup. Like half-melted aspic."

The chef didn't say anything more. He just clicked his pen a few times, then opened and closed a desk drawer. Cautiously, Konstantin opened his eyes.

Michel Beauchêne met his gaze. "Okay."

"Okay?"

"Okay," he repeated. "We'll give this a shot. Against my better judgment. You start tomorrow."

ON THE STREET outside Saveur Fare, Kostya felt lighter than he had in weeks.

His bank account had been wearing dangerously thin, and though he'd picked up a few extra shifts on Vanya's truck, he couldn't take on any more hours without the risk of it getting back to his mother. And that phone call—*Why you not tell me about job? You get fired and I must hear this from Vanya? I your mother! I always want help, and you never tell me nothing! You should do more with life! Be doctor! Be lawyer! Building super, at least!*—was a conversation so foul he'd rather eat dirt. But now he'd never have to have it. He'd preempt it with news of a new job—a respectable one! with health care!—which might even buy him a few weeks without his mother's daily calls to make sure he was still alive, the obsessive check-ins her way of overcompensating for the months she'd spent bereft in bed.

Kostya bought cheap coffee from a cart and made his way east. It was a pitch-perfect summer day, the sky cloudless blue, and still early enough that the haze of humidity hadn't descended to drown them all in their own body odor.

He texted Frankie the good news, then crossed Central Park West and walked a few blocks south to the nearest park entrance—72nd Street, near Strawberry Fields—where he wandered until he found an empty bench and melted into a lazy pose.

Frankie texted him back with three trophy emojis and three bottles of beer and a wolf and a puppy and a drunk face and a question mark, and Kostya was in the middle of responding that, yes, he *would* like to get drunk tonight at Wolfpup to celebrate, when he saw the little boy and his dad.

The kid was catalogue cute—blond and curly, dimpled, old enough to have control of his limbs but only just—and he ran down the path with his arms flailing, squealing delightedly as his dad—soft body, Yankees cap, embarrassing cargo shorts, and the kindest laugh Kostya had ever heard— ran after him.

"Sashen'ka, wait for me! Sasha! You're going the wrong way!"

Kostya watched as the dad caught up to his tiny son, swept him into his arms, and threw him in the air. The rush of breeze and height and speed cast a delighted look on the boy's face, and his dad mirrored it, caught him, set him gently down, and took his hand.

Kostya's heart was pounding. He could almost feel the fissure within him squirming, straining the seams, hairline cracks forming from the pressure behind his eyes, and he braced himself for the aftertaste that he was sure would pass across his tongue at any moment—the same one that had set his whole life askew. But it didn't come.

He tasted the sour remains of his coffee, but that was all. The liver dish— the liver he'd failed to re-create even with Frankie's help, the liver that could have given him just a few minutes of that kind of weightless joy, like a kid being tossed into the air, knowing that someone would be there to catch him—that liver was conspicuously absent.

Kostya felt afresh the disappointment of that night in Wolfpup. In the gleaming, stainless kitchen, surrounded by Frankie's gear, he'd tasted failure again and again. The problem, of course, was simple. Without being able to taste the dish himself, Frankie was shooting blind; if he hit upon it, it would have been more miracle than skill, no matter how good a chef he was. When he said as much, Kostya just shrugged one dejected shoulder and muttered that it probably wasn't meant to be, to which Frankie had replied the way his Irish grandmother would have, and told him that in this life, and probably the next, a man makes his own luck.

"If you knew how to cook instead of going through me, you could probably nail those flavors. You'd know *how* it was made, not just what was in it." Frankie had wiped his hands matter-of-factly on his apron, as if washing them of the whole conversation. "You want that ghost? Get your ass in a kitchen."

Kostya deleted his text reply and wrote instead: Not tonight, honey.

Frankie shot back: You washing your hair?

Gonna see if I can watch dinner service. Lot to learn.

Frankie sent through a laughing emoji, tears in its eyes. Then:

Oh, you got it BAD. Welcome to the jungle. Don get burnt.

Farineaux

The Konstantin Duhovny Culinary Experience

IMPRESSIVE, RIGHT?

Now speaking as a cook, Saveur Fare's just The Dream. Clean. Efficient. Top-of-the-line everything. Crew performing at their absolute peak. An eating experience second to none.

But speaking as your tour guide, lemme pull back the curtain. Even a place like this can have some unsavory shit in the kitchen. Not rodents—though you're kidding yourself if you think an A rating means no mousetraps—but people. Way some folks run things can leave you with a bad taste, and Saveur's no exception.

Matter of fact—and if anyone asks, I will deny, deny, deny—there's a Big NDA about what went down here with our guy. You won't believe this shit—this biz is ruthless! But, uh, I didn't sign the paperwork, so I'll go ahead and spill some tea.

Let's head up to the dining room—tell you 'bout the service from a real special night. And I hope you like drama, because this part—it is jui-cy!

Family Meal

SIX MONTHS LATER, grey city snow slushed into sewer grates, string lights twinkled from every retail display, and Konstantin grew quietly desperate for burns.

Getting burned would mean that he was working the grill or sauté or even the fryer, for crying out loud. That he stood an actual chance of accumulating oozing blisters and shiny scars up and down his arms, the kind of badass injuries real chefs wore like badges before tattooing them over with expensive, elaborate sleeves. It would mean that he was cooking with fire.

But Kostya was stuck on *garde-manger*—the salad station!—and the only thing that could burn him there (maybe?) was ghost pepper oil, though even that would only be able to eat away at him from within—something his insecurities already had well in hand.

He knew he should feel proud of what he'd accomplished, and grateful three times over. And he did, for the most part. To make it to a station—any station—at a place like Saveur Fare, with zero culinary cred and well under a year on the job, was almost unheard of. He'd gotten lucky—absurdly lucky. One of the busboys had quit his first week, and Kostya stepped in to pull doubles, bussing at lunch and then doing dishes at dinner, which turned into bussing at both, and then a stint on the finishing station, and on to *garde-manger*. Michel hadn't exactly taken him under his wing, but his sous, Tony, had seen something in Kostya, an eagerness he'd liked enough to let him learn.

Whenever there were quiet moments—early in the morning, before service; late into the night, after the last table left—Tony would teach Kostya technique. How to hold a knife. How to start a stock. How to see if a pan was hot enough to sear but not scorch. While he washed dishes, bussed tables, did any and every menial task—scrubbing the burnt layers of pans till his knuckles bled; carrying fifty-pound crates of shallots down into the cellar; shoving his arm pit-deep behind the walk-in to clear a decades-old air filter—Kostya watched the men and women around him, and took copious mental notes. At night, he practiced what he'd seen them do—how they tasted and adjusted their sauces; how they butchered and broke down meat; how they organized their stations; the confidence with which their fingertips seasoned, sautéed, and served.

He worked himself to the bone most days. He came in early and left late, with barely enough time between to go home, shower, and change before heading back for another shift. His only day off was Monday, when the restaurant was closed, and most Mondays he spent in the kitchen at Saveur anyway, watching Tony and Michel debate the menu, sample the week's produce, and talk shit about the soms.

Every minute he spent at the restaurant, each time he learned a new cooking method or honed a new skill, Kostya could almost feel the possibility of seeing his dad draw closer. Whenever he got an aftertaste now, he'd test himself, making mental notes about the flavors and textures and techniques he thought had gone into the dish, and trying them out later, when the Saveur Fare kitchen was abandoned to his own private ghost laboratory.

He hadn't actually summoned a spirit since that night at The Library, but Kostya suspected that had more to do with the other factors—the deceased's presence and the intermediary who needed to eat the food—than it did with his cooking. He figured that, in his dad's case, he could do the tasting himself, provided his father ever showed up again with that liver. Though the odds of a repeat taste didn't seem quite so hopeless now, not after that night with all the Reese's.

He wished he could go back there, to Seyoncé, and face the psychic again. Show Madame Everleigh how wrong she'd been, not just about the aftertastes, but about him. He thought about it a lot. About her. About how gorgeous she was, and how mean. About her warnings. About what he should have said. What he might say now.

He was different; Saveur had seasoned him. Every minute he spent in the kitchen made him feel like he'd found something he hadn't known he'd lost. He woke up buzzing. He *liked* coming to work. So much that it barely felt like work at all. He liked the chefs and the line cooks and the front-of-housers, even if they didn't always like him. He liked the scrupulous kitchen, the way everything had its place. He liked how hauling crates and being on his feet and sweating in the kitchen heat made his body feel. He liked working with the ingredients, learning the seasons by the harvests they yielded, the treasures he unpacked. He worshipped the food.

Sometimes, inspired, he'd experiment with variations on the house specialties, swapping sauces or modifying ingredients. He found he had a gift for knowing which flavors to pair, for intuiting how textures and notes and even the shapes of foods would combine in an excited mouth. And while he'd never dream of feeding the fruits of his labors to any of the staff, he thought, by and large, that his edits had improved their dishes. It wasn't that he thought he was a better cook, or that his measly months of kitchen drudgery outweighed their years of experience and toil. It was just that he thought he was a better taster than everyone there—Michel included.

Sometimes he'd even forget himself and toss unsolicited suggestions out to the kitchen floor. Mostly, this was met with vitriol. But once, Henri's—the saucier's—consternation changed to a look of surprised consideration when Kostya suggested lemon juice to resurrect a forgotten reduction that'd boiled into sludge. Another time, when Tony was swamped with a private party, he had Kostya finish his plates before sending them out to the dining room. And the sommeliers, who had a reliable hate-hate relationship with the line, found Kostya refreshingly approachable, took to shooting the shit with him after hours, and even occasionally solicited his opinions on food pairings. Even Michel—from whom he had about as much chance of extracting a compliment as he did of finding a pearl in a raw-bar oyster—had been caught actually smiling as he watched Konstantin work.

But all that still didn't change the fact that he didn't have any formal training and no one at Saveur was going to let him forget it. The kitchen was stacked with school snobs, which wasn't much of a surprise, since the fish stunk from the head. Michel (Le Cordon Bleu, '96) was notoriously nepotistic, and though he'd espouse egalitarian views about hiring the hardest-working chefs regardless of pedigree in interviews and glossy spreads from *Bon Appétit* to *Zagat*, the vast majority of his kitchen came straight from fancy schools and fancier apprenticeships. Still, even with the CIA or Le Cordon Bleu or ICE behind them, Kostya's colleagues couldn't do a lot of what he could. Decades of ghost tasting had trained his tongue better than their big degrees ever could.

All of which is to say, it came as both a surprise and not a surprise when Michel asked to speak with him before dinner service the Thursday before Christmas.

Kostya's hands got clammy on the walk over to his office. He barely ever went down this administrative hallway; he hadn't, in fact, stepped foot on the Moroccan floor tile since he'd first filled out his employment paperwork. His mind hummed with energy, speculating. Kostya could be getting fired. Promoted. Invited to an exclusive restaurant orgy. Framed for murder. Nominated to represent Saveur Fare as a marathon runner. His body sold to a science convention to pay for truffles by the pound.

He opened the door.

"Konstantin. Good. Come in. Sit."

Michel looked years older than the last time they'd sat in this office, and decidedly pissed about something.

"Uh, thanks. *Merci*, Chef."

His French sounded like he was asking for mercy, which, *well*, he wasn't not. Kostya swallowed and sat.

"I'll keep this brief since service is about to begin. I need a favor." Michel pinched a tiny speck of lint from his chef's coat and flicked it to the floor. "Henri's sister is getting married on Saturday" (uttered with the air of discussing something decidedly perverse), "and he begged off a year ago for the wedding" (as if this were a first-degree crime), "which means we don't have anyone making sauces that night . . . " (this with a sort of hopeful despondence).

"But Saturday's the Gild," objected Kostya, and Michel gave a small smile, pleased that he appreciated the seriousness of the situation.

Saturday, the restaurant would be shutting down for the private party to end all private parties—Bouche de Noël, the annual, by-invitation-only Christmas bash hosted by Gild, the restaurant group that owned Saveur Fare and Tutankhamen and a dozen other impressive New York institutions. The guest list was always a who's who of New York's culinary elite, plus the rich and famous who liked to rub elbows with them. Each year, Gild tapped one of their restaurants to host the soiree, and though it was an absolute pain in the ass of a night for the staff, it also guaranteed Gild's generous financial support—big, fat, year-making bonuses—provided it went off without a hitch.

Because it was such an important night, Michel had called in several artisans—a sugar sculptor, a wild-game huntsman, a guy who planted pearls inside edible oysters—as well as tightening his already prong-like grip on his regular kitchen staff. Kostya was supposed to tag-team salad and cold appetizers with Fernando, with Tony running sauté, Francois on grill, and Henri razzle-dazzling everybody with the new sauces he'd been concocting. Kostya had watched him prep for the better part of a week, sticking teeny-tiny tasting spoons into goop of every imaginable color and shade and making micro-adjustments to the tune of five grains of salt or a single turn of the pepper mill. And now he didn't understand how no one had planned ahead, or what, exactly, Michel expected him to do.

"So, what's the favor?"

Michel blinked rapidly.

"It appears that the gravity of Saturday isn't lost on you. Good. Fortunately, Henri is wrapping on his sauce plan and is going to prep everything we need before he goes. It should be a simple plug-and-play, but—just in case—I'd like you on saucier."

Kostya swallowed a throat lump so large he thought he might have ingested his Adam's apple.

"Me?"

"You've impressed me. I was sure you wouldn't, but you did. I'd like to give you this opportunity to rise to the occasion. I'll arrange for Henri to brief you tomorrow."

"Wow. Yes. Of course! Thank you, Chef. I won't let you down."

THE NIGHT OF the party, Kostya took over saucier, Fernando worked salads solo (with a visible chip on his shoulder), and Michel made rounds in the dining room in his chef's whites, occasionally popping his head in to give them play-by-plays or hiss at them to hurry it up.

Henri had left seven pages of meticulous notes in minuscule slant; if anyone was going down for a sauce-related snafu, it wouldn't be him. But what Michel had described as a simple plug-and-play was nothing of the sort. There were myriad dishes presented as bites to create the desired cocktail atmosphere, each with its own accompanying sauce, some with modifications for food allergies, general aversions, et cetera, et cetera, and enough variation in the flavors that mixing up one sauce with another could be damning.

If he weren't thoroughly convinced that Michel had no sense of humor, Kostya would have wondered if this was his idea of a joke.

Things went smoothly through the cocktail hour, thousands of morsels of scallop ceviche, cryo-seared lamb, endive and fig gratin, and foie gras parfait sweeping past Kostya's station just long enough for him to paint their corresponding sauces—preserved lemon butter, julep mint foam, raspberry-quince glaze, apricot preserve—on with tiny brushes before they were twirled round the room on enormous silver platters.

He got a brief respite during the raw-bar service, since the mignonette and cocktail sauces, clarified butter, Thai-chili vinegar, and lemongrass yuzu reduction that accompanied the oysters, shrimp, king crab, and caviar had been dished in advance into mother-of-pearl bowls and arranged within an elaborate ice palace.

He swigged water from a quart container, wiped the sweat dripping down his eyebrows and nose with a kitchen towel, and checked the clipboard. Pasta was next.

Kostya braced himself.

At Saveur, they made their own fresh pasta, cooking it to order à la minute. Even though the number of guests at this party more than tripled their average pasta orders for an evening, Michel had promised Gild that he'd deliver not only fresh pasta but seven different kinds, each with an inspired sauce and garnish.

Lorenzo, their *pastaio*, had come in at the ass crack of dawn to craft thousands of *gnudi*, *anelli*, *cavatappi*, *fideo*, *gemelli*, *orecchiette*, and *mafaldine*. Each pasta dough had been infused with a specific flavor—lemon zest in the *gnudi*, basil oil in the *anelli*, white truffle for the *cavatappi*, and so on—calibrated to complement the pasta sauces and create an orgasmic eating experience. The problem was that Kostya now had to oversee which sauce went on which pasta, with mere minutes between different batches flying in and out of water baths and sauté pans across three different stations, all hands on deck to cook, sauce, plate, garnish, and serve. And all this with two cream-based sauces, four tomato-based (two meat; two vegetarian), and one purple pesto, which meant that, aside from the pesto, he couldn't just yell, *Hot nut for mafaldine with the red jizz!*, because no one would know which red sauce he meant.

They'd agreed to try to keep just one pasta type on sauté at a time to avoid confusing the sauces and garnishes, and the plan seemed to be working. The first two had already gone out, and the third—lemony *gnudi* with almond–arugula–purple cauliflower pesto—was being plated. Kostya was just starting to feel a sense of pride, a new level of confidence in his culinary abilities, when he felt a tingle along the back of his neck.

It chilled him even though the kitchen was a fiery ring, his jacket soldered to his back with sweat. He took a deep breath and prepared for the aftertaste to pass over him, rolling in and out like an ocean wave, but as soon as it hit his tongue, his whole body went numb.

Gooey, sweet onions. Crispy morsels of liver that melted as he chewed. A zing of acid. Dill. And something bitter, just there, bringing up the rear.

He hadn't tasted this dish in twenty years, but it was exactly the same as the very first time, the taste he'd tried to re-create with Frankie, the taste he'd churned in his mind like butter, the absolutely irrefutable proof that his dad was here, *now*, waiting to see him, lingering for who knew how long before he vanished again, maybe forever. And for the first time in all those years, Kostya suddenly thought he knew how it was made.

"Oh shit!" he gasped.

"What?" To his left, Fernando jumped, alarmed, one pan in each hand, tossing *gnudi* coated with pesto into the air. "Didn't you tell us pesto?"

"Yeah. No! Sorry. Pesto's right."

Kostya's mind raced. There were whole chickens in the walk-in. He could pull the livers out of a couple, grab a lemon and white onions from the pantry; the dill was right there, on Fernando's mise.

"*Oy!* Konstantin! Cavatappi, what's the jizz?"

It was Tony, who was working a station and also directing the guys boiling the pasta. Kostya snapped back to attention.

"Meyer lemon Alfredo, garnish beluga!" He recited it automatically, the memory rote, and then hesitated. "No, wait! Sorry. The other Alfredo—the smoked salmon, garnish with Everything Bagel."

Tony raised an eyebrow. "You sure?"

Kostya thought. The cavatappi was the curly one, with the charred-onion infusion. The smoked salmon Alfredo was an ode to cream cheese and lox, paired to give the whole thing a New York bagel vibe.

"Yes, Chef!"

"You're the boss."

As Kostya hurtled toward the chicken, he heard Tony turn to the rest of the floor, raise his voice.

"I got cavatappi, smoked salmon Alfredo, Everything garnish! We gotta kick it up, people, shit's dying on the pass here, and Fernando, *Jesus!* Get your fucking *meez* in check!"

Kostya hunted in the walk-in, smacking his lips as he did, willing the taste to linger. He finally found the chickens tucked behind three boxes of duck breasts, and snagged the onions, the lemon. He was firing on all cylinders. He'd have to pull the giblets, toss the gizzards and hearts, keep the livers. Thin-slice the onion. Lemon into wedges.

He grabbed a sauté pan and jammed it onto one of Fernando's burners. Fernando was busy trying to clean up the mess on his station—garnishes everywhere—and almost didn't see him.

"What are you doing?" he finally asked, aghast, as Kostya started fumbling inside the chicken cavity.

"I got a VIP on the fly," Kostya lied. "From Michel."

Fernando moved one of his pans to make room.

"*Shit shit shit*," Kostya chanted under his breath, half from nerves and half to remember the flavor he was going for.

All this time, and he'd somehow never put it together. It was his father's favorite dish, but his *mother* had prepared it. His mother, who was always yammering away on the phone when she cooked, so absorbed in lecture or conjecture that she burned almost everything. Including *pechonka*.

Kostya wished that he could have just asked her about it. He wished she would have consented to talk about his dad, or cook the foods he loved, or keep the clothes that still smelled like him. He wished that she could have found a way, however small, to keep his father alive. Instead, it was like she'd blotted him out in her mind, an ink stain where the man used to be. A redaction. Everyone had their own way of grieving, and hers was denial.

He's no more, she used to say whenever Kostya brought up his father, the words bitter as a rind, *and he never will return now*.

Except now, maybe, with Kostya's help, he might.

He spooned a thick dollop of softened butter into the pan. It skipped across the surface, sizzling hot, foaming, turning brown. He threw on the sliced onions, flicked his wrist again and again to coat them, watching them soften.

"C'mon, c'mon," he willed them, "faster."

"Who's the *VIP*?" Fernando asked conspiratorially. "You know?"

"I gotta concen—" Kostya began, but then Tony was asking him what went on the *gemelli*.

"*Gemelli, gemelli*," Kostya repeated, adding a splash of oil and the livers to the pan. "Meyer Alfredo! Beluga garnish. And then the *fideo*, with the Mexican meat sauce, cotija, and cilantro."

That should keep the line busy for a while, and after that was just the *anelli* and the *orecchiette*—glorified SpaghettiOs and puttanesca—and they'd be home free.

"Konstantin, you gonna burn the liver, man."

Fernando tried to help him move the pan, but Kostya shrugged him off.

"Michel said *kill it*."

Fernando shrugged and got to work on the naked *gemelli* toppling into his station.

Kostya watched the outside of the liver fry and slid half—if it needed more time, he'd be able to try again without missing the window—onto a plate, seasoned it with Kosher salt, squeeze of lemon, sprinkle of dill, and a tiny pinch of parsley from Fernando's newly organized *mise en place*. He turned the gas off the burner.

He stared down at the dish, a vibration kicking up in the back of his throat.

The waitstaff were pirouetting in and out of the swinging kitchen doors now, delicate test tubes of *gnudi* and *cavatappi* glinting from the viper jaws of the Medusa-headed candelabras they were using to serve. (Talk about overkill.) The guys on the line were starting to boil *fideo*, switching to ultrafine mesh colanders to catch the hair's-width noodles as they came steaming out of the water. That gave Kostya just a couple minutes before Tony needed another direction.

"Yo, Tony!" he called. "Next up's *anelli*. Tomato broth, Parm crouton garnish."

Tony nodded. "Heard!"

Kostya grabbed his plate and shuffled to the pastry station, which was dusted with confectioners' sugar and flour and abandoned since dessert wouldn't be for another two hours. It was almost eerily quiet, just the occasional bang or sizzle from the kitchen. His hands trembled as he speared a bite of liver and brought the fork to his mouth.

He closed his eyes.

Chewed.

Tasted.

Smiled.

The bite was, note for note, what his father's ghost had slipped him. Only real.

Kostya swallowed, and something happened.

He could feel the aftertaste traveling down his throat, past his lungs, down into his stomach. He followed it deep into his gut, and somehow further, down into the chasm of his longing, to the lining between worlds. He could see it in his mind's eye, the way the morsel of liver—chewed, half-digested— ate away at the whisper-thin wall, dissolving it like an acid wash.

It was so bright on the other side, the kind of blinding luster that burned straight through your retinas. Just as the aftertaste was about to break through, tiny pinpricks of light beaming right into his insides, Kostya heard a crash in the kitchen and opened his eyes.

There, hovering over the floured stainless steel, were hundreds of blinking yellow lights.

The rest of the kitchen—well lit by rows of heatproof fluorescents— seemed almost dim by comparison. Kostya bit his lip, watching the lights pulse and twinkle, unable to peel his eyes away as they coalesced into the shape of a head, a torso, a waist.

There were more crashes across the line as the lights drew notice— murmurs and *holy shits* peppering the air as the cooks glanced up and witnessed the uncanny over in pastry, their sauté pans dropping with a clang as they lost concentration, utensils skittering to the floor—but Kostya barely heard them.

"*Papa?*" he asked, his voice on the edge of a sob.

The lights at the very top—the ones that were just now forming a forehead and jaw and oversized ears that were so excruciatingly familiar—gave an eager nod.

Кушай.

He heard the word like music, his dad's voice telling him to eat. He shoved another bite of liver into his mouth, found it hard to chew and swallow around the lump welling in his throat.

His dad got brighter, his edges more defined. He could see his face now, aglow in warm citrine light, like a prism passing through topaz. Every line in his forehead and eyes was exactly like Kostya remembered them. He felt his heart flutter in his chest, lifting him up as though he weighed nothing at all.

"Papa, *Papa!* Oh, God, it's so good to s—"

"*Duhovny!*"

Both Kostya and his father jumped in response to their name.

Michel burst violently through the kitchen doors. His face was rabid, flecks of spittle lining his mouth, eyes absolutely enraged. He pounced purposefully from station to station, scanning the room for Konstantin, the other chefs on the line all keeping their heads down, the work going. Whatever this was—though they'd gossip and shit talk and bust Kostya's balls endlessly about it afterward—they wanted no part now.

He shoveled more liver into his mouth, hoping it was enough to keep his dad materializing, and wove through the kitchen toward Michel. They met in front of the fry station.

"Here, Chef," Kostya said meekly.

"Instead of where you're supposed to be! Why aren't you at saucier?"

"I—uh—"

"You know what, I don't even care. What I really want to know is what the hell this is."

He held up a thin glass vial—plucked from one of the Medusa-headed candelabras—with spiral pasta curled inside, coated with a white Alfredo sauce, dots of black sesame visible in the garnish on top.

"The cavatappi, Chef?"

Michel shoved the vial at him, his furious face inches from Konstantin's, a vein in his neck throbbing.

"Eat."

Kostya nodded nervously, his mind a horrible blank—had he really fucked this up? given the wrong order?—and tipped the shot of pasta into his mouth.

The taste was instantly overpowering. Discordant. Wrong. It was bad. The creamy smoked salmon clashed horribly with the dough, which had been infused with truffle, *not* onion, offending his whole palate. In short order, it overtook the liver and onions, wiping the aftertaste entirely from his mouth.

Before he even realized what he'd done, the light in the room blinked, a bulb burning out, and Kostya whirled back toward the pastry station to find shadow.

"No!" he gasped.

"You shit the bed," Michel snarled. "The most important night of the year, and—hey! Where the hell do you think you're going?"

Kostya was darting back to pastry, bobbing around the stunned cooks at a half-dozen stations as he hurled himself toward the plate of liver, Michel hot on his heels. He shoveled it into his mouth with his bare hands—flatware be damned—but no matter how quickly he chewed, how completely he coated his mouth with the taste, the sparks didn't flicker back.

He had lost the tenuous connection, had severed the tie. His dad was gone.

Kostya felt the blood rush to his head. He grew faint and swayed on his feet. The kitchen was so hot, suddenly, so suffocatingly hot.

"I was speaking to you, Duhovny."

Michel's voice simmered, nearly a whisper. Kostya thought he looked mad enough to slug him, and he stared at Michel's thick, kitchen-scarred hands, waiting for them to clench into fists. Instead, he snatched the plate of chicken liver away.

"What is this garbage?" he asked, smelling it, sampling a tiny morsel on the tip of his tongue, his eyes growing wide, flashing dangerously. He strolled back through the kitchen, the plate held high. He wanted everyone to see this.

"Oh, I think I understand. We're getting creative now. We've somehow grown the balls to come into *my* kitchen during the most important service of *my year*, and fuck up *my* pasta course—so badly, I might add, that the president of Gild just told me he thinks I might be losing my touch—and in the meantime, we think we're *so* brilliant that we're coming up with our very own recipes, testing them out in the middle of *my* event, instead of doing our fucking job and overseeing every fucking bite of food that comes out of this fucking service like we were fucking supposed to. Fuck you, Duhovny. You're a waste of fucking talent. Now get out of my kitchen."

Kostya stood rooted to the spot, his mouth dry.

"Chef. Give me the plate back. Please."

He was desperate to try again, to somehow invite the connection, to make that dish perfect, one more time, to get his dad back and tell him—

"This plate?"

And with one furious motion, Michel threw the whole thing—plate, liver, lemon wedges, garnish—into the nearby fryer, which erupted so violently it sprayed Konstantin's entire right arm in a wave of flesh-curdling oil.

Potage

The Konstantin Duhovny Culinary Experience

OKAY, FAM, QUICK *show of hands—who saw that one coming? Wild shit, right? Lemme tell you, I saw KD's scars with my own eyes—this was before he got that dope sleeve—and it looked ripe. Like, I wasn't sure skin like that could heal, man. Nasty burn. Needed grafts or whatever, and even after, well, it didn't look right without ink. Like that.*

. . . .

Oh, it's more than fucked up, sis; it ain't legal.

And, look, I mean, kid was no fool. First thing he did out of the ER was call a lawyer—and he gets a letter written. This is all grapevine stuff I'm telling you now. I never saw the note and Gild did an outstanding job keeping it quiet. But apparently, Michel got scared. Figured he could lose everything if Bones wanted to press him. Which, you know, was true—room full of witnesses and his arm right there as evidence, plus the doctor's notes and all. So they settle. Our guy gets a nice little payday, plus a glowing review for anywhere he wants to go, because at this point Michel's not saying boo. Bones could've had his pick—Le Bernadin, Eleven Madison, Gramercy Park, all those fancy tasting tables would have eaten him up with a spoon after Saveur, and he knew it, too.

But he's done with fine dining now. Totally disenchanted.

He got a taste of what it meant to do his own little thing. To cook the food he wanted, on his own terms. He couldn't just go back to a new line in someone else's kitchen.

So he opened his own spot.

Here she is, up on the left.

A little hard to pick out from the street if you don't know what you're looking for. All these old Hell's Kitchen brownstones are, like, same make and model. There's no sign, no awning, nada. Just this cramped two-bed—first floor of this one here.

This, my friends, is Konstantin Duhovny's actual residence. Where the magic happens. Where the sausage gets made. Where you really hope the fuzz don't show up asking for permits because, uh, you're not operating with any.

Up the stairs here. You up front, my man, lead the way!

Let's see what's cooking at Hell's Kitchen Supper Club.

Soul Food

KONSTANTIN POSTED THE flyers under the influence of alcohol.

One near his apartment in the heart of Hell's Kitchen, taped to a sticker-book traffic pole. One in Washington Square Park, affixed to the gate of a dog run. One all the way downtown, at Trinity Church, stapled to the cemetery fence. One taped flat on the sidewalk in front of the New York Public Library, the stone lions, Patience and Fortitude, eyeing him disdainfully.

He'd been aiming (could you aim at that level of inebriation?) for places where ghosts might hang out, and where the people who wanted to see them again might go looking. When he couldn't think of any, he settled for foot traffic. The flyers read:

DINE WITH GHOSTS

Have you lost someone?

Recently bereaved, and reliving the past?

Mourning for the long haul, unable to let go?

Wish you had one more chance to tell them how you feel?

We can help.

Have a last meal together at the **Hell's Kitchen Supper Club**.

You bring the memories; we'll bring up your ghosts. (Literally.)

RSVP required. One diner per night. Seating at 8 PM. Pay what you can.

<u>Serious inquiries only</u>.

This was followed by a fringe of paper tear slips along the bottom, saying TEXT FOR DETAILS and giving Kostya's phone number.

Thinking back on the whole episode—the way he'd just dashed off the text at Kinko's, the way he'd printed the flyers without a single moment's hesitation—made him cringe. He'd been so confident. So convinced that this would work.

Granted, he'd been aided and abetted by several glasses of juniper-flavored courage. He'd spent the better part of the morning curled up on the couch with a bottle of Hendrick's, thinking about Saveur, and his dad, and how that hot, mean psychic had probably been right about him. He *had* been a coward, entrapped by his own hesitations. Unfit to handle the Dead.

"Maybe you should switch to decaf," Frankie suggested.

He'd walked out of the bathroom to find Konstantin becoming one with the couch cushions, in the exact same position as the day before, wearing the same clothes and the same indelible look of dumb disbelief on his increasingly plastered face.

"Or," Frankie reconsidered, "phew! At least change the bandages. Your arm smells like the Sunday special."

The doctors in the burn unit had talked him into a xenograft of tilapia skin, which meant that they'd applied the parts Kostya used to trash at Saveur Fare to the painful, searing open wound on his arm, and wrapped the whole thing in gauze. Just twelve to fourteen days smelling like fish sticks and he'd have a jump start on a new epidermis, they promised.

Kostya took another sip straight from the bottle.

He kept replaying it in his mind's eye, the scene with Michel. It scalded every time. His meekness, his spinelessness, his irrational fear. And of what, in the end? Michel Beauchêne's fury? His disappointment? Whatever awful lapdog instinct he had brought out in Kostya's subconscious, it had cost him his shot at seeing his dad again. Maybe his only shot.

Kostya had tried making the liver again—and he'd succeeded, over and over, the flavor precisely what he had eaten before Michel yanked the plate away. But his father hadn't shown. The aftertaste, it seemed, had to be fresh for it to work. The spirit had to still be there. All Kostya could do now was wait and pray that the aftertaste would reappear, that his dad would return on his own.

Frankie wrenched open their living room window.

"Alright, my guy. Enough. Outta the house." He snatched the bottle out of Kostya's slackening fist. "First, shower. Then go."

"Where'm I s'posed to go?" Kostya slurred back.

"Anywhere. Nowhere. Till you find some meaning, or a restaurant concept hits you. Maybe you'll figure out your next career move. At least till the room airs out."

Kostya shrugged and didn't move.

"Okay." Frankie tried again. "How 'bout this? Do me a solid—go by the FedEx on 9th and print me out a couple more copies of my résumé. Keller called back."

"Shit." Kostya sat up straighter. "You steppin' out on Rio?"

"I'm just taking a meeting," Frankie said, in a voice he usually reserved for conversations about commitment. "Anyway, you scratch my back, and how's *kadhi* and garlic naan sound? I'll hit Kalustyan's for asafetida."

A drunken smile curled over Kostya's mouth.

"Stop tryna get in my pants."

"You're a cheap date, Bones. Don't ever change."

IT WAS HALFWAY to FedEx, pressing the button for a walk signal, that the thought occurred to him. If there *was* still a chance to see his dad, however slim, he couldn't just wait around for his aftertaste to appear. While Kostya felt fairly confident about his ability to make the dish again, he couldn't risk tasting *pechonka* in a cab, or on the subway, or anywhere else he wouldn't have access to ingredients, to a kitchen. He had to learn to trigger the aftertastes for himself. To make them come when called. Like pushing a button.

And to do that, he needed practice.

By the time he got to 9th Avenue, the vague, inebriated plan had taken shape.

Flyers. A ghost test kitchen. One diner at a time.

Hell's Kitchen Supper Club.

KOSTYA HADN'T EXPECTED to receive any inquiries, not really, not based on his garbage ad, but barely a day later his phone exploded, firing off messages from several strangers all requesting reservations, the first of whom (Louise) he'd given his home address and a date (February 1) along with instructions to spend the day of her dinner stewing in thoughts of her dearly departed.

Louise was the music director at Our Lady of Sorrows on the LES and saw the flyer outside of Trinity Church after a workshop on organ maintenance. She seemed quaint, he thought, in her text messages. Mild. No-nonsense. Then again, she could easily have been an axe murderer, a religious zealot, or—heaven forbid—a social media influencer.

With Frankie's help, Kostya transformed their pocket-sized apartment into a workable restaurant. They hauled their stained couch, broken television, and cheap, particleboard console to the curb, and arranged a Craigslist dining set—PLANT YOUR ASS-CHEEKS IN JUDE LAW'S OLD CHAIRS!!! MANHATTAN PICKUP ONLY!—in the space to create a dining room. They strung up a shower curtain (a *Keanu Reeves Jesus with Dog* print, the last option left at their bodega) to separate the kitchen from the eating space. They scoured every visible inch of the apartment with bleach, and as they scrubbed some thirty years of grime from the ancient kitchen laminate and the crumbling brick of the exposed wall, Kostya—his melted arm still covered in a patchwork of fish-flavored bandages—made plans to pinball all over Manhattan to gather ingredients.

He'd asked Louise several questions about her ghost, trying to discern a category of food to focus on. She was maddeningly cryptic—*sister ate ascetic for years*—which, after more prodding, and answers like *oh, no, she couldn't have sugar* and *she liked meat, but had it very rarely*, Konstantin finally interpreted to mean that the poor woman had probably lived vegan or Paleo or some other equally Hellish half-life.

In the end, he decided that it was better to be overprepared than understocked. After all, maybe Louise's sister, Stacy, half-starved on bone marrow soup and rice crackers, had once stumbled into a Moroccan hole-in-the-wall to scarf down a secret helping of real food, and so it was prune-laced lamb—and not boiled tofu curd—that she'd need to find her way back.

For this to work, Kostya had to be ready for anything. He made a list of spices—from fenugreek to *furikake*—utilized in the myriad culinary traditions that someone living in New York City might encounter, and went shopping. By the end of his spice-gathering expedition, he felt like Vasco da Gama, unearthing new trade routes.

He'd wandered around Chinatown for a half hour before he found a place on Elizabeth without a single English character in the window. He bought star anise and red chili powder and Five Spice in there, plus a whole array of flavor enhancers that had no names, that he'd purchased on taste alone, dipping his pinky into tinctures and herbs and following his tongue. A few blocks uptown, on Broome, he snagged floral *yuzu koshō*, sinus-clearing *karashi* powder, *shichimi tōgarashi*, and Moshio salt from a Japanese standby. He bypassed Murray Hill and went instead to Jackson Heights in Queens, to a tiny Indian grocery that a Bengali busboy from Wolfpup had recommended, to get turmeric and garam masala, wild mushroom powder, plastic baggies full of curries ground to the most brilliant colors, gold and red and green. He took an Uber to the Bronx for Senegalese and Moroccan, West African and Northern, for *gejj* and palm oil, harissa and smen, *fufu* flour and suya and berbere and black cardamom, plus scores of base ingredients for dukkah and *bahārāt*, the blends so unique to each family that, if he needed them, he'd need the ghost to tip his hand. He hit up Ninth Avenue

International for handfuls of Mediterranean manna—tarragon, sumac, oregano, thyme. He scored truffle powder and *herbes de Provence* and bright strands of saffron from a small European market on Broadway.

And so on for seasonings.

The day before Louise's dinner he gathered the groceries.

Kostya got up in the dark to Citi Bike to the meat market on Bowery for the first pick of beef and pork and poultry and lamb. He got some more exotic stuff, too—venison and ostrich and rabbit and quail, even squab, which always tasted much more delicious than you'd think, considering most pigeons you saw squawking around the city were barely more than rats with wings.

He'd had to lie and say he was shopping for Saveur to get the suppliers to agree to sell him such infinitesimal portions—just one or two pieces of each protein, since he was quickly running out of fridge space—but he figured Michel still owed him one or a hundred, so whatever.

For good measure, he threw in chicken feet and pig hoofs and tongue and liver and heart, offal and marrow bones; someone could totally be jonesing for ramen in gooey, jelly-rich stock, and it was always possible the ghost hailed from green Scottish pastures and was craving haggis.

Frankie, with some prodding and more than a little groveling, had agreed to hit South Street on his day off for fresh fish—*You're the only guy in the world I'd sacrifice my beauty sleep for. You know how hard it is to stay this fresh all the damn time?*—while Kostya headed to the Manhattan Fruit Market in Chelsea for a truly staggering variety of produce.

Once that was deposited back in their apartment, Kostya caught the R train to Little Italy for canned Cuoco Milanese and San Marzano tomatoes in pretty glass jars, Nutella *fatto in Italia* (which put the American version to chocolatey shame), imported prosciutto and speck and ham sliced to translucent thinness. He scooped French bread straight from the oven at Balthazar. He picked up seven different kinds of rice, plus kasha, quinoa, farrow, and barley. And on his way home, he swung by the Food Emporium for dairy, tofu, tempeh, and seitan, as well as one of everything in the condiment aisle.

In the end, he'd spent a not-so-small fortune, but he'd grown increasingly okay with that. He felt empowered for the first time since he'd left Saveur Fare. He thought about his dad in his childhood kitchen, the way his whole face illuminated whenever Kostya guessed a mystery food, the way his mouth spread open, unable to contain his delight.

He was going to see him again, he swore, pushing a straining grocery cart forward on its broken wheel. He would find a way.

He'd do as many seatings at Hell's Kitchen Supper Club as it took for him to understand every rule, every nuance of the tethers he commanded—what triggered the ghosts, what stopped the connections, what might prolong them, what might entice them to be summoned in the first place—so that he could bring his dad back, and make him stay, and learn how to do it over and over. He'd never lose another chance because he was afraid, or intimidated, or trying to please. He'd never lose sight of what mattered again.

When his spirited guests showed up, he'd be their gracious host, their fearless leader. Their P. T. Barnum, full coat and tails and freaky pyrotechnics. Their Virgil, a voice of calm as they navigated the unknowable. Their Pac-Man, drawing them stealthily out of the maze with delicious fruits and no whammies. He'd be the maker of their dreams, the miner of their memories, the mouthpiece for their taste buds and tongues and every gut feeling.

Their Chef d'Esprit.

THE NIGHT OF the first dinner, that swagger was nowhere to be found. Kostya's intestines formed a queasy knot.

"You look like you're about to see a ghost." Frankie grinned as he pulled a coat over his chef's whites.

"You're funny, man, anyone ever tell you?" Kostya said sourly.

"Oh c'mon. You got this. What's the worst that can happen?"

"I dunno. Louise dies of food poisoning? Nuclear blast during dessert? Zombie apocalypse over apps?"

"Glad you thought this through." He punched Kostya's shoulder. "It'll work out. Just close your eyes, deep breath, picture yourself doing it. You'll be good, Bones."

"What if I can't be good?"

"Then be careful."

AN HOUR BEFORE showtime, Kostya positioned himself at the living room window. The street was deserted, already dark, the streetlamps casting ghostly halos in the night air. It smelled apple crisp and cold, like it was going to snow.

Kostya practiced his little opening speech under his breath, the words fogging the glass.

"Um, hi. Hello. Hey there. Welcome to the Hell's Kitchen Supper Club. My name's Konstantin, and I'll be your chef this evening."

Woof.

"Welcome, welcome!" he tried again, voice booming, "To a night of mystery, of enchantment, of otherworldly delights that will stun your senses and dazzle your . . . "

Jesus.

"Are you ready for some closure, because I'm about to serve it up— piping hot!"

What was wrong with him?

He'd just launched into another unfortunate monologue—"You ever ask yourself, what's the *deal* with ghosts?"—when the buzzer rang.

He pressed himself forward to catch a glimpse of Louise, but she was standing too close to the entry door, angled out of view. All he caught was a swish of long, black fabric, like a cloak. The buzzer again. *Great*, he thought as he dinged her inside, *dressed for Ren Faire and she's got an itchy trigger finger.*

A moment later, there was a timid knock on the door. Kostya pulled it open and had to pick his jaw up off the scuffed hardwood. Like the start of some bad joke, there stood a real, live, actual nun. In full habit.

She had an easy smile, lined by wrinkles that betrayed her age. Small, powdery hands. Eyes so watery it made him blink.

She blinked back.

He remembered, suddenly, what she'd said in her text, about eating ascetic. Somewhere, he was certain, God was laughing. So much for all that meat in his fridge. Maybe he could make wafers out of rice flour? Did nuns eat wafers, or was that just a communion thing—

"I'm here about the dinner? Louise?" she offered. "The ad said dine with *ghosts*."

She whispered the last word, like she was afraid it might escape.

"Yes! Louise! Uh, Sister. Hello. Welcome to Hell's Kitchen Supper Club. Please come in. May I offer you a seat in Jude Law's old chair?"

She stayed in the vestibule and frowned at his whites and checks, weighing his uniform against her own. "Is that supposed to be a Young Pope joke?"

"Oh, no! God, no!" Kostya fumbled. Louise winced at the Lord's name in vain. "I just bought this, um, this dining set"—he gestured absently to the table behind him—"that was rumored to once have . . . You know what, never mind."

Her frown was joined by an incredulous eyebrow.

"Is this some sort of scam? Because the ad said 'pay what you can,' so I thought you might be trying to do something charitable"—she eyed him suspiciously—"albeit unorthodox."

"Please," Kostya said, "it's not a scam. I just—look, it's sort of hard to explain, and I'd rather not do it in the hallway, if you don't mind?" He stepped back. "Just—come in, okay? Let me help you find Stacy. I'm not looking for any money."

At the mention of her sister—which Kostya now understood to mean "Sister"—Louise softened.

"All right," she said slowly, and crossed the threshold to his dim apartment. "But be warned. There's mace in my wimple."

THEY SAT AWKWARDLY across from each other, Sister Louise staring daggers at the Keanu Christ on the kitchen divider, her arms pretzeled over her chest, the glass of water he'd poured her untouched. After a few moments of this painful, judgy quiet, and without anything intelligible prepared, Kostya humbly slid off his toque, and started talking.

He introduced himself. Explained about his aftertastes. About the way his food brought spirits, briefly, back to life. Here, Sister Louise uncrossed her arms.

"How many times have you done this?" she asked. "Brought a ghost back."

"One," he answered slowly. "And a half."

"One and a *half*?"

He nodded. "Honestly? I don't know exactly how it works yet. Part of what I'm doing here is trying to find out. But in the meantime, I want to help people, if I can. Give them an opportunity to say what I—what they—didn't have the chance to."

She nodded slowly, studying him.

"Who did you lose?" she asked at last.

He hesitated. "My father."

"You bring him back?"

Kostya looked at his hands. "He was the half."

She nodded again. "Okay. What do I have to do?"

Kostya blinked at her, surprised she'd come around. He'd thought long and hard about this part, about what had made the spirits—Anna, and his dad—return. About what might have summoned them.

"Well, uh. Okay. You have to think about her. To . . . to reach for her. With your thoughts. You have to want her to come back. To miss her so hard it casts out a line."

Sister Louise rubbed her chest, right in the center. A tear slid down her face and vanished into her collar.

"I do."

"Then we'll wait. If she's around, I'll get a taste of what she wants to eat. Then I'll cook it, and you'll eat. And if I got it right, she'll appear."

"That's it?"

"That's it."

Sister Louise picked up the water and brought it to her lips. Took a sip. Set it back down. Looked hard at Kostya, gauging something.

"I'm not supposed to be here," she said then. "I told the other Sisters I had a headache. I'm supposed to be in my quarters, resting. If Father Mackenzie knew I was here, I'm sure he'd disapprove. He wouldn't support"—she gestured to the space between them, the flatware he'd set in front of her, the Keanu Jesus—"the occult. To say nothing of my Superior; she'd have my head just for tearing that slip off your flyer."

"So you're—sorry, what are you saying?"

"I'm saying"—she lifted the glass of water again—"do you have anything stronger?"

OVER SCOTCH, WHICH she drank like someone with a very different kind of habit, Sister Louise told Kostya about Sister Stacy. They met at the convent, both feeling the call in their twenties, Sister Louise after a stretch of horrible decisions that led her to seek the Lord and Sister Stacy after a string of good fortunes that renewed her faith in Him. They were fast friends, and though each entered into their sacred covenant with the deepest commitment to their Lord and Savior, they couldn't help feeling, too, that part of what drew them to the Church at the very same time was a divine wish for their two souls to meet.

"We were peas in a pod. And with our order being a closed one, we clung to one another for support. Each time I thought I wasn't good enough for this life, Stacy reassured me. Each time I had doubts—and I had many—she'd pray with me. I was so grateful for her. She had the wisdom of ages."

"How did she pass?" Kostya asked gently, and a dark look crossed Sister Louise, who drained her glass.

"That's just it," she said in a hushed voice. "I don't truly know. She was in the prime of her life. The picture of health. She'd run around the grounds for exercise, and one day, during her run, she just dropped dead."

"Jeez," Kostya exhaled, and she crossed herself. "Sorry. Did they autopsy?"

Sister Louise shook her head. "Doing so would imply that someone on the grounds at the time had harmed her. Which . . . we've all taken vows. We are women and men of God. It's inconceivable."

"So then . . . ?"

"Inconceivable," she repeated. "Not impossible. The thought bothered me so much that I requested a transfer. But even from a distance, it wore at me. I prayed and prayed on it. I asked the Lord to help me make peace with her demise, to forgive whoever had done it, but He never granted me respite. Which is why I'm here."

"To find out who killed her?"

Sister Louise nodded. "And to tell her how sorry I am, for not being there when it happened. She'd—she'd asked me to join her that morning. But I couldn't; I'd promised to help receive visitors from another parish, so she went without me. I can't tell you how much I regret that decision." She gave a small sob. "How many times I've wondered what might have been if her life hadn't been cut short. It's been almost thirty years, but I never stopped thinking about her. Wondering how. And why."

Kostya felt the sudden puff of air on the back of his neck, like somebody's last gasp.

"I—I think I got her."

He jumped up and barreled through Keanu Reeves and into the kitchen, Sister Louise's bewildered face vanishing behind him.

Flavors were blossoming in his mouth. Not the thin broth or stale bread or moldy old cheese he'd expected of a nun, but *heat*.

Hot cayenne. Smoky paprika. Tabasco. Lots and lots of Tabasco. The perfect, crispy crackle of golden fried chicken skin falling away from juicy morsels of dark meat. The characteristic tang of sour cream and the funk of Gorgonzola, but it wasn't . . . hm! Not a dip, but . . . soup? Hot and thick, creamy, roux-rich mouthfuls of baked potato chowder laced with lumps of blue cheese, and—yes! there it was, in the back of his throat—Guinness.

Kostya smiled to himself. There *was* some moldy old cheese in there, after all. And broth, he supposed. Plus a couple cardinal sins, like floating fryer-crisped goodness in anything that would make it go soft and soggy. Unorthodox and unexpected, the combination of heat and cream and crunch its own Holy Trinity.

He liked Sister Stacy already.

When he set the dish in front of Sister Louise, her eyes went wide.

SISTER LOUISE—NÉE Louise Mary-Ellen Fitzpatrick—stared down at the bowl in front of her. She knew this dish. It was the only outside meal she and Sister Stacy had ever shared, an ill-advised concoction Stacy's brother, Fred, had brought with him on a visit to the convent. They'd been too polite to refuse it, and had suffered mightily as a result, their bowels churning and cramping and threatening to vacate the whole night through. Unable to sleep, they'd stayed up talking, misery inspiring their love of one another's company. But there was no way this chef could have known that.

The soup's mere presence was a miracle.

Her hands trembled as she dipped the spoon into the bowl. Everything she was about to do—raise a spirit; defy God's will; consume this rich, decadent meal—reeked of wickedness. She might be struck down for this. Excommunicated. If not by the Heavenly Father Himself, then by the righteous women and men responsible for her actions. But she hardly cared. She had to see Stacy; she had to know.

Sister Louise tipped the soup into her mouth, the taste of it so potent it brought tears to her eyes.

The spoonful contained multitudes.

The lumps of potato with their skin, rough and brown and starched, were the tunics and stockings they were handed on their first day—*Cleanliness is godliness, Sisters!*—and the smiles they exchanged, she and the other novitiate, Sister Stacy Ann Robbins, as they donned them for the first time, their itchy, modest, new clothes. The tang and burn of hot sauce—Tabasco, heightened by cayenne—tore through Louise's throat just like her cough that winter, the only silver lining Sister Stacy's sweet concern, and the heat of the mustard patches from the medical ward, and the way she had applied them, hot and wet, to Louise's chest and back—*Breathe in now, deeply*—and how she kept applying them, long after Louise's cough had cleared. The chicken cracklings flaked with salt were the translucent pages of their Bibles, their heads bent low over their theology coursework, the crisp, righteous words that consumed their waking days and melted into dark meat, succulent conversation after lights out—*What do I miss? Romance novels. French fries. Being seen*—and a pause before Louise whispered back, *Nuns are supposed to be invisible. But I still see you.* And the chowder, smooth and creamy, sweet, the pale flesh of a wrist, a brow, a cheek, until the blue cheese crept in, ruining everything, like that afternoon in the gallery over the narthex, Sister Louise playing a hymn, the organ's rich, warm, brassy tone stirring life into stale air, Sister Stacy beside her on the bench, listening, humming, leaning close to watch, closer, until there it suddenly was, all those months of pious worship undone by this tacit meeting of their lips, and Louise could feel it again now, risen in this spoon, holy kiss! sacred! divine! a flush of heat in her face, a warm, ecstatic feeling coiling inside of her, cut suddenly short by a sharp, bitter sound that startled them apart, the click of the gallery door, the swift withdrawal of steps, the damning knowledge someone else had seen—penicillium, mold, bitter blue cheese—and a fortnight later, whoever it was taking justice into their own hands, agony rising in Louise like bile—Guinness, bitter and black.

The first firefly lights—blinding, electric blue—arrived as Louise swallowed. She saw them, streaky through her tears, and her mouth parted in surprise, her tongue still tingling with Tabasco as the sparks expanded around her, multiplying, pulling themselves into shape.

"Sweet Lord in Heaven," she whispered as Sister Stacy's dimpled face appeared, her smile enough to light cathedrals.

KOSTYA WATCHED THEIR reunion through the gap between worlds, his shower curtain severing the kitchen from the dining room, spaces special and distinct as altar and nave. These meetings were sacred. He wouldn't intrude. He would only observe, try to learn what he could, hone the tools of his craft. Hope that what he picked up would be enough.

Sister Louise ate slowly, and the nuns spoke for a long time.

There was more between them than she had let on. The way they looked at each other, how they laughed, what they said—it was obvious. They'd been in love. A quiet kind. New. A love that never quite got off the ground.

It was a love at odds with the Church, with the vows they'd taken.

"There is no penance I could do," Sister Louise said, wringing the skirt of her habit in her hands, "to atone for how you died. For my role in it. I've tried every prayer. Devoted myself every way I know how. It will never be enough. I—oh, Stacy! Can you ever forgive me? I should have been content to just sit beside you. To focus on my lessons and do God's work and live a humble, obedient life. If I wasn't tempted—if I hadn't deviated—you'd still be here."

Sister Stacy shook her head. She slid a glittering hand across the table.

"That is just absolute garbage, Louise. Catholic guilt! Listen to me, my darling: I made my choices, same as you. God knows there's nothing to forgive. Love has never been a sin. At least"—she gave a little eye roll—"not in my eyes."

Relief melted over Sister Louise's face. "Nor in mine."

"Murder, on the other hand," Sister Stacy continued, her light flickering in warning, "'*Thou shalt not kill.*' Exodus. Deuteronomy. Genesis. It's all right there. It's Sister Agnes who should have paid attention to her lessons, not you."

"*Sister Agnes?*" Louise gasped, choking on her soup. "But she was next in line for Superior!"

Sister Stacy nodded. "And a scandal—two novices under her charge quitting the Church, running away together—would have ruined her. She couldn't have it. So she put poison in my water bottle."

Sister Louise sat shellshocked for a moment, before uttering some choice phrases Kostya was sure didn't come from the Bible.

"And she's a Reverend Mother now! Thirty Sisters under her charge!"

"Which is why you should bring her to justice," Sister Stacy agreed. "If only to protect her order. But then—Louise, you have to let it go! Leave the burden of her judgment to the Afterward. It isn't yours to carry."

Sister Louise hesitated a moment, then nodded.

"Can I ask you something?" Sister Stacy studied her. "Why did you stay in? Why not refuse the vows and leave? Just start over, after everything? We were so young. You had your whole life."

Sister Louise swallowed more soup, then examined her reflection, inverted, in the spoon.

"The Church—the Sisterhood—it was the only thing I had left of you. Leaving it would have meant . . . putting you away. You were brief, in my life. But you were the truth. Maybe the most honest thing about me."

"I wish we'd had more time."

"So do I." Sister Louise scraped chowder from the bottom of her bowl. "It was difficult, holding two truths inside me all these years. What the faith teaches, and what I know in my own heart—they don't always reconcile. But

I found peace, eventually. Not in religion so much as in God. It's a different kind of love, but it sustained me when you couldn't anymore." She reached across the table for Sister Stacy's light-beam hand, their fingers occupying the same space, spirit layering through flesh. Then she smirked. "Can you at least level with me? What happened on the other side? Did you find peace? Did you meet God?"

"Oh, Louise!" Sister Stacy's eyes twinkled as she spoke. "There's so much I wish I could tell you! So much that surprised me! I always believed that if there were a Heaven, I'd be a shoo-in. But it wasn't that simple. Peace requires closure, not only faith or love." She hesitated. "I trust you'll do what it takes now, to let me rest?"

Sister Louise looked down at her plate, at the last buffalo wing there, coated in soup.

"I will. Of course I will. I just—will I see you again? After this?"

There was a long pause between them.

"I don't know," Sister Stacy said at last. "But I have faith. Love is patient."

Sister Louise nodded, her eyes filling with tears. "'It always protects,'" she quoted.

"'Always hopes. Always trusts,'" Sister Stacy supplied.

"'Always survives.'"

Sister Louise lifted the last wing to her mouth.

"Love." Sister Stacy gave a small, decisive nod. "The closest thing to godliness we'll ever know. The chef who prepared this meal, for instance." She glanced back toward the kitchen, straight into Kostya's prying eyes. "He did a selfless thing, reuniting us. An act of love."

"It really was." Sister Louise chewed, nodding. "I feel a burden lifted from my soul."

"Me too." Sister Stacy turned slowly back to face Louise. "Tell him it's important. This work he's doing. There are so many here, suffering. Seeking just this kind of aid."

"Suffering?" Kostya breathed from behind the curtain, his chest going tight.

"All right," Sister Louise agreed, absently biting the wing again, tearing the last morsel of chicken from its bone. "But why," she asked with her mouth full, "is there suffering in Heaven?"

She swallowed.

And before Sister Stacy could answer, before she could, in fact, say another word, her spirit scattered like a sparkler, her final flickers dying blue in the dark, dotting Kostya's ceiling like so many stars.

Entrée

The Konstantin Duhovny Culinary Experience

ALRIGHT! HOW WE DOING?

Getting a taste for our guy's secret sauce?

This is the place to do it, because Hell's Kitchen Supper Club was a real turning point.

Every chef's got one, that kitchen where you feel it for the first time, how you're touching people with what you do. Where the food becomes more than just food. Mine was at Wolfpup, first time I saw my take on Sancocho on the menu. And this right here—it's Konstantin's.

The Sister Act was just the beginning. Planted a seed for him, for what came next. See, his big motivator up till now's been his daddy issue, that big reunion. Whole point of Hell's Kitchen was getting him back. But what that Flying Nun said got his wheels turning. This was bigger than him. An opportunity to really help folks. Folks who, by the sound of it, really needed help. He do this thing right, he could change the world a little bit. Leave it better than he found it.

Go zero to hero.

But I'll keep it real: it wasn't all sunshine. There were hiccups, too. Always are with a restaurant. For one thing, our guy was getting low on cash. For another, spirits didn't always answer when he called.

Still, he made it. He opened.

More than a lot of spots can say, especially in New York.

So time to break out the champs, right? Toast to the future!

But it's a funny thing, the future.

Ain't never promised.

En flambé

A DINER BAR is an odd place to drink. Especially before noon. On a Tuesday.

But there Kostya was, seated at the bar of a greasy spoon called The Flame, sandwiched between Fordham sweatshirts debating a problem set and an early-bird geriatric considering the crossword, nursing a pale ale and soggy fries by the dawn's early light.

February had eighty-sixed, and after a month of service at Hell's Kitchen Supper Club, he had, too. What began as a home run (Sister Stacy! Buffalo soup! Easy-peasy!) had quickly devolved into a series of swing-and-a-miss. Night after night, diners arrived at his apartment aching to see their Dead, and Kostya struggled (and usually failed) to reunite them. He was burnt out. (Emotionally. Spiritually. Physically. Not to mention financially; the pay-what-you-can model had turned out to be kind of a money pit.) He was frustrated. (Who wouldn't be after twenty-eight consecutive dinners—no nights off; no breaks; no life outside death—with a measly six ghosts to show for it?) He was concerned. (No shit.) So while he knew he'd live to regret the morning booze, last night at Hell's Kitchen had been another flop, and he just needed something to soften the blow.

The customer had been a young guy, a freshman at NYU double majoring in history and East Asian studies. He'd wanted to see his granddad, to show him that he was finally learning Cantonese. The request was so sweet and simple and uncomplicated that it made Kostya smile. There was no grand drama playing out here. No high stakes. Just a kid, wanting to see his *Yé ye*, who had passed peacefully in his sleep a few months prior.

Except, after nearly an hour of romancing an aftertaste, Kostya hadn't gotten so much as halitosis. He felt awful. Not only a failure but a fraud.

Frankie had been helping in the kitchen—sometimes, on days off, he stuck around in hopes of feasting his own eyes on the mysteries of the unknown—and attempted to cheer him up.

"Don't sweat it, Bones," he said, wiping down the counter. "There's always next time."

Kostya slapped lids onto a half-dozen plastic containers—the remains of his untouched *mise en place*—and labeled them with the date.

"Except I'm on a losing streak, so next time's probably gonna flop, too."

"Always looking on the bright side."

"I just thought it would get easier with practice." He shoved the containers dejectedly into the fridge. "I wish I knew what I was doing wrong."

"Maybe it's not you." Frankie finished with the counter and dried his hands on his apron. "Maybe it's them. Maybe not every spirit wants to come back."

"But these ghosts are supposed to be suffering! Sister Stacy said so. Don't they want my help?"

"*They* probably do, but how do you know they're the ones you're getting?"

"What do you mean?"

"Take this kid tonight. All he wanted was to show off his homework, right? And Grandpa died peaceful, from what he said. No regrets. No big deal. Doesn't sound like suffering to me. So maybe he didn't need to come back."

Kostya frowned. "Maybe. But if you were dead and had the chance, need or not, wouldn't you just go?"

"If it were me," Frankie said, untying his apron, "I'd just stay dead."

"Bullshit. You'd be first in line to get back here!"

"Not a chance! There's some things I won't fuck with." He reached into the fridge for a bottle of Coke—the good kind, *Hecho en México*—and popped the cap on the edge of the counter. "Know how many stories my *'lita*'s got about spirits who fucked around and found out? One for every damn day of the year."

He handed the Coke to Kostya and got a second for himself.

"And yet"—Kostya took a sip—"you have no problem helping me bring them back."

"That's just cooking." Frankie swatted the thought away. "Same as any other kitchen. I don't gotta eat tripe to be able to serve it."

"Oh." Kostya laughed. "*Okay*. So it's fine for everyone else?"

"Look." Frankie held up his bottle. "It's like Coke. You got Diet; you got Zero; you got Freestyle if you're nasty. Call me a purist, but I like it classic. Everybody's gotta make up their own mind about what they want. And me? When I'm dead, I wanna stay dead." He took a long sip of soda, smacked his lips. "Matter of fact, gimme your word."

"On what?"

"That you won't bring me back if I go."

"Okay? Sure. You have my word." Kostya frowned. "But what if something happens? What if you're suffering? Don't you want to at least—"

"Nope." Frankie shook his head. "Save your hocus-pocus for the other guys, Bones. Folks with baggage." He polished off his Coke. "I plan on dying without any."

"Right. Naturally."

"I got it all figured out." Frankie grinned. "I'll win a James Beard or three. Couple Michelin stars. Get famous. Make a name. Open my own spot. Fuck around until I do because, well, when you look this good—but once it's set? Settle down. Give my mama her grandkids. Live a nice long life and die in my sleep around ninety. Before I need Viagra."

"Sounds pretty nice. We still living together in this scenario?"

"Oh, no, you'll be out on your ass. Better start looking for a new place to raise the Dead."

"Gotta keep my kitchen open that long first."

"Ah, shit. Speaking of kitchen"—Frankie checked the time: nine o'clock—"I gotta head back to Wolfpup."

"*Now?* I thought you were off."

"I am. But we're wrapping spring menus tomorrow, and I need to test a few more recipes. And then I'm going by Delia's." He winked at Kostya. "Don't wait up."

"Jeez, when do you sleep?"

"I run on hustle, baby, not sleep. But look. Don't worry so much. The aftertastes—an answer'll come. Don't overthink it."

BUT OVERTHINKING, KOSTYA thought now, finishing his beer and signaling The Flame's grizzled waitress for another, *is my Olympics.*

He had analyzed and dissected and pondered the problem all morning. How come Sister Stacy came right back, but NYU kid's granddad didn't? How come he vomited up that meat-headed rock-climber as soon as his yogi sister Om Shantied through the door, but couldn't get so much as a whiff of that nice widow's husband after three hours of tearful reminiscence?

His customers had all been understanding about it. Some even got competitive, making another reservation right away, determined to make it work. Still, Kostya knew that eventually people would grow tired of waiting.

He picked at the label on his beer.

Why did some spirits show and others—pun very much intended—ghost him? Were his taste buds off? Were his diners out of sync? Did they need a special way of connecting with the Dead that he couldn't seem to tap into? Or was it like Frankie had said, that not every spirit wanted to come back?

"Hey," he asked the old-timer to his right, "can I borrow a pen?"

Kostya fished a notebook from his coat pocket (an Italian leather order pad he'd lifted from Saveur Fare) and began a list. The dates, locations, foods, conversations—all the details he could remember about every ghost he had managed to resurrect.

He was looking for patterns, or at least clues.

The first few were easy to recall. Steven Tyler's ghost bride, Anna. His dad (sort of) at the Bouche de Noël. Sister Stacy his first night at the Supper Club.

The most recent one was easy, too.

Tad, that California *bruh* in climbing gear, who'd died when the rope snapped (*eeesh*), retrieved by a sardine sandwich and his yoga-pose-for-a-selfie sister. That left four more, Kostya straining to remember.

There'd been that bland turkey meatloaf the night Frankie was helping out—a Juilliard instructor, Marguerite, bringing back a dance protégé, her pupil dead from diet pills. There was Jaden, a high school senior whose Captain Crunch and Cheerio blend had produced—it made Kostya ache—his little brother Michael, a wrong place, wrong time, *should've-been-me-instead* tragedy. There was Erica, the mom who had wept on Kostya's shoulder, who blamed herself because she'd held on too tight, had never let her daughter live, was so stifling that Ashley snuck out one night to meet a boy she'd met online, who turned out to be a man, a terrible man—carrot cake smothered in thick, cream cheese frosting.

But the last one really stumped him.

It was the second ghost at Hell's Kitchen, the one he'd used to convince himself that the lull following Sister Stacy's resurrection was just a fluke, opening-week jitters. What'd he make the night after that string of failed services, his confidence shaky?

When he finally remembered, he was ashamed to have forgotten.

He'd been nervous, afraid he'd lost his touch, and the diner who shuffled in was an old man in a baseball cap. He didn't speak much English, and had pantomimed alongside slow, enunciated Spanish, as though lengthening the syllables would somehow make Kostya understand. The language barrier made it difficult to warm the guy up, to ask the questions that might have prompted the ghost to reappear, and in the end Kostya just sat down across from him and took his hand, squeezed gently, said something like, "Let's see if they show."

When the aftertaste hit him, it was unmistakable, though for a second he did the lingual equivalent of a double take.

It was a memory from Kostya's own childhood, the year after his dad died, when his mother fell into a depression so dark she spent weeks on end in bed, covers drawn, shades dampening the room. Kostya had kept them fed then, had trudged twenty minutes to the only grocery store that took their food stamps, had hauled home milk and bread and cheap orange cheese in a tearing plastic bag, its yellow smiley stretching to a frown by the time he huffed through the door. Anything they couldn't afford on the stipend, he supplemented with freebies: sugar packets from the bodega on the corner, ketchup and mustard from Burger King, oyster crackers abandoned by the people who could afford the overpriced soup at Hale and Hearty. There were weeks when their food ran out before their next set of food stamps arrived, and Kostya had survived them with what he was about to make for this spirit.

Seven Heinz packets dissolved in boiled New York tap. Mix with a plastic spoon in a Styrofoam cup. Serve with broken saltines, if available. Ketchup soup.

He sucked back tears as he stirred.

When the ghost materialized, a kid in his teens, Kostya just wanted to hug him.

That dish was proof—the aftertastes didn't have to be sophisticated. They didn't even have to taste good. To anyone who tried this Campbell's Tomato knock-off without knowing what it was, it probably ranked somewhere between awful and inedible. But that was the thing about food you ate when you had nothing: the smallest things—warmth, crunch, calories, someone making it for you, taking care of you even if only in some small way, or making it for yourself, proving that you could survive even when the world didn't want you to—could make it the best thing you ever ate.

Something in Kostya's gut lurched.

The best thing you ever ate.

Anna, his very first ghost—the drink that brought her back had been a cocktail she and her husband had shared, from a night they'd both agreed had been special.

The best, she'd called it.

And hadn't Sister Louise said something similar, when Kostya was clearing her plate?

That soup was the one meal we shared that hadn't come from the convent. A taste of what might have been. The best things.

Kostya read his list again. Reread. Summoned back the aftertastes that had flitted across his tongue over the decades, across space and time, across death. It struck him, suddenly, how specific each one was; not always delicious, but always distinct. Even the Reese's at that warehouse party, he'd be willing to wager, had a story behind it, something that made it unlike every other Reese's Cup the good people at Hershey mass-manufactured. Unique enough to trigger an individual moment, some unmistakable instance in a person's life, strong enough to reach across the Afterlife and yank them back.

Madame Everleigh—at that party—had accused him of having no idea what he was tasting, and maybe he hadn't then, not really, but Kostya felt sure now. *This* was what the flavors in his mouth were: the single best thing any spirit could remember consuming. But the reasons for a food's greatness were as personal as a fingerprint. That, maybe, was the point. *What* they were eating didn't matter nearly as much as *why*. If he could just figure out the *why*, understand it, find some way to prompt it for the Living reaching out for their Dead, maybe that could trigger the spirit to come.

It still didn't explain why sometimes he got an aftertaste and sometimes he didn't, unless not every spirit *had* a memory like this to guide them back. Something powerful. Life-changing. Linked, inextricably, to food. Something they *needed* to taste again, a craving that demanded satisfaction.

A sort of suffering only he could relieve.

Kostya closed the notebook and slipped it back into his coat. His hand twitched as he felt his phone there, and he pulled it out and stared hard at the screen.

He was itching to make the call but fighting the urge.

No. He shook his head. *Uh-uh.* It was too painful. Every conversation with her was excruciating.

His hand hovered over the screen, about to slide it back into his coat.

But then . . . he *had* to know. The *why*—only she could give him that.

His knee bounced as the phone rang. One ring. Two.

"Mama. Hey."

"Kostya? Everything is okay?" She always jumped to the worst conclusion.

"*Da.* Listen. I gotta ask you something, but I really need an honest answer. It's important."

"I always tell you truth. Maybe if you call more, you remember."

He could feel the barbed edge to her voice but took a breath and pushed around it.

"When you cook *pechonka*, do you burn it on purpose?"

He heard her laugh.

"What's a strange question from Mister Top Chef! I think you know all cooking already! See, if you go culinary school, they—"

"Mama!"

She huffed. "Okay. *Nyet.* I cook few minutes each side. Burnt *pechonka* unbearable thing. Everybody know this."

"How about when you made it for Papa? Did he like it burnt?"

She got quiet then, so eerily silent he could almost feel his father there, hovering in the empty airwaves between their cell signals.

"Papa—I only made it for him special times. One," she said slowly, "was when I make it to tell him about pregnancy. Oh, Kostya! He dance me through kitchen! It burn while we celebrate. He ate anyway."

Kostya swallowed a lump in his throat. He wanted to ask more, to understand, to remember his father with the only other person in this world who could help him to, but his phone beeped through another call then, the ID flashing out a number he recognized instantly, one he'd memorized after staring at it for hours a day on the Restaurant Sanitation poster that hung over the dishwashing station at Saveur Fare. The New York City Department of Health and Mental Hygiene.

"Mama, lemme call you back."

THEY SHUT HIM down right over the phone. By the time he paid for his beer and walked home, there was a pink Cease and Desist notice taped to his door.

Turned out the fresh-faced yoga chick he'd pegged for an Instagram influencer (last Tuesday, *sardines on toast with preserved lemon*, resurrected the aforementioned Tad) had actually *been* an Instagram influencer, and she'd posted a picture of the outside of Kostya's apartment, street number fully visible, along with a gushing entry about how excited she was to eat at the hottest underground restaurant in NYC—*get in my DMs for deets!*

All it had taken the City of New York was a casual message and a quick database search to confirm that he was, in fact, operating without a license.

Kostya was numb with rage. Angry at this stupid influencer (she had completely blown up his spot!) and at himself (would it have killed him to actually file some paperwork?!). He had been toiling all month, and now that he'd *finally* made the babiest of steps forward, he was back to square one.

He tried calling Frankie, hoping for a pep talk or at least some commiseration, and when he didn't answer Kostya did the next best thing, and proceeded to eat his feelings. He had made his way through half their fridge and was just setting sights on the kitchen cabinets when his phone rang again—another 212 number that he could only assume was a Health Department lackey calling to follow up with outrageous, insult-to-injury-adding fines.

"What is it now?" he shouted into the receiver by way of greeting, his mouth half-full.

The NYPD officer on the other end cleared his throat authoritatively, and asked if he was speaking with a Mr. K. Duhovny, listed as the cosigner on the lease with Mr. Francis K. O'Shaunessey?

"Yeah," Kostya said, swallowing. "I'm Frankie's roommate. Everything okay?"

The officer cleared his throat. "There was a fire at Mr. O'Shaunessey's place of employment. A—um—" Kostya heard papers flipping.

"Wolfpup?"

"Yes, that's right."

"What? *When?*"

"Late last night. This morning, technically."

"Well, where is he? Is he okay?"

The officer cleared his throat, and Kostya's flesh went suddenly cold, goose bumps rising up and down his arms.

"Mr. Duhovny, do you have contact information for Mr. O'Shaunessey's family?"

"Where is he?" Kostya repeated, his heart beginning to pound, adrenaline flooding his ears. "Which hospital?"

"A cellular or home phone number, maybe? Or an address?"

"No—you're not hearing me. Frankie's my best friend. Just tell me the damn hospital."

"Mr. Duhovny," the officer said after a long pause, "he isn't in a hospital."

Kostya couldn't speak, was numb all over, was trembling.

"I'm sorry to have to tell you—Mr. O'Shaunessey is dead."

Entremets

The Konstantin Duhovny Culinary Experience

AIN'T THAT JUST the way? Shit starts getting good and pfffft, there's the fan.

This is the part that always gets me—the pang, right here in the chest. Reliving how you died—it never gets easier. Deathday blues, postmortem depression—whatever you wanna call it, it's real. See those therapists, fam. Don't let it haunt you.

Haunt.

Get it?

Yeah . . . even the jokes lost their fizz.

Listen, let's take a quick five, alright? Gimme a hot New York minute. Hit the reset.

We'll circle back and pick right up again for the throwdown—little cooking contest you're gonna love. Just . . . gotta get my head back in it.

.   .   .   .

Hey there. You looking for something?

.   .   .   .

Yeah, that's us right here! Come join up; we're taking a breather then heading over to the next stop. More the merrier.

•   •   •   •

Safe? Course it's safe. Just a little food tour. Why wouldn't it be safe?

PART THREE

Sweet & Vicious

*You will need a pure heart, and a
soul, meaning you are cooking for the right
reasons. . . . You need passion, curiosity, a full
spectrum of appetites. You need to yearn for
things. . . . You need love.*

Anthony Bourdain
Anthony Bourdain's Les Halles Cookbook

!

WHEN YOU GET to the Food Hall, you eat and you drink.

You're starving by the time you arrive, so you pretty much stuff your face with everything.

Pomegranate pips. Mushroom caps. Blood-red wine.

Soda pop. Cinnabuns. Spicy Girl rolls.

This thing you had once on vacation with your parents, at a bed-and-breakfast that hasn't been there for a decade. This other thing you couldn't have eaten while you were alive, even if you wanted to, because the restaurant that makes it won't open for years.

That's the cool thing about the Food Hall. It serves, like, everything. Anything. Whatever you want. Whatever you feel. It's full of coffee shops and grocery stores and restaurants. There's bodegas and clam bakes and a whole island of cheese. Imagined places to hit up for imaginary meals. Carbon copies of your favorites from the Living world.

It's endless. All-you-can-eat. Edible Eden, basically.

And it's all there to feed you because that's the whole reason the Food Hall exists—to nourish the spirits of the Afterlife. To help us get full so we can move On to our next lives.

Some spirits are satisfied by a single bite of a particular dish, or a sip of *just the right drink. Others take longer to feel full—days in the Hall, or weeks. Months of eating. Some even need years to digest—each meal a way to work through the life they just lived, the memories they need to process, every bite a step closer to fulfillment.*

Sooner or later, most spirits get to board the glittering trains departing the Food Hall and move On.

But some of us don't.

Some of us can't feel full no matter what we eat.

There's a Hunger inside that won't be tamed. Our Living put it there.

See, when we died? Their grief was bottomless. So vast and deep it swallowed them whole. They couldn't process our loss; they couldn't let us go. They held on so tight that it held us back. Kept us here. Made us Hungry.

That's the uncool thing—like, deeply uncool—about the Food Hall. If our Living don't move on, then neither can we.

We get stuck.

Destined to spend all eternity eating Snickers that won't satisfy.

Chef's Kiss

LAST RITES TATTOO is cramped and dark and probably a gateway to Hell.

It's in a basement sublevel beneath an old meat plant, and while the street above has long since been recast as a gleaming mecca of trendy nightclubs, gimmicky eateries, and unattainably beautiful people, the tattoo parlor looks like something out of Satan's sketchbook.

The walls are covered in thick, grainy plaster, out of which skulls and bones and whole skeletons protrude. The lighting makes everyone look kind of undead. The tattoo stations are fashioned after old-school electric chairs, with belts and restraints and a place to bite down, so you know right away that it's going to hurt.

Kostya was sitting in one of these chairs, unrestrained but squirming, while Cal, an overly effervescent tattoo artist, burned a chef's knife onto his left forearm. Frankie had had one just like it, in the very same spot. It had been his first tattoo, the start of a sleeve he was working on, accumulating ink like belt notches—a knife covering an oil splatter, a sprig of rosemary reconfiguring a kitchen cut, a flame-kissed sauté pan in the place where steam had rubbed his skin raw. Kostya had wanted a tattoo for a while, and though his right arm still hadn't healed to the point where he could handle blistering needles with ink inside, he couldn't wait anymore, and offered up his left.

He had thought—somewhat delusionally—that if he just came here, sat where Frankie had sat, chatted up Frankie's tattoo artist, got the same damn thing seared onto his body that Frankie had, Frankie might feel him on the other side and consent to sending him a sign. To let him know he was okay, wherever he was.

It was a long shot, but Kostya was getting desperate.

That first night, the apartment stone cold and empty, he'd hung up the phone with Frankie's mother and stood in their kitchen—his kitchen, now—in the dark, waiting. He closed his eyes, felt the raw opening inside of him tearing at its sutures, felt the notches in the countertop where Frankie had banged scaloppini thin with a mallet, felt the air around him shift and maybe—maybe—maybe—

But no.

Frankie didn't show up that night. Or the next. Or the next.

He didn't show up in his old bedroom, Kostya sitting on his stained—*ew*—comforter in eerie silence. Or at his own funeral, when the Wolfpup staff cut through the grieving crowd to present Frankie's knife set—salvaged from the fire and wrapped in white linen—to his mother, who cradled it to her chest and wept. He didn't make an appearance when Kostya helped ease his casket—featherlight; there was so little left to bury—down into the ground, like slipping sage into the cavity of a fish. He didn't even show up at the charred ruin of Wolfpup, where Rio held a candlelight vigil in his memory.

Kostya had stared into the flame of his votive, willing Frankie to appear, send a smoke signal, *something*. Make some sort of contact to stop the awful thoughts that kept creeping into his head. Thoughts about how Frankie's death had been his fault.

A couple weeks before the fire, Frankie told Kostya that he'd seen something strange in the Wolfpup dining room.

"A face, man."

"A face?"

"Yeah. You remember that ghost we did a couple Fridays back? Real skinny? Sad turkey meat loaf?"

Kostya did remember. No salt in the mix. No pepper. No seasoning at all. Baked just till it was cooked through—nothing brown or crispy about it. A gross, flesh-colored mound of meat.

"The dancer," Kostya said. "From Julliard."

"Yeah. Right. So it was definitely her—I don't forget a face."

"And she was in the Wolfpup dining room? Doing what?"

"Straight-up lurking."

"Why?"

"I dunno, man." Frankie hesitated. "I'm not even sure I really saw her. I been pulling graveyards all week, then camping at the bar, partying with Delia, downing espressos, and doing it all again."

"Delia's the artist?"

"That's Celeste. Left me for that ball player, remember? Dee's an heiress."

"You should get some rest."

"I'm hustling, Bones. I'll sleep when I'm dead."

And then, just like that, Frankie was gone.

Was it really such a stretch to imagine that Kostya had somehow been responsible? Guilt rose in his throat whenever he considered the possibility that a ghost—one of his—had done this. The other possibility, of course, was that it was just an accident—a horrible, freak, life-altering but totally explicable accident—like the cop on the phone had claimed. And either of those theories was still better than the *other* alternative, the truly unhinged notion Rio had posited at Frankie's repast.

After the fire, Rio had scrambled to get the insurance company to pay out damages so he could reopen Wolfpup someplace else, or at least pay his staff till they found other gigs. But they wouldn't give him so much as a cent.

"You kidding me?" Kostya had asked, stunned. "Why?"

"They say they're still 'investigating the incident,' whatever that means."

"What's there to investigate? There was a fire."

"Yeah." Rio took a long sip of coffee, waited for Frankie's mother and aunts to get out of earshot. "Except they're saying Frank mighta started it. Which, I know," he added, catching Kostya's expression, "I *know*—but if he did kill himself, set the fire on purpose, insurance won't pay."

"He'd never do that."

"It don't make sense to me either." Rio looked away, at a photo on the wall, a five- or six-year-old Frankie on his father's lap, his mother standing behind them, a grandmother on either side—one draped in patterned scarves, the other in clerical black—looking dotingly at their grandson. "But thing is, that walk-in? Lock's got a safety release on the inside. Glows in the dark."

"He could've gotten out?"

"That's what they're saying."

Kostya sat with that information a moment, feeling a gnaw in his chest. He knew Frankie was far from suicidal. There were plans he was making, big things in his future.

"I just don't get it," Rio continued. "I mean—anyone who knew Frank, guy had the world by the balls. Seems stupid to end it. And he was no fool."

NO FOOL AT ALL, Kostya thought to himself as he watched the shape of the knife being seared onto his forearm, the letters etched onto its handle— WTFWFT. *What The Fuck Would Frankie Try.*

Please, he thought at it, *talk to me.*

But all Kostya tasted was that morning's breakfast.

"And . . . done!" Cal exclaimed, lifting his headlamp off and turning the machine down. He plucked the latex gloves from his thick fingers and grinned at Kostya through gapped teeth. "How's it feel, champ?"

"A little sore," Kostya said, flexing his forearm and wincing at the tingling sensation that followed.

"Lots of lube," Cal advised, handing him a tub of Vaseline. "Ice if you're itchy. Don't scratch."

Konstantin stared down at his new ink, at the raw, red skin around it, the pin-sized blisters puckering up around the edge of the blade burnt onto him. In this moment, he liked the pain; it was something to focus on that wasn't the dead end he'd hit—Frankie gone, his supper club gone, his life back in the toilet.

"Hey," he said to Cal, "how long to turn this bad boy into a sleeve?"

Cal surveyed him. "You got a design in mind?"

THEY STARTED WITH a sketch Cal had done for Frankie and made modifications, adding a little more Death and a little less Wolfpup. The tattoos were gorgeous. Cal was an artist, truly gifted; Frankie had done his research. By the time they'd finalized the art—Cal adding skulls and bones and cookware and tons of intricate detail, more than would fit on one arm—Konstantin had agreed to not one sleeve, but two, planning to go all in once the burns on his right arm had healed. Cal assured him that the ink would help camouflage his scar tissue, and besides, he couldn't just look badass from one side, after all.

For now, Cal detailed Kostya's left arm with an undead cornucopia—flowering skulls surrounded by fruit and grains and veggies, their eye sockets and mouths and nose holes all blooming with herbs—rosemary and thyme, Thai basil and cilantro. The bones were nestled among other culinary delights—*fruits de mer*, oyster shells and curling pink shrimp, crab legs and lobster claws, cuts of meat, steaks and chops and poultry, dumplings and noodles, pastry and bread; and tools of the trade—knives and forks and spoons, spatulas, cleavers, balloon whisks, kitchen twine. The detail was otherworldly, each element real enough to touch, and, surrounding it all, the frothy flow of rich, dark wine—Cabernet, Petit Verdot—cascading down from an upended glass on his shoulder, dripping along the entire length of his arm.

It hurt like a mother—like *his* mother—having it done. But every moment of discomfort was one he spent thinking about Frankie, willing him to be okay, to be safe, swearing that he'd find out how he died, make it right however he could.

"Well, my friend," Cal said as he put the finishing touches on the last layer of color, the red that made the wine shine, the tomatoes ripen, the apples glow, wiped the fresh ink smooth with his towel, "there . . . ya . . . go."

Kostya turned his arm over and over in the mirror, feasting his eyes. Every inch had been illuminated, made new. The guys at Saveur Fare would have lost it if he strolled in with this ink. If he ever made it back into a kitchen, he'd be giving Cal's number out left and right.

Sure, he'd still have to hide it from his mother. He could practically hear her now, shrill in judgment—*What you thinking, getting tattoo? Is for rest of life! What if you drop cooking? You see, Kostya! If you only talk to me, I tell you all this before too late, but you say nothing and now is forever!* Ever since *the pechonka incident*, his mother had always leapt to the worst possible conclusion. Which was exactly why she didn't get a say in anything he did.

This wasn't just some frivolous decoration. He *needed* this. A memory of Frankie. His friend, his best, one he'd never let himself lose. Frankie was part of him now. Indelible. Wherever Kostya was going, Frankie would come, too.

The front doorbell—reminiscent of the bowels of Hell—shrieked through the room.

"Ah, my eleven's here." Cal stood up. "I'll go let her in. Meantime, you take a good look. Let me know if there's anything you want touched up. I think it looks pretty sick, myself."

Kostya's eyes traced the River Wine, part vintage and part blood. *Yeah,* he silently agreed. *Sick. So sick.*

And then, amid the appraisal of his own illness, there came something actually infirm. Off. Not like it should be. The burgundy rapids foaming around his elbow—where an elaborate fish with iridescent scales dove into the flow—seemed to be growing, expanding, engulfing the fish's head. His whole arm now, in fact, seemed to be swimming in pink, tingling, and—his eyes began to water with pain—burning. His skin was swelling like a balloon. *No.*

No-no-no-no-no.

"Uh, Cal . . . ?" Kostya asked, voice rising an octave. *"Cal?!"*

"Yeah, champ?" Cal bounced down the steps, someone trailing behind him, only her black boots visible on the stairs. "I miss a spot?"

"My fucking arm's on fire."

"Oh. Um . . . shit."

Cal bent over Konstantin's ink—which grew more painful by the moment—tsked, shook his head, started to mutter something that sounded like *Yeah, that doesn't look good* but was drowned out by the woman who'd arrived downstairs just in time to witness the inflation of Kostya's arm and the air being let out of his ego.

"Oh! *Hey.* It's . . . Konstantin, right? What are the odds?"

Kostya looked up, saw her, and thought to himself, *Figures.*

Madame Everleigh—Maura—looked far less psychic without the striped tent and tarot deck of the Seyoncé party, and far more beautiful, even, than he remembered. Her hair was longer now, strands of silver fading to periwinkle, then plum. She wore boots and jeans and a slouchy black sweater. A grey scarf covered in little skulls. Also, a frown.

"Um"—she waved a hand in front of his face—"you okay?"

Kostya swallowed.

He wanted to say something venomous to her, to pay her back for all those months ago, the way she'd shat all over his gift, everything he'd gone on to do since she'd tried to talk him out of it. But he found, face-to-face now—and *oh*, what a face!—that he couldn't.

It wasn't just that she was gorgeous, or that he'd thought about her an inordinate amount. It wasn't that, of anyone he'd ever met, he thought she might know something—like, *really* know—about his aftertastes. It was simpler than that, just something in his gut—a strange intuition, a funny feeling—like this couldn't be coincidence, meeting her again. After all, what *were* the odds that on the same day Kostya got the sleeve Frankie was supposed to get, by the artist Frankie had handpicked, he'd suddenly see her again, the girl Frankie had nudged him toward?

It was almost like someone was sending him a sign.

Yes, Kostya thought suddenly. *YES.*

Maybe this was the contact he'd been waiting for, Frankie giving him a fist pump from the other side! It seemed exactly like the kind of thing he'd do—play wingman, shoot Kostya a second chance, force him to face his fears, prove to his biggest critic that she'd been wrong about him.

Kostya wouldn't let him down.

"Uh, sorry. Yeah. Konstantin. Hey. Hi. *Ouch!*" Cal had poked something on his arm that felt like the flesh was melting off. "You're . . . Maura, right?" he added, wincing, trying to sound nonchalant about it, as though he'd nearly forgotten (as if he could ever).

"Good memory." She smiled, genuinely surprised. "You were at Seyoncé, right?"

"Uh-huh. Yeah. I didn't think you'd—*yow!*"

Maura glanced at Cal, who was gingerly probing Konstantin's ballooning skin. "What's with his arm?"

"Allergy to the ink, I think." Cal shrugged. "Nothing my house special won't cure."

She turned back to Kostya, one eyebrow arched. "A whole sleeve, huh? Can't say I pegged you for a tat guy."

"Some psychic," he shot back, and she laughed.

"Let me see."

Maura leaned across him for a better look. She smelled incredible, like oranges and eucalyptus and cedar, and Kostya tried not to look like he was inhaling her.

"That looks nasty. Does it hurt?"

Cal poked him again, and Kostya gave a little shriek.

"Nope," Kostya said, his voice like helium. "Feels awesome."

The pain was really spectacular now, his whole arm dancing with it. It felt like he was blistering from within, like thousands of tiny water balloons were bursting through his skin.

"This might sting a little," Cal warned him, unscrewing the lid of some foul-smelling mystery goop, the stench from the jar like something had drowned in it.

"More than it's stinging now? I'm gonna pass out."

"Hey." Maura bent down to Kostya's level, her eyes locked on his. "Here. Focus on me." (No arguments here.) She took his unswollen hand, turned it over, traced her fingers over the lines of his palm. "I'll distract you." (You sure will.) "I'll read your fortune."

"Here we go," Cal said, and Kostya braced, tunneling his focus into Maura's wide brown eyes.

"What do you see?" he gasped.

"Okay, interesting! Your love line—it's really pronounced. But short. You love deeply, but it doesn't last."

Cal dabbed the wound, the feeling like spreading acid over a swarm of bees. Kostya forced himself to breathe, to squeeze Maura's hand, to not look at what might be an ER visit in the making.

"That's . . . depressing," he wheezed. "What else you got?"

"Your life line—here. It's superlong, but it sort of breaks in two. Like a before and after."

Cal was sealing his arm with gauze now, tight, the pressure like being stabbed.

"Ow! Ow! *Ow!* Fuck! What else?"

"You're doing great, champ!" Cal said, way too cheerful for how much pain he was inflicting. "Just gotta get the plastic wrap."

"*Plastic wrap?!* Tell me more!" Kostya begged Maura, his eyes streaming.

"Your—your head line—that's this one. See how it breaks? It's all dashed."

"Nervous breakdowns?"

Cal began embalming him in cling wrap.

"Epiphanies! Aha moments. You have a lot of them."

Kostya released a long, painful breath.

"All right, my dude!" Cal exclaimed. "All set!"

Kostya took a reluctant look at his arm. It had gone from sick ink to sad deli sandwich faster than you could say "antihistamine," which felt like some sort of metaphor.

"Just breathe," Maura said, and he did, slowly. "It'll heal. Eventually."

"Pain before beauty, right?" he choked out.

"Totally. You're gonna be a priceless work of art."

He stared at his arm again. (Well, what was left of it.)

"Thanks." He looked back at Maura. "For um, yeah." He waved his palm at her.

"No problem. That'll be twenty-five bucks. Cash or check?"

"Wait? Are you—you serious?"

"Of course. I charge for my services."

"But you just—"

"Or"—she shrugged a shoulder—"just this once, maybe you can pay me in drinks."

He nodded, not entirely believing his luck.

AFTER MAURA'S TATTOO—which only took a few minutes in a back room—they left Last Rites and wandered southeast, which led them on a meandering tour of the Village and Soho, and a long conversation about restaurants. Which led to Maura raving emphatically about her favorite spots, some of which, to Kostya's surprise, were solid recommendations (*I've never heard anyone who wasn't on a line talk about Frenchie's!*), which led to Kostya revealing that he'd become a chef (*Seriously? Wow. That's . . . unexpected.*), and to him dishing out what he'd heard went on at this oyster bar she swore by (*So steer clear on Tuesdays unless you're into casual hookups. Actually, wait, what are you doing Tuesday?*), which led to Maura turning an endearing shade of pink, and to her shoving Konstantin, in the painful arm by mistake (*Oh, shit! I'm so sorry! I didn't mean—wait, are you crying?*), and to him doubling over and needing to sit down, which led them to duck into the nearest bar (*Booze! Need booze!*), a spot called Mother's Ruin, which served unexpectedly good old-fashioneds, and shots of tequila, and, because Maura was a bully, a flight of cheap champagne. *That* led them to a trash can on Crosby Street, where he held her hair back (*This has never happened to me before—reeech—I swear to God!*), and then to greasy burgers at Soho Park to absorb the rest of the liquor, except she wouldn't let him pay (*I owe you, for what I just subjected you to!*), which led Kostya to figure that any minute she'd tell him he was *such* a nice guy, a *great friend*, that she'd love to grab breakfast sometime, or coffee, the kind of thing women always said when it fizzled, but instead her eyes lit up and she grabbed his uninjured wrist, asked if he wanted to have some real fun, which he thought was code for sex, but which wound up leading them to Chelsea, to a warehouse along the High Line, to *No Turning Back*, four stories of immersive theater (*. . . Oh. A play? Yeah . . . sounds, um, great.*) from the people who produced *Sleep No More*, and to silver plague masks hiding both their faces, to the embrace of the velvet dark as they wandered the levels of an Afterlife (*Okay, fine, this is pretty cool. . . .*), to Maura's hot hand in his, leading him through secret passageways, each intricate space filled with the most amazing things: dancers in flight, books stained with blood, Orpheus and Eurydice singing and falling and fucking and drowning in an indoor swimming pool, a masquerade ball, Hades and Persephone in a palace of fire, Hermes at a card table (*Place your bets!*), but despite the miracles of light and costume and set design around him, the visual feast, Kostya's eyes were otherwise occupied, fixed only on Maura.

In the final scene, when Orpheus looks back and loses Eurydice forever, Maura leaned close and whispered, *What an idiot*, and Kostya grinned beneath his mask, nodded, breathed back, *Punk move. If it's love, you hold on.*

They stayed so long the performance began again, looping anew, Orpheus playing his lute, wandering through a star-filled mist toward Eurydice, alive, resurrected, uplit in the next room, and Konstantin turned to follow them for a second time, but Maura squeezed his hand, pulled him into a stairwell instead, into a long kiss on the scooped stairs.

"Wanna get out of here?" she whispered, her breath hanging in the cold air.

It had been a long time since Kostya had been with anyone, since he'd felt the draw of desire for anything other than otherworldly answers, and he was so taken by it, swept up so completely by this impeccable moment, this sublime girl, that he dismissed the puff of cool air on the back of his neck, ignored the sensation climbing up the back of his throat, and barely registered the aftertaste spreading, for the third time, over his tongue.

The Reese's Cup—the unmistakable texture of smooth peanut butter, of impossibly soft chocolate—should have given him pause, but nothing was going to stop the momentum of this night for him, especially not some needy ghost with a candy crush. He swallowed it back down, put it out of his mind, focused instead on Maura's mouth as he kissed her again, the taste of her tongue, like beer, like butter, like salt, like everything he'd ever craved.

She kissed him back, deeper, hungrier, and he got the hint of something else, something familiar—delicious, smoky, sweet. Something indolent he couldn't quite identify. It would be a long time before he understood what it was, why the death in her tasted so good to him, but here, in this moment, her fingers tugging his hair, her body pressed against his, he didn't care what it was, only that he wanted it.

"Lead the way," he whispered back, and followed her into the street, into a cab, into the perfect magic of a Manhattan night.

THE RIDE TO her place—city lights blurring through the windows as he kissed her mouth, her neck, inhaled the way her perfume mingled with her skin, like some kind of drug—was the longest seven minutes of his life.

They fumbled in the dark of her entry, kissed their way onto the rickety old elevator, tumbled through the wide mouth of her apartment door, insatiable along a never-ending hallway where they lost her sweater, his coat, her jeans, his shoes, and into the kitchen where she eased his tender left arm from his sleeve, the plastic still taut over his new tattoo, and paused for half a beat, tracing the scarred, glossy flesh of his right.

He scooted her onto the counter and she kissed him again, ravenous. He asked her what she liked and she whispered back words that made him see stars, blistering hot.

I want you to fill me up.

When she slipped his hand between her legs, made that sound, he stopped caring what room they were in, what city, what planet.

When he pressed his mouth there, to sweet, wet heat, when it traveled over his tongue, into his throat, the taste of her, he knew he'd never tasted anything—from this world or the next—that had ever made him as helplessly hungry.

In her bed, silk sheets, slick as glass. Skin damp. Hair sticking.

Konstantin. The way his name stops in her throat.

Watch me. He never wants to stop.

And in the dark, for half a beat, she's gone, as if the life has left her eyes.

A trick of light, surely, this little death.

Because then she tumbles down beside him.

Gasping, laughing.

I want seconds.

Undeniably alive.

!!

ON A SCALE of one to suck, the Hunger's an eleven.

You eat around-the-clock but never once feel full.

You're trapped in the Food Hall, unable to move On.

You keep hoping things'll get better. That your sister—the one who couldn't let you go—will get therapy. Get laid. Find some other way to get her mind off you.

Spoiler alert? She doesn't. She just stays angry, and sad, and stuck.

And so do you.

As time goes on, you feel a shift. Your hand, you think, has it always been this grey? Did your voice always echo when you spoke? It isn't your imagination; this Hunger changes you. It transforms.

(Honestly? If you'd known it would be this much trouble being Dead, you never would have killed yourself.)

You wonder how it might end. What you might become if you never move On. If Maura—that's your sister—dies before she ever lets you go.

Then you find out.

In a dark corner of the Food Hall is a place full of shadows. Filled with the empty husks of spirits who were once like you—haunted by their Living and never released. Only they're not spirits anymore, and they're worse than Hungry.

They've become ghosts.

Hangry Ghosts.

(Try not to laugh, okay? It really isn't funny.)

Hangry Ghosts are soulless things with torment in their eyes. Grief for the incarnations they'll never get to live. Cravings for the satisfaction they'll never feel again. Fury, at the way they've been bound. They are cold, and dark, and desperate. Scared. Impulsive. Violent, too. Powerful enough to rip anyone who gets too close to shreds. If they were ever to get out, the Hangry Ghosts could tear the veil between the Living and the Dead apart. And they would, too. They'd go to any lengths to try and sate their urge. Which is why the Hall locks them away.

It isn't fair, not really, what happens to them. What's happening to you.

It reminds you of your dad, of how he got when his depression hit. All the joy sucked away. Hollow and drowning and unwilling to swim until the moment when he snapped, a pin from a grenade.

You refused to live that life. You didn't want it. It's the whole reason you chose death. Because you'd been diagnosed with what he had.

But now you might contract it anyway. For all eternity. With no way out this time.

Well screw that, you decide.

Just Desserts

IN THE MORNING, still intoxicated—his liver and his mind—and hoping it wouldn't be an absolute creeper move if she woke up and caught him, Konstantin watched Maura sleep. It was like staring into the sun—mesmerizing, blinding, an image with an afterburn.

Her hair glowed against the pillowcase, pooling like spilt ink. He wanted to bury his face in it, to breathe in the scent of what he imagined would be sugared violets, grape soda, blackberry jam. Her roots, up close, surprised him; they weren't bleached white but grew in that way, as if the shock of something had blanched her follicles.

Her eyeliner was smudged, everything softening in the dusty light. Her mouth was smudged, too, last night's lipstick faded, patches of it smearing her pillow.

Her skin was dotted with constellations, so many marks he hadn't noticed in the dark. She had a tattoo on her collarbone, a tiny skull. Another on her shoulder, beneath a thin slip of plastic, raised and red around the edges—Cal's work from yesterday—the words *Memento Mori* in slender black strokes. A larger, more elaborate design that began just beneath her breasts and curled down her side toward her left hip—a skeleton hand holding three cards: Death, The Lovers, The World. There was a galaxy of freckles across her waist. A small, straight appendectomy scar. Another series of tattoos on her thigh—three jagged strokes of ink in ballpoint blue, as if she'd done them herself—like a tally being kept.

Maura shifted in her sleep and Kostya caught sight of her forearm, her wrist, drank in the scars there for a long time. A failed attempt to meet her maker. He wondered why, and then, like a cord being pulled, an answer spread across his tongue.

A candy cup so soft it barely qualified as chocolate, warmed and half-melted in someone's hand. Peanut butter so sweet it hurt his teeth.

"Hey, stranger." Maura stirred awake then, smiled.

"Morning." He grinned back, the taste of Reese's circling his mouth.

"How's your arm?"

"Never better." It felt like the flesh was congealing, actually, but who needed arms?

"I'm glad."

"What time is it?"

"Time is a construct." Maura felt around on the nightstand. "But in this reality? Ugh. Six thirty. Whoops, this one's yours."

She handed him his phone, which displayed (5) missed calls from some 917 number. He flicked it off silent.

"So, you really a chef? Or was that just a line to get me into bed?"

"Hey, you took *me* home. But I am a chef. At least, I was. My place—my supper club—it shuttered."

"Bummer. Sorry to hear that." She sat up, pulled a T-shirt on. "But my kitchen's still open, and I'm starving. Coffee first. And then, Chef, come show me whatcha got."

HER KITCHEN WAS a disaster. Instead of utensils, one whole drawer housed restaurant matchbooks, half of them from places that had been closed for years. She owned only one frying pan and every knife in her collection was dulled to the point of futility. Her oven—this really took the cake—was storage, but not for shoes or sweaters or any of the other things New Yorkers lacking space might put in there. It held a laptop, two landline phones (*Did we time warp to 1999?*), and a half-dozen paperback editions of *Chicken Soup for the Teenage Soul.*

"That stuff's for work!" she said defensively.

"What, for a junkyard?"

"Suicide hotline," she informed him. "For teens. One of my side hustles."

"Shit. Well now I want to crawl into a hole."

"Think you could make me some coffee first?"

Kostya messed with the coffeepot while Maura frowned into her fridge and began pulling ingredients out of it—leftover slices of salami, half a container of strawberries, a jar of gherkins, three brown eggs.

"You gonna put all that in a mystery basket?"

She looked down at the counter. "Julia Child I am not."

"Julia? The school lunch lady wouldn't touch that combo."

"Don't make me deduct points."

"Oh, so there's points now?"

"Obviously."

"What about prizes?"

Maura slapped two Kraft singles onto the pile, gave him a mischievous smile.

"You make all that into something edible and I'll see if we can top last night's performance."

Kostya processed this a moment. *Holy cannoli, Batman.*

"Set your timer."

FORTY-TWO MINUTES LATER, Maura was moaning.

"Oh my God. Oh my *God*." She took another bite of strawberry soufflé. "This is some next-level tantric Kabbalah shit."

"That's *supposed* to be dessert," Konstantin tsked.

"Life is uncertain." She wagged the spoon at him. "Eat dessert first."

"Try the Benedict."

He slid the plate over, watched her crack the crispy salami basket with the edge of a fork, the yolk of the poached egg beneath oozing out, mixing with the Hollandaise, five stars for the preparation. She closed her eyes as she chewed.

"I think I love you," she said, swallowing. "Where'd you learn this?"

"Saveur Fare, mostly."

"*Saveur Fare?*" she repeated. "As in three Michelin stars, exec'd by culinary legend Michel Beauchêne, reservations six months out Saveur Fare?"

"You side hustle as a food critic, too?"

"Just as a foodie." She dug her fork back into the eggs. "Saveur's been on my bucket list for ages. Look at you, fancy pants."

"It wasn't like that. I was a glorified dishwasher."

"Isn't that how all apprentices start?"

"That makes it sound more . . . intentional than it was. I just—I got lucky. Guys on the line quit, I moved up. Don't get me wrong; I'm grateful. Saveur taught me everything about how a restaurant works, how a kitchen operates, how to make something out of just about anything. But the flavors—the spices, the combinations, the mouthfeel—that education, that's mostly the ghosts."

He said it without thinking, without any reflex to hide or deflect or explain it away, because Maura already knew. There was something so freeing in being able to tell her, in having someone he could confide in again, confess what it felt like to live with the Dead. It made him realize, with a pang, just how much he missed Frankie, how alone he'd been with his secret since he died.

"You must taste them a lot, if they changed your palate."

Yes! It was like she understood him.

"All the time. But, I mean, can't complain, right? Gave me a leg up over all the culinary school snobs."

"It must be exhausting, though, communing with the Dead like that."

"You get used to it. Sort of."

"And cooking," she went on, "becoming a chef—that's been your release for it all?" She shook her head in awe. "Pretty brilliant. Getting the aftertastes out of your system without messing with the Dead."

Wait . . . what? *No.* She didn't think . . .

"I mean that *is* what you're doing, right?" She gave him a look he couldn't entirely read. Expectation? Suspicion? Hope? "You're not still . . . experimenting?"

This felt like a trick question.

"Uh, well . . . "

He *wanted* to tell her the truth. He *should have* told her the truth. Fess up. Admit the whole thing. About his dad at Saveur Fare. About the revenant souls over at Hell's Kitchen Supper Club. About the fact that he hadn't left his clairgustance behind. Instead, he hesitated. Because she'd warned him. Months ago. Had told him that he should not, under any circumstances, keep messing with the Dead.

"You know, it's actually kind of a funny story?"

She raised one eyebrow. "Funny how?"

He swallowed.

If he came clean, this thing between them—whatever it was, whatever it could be—might be over before it even began. It had only been a handful of hours, but he already felt more spark, more thrill, more desire with Maura than he'd felt in years of fruitless dates and passionless relationships. He couldn't just let her go. Not without giving her the whole picture. He would find some way to show her all the good he was doing, all the people he was helping, that it was safe, that he was figuring it out, then maybe—

"Konstantin?" she prompted, and he Animorphed from a man into some invertebrate jelly.

"I . . . um . . . *well* . . . remember at Seyoncé, when I told you about that drink?"

"The one that brought back a ghost?"

"Uh, yeah. That drink. *Well*, I thought a lot about what you said at the party." He chose his words very carefully; this was all technically true. "If I'm being honest, it was hard to hear. It wasn't exactly what I was hoping you'd say." Also true. "And I was pretty pissed that you rained on my parade. So becoming a chef, opening my own spot—in a way, that was my big F you. To, um, to you." He was practically Abe Lincoln, with all this honesty.

Her expression softened. "Look, I know I came on strong. My delivery was . . . unkind. But that had nothing to do with you. I—I actually tried to find you that night. After you left."

"Really? Why?"

Maura shrugged in a way that tried—and failed—to appear nonchalant.

"To apologize. I could tell I'd crossed a line. You were cute, and sweet, and *clueless* about what you were getting into. And you didn't deserve that."

Cute? Kostya was about to levitate off the kitchen tile.

"Anyway," she added, "I'm kind of surprised you took my advice. About the Dead."

"What makes you so sure I did?" he asked, trying to stay on the right side of history while keeping it fun and flirty. "I mean, I'm a tat guy now. Maybe I live on the wild side. Maybe I've brought back hundreds of them."

Maura fought to suppress a laugh. She slid her hand up his arm, pressed a little piece of plastic wrap back down against his elbow, where the edge of his bandage had come up. It hurt and he wanted her to do it again.

"Okay, Wild Thing. Sure. You screwed with the cosmic order and walked off without a scratch. Get real! If you'd really been fucking with the Dead, after all this time . . . "

She trailed off, that ellipsis like a death sentence.

"After all this time what?"

"I dunno? They'd probably come for you."

"I take it you don't mean that in a sexy, Patrick Swayze–pottery wheel kinda way."

"I was imagining more of a 'There is no Dana, only Zuul' sort of scenario."

"Oh. Cool. Cool cool."

She laughed. "But you just did it the one time, right? With that drink?"

"Uh, yeah." He nodded, unable to meet her eye. "More or less."

"And you're gonna keep it that way?"

"That . . . that's the plan. One and done."

He told himself it wasn't an outrageous lie. More like a fib. A fiblet. And he hadn't prepared a dish since Hell's Kitchen had been shut down, over a month ago. So who knew? Maybe he'd never bring another ghost back. And he'd tell Maura the whole truth. As soon as they gave this a chance.

"Okay. Well. In my experience, it's repeat offenders that get on the naughty list." She gave him a decidedly subject-changing look. "Speaking of which"—she nudged him back against the counter—"winner, winner, chicken dinner, I think I owe you a prize."

A tingle went up his spine, his pulse blending through his body—mix, stir, liquefy. She leaned in, kissed him like she meant it. His hands slipped beneath her shirt. She gave a little moan. Check please.

And right on cue, his phone exploded, a badly digitized rendition of "Afternoon Delight" (Frankie's idea of a joke that Kostya couldn't bring himself to deprogram) belting from the speaker.

Seriously!? He tugged it from his pocket. That 917 number again.

His immediate instinct was to chuck it across the room, but a small voice in the back of his head wondered if his mom was okay, if Lower Manhattan was underwater, if some apocalypse had befallen the world while he was over here acting out several fantasies.

He groaned. "Sorry. I better get it."

"Should I start without you?"

"Don't you dare," he told her, and picked up the call. "Hello?"

"*Da*, hello," the voice on the other end said, in an accent so unmistakably Russian it could have been a Bond villain. "I looking for Konstantin Duhovnik."

Oh, *come on!*

His mother was probably behind this, trying to get Uncle Vanya to give him his old trucking gig back. She never trusted him to figure things out on his own. Well—Maura fiddled with his belt buckle—this was *not* the time.

"It's Duhov*ny*. And this is Kostya," he said quickly, "but look, I told Vanya I wasn't going to drive anymore, so—"

"Drive? *Nyet, nyet.* My name Viktor. Musizchka. I own *Taina* club Miami, *Passage* in Brooklyn, *Russian Doll* LA. You know these?"

"No."

The belt clattered to the floor.

"I want you be chef."

"Thanks anyway, but I don't really do Russian cuisine—"

"No Russian. New place. I hear about Hell Kitchen Supper Club. Ghost food, yes or yes? I want make restaurant like this. In Manhattan. High-concept. High-end. Five-star. You interesting?"

Maura was kissing his neck. Somewhere, Satan was cackling.

Kostya gave her a stricken look, mouthed, *One sec.*

"Yeah," he said into the receiver. "Very interested."

!!!

YOU'LL DO ANYTHING *to avoid becoming a Hangry Ghost.*

So you start searching for a way back.

A way to make peace. A last conversation. A chance to explain. To tell Maura to let you go. To stop hurting you. To stop haunting you.

You know there are ways to travel; you heard the stories even when you were alive. Spirits returning for festivals. For offerings left in their name. For Halloween. There were spirits that haunted old Victorians, and gas station bathrooms, and amusement parks. It can't be that hard.

But when you start asking around, other spirits—Hungry ones who've been in the Food Hall much longer, old-timers with sunken faces, shadowed limbs—tell you that there's only one way back that can sate the Hunger.

They call it the Magic Meal. A Reincarnosh. An Aftertaste.

It has a lot of names, but if you find yours, it's a Golden Ticket. A way to return to your Living. A last meal to help them finally let you go.

All you have to do is find the right dish, the combination that unlocks your pathway back to them. Only, no one's ever managed to do it, and no one you ask can agree on what it is you're looking for.

Some say it's supposed to be the best meal you ever ate. Others are convinced it has to do with your Living, a dish you ate together. Some claim it's the flavor of your Living's grief. Others, the flavor of their love. One guy says it isn't about the food at all, but about how it makes you feel. Some lady has this whole theory about meals, and memory, and ties that bind.

In the end, you hedge, and take all of their advice.

It doesn't bother you that it hasn't been done before; you don't mind being the first.

But that doesn't make finding your Aftertaste any easier.

Backburners

KONSTANTIN MET VIKTOR the next afternoon for zakuski—hot and cold appetizers, basically—at the Russian Tea Room, which was exactly the kind of place he expected a paunchy old oligarch to conduct business. (Either that, or a *banya*, where they'd sit naked in a steam room talking shop before beating each other raw with birch branches and plunging into ice pools. Fun.)

What he hadn't expected was the guy waiting for him at the table, or the baffling tear in the time-space continuum that had paired Viktor Musizchka's voice with his body. While his accent was goofy, all *Rocky and Bullwinkle*, Boris and Natasha in fedoras and furs, his face was early-era Brad Pitt, the rest of him an Armani underwear ad, his confidence reeking like too much cologne.

Viktor Musizchka (muted) was a force.

The kind of man you'd want to do business with. Capable. Sophisticated. Someone who got shit done. He was mid-thirties—unfathomably, Kostya's age—and the kind of athletic that required discipline and green juice and early-morning Peloton rides. His thick blond hair and trim beard were meticulously styled to appear both boyish and mature. He practically glowed.

Kostya kept getting distracted by it—Was that dimple real? How'd he get his skin so dewy? Did he moisturize? Should Kostya be moisturizing?—and if not for his voice, bootlegged overseas and dubbed by Yuri's Unauthorized Audio, he'd almost certainly be on television, selling people things they didn't need.

Luckily for Kostya, he'd gone into business instead.

Viktor gave his spiel after he ordered their food, barely glancing at the menu, the kind of patron for whom the kitchen delivered off-piste delights, seasonal secrets, amuses the average schmo never got anywhere near his bouche. He'd grown up in St. Petersburg, attended university in Moscow convinced he'd be a poet, then graduated and went to work for the family business (some hand-wavy import-export deal). Turned out he had a knack for it, made a killing, and moved to the States to expand his operations into a global affair. Along the way, he'd sponsored several pet projects—Russian restaurants, a nightclub—and was looking for his next great adventure.

"Which bring me to you. I want know everything."

Kostya was sure Viktor would pepper him with inquiries about his clair-gustance, his prior restaurant experience, what qualifications he might have to head a kitchen. These were the questions he'd prepped for, but Viktor never raised them. Instead, they spilled the chai about Konstantin's upbringing, where in the USSR he'd hailed from, what family he had in New York. Viktor asked about Kostya's mother, whether she worked, whether she was married.

When Kostya mentioned Uncle Vanya—Ivan Vasil'yevich Kozlov; not his real uncle at all, but his mom's light-switch boyfriend, on-and-off-and-on-again for the better part of two decades—Viktor grinned broadly, as though Konstantin had just told him exactly what he'd needed to hear. Unlike Michel Beauchêne, Viktor Musizchka *had* heard of Vanya's Victuals—*That's your uncle? What small world! Vanya been supplying me long time!*—and it seemed to tick a certain box, to somehow cement Kostya in his mind as his kind of people.

Viktor lit a cigarette and inhaled deeply.

"We have opportunity here," he said, tapping his ash into an empty glass, none of the waitstaff daring to tell this demigod that you couldn't smoke in a New York eatery anymore. "A major restaurant. We just needing chef with big idea. I believing very much in concept. Anyone can have restaurant, but we"—he pointed to Konstantin, to himself, to the space between them as though they were already one entity—"interested in experience."

He paused, took a quick shot of vodka, a little nip of caviar from a mother-of-pearl spoon.

"Is good here, yes? *Ikra* like in Moskva. You see—concept! Anyone can serve caviar, but Russian Tea Room is institution. The place to go for authentic experience."

Kostya looked around the dining room—emerald walls with elaborate inlays, soaring firebirds in gold relief, crystal caviar bowls, etched silver trays—the cumulative effect of which felt like being trapped inside a Fabergé egg. This experience was authentic for only a small portion of actual Russians, the kind who used to live in palaces and rub elbows with Romanovs. It was a fantasy, a way to imagine yourself at the table with a tsar, breathing in the air of lost aristocracy, that excessive, exclusionary, gilded age.

He remembered, in stark contrast, something his father had once told him, how in the Soviet Union a meal out at a restaurant cost a month's pay and the food you got was never better than your grandmother's. His dad had been amazed by American eateries, by pizza parlors and diners and hamburger joints, by the idea, the thrill of it, a place you could sit and eat and still afford to pay rent after, where the food was good and fast and cheap, a holy trinity. *This*, he told Kostya once, *is truly American. Everyone equal in pizzeria.*

It was what he aspired to in his own kitchen. A place where everyone was welcome. Kostya wasn't sure, watching Viktor pour another round of Imperia into a slender shot glass, whether he was the kind of person who could appreciate that.

"So." He cleared his throat. "How did you hear about me?"

"On the Instagram. I see post from NamastayHigh."

Kostya had to remind himself to relax his jaw. NamastayHigh was that influencer, the one who had gotten him shut down.

"I'm . . . surprised you saw that."

"Everyone see it! She gets fifty thousand likes." Viktor took another shot of vodka, a flush coming into his face. "People very interesting to know what is secret, how she see brother again, how she get this closure. So I ask her: Is this joke, dinner with ghosts? Is she making metaphors? And she tell me, no. Is chef who brings back Dead. And I know then I must meet you."

Kostya sat back in his chair.

Fifty thousand likes! That many people thinking about his food, excited to discover it! That many people who might need his help.

"And you'd really want to back a restaurant? Just like that?"

"Listen," Viktor said, spreading a thin layer of caviar onto buttered toast. "I have many business. Very successful. I know restaurants. And I know people. Idea, I think, is amazing. Ghosts very scary. Very sexy. Like Halloween, and people love this." He took a bite, chewed. "Is like old spiritualists, yes? Fortune-telling? Talking to ghost through crystal ball and flying scarf. What you use now, projection? Hidden speaker? We will upgrade tech. My associate, Maksim, has—"

"What? No. No, no, no. It's not a trick." Kostya felt himself grow warm, his shirt too tight, the cuffs, the collar. "What I do—it's not a show. It's real."

Viktor laughed like he was in on the joke. "I sure you make feel very real, but Kostya, my dear, if I'm investing, I must know truth."

"That *is* the truth. There's nothing fake about it. The ghosts are real."

"I not believing in ghosts."

"It doesn't change the fact that they exist."

"This we can debate. But people not want real! They want fantasy."

"Look, you might think that, but authenticity is everything. You need it for connection. For food, too. I was at Saveur Fare for almost a year—"

"Yes, yes." Viktor rolled his eyes, took another bite, laughed with his mouth full. "Michel Beauchêne, I guessing, not believe in ghosts either. According to my source, he fire you in middle of service."

"Because he saw me do it!" Kostya blurted out. "You want proof?" He tore open the buttons at the cuff of his shirt and pulled violently at the sleeve, revealing the shiny, scarred flesh beneath. "Here. I raised a ghost right there in the middle of his big holiday party, and he didn't like it. Gave me this as a Christmas bonus. They're real, okay?"

Viktor's eyes drank in Konstantin's arm, the puckered skin from wrist to elbow. He set down his toast, wiped the corners of his mouth with a napkin.

"Okay. Let us say is real. How many times you do this, raising ghost?"

"What?"

"How many you bring back?"

Kostya dug his fingernails into the palm of his hand. Breathed.

"A couple dozen." If you rounded up. And multiplied.

Viktor nodded slowly, calculating something. "And you can always do this, for every customer? It always work?"

"Well, no, but—"

"You can do this ten, twenty, thirty times each night, every night of week?"

"Sure." Konstantin swallowed, his spit thick and unpleasant. "Probably."

"You do this before, at supper club? Multiple seatings?"

"Not—not exactly."

Viktor raised his eyebrows. Nodded again. Lifted a glass of champagne to his lips. Took a long, relaxed sip.

This wasn't good.

"Maybe we misunderstanding each other," he said at last. "I like very much your concept—"

"It's not just a concept," Kostya said quickly. "I can do it. My dishes—my food—I serve closure. It matters. I'll work hard, harder than—"

"I like very much your concept," Viktor repeated, cutting him off, "but I looking to open restaurant. You not ready. You need practice. Test kitchen, not restaurant. This not for me. I no longer interesting."

They didn't stay for dessert.

KOSTYA TRUDGED HOME in the cold.

As he passed the Times Square McDonald's, an old standby in moments like this, he resisted the urge to go in, to order several combo meals and shove them, one after the other, into his mouth. He didn't want to be that guy anymore.

Then again, that guy's life had been simple. Predictable. Safe.

That guy had had a job—a shitty, soulless, dead-end delivery job he hated, granted, but most of New York seemed perfectly at peace with that kind of arrangement. He'd had Frankie, who always knew what to do. He'd had a quiet, stable existence rather than this Macy's Thanksgiving Day Parade of fuckups, each one more spectacular than the last.

When Kostya finally made it inside, his apartment was a Popsicle. Had the furnace busted? Had he missed a bill? Was it just the universe, icing him out while he was down?

He retreated to Frankie's old room, the most interior, for warmth, and wrapped himself in the comforter. It was so cold he could see the puffs of his jagged breath as he sat there trying not to wallow, which wasn't exactly easy when he was shivering in an apartment he'd shortly be unable to afford, smelling his dead friend's body spray on the sheets, reliving in his mind how catastrophically it had gone with Viktor.

It'd be almost funny if it weren't so sad. He hadn't raised enough ghosts to satisfy Mr. Musizchka, but too many (if she only knew) for Maura's taste. One kasha too cold, the other too hot. Maybe it was good, he told himself, that Viktor had passed. Kostya didn't think he could open a ghost restaurant and be with Maura, too. It'd be like running a steak house and dating a vegan.

You kind of had to pick a side.

He wanted Maura; that was as undeniable as the alchemy between butter and salt. It was more than mere attraction, though there was plenty of that. Being with her was like cooking by intuition, without a recipe, just a feeling that this thing and this other one would be magic if you put them together. If it were anything else he needed to give up, any other obstacle he'd have to overcome to be with her, he wouldn't hesitate.

Never drink again? Done.

Disown your family? Okey dokey.

Rob a bank? Citi or Chase?

But his *aftertastes*? Even with all their setbacks, the inconvenience and disappointment and frustration they'd invited into his life, he couldn't just leave them behind. The good of them was too good.

Each time he succeeded in raising the Dead, the rush was like rocket fuel. It made him feel like he was more than a fluke. Like he was worthy. Impressive. Exceptional.

With every spirit he brought back, he felt like he was changing a life, like what he was doing mattered. He wasn't sure he could just abandon them—the ghosts, the dishes, the Living—or his decades of flavor profiling, his months of kitchen toil, the shadow parts of himself that he'd only just begun letting into the light.

Then again, maybe Maura was worth that. How he felt when he was feeding her—that was life-changing, too. He could picture it with her. Something real. Long-lasting. He could imagine growing old—his body too stooped to lift a cast-iron pan, his fingers so gnarled they could barely crack eggs—and still working each day to make Maura a meal. To feed her something that would draw out that smile.

But that was insane!

Months of fantasizing notwithstanding, he'd barely spent twenty-four hours in her actual company. He couldn't throw away everything he'd been working toward for a crush!

. . . Or could he?

He plopped down onto Frankie's pillow, wanting the darkness to ingest him, to make it so he wouldn't have to think, but a sheet of paper fluttered down from the bedside table and he leaned down to fetch it.

It was a daily calendar page featuring a questionable recipe for English Muffin Pizza Bites: *If you don't have pizza sauce handy, sub in pasta sauce or catsup!*

This aberration was probably a gift from one of Frankie's many hookups, someone who actually believed that what a professional chef wanted most for the holidays was 365 days' worth of bad ideas.

The other side was a menu. Frankie had written it, his cramped block letters dashed off in a flurry, the ink smeared:

Aperitif—Spectral Sour (Library of Spirits, Fall 2016)

Amuse-bouche—Sautéed Liver & Onions (Saveur Fare, Winter 2016)

Potage—Buffalo Chicken & Baked Potato Chowder (Hell's Kitchen, Winter 2017)

Entrée—Fried Sardines with Preserved Lemon on Toast (Hell's Kitchen, Winter 2017)

Special Seatings—Chef's Tastings (Limited)

Once he realized what it was, Kostya had to take a minute.

They were all aftertastes, dishes rooted in the Dead that he, Konstantin, had shepherded back to life. Frankie had seen the possibilities; he'd believed in him. Always. So much, apparently, that he'd imagined what a restaurant serving Kostya's food would look like. How he could structure his courses.

Longing gathered in Kostya's gut, making him simultaneously empty and full.

He wished more than anything that Frankie were there. He wished he could ask him about this menu, about what to do, whether he should choose the ghosts or the girl, a shot at a legacy or a shot at love. Most of all, he wished he knew what had happened that night at Wolfpup. Whether Frankie was okay. How he'd died.

"I miss you, man," he whispered, the room growing colder in response. "So damn much."

Kostya shivered, pain and loss moving within him like a physical thing, a finger burrowing into his chest, paralyzing his lungs.

And then, air. A puff, hitting the back of his throat. Melting into flavor.

Irish Whiskey. Not Jameson. Not Teeling. Sexton. Strong and toasty, honeyed fruit stinging his nose. Sweet sponge cake. Soft, so soft, sopping with booze, oozing into his throat. Coconut Cruzan. Flavored Dominican rum, the scent of an island breeze. Beeswax, from a birthday candle, crackling between his teeth.

He'd know that rum cake anywhere. Warm and heady, half-Irish, half-Dominican, with the promise of a good time. Just like the man himself.

In all the time they'd lived together, Frankie had never had a sweet tooth—preferred heat and spice, salt to sugar—but whenever he went home to his mama's, he'd come back with a Tupperware of this. It was what she made every birthday, every holiday, every time her baby visited. It was the stuff of Frankie's childhood memories, the magic of his sweetest moments baked into a bundt and soused with sweet booze— a shot of Cruzan for his *'lita*, his mama's mama; a shot of Sexton for his grandmam—and served to him in increasingly large slices as he aged up and learned to hold his liquor.

Kostya could almost see him, coming through the door with the container swinging in a plastic bag, digging a spoon out of the drawer, leaning over the kitchen counter to shovel it into his mouth, no plate, no chair, just a look of ecstatic nostalgia on his face.

Y'all can have the foie and lobster, he once said, scooping crumbs into his mouth. *This is my death row dish. Want a bite?*

"F-Frankie?"

Kostya's heart beat six cups of coffee. He knew what he'd promised Frankie. That he'd sworn never to raise him. But after all these months of nothing, the sudden appearance of his aftertaste might mean a change.

Maybe Frankie had reconsidered. Maybe he was in trouble. Suffering, like Sister Stacy had said. Maybe he needed Kostya's help.

The heat rushed back into his fingertips. He disentangled himself from the sheets, found his shoes, jammed his feet inside. He was tracing a mental map to the nearest grocery store when his pocket lit up, vibrated.

Maura.

He stared at the screen, tearing in two. If it had been anyone else, he'd have already sent them to voicemail. Instead, he stood there, the hint of whiskey on his breath, rereading her name.

It rang for a second time, his thumb hovering just over the slider.

Frankie or Maura. *Maura or Frankie.*

Would Frankie wait? Would he come back again if Kostya didn't act now? Or was this his only shot? He could already feel him starting to slip, the tingle of sugar dissolving from his tongue. If he sprinted, he might make it to the bodega for ingredients. Or it might already be too late.

Maura's name flashed up at him again, and he recalled what she had said.

It's repeat offenders that get on the naughty list.

They'd probably come for you.

"No Dana, only Zuul."

Maybe it was a bad idea, bringing Frankie back before he could at least investigate those claims. He might cause more harm than good. He might piss Frankie off. And besides which, he reminded himself, he'd promised not to.

His phone buzzed again.

"Maura? Hey."

The aftertaste vanished as soon as he picked up.

!!!!

YOU SCOUR THE Food Hall searching for your Aftertaste, eating everything you can remember.

You try birthday cake from every year you were alive. The chicken soup your mother made before she left. Your sister's soggy breakfast tacos. Your dad's trademark microwave dinners, still frozen in the middle.

You eat school lunches, and your Grandma Perry's pies, and Aunt Sarah's ambrosia, which you can't stand but Maura loves.

Each dish is a memory, a way to relive something you shared. You eat things that make you feel angry and sad and happy and loved. Scared. Lucky. Curious. Calm. None of them is it, but it still feels like progress. Like in some small way, you're getting back control. There's a purpose to your days now. A mission. A goal.

It feels good, despite the Hunger. You feel better.

And then, without warning, Maura shows up in the Hall.

One minute you're eating pizza from Game Zone—the arcade you used to go to together after school, two bucks for a slice the size of your head—and the next she's there, beside you, just standing in the Afterlife, the very person you were trying to see before she died.

You blink at her, your pizza growing cold. A kernel of fear blisters—pop!—inside you. If she's here, then any moment now you won't be.

The Hanger will come for you. The emptiness. The pain.

She asks if you're okay, and you shake your head. Of course you're not.

Then you just start talking, telling her what you'd been planning to say—that you're hurting, that you need help, that she has to let you go. But before you can finish, she's gone again.

Poof.

You don't understand; it doesn't make sense. She couldn't be in the Food Hall, not unless she were Dead. But now she's gone, which would mean she's . . . still Living? Had she somehow, in her grief, found a way to visit here? To die, and then return? And had she done it to help you? To save you? Would she do it again?

It shouldn't be possible, but then, Maura never did play by rules.

You hold on to it, tight, the hope of seeing her again. To the memory of your sister, the person you loved most in the whole world. You can't let it go.

You wonder if this is how she felt, holding on to you.

Another Round

KOSTYA MET MAURA an hour later, at an address she texted him in Alphabet City.

"I was thinking," she said instead of *hi*, "you should call him back and demand a do-over. Musicman, I mean."

"Uh, hey. Hi. Nice to see you, too."

"I'm serious!"

"Look, you didn't meet Viktor. I just . . . It's over. It's done."

"Nothing's done until you're dead, and even that might be negotiable. Convince him to try your food!"

"Can we talk about something else? Like why we're in StuyTown?"

She shrugged one shoulder. "You sounded really down. I'm cheering you up."

"Here?"

"Uh-huh. I'm gonna show you the city, Stan."

She swept her arm out before them. A rat skittered out from beneath a dumpster.

"You know I live in Hell's Kitchen, right?"

"But you don't walk around with your eyes open."

———

NO TWO PEOPLE, it seemed, experienced Manhattan in quite the same way, and the places Maura frequented, all her beloved haunts, made him feel even less cool than usual. Her version of the city was a different world. Full of nooks and crannies, holes-in-the-wall, secret entrances, spaces you'd never see unless shown.

SHE TOOK HIM for zombies (warning: one per customer) at Fuego's Shrunken Head, a Polynesian tiki bar above a laundromat, carpets sticky with decades of syrupy rum.

"They're limiting the signature drink?" Kostya asked. "Tough look for a bar."

"I don't think they have a choice," Maura said, plucking a paper umbrella from the rim and skewering a cherry. "These things are deadly. I sweet-talked the bartender into sneaking me a second one once. Blacked out an entire weekend."

AFTERWARD, THEY STUMBLED around the corner to Big Apple Handyman, a hardware store wedged between a barbershop and nail salon.

"Our next stop," Maura announced as she led him down the paint aisle, toward a door marked *Danger: High Voltage*. "Courtesy of my former employer."

"You worked *here*?" Kostya asked.

She nodded, entering a four-digit code on the door's pinlock. "In art school. Before I dropped out."

"You went to art school?" Lord, he knew astonishingly little about Maura.

"For visual effects and 3D animation. Lots of coding, logic, world-building—which is why I fought so hard for this job." She turned the handle down slowly, felt the lock click open.

"In a hardware store?"

"No." She pushed open the door. "In High Voltage."

It was a private arcade—ten or twelve video game cabinets lining the walls of a small room, a machine in the corner that traded bills for quarters, and a tiny (no liquor license, surely?) bar in the back. It was an insider's place, and, unlike The Library of Spirits, an *actual* secret. A few groups huddled around two of the older-looking consoles, the players focused, the spectators watching, breath held.

"You play?" Maura asked him.

"Never had the money."

"Well," she said, loading a bill into the change machine and scooping out a fistful of quarters, "allow me to make up for your horrible childhood."

MAURA CREAMED HIM at every game.

It wasn't just that he was a novice, prone to button mashing; she was uniquely skilled, so good that other gamers paused to watch. Her eyes never left the screen, her fingers flitting across combinations of buttons, maneuvers of joysticks. It reminded him of the way she shuffled cards.

She moved to the next cabinet, sliding a quarter into a Japanese version of Ms. Pac-Man.

"This is the one I actually brought you here to play," she said, her hands settling expertly onto the controls.

"You get this good just by working here?" Kostya asked.

"I've been gaming since I was a kid." Ms. Pac-Man appeared on the screen, a maze loading, and Maura's face shifted in concentration. "There was an arcade in town, and my sister and I—it was our happy place. We were safe there."

Something about the way she said it unsettled Kostya.

"In a game," she continued, "no matter how much you messed up, no matter how many times you died, you could come back. Play again." On-screen, she chased down a set of flashing ghosts, swallowing them one by one, orange, then pink. "We spent hours playing after school. I loved everything about it. The puzzles. The levels. The way games follow rules. There's a perfect logic to a game world. Orderly. Predictable. Not like real life."

"You can see the bad guys coming."

"Exactly." She ate a cherry, then a Power Pellet, then swallowed the cyan ghost, sending him back into his little box. "And if you get really good, you can learn which rules to break. Unlock secret levels. Have an experience the creator intended only for a select few."

She took her hands off the controls and turned back to Konstantin. He watched as the last ghost—the one she hadn't yet eaten—stalked closer and closer.

"Watch out!" he warned, but it was too late.

The red ghost overtook Ms. Pac-Man, sending her spinning. Dead. The maze went blank, all the little pellets vanishing at once. Some Japanese characters flashed across the center of the screen. Game over, he figured.

"Ouch. Didn't think I'd get to see you lose."

"You didn't." Maura tapped the bottom left of the screen with her finger, pointing out the two life icons still displayed. "Watch and learn."

The maze reappeared, in ghostly blue this time, the pellets punctuated by countless miniature foods—not only fruits but pixelated pizza slices, tiny sushi rolls, petite hamburgers. Ms. Pac-Man faded onto the screen, not in the bottom half, where she usually started, but in the central box, where the ghosts usually did. Instead of her trademark yellow, she appeared blinking, in blue.

"She's—she's one of the ghosts?"

Maura took up the controls again. Kostya watched her move through the maze, eating everything in sight.

"It's a secret level," Maura told him. "Only available in the 1983 rerelease of the Japanese cabinet. It's called the Hungry Ghost Maze."

"So it's a bonus round? The point's just to . . . get more points?"

"The points don't matter in the ghost realm. To clear this level, you have to find the Happy Meal. Hidden in one of these fruits is a portal that gets you back to the real world."

"But there's no opponent!" Kostya balked. "No timer. This seems too easy."

"It would be, without the second player. Get ready." She nodded at him. "You're almost up."

"Wait, what?"

"On the floor, to the right. There's another controller."

A handheld joystick was jerry-rigged to the back of the cabinet, a thick black cord tethering it in place.

"But I don't know—"

A moment later, the screen divided, Maura continuing to eat in the ghost realm on the left and a new maze appearing on the right, the original Pac-Man in his first level, caged ghosts breaking free one by one to chase him. Kostya fumbled with the joystick, running Pac-Man straight into an oncoming ghost and losing one of his lives.

"Careful! Ms. Pac-Man only gets to stay on this side as long as Pac-Man survives on his. True love, right? If I don't find the portal before you die," Maura warned him, "I vanish. Literally. We'll have to reset the game to get her to show up again."

"Happy Meal, huh? To bring a ghost back from the Dead?" Kostya maneuvered Pac-Man around a corner. "That's kind of on the nose."

"Well, Hungry Ghosts are the kind that come back." Maura grinned. "Feeding the Dead to help them cross—it's a whole thing in, like, a dozen different traditions. Japan. China. Mexico. Ancient Egypt. I figured it'd be up your alley."

Another ghost attacked then, catching Kostya in a pincer. Womp-womp.

"Except you really suck at getting away," Maura scolded, snatching his controller. "Here. Let me."

AFTER THE ARCADE, they wandered through Tompkins Square Park, darkness falling around them. Maura's hand laced through his felt so right, a warm feeling gathering in Kostya's belly like a big bowl of soup. She led him along a dim, tree-lined path, finally stopping at a bench where they sat, his arm draped around her shoulder.

"So," he asked her, "there some secret in the park, too? Some tree branch you pull to get into a rave?"

She laughed. "I just used to come here a lot. Most of my classes were across the street."

"Visual effects, right?"

"Yeah." She gave a tight smile. "I really thought I was gonna make games for a living."

"What happened?"

Maura sighed, her eyes carefully fixed on the ground. "I made it through fall of senior year. Started my big thesis project. But then I dropped out. Because Everleigh died."

"Everleigh," Kostya repeated. "Like Madame Everleigh?"

"My sister." Maura nodded. "Spiritualism was always her thing. The psychic stuff, for me, that . . . "—she gave an ironic laugh—"*career path*? It's just one of the ways I try to keep her alive. After she died, I couldn't let her go. I did a lot of stupid things, trying to hold on."

"Holding on isn't stupid." Kostya had been doing it his whole life—was, in fact, trying to make his own career out of it. "How did she—was she sick?"

Maura shook her head. "A car crash."

The air went out of his chest. He thought of his dad. The bus. That phone call. The sharp knife of sudden loss.

"I'm—God, I'm so sorry."

"Ev crashed it on purpose." She sounded numb as she said it, like it was something she'd relived a million times, the memory threadbare. "I was away at school, and she needed me, and I wasn't there."

"Fuck."

"Yeah." Maura shivered beside him. "I didn't even see it coming. I couldn't understand why. Like, our dad has issues. He's bipolar, and our house was never really stable growing up. One day there'd be food in the fridge, lights on, and the next he'd be slamming a wall. Losing his job. Or catatonic, barely there. We never knew what we'd find when we walked through the door. I took the brunt, I guess, when I was home. But for Ev to be hurting that bad? To feel like her only choice was an ending?" She dug the toe of her shoe into the ground. "She never even said anything."

"You can't blame yourself."

"Yeah, that's what people say to make you feel better, but honestly? Our mom was gone, and then I left, too. I was her big sister. I should have stayed home. I should have—" Her voice cracked, and Kostya pulled her closer. "She must have lived with so much darkness. And now I'll never know."

He chewed his lip, the answer right there between them, close enough to touch.

"What if you could?"

The aftertaste had thrown itself at him the very first time they met. He could almost taste the chocolate on his tongue now, the peanut butter, the memory a ghost of a ghost. All those times, all those Reese's, only and always around Maura.

Everleigh had been there all along.

"I could help you," he said slowly. "You could see her again."

Maura turned toward him, her mouth so close. Her lips. Her warm breath.

"I—I thought you said you were finished. One and done."

There was something different in her voice. Not accusation, or anger, like he'd expected, but possibility. Hope.

"I know what I said." He slid his arm from her shoulder. "But it wasn't true."

His heart was sprinting inside him. Was he really doing this? Here? Now? He looked at Maura, into her eyes, and he couldn't lie anymore.

"My supper club? The one that closed? It was a ghost kitchen."

She scanned his face, as if trying to read something, but said nothing.

"And this restaurant with Viktor? It was going to be the same thing," he continued. "Channeling spirits. Cooking their aftertastes. Trying my best to bring them back."

"Why'd you lie?"

"I'm sorry I did. *Really*. It's just, the other day, when it came up—I panicked. Because I like you. A lot. And I thought it would fuck things up between us, the ghost stuff. I know how you feel about it."

Her face gave nothing away. All he could see was a flicker behind her eyes, like she was thinking very fast.

"You know how I *felt*," she said at last. "During one snap judgment at a party. A lot's changed since Seyoncé."

"So all that stuff about ghosts coming for me? No Dana, only Zuul. You didn't mean that?"

"Oh, no," she relented. "I totally did. If you keep fucking around, sooner or later, something's gonna give."

"Then nothing's changed."

"*I've* changed." She found his hand and traced her thumb across his palm, along one of the lines there. "And on some reflection, I think the benefits might be worth the risk."

He stared at her, unsure if he'd heard right.

"*Seriously?*"

"Yeah."

"What, um, brought you around?"

"The restaurant."

"The . . . the one I lied about?" He didn't follow.

"The one you took the trouble to open when you didn't have to. You could have just brought back your own friends and family. Left it there. Instead, you raised the Dead for people you barely knew. Strangers."

"Yes?"

"Why?"

"I—" Kostya chewed his cheek. "Because of my dad? I guess? Because I know how it feels to need more time? When I lost him, it was sudden. He was in an accident, and we'd—we had a fight that morning. A fucking stupid fight. And I spent my whole life wondering if he died mad at me.

If the very last thing I ever did was hurt him. I've been there, wanting so badly to make things right. Thinking I might never get the chance. So if I can help someone not feel that way? It's worth it."

"You're a good person, Konstantin. Selfless." Maura stared down at his hand in hers. "Even if you are a liar."

"Does that mean I get a second chance? Or does lying trump selfless, so I can still go fuck myself?"

She smiled at him. "Did you mean it, about Everleigh?"

"Of course."

"And you wouldn't think I was a hypocrite?"

"I mean, I totally would. But that's being human, right? You're allowed to change your mind."

Frankie flashed through his head then—his wish to stay dead; his sudden, contradictory aftertaste.

"I'd like to see Ev again," Maura said softly. "To help her."

"So let's do it."

He started to rise, was mentally mapping their path to the nearest candy aisle, but Maura reined him back.

"No! Not yet. I just—I need to be sure it's the right thing." She looked away from him, at a cluster of trees. "Every time I try to process her death, it only makes it worse. Grief's like leftovers that way. Like you made this four-course meal out of your love, but they only got to eat one little bite. So now you're stuck with all this food you can't bear to throw away, and all you can do is shove it in the back of the fridge to rot, or make yourself sick trying to binge it on your own."

"Or maybe," Kostya said gently, "you could invite someone else to dinner. Someone hungry."

She looked at him for a long moment, the way you look at something you can't have.

"Just . . . I'm here, okay?" he said, breaking the silence. "If you ever decide you do want . . . leftovers. I get it."

"I know you do. It's just that—" She started to say something else, the words right there, tongue tipped, but her stomach gave a roar, and she laughed instead. "Apparently, I'm still starving. You up for some food?"

Kostya blinked at her, amazed. No, impressed.

He was still stuffed from the tiki bar, from the dozen apps Maura insisted they order there, and from the beer and pretzels at High Voltage, *and* the jumbo package of Nuts4Nuts she'd bought on the walk over to the park. He couldn't imagine consuming so much as a cocktail cherry.

Maura's metabolism was unreal.

Another mystery to solve, right up there with those scars on her wrists and that mid-coital blackout. Not to mention all the stuff she knew about the Dead. But that was probably just an occupational hazard of being a psychic. And she'd just let him in about Everleigh, so it was only a matter of time before she'd share the other stuff, right? *Right?*

Sure. Yup.

It was fine. This was fine.

Fine, fine, totally fine.

"Stan?"

"Hm?"

"There's a good Cuban place a few blocks away. You haven't lived till you've tried one of their cigars. Or we could go back to your place . . . order in. . . ." She twirled a piece of purple hair around her finger. "Find *some* way to kill half an hour . . . Unless you're not hungry?"

He was, suddenly. Very.

"I could eat."

MAURA LEFT HIS apartment around midnight, her scent still lingering in the air, perfume and shampoo and sweat like olfactory ghosts. He'd wanted her to stay, had nearly begged, but she had work early the next morning, an aura cleansing for some celebrity—*You'd die if I told you who*—and needed to prep.

She'd liked his place, had asked for the grand tour—*Oh my God, there's* another *bedroom?*—astonished by the square footage until he explained that he hadn't always lived alone, that his best friend had been his roommate.

"Is he coming back for his stuff?" she asked. "Because you could totally sublet."

"No, he, um . . . he died. Couple months back. He—he was a chef, too. There was a fire. At his restaurant."

Her eyes grew wide. "Oh my God."

"Yeah. Wolfpup. On the Upper West Side. Frankie was the sous." Kostya pulled up a photo on his phone, Frankie in his chef's whites, plating a dish with one hand and flipping him off with the other. "He ran that ship."

"Whoa." Maura stared at the picture for a long time. "Can you taste him?"

Kostya thought of the rum cake from earlier that night, the flavors appearing right there in the room.

"Sometimes."

"It must be nice," Maura said. "To know he's there."

"It is," Kostya agreed. "But it's hard, too. Most of my life, I've felt more connected to the Dead than the Living."

Maura moved closer. "Maybe you just need to live a little more."

He breathed her in, her smell intoxicating. "Maybe you can show me."

She swallowed the space between them, kissed him slow. The sensation of her mouth was honey, sweet and sticky and thick. He kissed her back, and it was agony, this kiss, the way it consumed him. She pulled him in, close, closer, desire pushing every other thought to the back of his mind.

AFTERWARD, ALONE, KOSTYA stood in his kitchen, and stared at Frankie's note, the menu he'd scrawled a message from beyond the grave. He read it again. The last line, over and over.

Special Seatings—Chef's Tastings (Limited)

Yes.

This was it. *Of course.*

This was how he opened a restaurant—one that could seat lots of people while still raising just a few ghosts a night. *This* was how he solved Viktor's volume problem.

He would offer a permanent menu of the best ghost flavors he'd tasted from beyond, prepped and ready for ordering à la carte. And then, for the more adventurous eaters, a special dining experience to reconnect them with their own personal ghosts, the seatings limited to a select few each night. Chef's Tastings.

Chef's *After*tastings.

Arranged in advance, with private rooms and a manageable number he could control.

Maura had been right, about needing a do-over. Giving this thing another chance.

It was late, but Kostya didn't care. He picked up the phone, dialed the number. Viktor Musizchka answered on the fourth ring, voice thick with sleep.

"Viktor? It's Konstantin."

"Is one in morning. This spank call?"

"Don't hang up! Please."

He heard Viktor yawn. "I give ten second."

"Ten se—jeez—okay. You were wrong. I don't need a test kitchen. I'm ready. I can scale this. I figured out how."

There was a moment of silence, and then, "Thank you for call, Kostya, but ship, I think, already on sale."

"Just let me prove myself! Let me cook for you."

"We already talking to other chefs—"

And, desperate, Frankie's menu in his perspiring palm, Kostya played his card, the one he knew Viktor would fold for.

"But none of them would have anything like the buzz we could create. With the ghosts, with my concept—you'd make a killing. And we could seat as many people as you wanted. A full house every night. But the ghost experience—that would be exclusive. Like a club within a club. A restaurant within a restaurant. VIP rooms."

Silence on the other end.

"Think about it," Kostya pushed on. "What would you do, to see some-one you loved again? Someone who died, someone you thought was gone forever? To have one last conversation? Ask their advice? Hear their voice?"

Viktor cleared his throat.

"What would you give," Kostya pressed, "for one last meal together?"

An aftertaste shimmered into his mouth then—*pickled herring, white onions, diced egg, grated beets, mayo, mayo, so much mayo, drowning in it*—and he knew he had him.

[illegible] many people spent [illegible] money [illegible]
[illegible] that would be enormous. I should [illegible] and decide whether we were
[illegible] in a pause give [illegible]
Come in, one and [illegible]

'[illegible],' K says, [illegible] would you [illegible]

'Would you like,' K says, '[illegible] and [illegible] because—'
'[illegible] extraordinary thing to ask. Is this really because—' [illegible] were
[illegible] because I should never [illegible] was going
[illegible] could not [illegible] Beatrice [illegible]
'[illegible],' he replied just then.

!!!!!

AFTER VISITING THE Food Hall, Maura gets worse. So your Hunger does, too.

It's simple math: the more your Living suffers, the more their life is ravaged by your death, the worse you crave. And Maura? She'd been wrecked enough to die.

You watch the changes taking hold. Your fingertips first. The ends of your hair. They aren't solid anymore, but dimmed. Fading to shadow. A bulb, burning out.

You've got to fix it. You need to see her again.

You need that Aftertaste.

So you redouble your efforts. Eat more. Chew faster.

Nothing helps.

You feel time slip through your fingers, a fistful of sugar, and you get desperate enough to try anything. And still, when the new soul arrives, with his big talk, his slick smile, his assurance that Yeah, going back's easy—I seen it; my guy does it, you don't entirely believe him.

But then other souls you see around, Hungry ones, start to talk.

You hear rumors, that the New Guy's legit. That he used to be a chef and knows all about food. That there's someone on the other side working with him. That they can bypass the Hall, summon Aftertastes on demand.

That they can smuggle you through.

How the Other Half Eat

VIKTOR WAS BACK in. Sort of.

There was a dinner—short notice; no notice—at his place, and he wanted Konstantin there, a final hoop to jump through. One that may or may not have been set on fire.

"You want prove yourself," Viktor asked without asking. "Tonight big chance. I hosting small circle friends for dinner. They interesting in restaurant. You impress them, we in business."

Kostya's mouth went sour. "I thought we were already in business."

"These just discussions, Kostik! Not business yet. See, for you, no risk. But for me? Is big investment. Maybe five hundred thousand, half lemon, to build space, hire staff, make marketing. But no problem, I pay. We make beautiful. But I must be sure what I pay for."

KOSTYA SPENT THE morning trying not to panic.

He'd been an idiot not to anticipate some sort of test—Viktor wasn't just going to hand him a restaurant, *obviously*—but now his future depended on schmoozing a bunch of New Moneybags for their glowing endorsements.

What could he say to gain their approval? What did people with money even talk about?

His immediate instinct had been to call Frankie. He'd unlocked his phone, his thumb hovering over the speed dial before he remembered. It hurt every time his mind slipped back into old habits, into a world where Frankie was still alive. He'd been gone two months, but Kostya still couldn't bring himself to remove Frankie's name from his favorites list, to trash their text chain with the record-breaking number of eggplant emojis, to delete the handful of voicemails he'd left.

What he wouldn't give, just then, for another taste of that rum cake.

Instead, insult to injury, his phone buzzed through a message from his mother.

Kostya, call me.

He locked it without answering, and she dinged through another text.

Is important!!!

Frowning, he set his phone to silent and went to take a scalding shower. His apartment was still freezing, and Kostya had to find some way to decompress before the party. If he didn't get out of his own head soon, he was going to have a nervous breakdown before he even had the chance to die of shame.

THREE HOURS LATER, a thick film of sweat undoing all his ablutions, he stepped out of the elevator into Viktor's Tribeca penthouse.

Opposite the elevator doors, taking up an entire wall, were two enormous pencil drawings, one depicting a twisted Hermès scarf, which barely earned a cursory glance from Konstantin, and the other immortalizing a six-foot-tall strap-on, which triggered a wave of nervous laughter so violent it prompted the arrival of a thick-necked, Soviet-issue bodyguard.

After several deep breaths that enabled Kostya to finally gasp out his name, his new Comrade issued a stern grunt and led him through a sprawling living space—two-story windows overlooking the Hudson, everything shiny and modern and the color of Candy Buttons—where he poked a meaty forefinger into Kostya's spine and prodded him toward a library. Kostya gaped at the floor-to-ceiling shelves—wall-to-wall built-ins in high-gloss lime, hundreds of tomes cased behind doors of iridescent glass—so absorbed by the psychedelic effect that he didn't immediately notice the copper French doors at the end of the room, a dinner party in full swing on the other side.

But they noticed him.

The sounds of their cocktail hour—pockets of laughter, chittering talk, the rattle of ice in shakers—dwindled to silence as he came into view.

Kostya peered through the glass panels in the door. Viktor scowled at him from the head of the table. His friends, six of them—posh, polished women, nipped and tucked and sheathed in brands Kostya could barely pronounce; titanic men, flushed and vodka-faced, ties coming loose—drank him in, head to foot—his scuffed black shoes, his off-the-rack jeans, his wrinkled Gap button-down with the ghost of a sauce stain on the collar— before spitting him back out, unimpressed, their gazes tennis-balling back across the polished chrome dining table toward their host, waiting for an explanation because this guy, surely, wasn't here to sit with them?

It felt like fifth-period lunch.

Normally, Kostya would have made himself small, as invisible as possible. Instead, on a mission to impress, he forced himself to grin broadly, wave, wrap his fingers around the handle of the door. At this, The Comrade death-gripped his upper arm. He hauled Kostya away, muttering a string of colorful Russian endearments (*What the dick kind of cock-braiding?*), and hustled him through a small passage to the right of one of the bookshelves, a corridor that spat them into an enormous, double-island kitchen, where three chefs—two women, one man—were already in the throes of prep.

"I think there's been a mistake," Kostya began. "I was invited to dinner."

"You"—The Comrade slapped the unoccupied side of the second island— "work here!"

"But I'm not cooking tonight! I was just supposed to meet his friends.

To—to talk to them. To get them interested. In me." Kostya looked imploringly at the other chefs, as if one of them might intercede on his behalf. "I'm a guest!"

Even coming out of Kostya's mouth, it sounded stupid. The people in that dining room had looked at him as if he were a piece of primordial ooze that had washed up on the shore of their private island, an aberration they hoped the next wave would dispose of before anyone stepped in it by mistake.

The Comrade began to laugh. Kostya gave a nervous chuckle. One of the chefs—beak nosed and too skinny to be trusted—snorted. The other two— one with perfect posture and a plait of black hair escaping a silk kerchief; the other with a shaved head, brow ring, and mermaid pinups tattooed on her forearms—exchanged wry looks from their territories on the adjacent isle.

"You," The Comrade choked in English, the laughter flooding out now, tears streaming from his eyes, "a guest? You!" He gasped for air. "A guest!? You an asshole!" He steadied himself on the edge of the counter. "You serving last, *Dîner de Cons*!"

And with that, he swept from the room.

The chefs settled down again, went back to mincing, peeling, grating. They all wore unsullied coats in solid colors, with their names embroidered over the breast pockets—Louis-Jean Volière, 朽木 Yume Kutsuki, Val Ibáñez—and moved with the untroubled ease of people unaccustomed to pressure—an inertia Kostya had never seen in a professional kitchen.

No, he decided, these weren't restaurant vets; more likely personal chefs, the kind who made big bucks summering in the Hamptons and nine-to-fiving for flush Upper East Siders in the off-season.

"Welp," Kostya said, hoping the others would somehow find him pathetic and endearing, "joke's on me, I guess. So, what are we making? Where do you want me on the line?"

"We?" Volière sniffed, not even deigning to glance up from his station, where he was plucking an infinitesimal bird. "*Mais non, mon ami*. We are every man for himself."

Kutsuki, to his left, put her knife down, and leaned below the counter for a cooler.

"We each bring our own dish," she explained, hoisting the Igloo up, the sound of water sloshing inside. "The more exotic, the more impressive it tends to be. My employers—the ones with so much Botox their faces barely move?—they've been trying to win for over a year."

"Win?"

"It's their own personal *Iron Chef.*" Ibáñez sounded disgusted. "They trot us out once a season for this freaking dog and pony. They love a pissing contest so much, why don't they just buy some wild cocks and have a cage match? Keep us out of it."

She slammed a cleaver against the top of a jar of caviar, Frisbeeing it across the room.

"What's the winner get?" Kostya asked.

"Five thousand bucks." Ibáñez shrugged. "Bragging rights. To keep their job."

Kutsuki nodded; Volière pursed his lips.

"And you *want* to keep working for the people putting you up to this?"

"You gonna point me to another easy six-figure gig? Plus benefits. Room and board on the Upper West Side?"

"I see your point."

"You're not on Viktor's staff?" Volière asked. "This is your interview? *Merde.*"

"I'm not here to join his staff," Kostya said. "I'm going to EC his new restaurant. If I win, I guess. What are you making?"

Volière didn't answer, just kept plucking the pathetic creatures on his station, a dozen or so palm-sized birds, their feathers tan and black and bright, bright yellow, their beaks and feet still on, dead eyes glinting.

"Fugu," Kutsuki cut in. "Hand-delivered from Tsukiji."

She'd cleared her station of everything but a sharp fillet knife and the cooler, which she uncapped with a flourish. From inside, she withdrew an enormous, scaleless fish, grey on top, white bellied, thick lipped, still thrashing in her slender hands. She gave a squeeze at the back of its belly, and it inflated like a balloon, spikes extruding across its body like dangerous goose bumps. She laid it on its side and gave a quick, sharp slice through the back of its head before beginning to peel the skin away from the flesh. The fish bled out across the counter while her blade moved through its body, each cut surgical, designed to keep the poison in its liver and ovaries—more potent than cyanide; no known antidote—from tainting the meat.

"Blowfish," Kostya breathed. "Wow. Well, try not to poison them before they taste our food. Or, actually, maybe do."

Kutsuki gave a small, satisfied smile. "Don't worry; I'm licensed. Took years of training, but it was the whole reason the Stolis hired me." She frowned. "They like to surprise their friends on sushi nights. Have them think they're eating fluke until their tongues go numb. Totally unethical."

She sliced open the belly and scooped out the interior—the fish's tiny heart still beating in the palm of her hand—then dumped the guts back into the cooler.

"But no one's asking your opinion, right, sugar?" Ibáñez cut in. "Me either. You deal with one percenters long enough, you learn to look out for number one. That's why I spent ten grand of their blood money on this." She held up what looked like a shriveled old stone, greyish brown, streaked with white. "I like the idea of feeding them shit while they thank me repeatedly."

Kostya squinted at the specimen. "I take it that's no truffle."

"Guess again."

"Something calcified. Rotten porcinis? Ancient cheese? Dehydrated lung?"

"Ambergris." Ibáñez gave a little bow. "The fecal matter of the noble sperm whale." She took a sniff. "Got a nice musk, actually. Pairs great with Rocky Mountain oysters." She winked. "If you're gonna screw around, may as well go balls deep."

It took Kostya a second to remember what Rocky Mountain oysters were: *animelles* in Canada; meatballs everywhere else; bull testicles in plain English.

"She thinks she is on *Fear Factor*." This from Volière.

"Cojones don't scare me." Ibáñez shrugged. "But maybe that's 'cause I got more of 'em than most little boys running around with big knives. Don't misunderstand, Frenchie. I play to win. I just won't do it on their bullshit terms."

"Yes, you are *so* noble!" Volière spat, unable to contain himself. "Lying by omission! Worse even than Sunday brunch in Midtown."

"What lying? I'll tell them straight up what's in it." Ibáñez grinned, and began Microplaning the ambergris, the smell of it floating, heady, through the kitchen. "They'll suck it down and ask for more. And you're one to talk integrity, Lou." She stared knives at the little bird in his hand. "Least *I'm* not serving black market."

This smacked Volière as intended, and he shrank bitterly back to his work, squinting at the tiny fowl scattered across his station, inspecting them for rogue feathers.

Kostya peered again at the miniature bird bodies—what *were* they? Young squab? Cornish game chicks? Fetal ducklings? Then he noticed several empty bottles of Armagnac, cognac's spunky cousin, glinting golden on the counter just behind Volière, and the way the birds' feathers were slicked down, wet. His eyes grew wide.

"No," Kostya breathed. "No way."

Ortolan.

Michel Beauchêne had told Konstantin about it one night after a late close, a dish so exquisite, so absolutely enthralling, that he'd measured everything he'd eaten afterward against it. Michel had tasted it just once, in the private home of a French chef whose name he refused to reveal, and it had been the single greatest dining experience of his life, an edible nirvana that, he said, had made him see Heaven even as he hid his face beneath a napkin veil, the traditional way, shielding his indulgence from God as the songbird—drowned alive in Armagnac; fried and eaten whole—sluiced boiling guts and juices and hazelnut-flavored fat down his throat, its little bones breaking beneath the weight of his jaw.

Ortolans were endangered—killed off by centuries of human glut—and unlawful to poach, the dishes made with them wiped off restaurant menus and struck from the collective culinary consciousness in the nineties. Barely anyone knew how to cook them anymore—only those who had trained with old masters.

"But you couldn't," said Kostya. "They're illegal."

Volière shrugged one shoulder, almost imperceptibly, and Kutsuki made a loud clang on her board, the pufferfish tail flapping off in one piece.

"He didn't," she said softly. "Those aren't ortolans."

"As if you'd know!" Volière shot back. "It's a bit out of your league."

But the look on his face—like he too was looking at the prospect of being plucked and drowned in Armagnac—said more than his words.

"I bird-watch. For fun. I'm quite good." She gave a low whistle that sounded undeniably tweet-like. "But even an amateur birder would know that what you have there"—Kutsuki switched to a fine fillet knife and shimmied it beneath the blubbery skin of the puffer—"with the characteristic golden chest, far yellower than the ortolan's greyish brown, is American goldfinch."

Volière looked like a large bone had lodged in his throat. Ibáñez laughed so hard she dropped a bull testicle on the floor. Kostya—who couldn't help laughing, too—almost felt bad for the guy, *almost*, until Volière muttered that these idiot oligarchs wouldn't know the difference, anyway.

"But *you* will," Kostya said. "Good food's about honesty."

"But fine cuisine," Volière replied, impatient, "is about perception. Tradition."

"Look, either you tell them the truth," Ibáñez said, suddenly serious, "or I will. I'm not losing to you on a lie."

Volière tightened the grip on his knife. Ibáñez started to say something else, but Kostya cut in.

"Say you're reinventing it. Tell them they'll be the first to taste ortolan reimagined as goldfinch—a New American dish, inspired by the Old World. Just like them."

Volière looked humbled for the first time. "*Merci*, Chef."

Ibáñez gaped. "Why the hell would you do that?"

"Because when I win," Kostya said, "I want it to mean something."

"*When?* Check out the Saturn-sized man nuts on you! Wasn't sure you had it in you, Chef—uh—"

"Duhovny. Konstantin."

A glimmer of recognition crossed her face. "The same Duhovny that got scalded at the Gild Christmas Circlejerk?"

Kostya held up his arm, scar tissue shimmering beneath the tattoo.

"I was told Beauchêne put you in charge of saucier," Volière said, awestruck.

"I heard you told the head of Gild to suck it," Ibáñez said, grinning.

"I heard you had a skin graft made of tuna," Kutsuki added, beginning to plate, translucent slices of puffer fillet arranged in a lotus shape.

"Tilapia, actually. I reeked for weeks. But I didn't know anyone had heard anything," Kostya said. "They paid me not to say a word."

"There are no secrets in a kitchen," Kutsuki said.

"Ours is a small, incestuous little world," Ibáñez agreed, pouring peanut oil into a cast-iron pan, lighting a burner. "Cooks like to talk." She was silent a moment, then wiped her hands on a kitchen towel and stared at him, squinting as if she were trying to read something. "My cousin was in the kitchen that night. Fernando Rodríguez. Remember him?"

Kostya did. They'd worked *garde-manger* together, Fernando's *mise en place* a constant mess.

"He said he saw some shit go down right before Beauchêne stormed in. Lights glowing. A face, hovering midair. You talking to it. Now, Nando's a good kid, but he likes to hit the bottle, so I don't buy half of what he's selling normally. But something tells me you're more than just a pretty face, eh, *papi chulo*?"

Kostya swallowed, deciding whether to confirm or deny. There had been times in his life when it would have been a no-brainer: downplay the bizarre, deny anything unnatural, keep your head down and your mouth shut.

"You're not wrong."

"Huh," Ibáñez said, eyes going wide. "So, share with the class—a guy who walks out on three Michelin stars, who may or may not be some sort of Russian *brujo*—what are you gonna make to impress the judges?"

Kostya licked his lips.

There was only one thing he *could* make to compete with what these three were throwing down. He'd win, too. If it worked.

It was a big if.

It had been a couple months since Kostya had attempted a ghost dish. He'd be rusty for sure, and he still didn't know exactly what he'd done right (or wrong) at Hell's Kitchen, or how—beyond a potent memory—to make contact with the Dead. Would Viktor scrap the whole thing if Kostya didn't deliver? Would he give him another chance? No, Kostya answered himself. There would be no do-overs. It was sink or swim. Now or never.

"I'm Ukrainian, actually. And I'm making my signature dish," he said slowly, meeting Ibáñez's stare. "More shocking than Rocky Mountain oysters." He nodded to Volière. "Rarer than ortolan. Maybe just as taboo, though." He turned to Kutsuki. "And it does more than just dance around death. It reverses it."

There was silence in the kitchen as they waited for the punch line, anxious to learn if the things they'd heard through the grapevine were true.

"Well?" Volière prompted. "*Qu'est-ce que c'est?*"

"I don't know." Kostya shrugged. "The Dead haven't fed it to me yet."

ONE BY ONE, Kutsuki, Volière, and Ibáñez all served.

After, they returned to the kitchen to sip wine and rehash play-by-plays.

When Kostya was up, he downed his Malbec and waited for The Comrade to come escort him into the dining room, the way he'd done with all the others. What happened instead was a violation of the unspoken rule between the Kitchen and the Front of House: you don't come back unless the chef invites you.

Kitchens were private places, where alchemy occurred, where sausage was made, where, once in a while, the divine was summoned and baked into a pie. Every kitchen where Kostya had ever felt comfortable had been intentionally divorced from the goings-on of the dining room, the heat and cursing and shouting of orders incongruous with the serene environments required for white tablecloths and sophisticated banter.

Sure, there were restaurants that put their kitchens on display—right in the middle of the dining room, even, encased in glass—and they worked in perfect silence, never spilling a single drop of demi-glace, never colliding with runners carrying trays, never shouting about the jerk at Table Four who demanded that they kill his steak. Sociopaths ran kitchens, too.

Kostya would never have chosen to be put on display like that, both dinner and the show, but Viktor hadn't consulted him (he was beginning to notice a pattern) before leading his retinue straight into the kitchen. Kostya watched helplessly as they overtook the room, contaminating the air with perfume and hairspray, cigarette smoke, amuse-bouches they'd transported from the dining room. They draped themselves around the islands, besmirching the counters with fingerprints and grease stains, commandeering Volière's station and Kutsuki's without asking for consent from anybody. The other chefs retreated to a corner—so much for comrades in arms—and watched, wide-eyed, eager to learn if Kostya's would be a tactical victory or a bloody massacre.

Viktor cleared his throat, and Kostya understood that they were waiting for him to say something, to perform, to dance. His heart pounded, dissolving what little courage he'd nipped from the wine, and he pushed up the sleeves of his shirt, bracing himself, revealing his tattoos in the process.

His gaze hovered on the knife on his forearm, *WTFWFT* inked on its handle.

What *would* Frankie try, if it were him up here? How would he dazzle them?

He'd regale them with stories on the line—hilarious *Kitchen Confidential* antics—charisma flowing like honey from a comb. He'd play up the food, have them believing in what it could do before they took so much as a bite. If he were there, he'd . . . *make them think they're the most interesting people in the room, and then show them that, actually, he was.*

Viktor cleared his throat again.

"Uh, right." Kostya nodded at the crowd and they stared back. "Ladies. Gentlemen. I want to begin by saying what an honor it is to feed you tonight. Though as you can see, I, uh, don't have anything prepared just yet."

The guests exchanged glances, wondering if there had been some mistake.

A Rapunzel-haired woman crossed her arms. A man in a grey suit fingered his goatee. A petite, curvaceous brunette squinted at Kostya. And Viktor struck a match in a way that communicated his displeasure, and lit a cigarette.

Kostya locked eyes with him.

It was time to face the Musizchka. Prove that he was worth every penny of this investment.

"When Mr. Musizchka first told me about this dinner," he continued, speaking directly to Viktor, "I was intrigued. And when I spent time with your chefs this evening, I went from intrigued to impressed. It's not every day that I'm invited to feed appetites as discerning as yours. Fugu, ortolan, ambergris—these are some of the rarest delicacies of the living world. But what I'm prepared to offer you is rarer still. A taste of the Dead."

"Did he say *dead*?" one of the women hissed.

"Oh, no, not that cannibal shit again," a round man in a paisley shirt whined.

"I have a unique palate," Kostya continued. "Singular, perhaps. It offers me a culinary connection with the spirit world. With the proper triggers,

I'll taste a meal from one of your Dead tonight. When I prepare it, and when one of you eats it, it will bring that spirit back here to dine."

Several people shifted uncomfortably.

"If this disturbs you, please, feel free to go."

A slender woman dressed all in black walked silently to the door. A moment later, a red-faced man followed her.

"Anyone else?"

He looked from person to person, meeting their gazes. Behind him, he heard movement, and turned in time to see Kutsuki shake her head and dash for the door, whispering something that sounded like *idiot* and *raise Hungry Ghosts*.

"All right," Kostya continued, unfazed. "To begin, think of someone you've lost. Someone you'd like to see again."

Several people closed their eyes; several others gave Kostya an incredulous stare.

"Concentrate," he urged them, "on the Dead. Remember them."

"What kind of memories?" the brunette asked, her eyes squeezed shut. "Like happy? Or sad? A memory about food, or eating with them? Our first memory of them, or our last one? What, exactly?"

Kostya opened his mouth to answer and closed it again. Frowned.

At Hell's Kitchen, he'd never dictated a *type* of memory; he'd just talked to each diner about their deceased and either something appeared in his mouth or it didn't. But the way she posed the question—what *kind* of memories?—made him pause.

He thought about Sister Louise. It had taken a while for Stacy to appear. She hadn't been waiting in the wings to see her; there had been a trigger. She'd come along once Louise thought about her murder, once she'd blamed herself, once she'd missed Stacy so much there had been an almost palpable ache in the room, peppered by regret—the guilt of not being there when she died.

He thought about Steven Tyl—*no*; Kostya stopped himself. His name had been Charlie. His dead wife was Anna. And he'd come down to The Library of Spirits practically paralyzed by grief, unable to move on with his life, his desperation so strong that the moment he invoked her—*my poor, dead, beautiful wife*—Anna came barreling up through Kostya's digestive tract. The toll those thoughts had taken—it had been written all over Charlie's face.

He thought about his own dad. He'd appeared in the moments Kostya felt his absence most, the awful resentment at the pool when he was young, the piercing yearning at the Bouche de Noël a few months prior. Just before he'd tasted the *pechonka* at Saveur Fare, Kostya had been watching the line at work, swelling with pride each time he'd yell a direction and the whole brigade would shift in response, amazed at the place he'd made for himself, the respect he commanded. And he couldn't help but think it: *Papa, how I wish you could see this.*

Kostya closed his eyes. He felt very close to something, his fingers twitching toward a pulse. Overhead, the white lights shivered.

"A memory that costs you something," he said aloud, almost to himself. "One that hurts to remember. That makes you regret what you did or didn't do. Or makes you remember how happy you used to be when they were here. Something that makes you really feel your grief."

Those were the memories that summoned the ghosts: the ones that came at a price, that took a little something from the person remembering. These were emotions complex as flavors, sweet articulated by bitter, acid cutting through umami, fat neutralizing heat.

Like a burner catching fire, things began happening inside Konstantin's mouth. Flickers of flavor—not aftertastes, exactly. More morsels than meals. A whole lot of them.

Boiled-chicken-Kiev-chocolate-cake-kielbasa-tart-red-currant-Wonder-Bread-kvass-coconut-amino-thin-sliced-cow-tongue-pickled-cabbage-bitter-wine-oyster-mushroom-pork-fried-sprats-on-toast-Nutella-morel-syrup-cognac-tuna-tartare-herring-in-a-fur-coat-honeydew-vinegar-burnt-brûlée-mortadella-sunny-side-pineapple-upside-down-marzipan-Jolly-Rancher-

grape-fruit-snack-peanut-butter-pesto-escargot-lemon-jus-saliva-stomach-acid-prelude-to-a-puke—

Kostya gripped the edge of the counter for support. It was like drinking the pool of goo at the bottom of the kitchen trash. Dietary discord, cacophony, the notes all sour, curdling. He could feel bile clawing its way up the back of his throat; he was going to hurl.

"Stop!" he gasped. "Stop!"

The diners startled out of their thoughts, the flavors vanishing from his tongue with a little pop. Except for one, which fluttered to the surface now, enveloped his mouth, revived him like smelling salts. A real aftertaste, complete in its complexity.

Sweet, tart, tangy soup. Slim strips of boiled cabbage. Carrot. Potato. Cubed and stewed. A single chunk of beef chuck, boiled so long it dissolved in the broth. Beet, cubed and blanched till its color faded to pink and dyed everything else in the pot maroon. Something zesty, below and above—tomato paste? Pizza sauce? Oh, gross—ketchup (?!!!) and a swirl of (blasphemy!) Miracle Whip. Borscht. With unorthodox trimmings.

"Who puts ketchup in borscht?" Kostya wondered aloud. "Or Miracle Whip?"

The petite brunette gasped.

"Babushka Fira! But how did you—" she began, though Kostya wasn't listening.

The kitchen seemed to go dim, everything muted but Viktor's face across the island, stunned surprise registered in his raised brows, his smirk.

"Now we're in business," Kostya said.

THE REST WAS easy. Kostya dashed off the ingredients and Viktor sent one of his many minions to the grocery store down the block. Volière had brought a sous vide and a pressure cooker with him and was only more than happy to let Kostya borrow them. (*But of course! This I must see.*) Fortyish minutes later, Baba Fira was coalescing in scarlet fireworks above their heads, the audible gasps and expletives from the spectators filling Kostya with a sort of buoyancy. It never got old, granting people's wishes.

It made him wish that he could grant his own.

He ached to see his dad. To test his sudden revelation about triggering the aftertastes. He wondered whether embracing his grief would make him taste *pechonka* again, and how to draw that flavor of agony out of himself, something deeper and more raw than the dull pain he usually felt. He watched jealously as the brunette reached for her grandmother's glittering hand, thought about how easy it would be to sneak away, to rush back to his apartment and try to conjure up his dad.

But something held him back. A kernel of fear, of doubt.

He'd already missed his father twice. Two strikes. He couldn't risk a third, not if it might be his last chance. He had to be sure this worked beyond this party. That it worked every time. Airtight. Because what Maura had said—if he kept this up, sooner or later, something had to give—if that was true, he couldn't let that something be his dad.

He smiled across the room at the old woman's spirit. One day, when he was sure, it'd be his turn. She looked up, and, through glowing, burgundy tears, smiled back.

AFTERWARD, VIKTOR INVITED him back to the living room for a champagne toast, the clink of their glasses as good as any handshake.

"To partnership," Viktor toasted.

"And success," Kostya added.

The bubbles were so fine in Kostya's mouth, notes of caramel and vanilla undercut by mineral, salt, metal, the limey acid transforming into warmth in the back of his throat, sweetness like bruised fruit. He held the flute up to the light, watched the slender streams of fizz dance across the glass, the almost green glint of it.

"You like the Krug?" Viktor asked. "Is Blanc de Noir. From black grapes."

"It's wonderful."

Viktor studied his own glass. "I always like name. *Krug.* Like circle." He took a sip. "I save for special people. My partners"—he nodded at Kostya—"join this circle. Like family. Closer."

On cue, Kostya's phone buzzed loudly in his pocket. He silenced it. It rang again.

He pulled it out, his mother's photo flashing across the screen, a tiny thumbnail of her wedding photograph, she and Kostya's father in profile, grinning.

"I—I'm sorry, it's my mother. Please . . . excuse me a minute."

He shuffled a few steps away, picked up, didn't even have a chance to say hello before the barrage began.

"Kostya, thanks God! You completely step off your mind?! I text in morning! Say important! You not call back. I have eight stroke while I waiting. You want kill me, you doing good job."

"Mama, sorry. Busy day."

"I hear! Vanya call me yesterday night, and say you talking to Viktor Musizchka—"

"Well, yeah, actually I—"

"—and I tell Vanya, what kind of garbage nonsense you carrying me? Kostya smart boy, he know better. He never talk to thugs like this! Musizchka family all gangsters."

Kostya's tongue felt glued to his mouth.

"New money but no better than old KGB," she continued. "No rules, no moral, bang bang left right. I tell Vanya, you not get involved. You stay away."

Kostya tried to swallow, couldn't manage even that.

"Kostya," she said slowly, "tell me I right. Tell me you not talking with murderers and thieves. Tell me—"

"I don't know what you're talking about," he said quickly, which was true. "He's great."

The Viktor he knew seemed totally legit. A businessman. A well-dressed hunk standing on the other side of the room with expensive champagne and an open checkbook, Kostya's ticket to a restaurant, to making a difference, to finding Frankie, and his dad, and all the lost pieces of himself again.

"*Bozhe moy!*" He could hear her clutching the fabric over her heart. "You lose completely sense of smell?! What you messing into! You gonna get yourself killed."

"I gotta go."

"Kostya? Kostya! Don't you dare hang phone! Don't—"

He hung up and turned back to his host.

"Everything is okay?" Viktor asked him.

"Oh, yeah. She, um—she likes to worry."

"Well, you have no worries now."

Viktor raised his glass, and Kostya mirrored him. When they drank, the champagne seemed flatter, duller. Less sweet, more metallic. The iron like blood.

"Welcome to family."

!!!!!!

THE NEW GUY *is starting a food tour.*

The Konstantin Duhovny Culinary Experience.

A stupid name, you think but don't say. Instead, you ask him how it works. If what you've heard about the, uh, itinerary is for real.

Think of it as a hop-on, hop-off, the New Guy tells you.

He winks as he says it, which you take to mean that the rumors are true. That you'll be hopping neither on, nor off, but through. You try to probe further, to understand how it happens, whether they really can make Aftertastes outside of the Food Hall. But the New Guy deflects. Either he doesn't know, you decide, or he isn't saying.

You ask when the tour leaves, and he tells you that his guy is opening a restaurant on the other side. That the tour's gotta be there opening night.

Why? *you ask, unsure what a Living restaurant has to do with the Dead.*

'Cause that's what his spot's for! Aftertastes. Spirits. He'll bring us all back there. Long as you're down for the ride.

The Hunger lurches, hard, inside you.

Okay, *you tell him.* I'm in.

He says he'll reach out about the date, but it shouldn't be long now. No time at all.

You just hope Maura lasts until you make it.

That she doesn't do something reckless. Impulsive. The kind of something that spells trouble.

But then, because she's Maura, of course she does.

Hau(n)te Cuisine

IN THE SEVENTIES, Swingline was a glitzy, superfly spot, a boutique hotel far downtown, catering to the grooviest cats and foxiest kittens, the kind of beautiful people who shook their asses and snorted their drugs in Studio 54 and Max's Kansas City. In the twenty-teens, not so much. Now it looked old. Run-down. Decidedly—Kostya frowned at the peeling gold siding and mirrorball door—*retro*. And not in a good way, like a first-press vinyl or vintage tee. More of a *should-have-died-with-disco* vibe.

Inside was worse. The walls were wood paneled, a take on somebody's uncle's basement; the carpets red shag, a communal grave of Elmo dolls. The reception desk—which you got to by trudging through a sunken seating area (more shag, puce velvet sofa, vomit-inducing floor pillows)—was mirrored, scuffed, and tagged with graffiti. It was also the last resting place of a dead mouse—one look at the lobby must have killed it—and an ominous pile of lease paperwork, some of it already bearing Viktor Musizchka's signature.

Kostya shoved his fingers into his eyes, trying not to judge this dumpster fire by the height of its flames. He hadn't seen the main attraction yet—Viktor said this place used to have a restaurant—but Kostya could already imagine what "charming, period brasserie and commercial kitchen" translated to if this pimply ass-cheek had been passed off as "seventies glam Manhattan legend, nostalgia chic" by the fast-talking broker.

It almost didn't matter what they did to fix it up either. Even if Viktor was willing to throw money at the obvious problems, it still couldn't fix the biggest issue of all: a restaurant located right in the sphincter of Manhattan dining.

Swingline straddled the border of the South Street Seaport and Two Bridges, right at the tippity top of the Financial District. This was the dead zone bordered by the NYPD, County Supreme Court, and Metropolitan Correctional Center, a culinary wasteland that barely attracted leisurely lunchers during working hours and was cursed, like the rest of FiDi, to become an absolute ghost town after 6:00 PM, when all the Wall Streeters emptied from its bowels. They'd be the only sit-down for blocks, which Viktor saw as a first-mover advantage, and which Kostya knew was the first nail in the inevitable coffin.

There was a reason all the hot restaurants clustered in certain locations—Soho, the Village, the Upper East and West, Gramercy and Flatiron and the Meatpacking District—and it wasn't because they all wanted to be next door to their competition. They went where the people went, where other restaurants had had a good run, or at least an enviable sprint. It was no big secret that most restaurants shuttered within the first six months; the big-deal places, the success stories, those you could count on one hand. In this business, the only surefire option was a deal with the Devil, and Restaurant Satan was booked three years out, last Kostya had heard.

"Kostya, *privet*! Thanks you for coming."

Enter Viktor, stage left, materializing from a room behind reception. Dressed as if his stylist had the day off.

Like all new-money Russians, Viktor liked his luxury brands—Gucci and Hermès, Armani and Prada, Burberry and Louis V—but Viktor donned his attire a little too enthusiastically, from head-to-toe, *the more expensive, the better to see you in, my dear*, which sometimes, like right now, wound up looking like the storefronts along Fifth Avenue had gotten into a brawl.

"Viktor," Kostya said, "hi. So this is the place, huh?"

Kostya was hoping Viktor would confess he'd just been screwing with him, take him by the arm, and whisk him into a private car, to another location far, far away. Instead:

"Well, what you think? You like or you love?"

"Love's a strong word."

"Love, yes? Me too. Very much."

He removed a Tiffany lighter from the pocket of his slacks, lit a cigarette, and exhaled smoke in the direction of an exasperated No Smoking sign, its peeling paint—like the rest of this place—having given up long ago.

"I think we make lobby into *cocktailnaya*." Viktor took another drag. "People come in, drink while wait for table." He exhaled. "I thinking black glass here. Obsidian. Modern. Very clean. We put hosts in front by door. Sexy girl and guy, dress in white for *kontrast*. What you say?"

"I think we should see the kitchen first."

"Okay dokey. Follow me, is downstairs. Very cool features. I think you be surprised."

"Well, if it's anything like that lobby . . . ," Kostya began, inhaling Viktor's secondhand smoke and heady eau de cologne as he followed him through the little door behind reception, past a couple of administrative offices, and into a cramped stairwell, " . . . then it'll take a lot of dough to bring it up to code. Maybe more than you want to invest. Might be worth seeing what else is out there. We could even look in Brooklyn. Or Astoria's got a solid food scene. . . ."

They took the steep flight down, passing evidence of several infestations— gnats, rats, cockroaches—on the steps.

"Man," Kostya said, making a show of squelching a roach beneath the heel of his sneaker, "this place looks like a plague hit it. I mean, are we gonna have to give up a firstborn? 'Cause I left my lamb's blood in my other pants."

Viktor—either not following or not interested—ignored him and waved his phone around, searching for the light switch. He found it, and Kostya braced himself for the shock of fluorescents and whatever other horrors awaited this kitchen reveal. But when the bulbs blinked awake, when the generous space expanded before his widening eyes, when he took in the high ceilings and wide prep areas, the industrial beams, the cement floors, the enormous arched windows on to—was that a subway station, visible on the other side of the glass?—he grinned despite himself.

Kostya felt it in his gut; there was something here, a diamond in the rough.

"It need update, of course," Viktor said quickly. "We can lay out any way you want. But space, I think, is good."

"Better than good," Kostya said. "Those windows, what do they—"

The answer came barreling past them. The 6 Train as it made its loop through this defunct stop onto the uptown track, its strobing light bathing the shuttered station in momentary illumination, like a flashbulb from the past. Kostya took in the soaring half-moon archways, the braided tile, the art deco stained glass, all blinking like stop-motion as the cars advanced, souvenirs of another era. He could almost picture New Yorkers of yesteryear waiting on the platform, all trenchcoats and wool, briefcases and newspapers, cigarettes and handkerchiefs. Ghosts only the track remembered.

"We can Sheetrock," Viktor offered. "If is distracting."

Kostya could see it so clearly, what this place could be. The way even the walls had history.

"It's perfect," Kostya breathed. "It's all perfect. Where do we sign?"

OTHER THINGS IN his life felt perfect, too.

When Kostya got home, still riding the high of his new kitchen, he found Maura sitting on his stoop, nursing a coffee and an almond croissant, a paper bag fat with pastries on the step beside her.

"Hey, Chef." She grinned, wagging the bag at him. "I went to Balthazar."

"I have never been more attracted to you." He kissed her, tasted the sugar and butter and almond paste coating her lips. *Yum.* "What's the occasion?"

"Oh, just your average Tuesday morning bribe."

"Oh, yeah?" He unlocked the entryway door. "And which of my many services are you trying to buy? Because there aren't enough croissants in the world to get me to clean your kitchen."

She laughed, the sound thinner than normal. "Guess again."

"Well, if this is about using me for some sort of kink," he continued, letting her into the building and unlocking his apartment, "like really dirty, filthy stuff, then save the pastries. Truly. I volunteer."

She gave a queasy smile. "Maybe after."

"*After?* Don't tell me we're assembling IKEA furniture."

She followed him inside, something definitely off. She twisted the top of the pastry bag so hard it threatened to tear.

"Maur?" he asked, rescuing the bag. "Seriously, what is it?"

"I—" She looked petrified. "I'm ready."

"For . . . ?"

"I want you to bring back my sister."

"Oh!" Kostya laughed with relief. "Is that all?"

Her eyes were enormous, full of emotion that threatened to spill into tears.

"You'll do it?"

"Of course! I gave you my word. I just need to run to the bodega."

"Why?"

"For the Reese's," Kostya told her. "I've tasted them around you since the night we met."

BACK IN HIS apartment, a dozen packages of peanut butter cups cluttering his counter, Kostya coached Maura through the visit. He explained about the memory she needed, about sitting in her grief, about reaching out with it. He told her about the rules—that Everleigh would only stay as long as Maura ate. He promised to be with her the whole time.

"Actually," Maura said, her eyes not meeting his, "if you you don't mind, I'd rather see her alone. In private."

"Oh." He tried not to sound hurt. "Sure. Totally. It's such a personal thing. I'll, um, I'll get things started and then I'll leave you to it."

"Thank you." She took his hand, kissed it. "You have no idea what this means to me."

He gave her a sad sort of smile. "Actually? I really do."

MAURA ELIZABETH STRUK sat at her boyfriend's dining table, an empty white plate before her. She reached for Everleigh, through the otherworldly Hunger writhing inside her, through her endless regret and guilt, through all the risks associated with raising her sister from the Dead. She combed the tendrils of her mind for the memory, the one that hurt the most. That made her feel her grief most profoundly, just like Konstantin had said. It was obvious, once he mentioned the Reese's.

Halloween night, a decade ago.

Maura was fourteen, and Ev was ten, and they were both still alive. They'd been trick-or-treating. For the very last time, only Maura didn't know it then. They were on the porch, combing through their candy, taking inventory. Ev loved Reese's, hoarded them every year, kept them under her bed to eat at night, especially on their dad's bad days. Sometimes, in the dark, Maura could smell it from the other side of the room, chocolate and peanut butter, and she'd roll out of bed and curl up with her sister, saying nothing, just listening to Everleigh chew.

But that night, that Halloween, Ev didn't hoard them. She didn't ask Maura to trade—an even swap for Snickers or those paper packs of M&M's, two Reese's in exchange for Nerds, or, on rare occasion, three for an Airhead.

Everleigh ate them instead. She shared them with Maura.

They sat there, the air like ice, Everleigh's Ayane wig (*When I'm older, I'm gonna dye it purple for real!*) and Maura's Super Mario mask (*I can't breathe in this thing!*) cast aside, eating every one of their collective peanut butter cups. It felt indulgent. Fun. They licked the chocolate from their fingertips. They threw the paper cups across the floor. They feasted. And then there was just one package left, a full-sized score, two final cups inside. They lifted them, and then, as if they were older, an age Everleigh would never live to see, they clinked them together like glasses of champagne, dinging the chocolate, a toast to themselves.

"Let's do this every year," Everleigh declared.

"I'm in," Maura agreed, mouth full.

"I mean it! Promise. As long as one of us wants to go."

"Of course we will. Always."

It was the happiest they'd ever been.

SOFTLY, BESIDE HER, Konstantin gasped.

"I got her, Maura. She's here."

Maura felt her palms go slick. She opened her eyes and watched him peel apart a package of Reese's, slide a peanut butter cup onto her plate.

"Wait," she said. "Pick up the other one. Cheers me."

His eyes went wide. "The dent! I was wondering what that was."

He smiled, lifted his candy, tapped it against hers, and she was so glad that it was him there, that the first person she'd let in since her sister was gone, the first person who made her feel like she might be able to love again, was the one who'd help her bring Everleigh back.

And then Maura was eating the Reese's.

She hadn't had one in years. They didn't taste good to her. Not anymore.

She bit through the crimped chocolate shell, snapped it the way she'd snapped at Everleigh on the phone the day she died—*Trick-or-treating!? Aren't you too old? I'm in college, Ev! I have plans! I'll see you next weekend, okay?* The peanut butter stuck to the roof of her mouth, gluey, clung the same way she had—first to the sheet in the morgue, where she'd gone to identify Everleigh's body; then to the box of her ashes; and then to the memory of Ev herself, her funky clothes, her violet hair, her brief, passionate, glittering life. The sugar laced everything like poison, like all the things Maura had pumped into her own body afterward—booze and drugs, pills of every color, anything to keep herself from feeling—until that time it went too far and she'd seen, firsthand, how Ev had suffered. And as she swallowed, the cumulative effect of the Reese's Cup—how you couldn't stop at just one bite; how it tasted fake, manufactured, but you wanted to finish anyway; how there was a second one waiting to follow up the first—became that loop of addiction, of lying, of one thing leading to the next, the avalanche she had found herself in, Maura's slippery slope, the one she'd been trying for so long to outrun, and which this last, desperate attempt—right here, right now, Everleigh, and her, and this fucking piece of candy—might finally bring to a close.

KOSTYA WAITED UNTIL Everleigh appeared. Her lights—he should have guessed—materialized in lilac, delicate orbs that arranged themselves into someone he almost recognized. Like a younger Maura—those same wide, flickering eyes; the same stance; the same (he smiled when he saw it) purple hair. He kissed the top of Maura's head as he left, squeezed her shoulder.

"I won't be far," he told her, "just in case."

But she didn't call.

Instead, an hour and a half later, on his second milkshake at The Flame, Kostya tasted something strange.

A Reese's. Another one. That same notch in its side, like a calling card.

Everleigh's.

But that was impossible, wasn't it? Especially since—he checked the time—no matter how slowly she had eaten, surely Maura had finished that Reese's by now.

Surely, Everleigh was gone.

WHEN THE AFTERTASTE appears it's just a shimmer in the air, liquid and melty, like someone's cracked an oven door. An aroma pours out of it, mouthwatering. Soul shaking. Like Reese's, but also like memories.

You follow it right back to Maura's embrace.

SEEING HER AGAIN is everything you'd hoped. There's laughter and secrets and the slowest possible way to eat a peanut butter cup. She tells you everything. That after you died, she screwed up her life. That she tried so hard to help you. That all she wants now is to leave Death behind. To live. To love someone again, this man who makes her full.

She doesn't want to hold you back anymore.

You can feel it, the moment she lets go, your Hunger spirited away. Chased out by what's now spreading through your chest: relief, and closure. Love.

You let her go, too.

When you tell her goodbye, when you say you love her one last time, you're so sure. Stupid hopeful. Convinced this has worked out like you'd imagined, that any minute you'll be on that train, leaving the Food Hall far behind. Moving On.

Only it doesn't work that way.

When the Reese's is done, the wrapper licked clean, you disappear, but you don't return. You stay in the Living realm.

Helpless, invisible. Unable to leave.

You bang on the veil. You kick. You cry.

But there's no way back. No exit at all.

No way forward either.

Turns out the Aftertaste you followed here—made from the food of the Living; cooked by someone alive—doesn't work the way the food of the Dead does. It isn't anchored to the Afterlife, a product of the Food Hall, a tether to lead you back to Death. This Aftertaste is anchored to Life. To a person.

To the Chef.

And now you are, too.

You go where he goes, can only visit where he's been. You try to make contact, to chill the air and spoil his food and flick his lights, but you're too weak for him to notice. The most you can accomplish is to make him taste again, his forehead furrowing when he recognizes your dish, one he thought he'd already handled.

The only silver lining is you aren't here alone.

Fleur de Sel

THE LEASE WAS signed.

In a few shorts months they'd have menus. Dinner service. A bona fide grade A (Viktor would make sure) from the Health Department. They'd have butts in chairs. A bar with bartenders. A reservation book. A kitchen spitting tickets out for orders and waitstaff and Konstantin helming it all. It would be an actual restaurant. Made to bring back actual ghosts.

It almost didn't feel real.

Maura was coming over to help him celebrate (*This calls for a toast! Dinner at your place?*) and Kostya was peering into his fridge (someone had to come resuscitate this thing; food was rotting by the hour), trying to determine what to make her. He'd asked what she was in the mood for, and the answer was typical Maura: *Something that thrills me.*

Their relationship didn't quite feel real to Kostya either.

Since the tattoo parlor, they'd spent most of their free time together, hours of witty banter and great food and multiple—ahem—courses, with no indication that Maura wanted to slow down or just be friends or see other people. It was almost the opposite; she couldn't get enough of him. If he were a different person—someone allergic to commitment; Frankie, say—it would have shot up red flags, triggered an analysis of her as a Stage-Five Clinger, a plan for escape, but Kostya reveled in the attention. He'd never felt so wanted.

They traded secrets, shared parts of themselves other people never saw. He, peak boyfriend material, had brought her kid sister back from the Dead. Sure, he still had no idea what had happened when she returned—but then, he hadn't asked. Because he respected Maura's privacy! He trusted her! She'd tell him when she was ready. Which would probably be any day now; she had a drawer of things at his place, after all. And he—the height of intimacy!—had left several knives and a carbon steel pan in her kitchen.

He was falling, hard, and he wanted to tell her. To show her.

What he cooked tonight had to be special. Food that would let him reveal himself to her, not just the chef part, but all of him. Who he was. Where he came from. What he believed in.

Food could do that. It could tell stories. Not just cuisines or component parts, but histories—of the people who'd prepared the dishes, the way they evolved them over time, the way they made them theirs. Leaving behind a recipe was a way to be remembered and savored and loved even after you were gone. A way to live forever.

When Kostya ate the food his dad had made him as a kid, it always felt like he was still there, right in the room, his hand guiding Kostya's as he chopped dill or scooped sour cream, his bright laugh just out of earshot, ringing out behind a door. A meal could contain so many things he couldn't say, every bite a way to travel through time.

He shut the refrigerator and opened a cabinet.

There was an embarrassment of spices, assorted cans (tuna, black bean, coconut, condensed milk), a half-dozen dry grains. And then he saw them—Morello cherries in a jar.

In their current form, they were too sweet for anything other than an old-fashioned, but before they were preserved, they'd been sour. Deliciously tart.

He knew immediately what he should cook for Maura, the journey he would take her on.

They could make them together—*varenyky*. Thin-skinned dumplings bursting with lightly sugared sour cherries, their warm, dark juice flooding your mouth. Or the cheese kind—soft, sweet kernels of curd luxuriating in a pool of liquid butter. The meat ones, his dad's take on pelmeni, beef and pork and black pepper and onion, boiled first and then pan-fried, brown and crispy, doused in a poultice of white vinegar and sinus-clearing Russian mustard and thick sour cream.

Hell, he'd cook all three.

They used to make them in the summer, Kostya and his father and mother together. A weekend-long event, kneading the dough, mixing the fillings, shaping and pinching and sealing the delicate pouches by hand. They used to make hundreds of them the first hot weekend of the season, freeze them in bags to eat year-round. An assembly line—his dad rolling the dough into rounds the size of his palm; a small Kostya spooning fillings; his mother's fingers white with flour, her fingertips flitting in and out of a water bowl, crimping the sides. He hadn't thought about it in years.

It was the sort of thing that might not have moved the needle at Zagat, that Michel Beauchêne might label quaint or homespun, but it was honest. His best memories of childhood, on a plate. He hoped Maura would like it.

He wanted so badly to impress her, to astonish and electrify and awe her, to see that look on her face when it tasted good, to hear that little moan, her eyes half-closed. He still had trouble wrapping his head around the two of them, how someone like her could be interested in him, but his food, the way it felt to feed her, to watch her eat—that was the real thing.

AROUND FOUR, HE started prep.

Huge pot of water, salted, set to boil. Ground beef and pork coming to room temperature on the counter in trim, brown-paper packages. An onion, peeled. A bag of frozen Montmorency cherries draining in a colander, a bowl beneath catching their acrid juice. Another colander lined with cheesecloth, white vinegar and salt and lemon juice curdling hot whole milk, the start of a soft farmer's ricotta. Flour and salt and oil from the cupboard, measured out in cups, plus sour cream. An egg. Whole milk. The entire countertop cleaned and floured, lined with parchment.

Cooking this food—his dad's food—sent a dull ache through the center of his chest. He still hadn't tried to trigger the *pechonka*. Not yet. Not even after Everleigh. Kostya knew it would work; Everleigh's return confirmed it, though deep down, maybe he'd already known. Faced with the reality of seeing his dad again, he'd hesitated. Was he really ready for a reunion? Did he know what he wanted to say, how to express all the things he needed his dad to understand? They'd have *one meal*. An hour. Maybe two, if he took tiny bites. And that conversation would have to last him the rest of his life. He couldn't squander it.

Kostya had just begun mixing the dough, his hands sticky, kneading and folding on his counter, when Maura buzzed.

FRAMED BY THE threshold, she was like one of Mucha's *Seasons*: the tingle of Winter, the seduction of Spring, the kiss of Fall, the warmth of Summer. She shrugged out of her coat, her violet hair spreading like ink across her loose white tee. Her lips were so red, stained like cherries, the tart kind that grew by his father's childhood home. *Vishnya*—the word came back to him, his dad handing him a newsprint pouch, soft fruit inside.

He almost dropped the kitchen towel.

"Maura, hey. Wow."

She handed him a chilled bottle of Moët & Chandon.

"Wow yourself." She peeked past him, into the kitchen. "You've got a whole assembly line."

"Hope you're hungry." He smiled, stepping back to let her in.

"Always."

THEY POPPED THE champagne, and then Kostya got to work.

She watched him make the dough as she sipped, her eyes feasting on his movements. He kneaded it into pillowy softness, added flour, rolled it into a long log. Then he sliced it with a sharp knife, portioned it out into neat little lumps.

"What do you do now?" she asked.

"Now *I* make fillings, while you roll these into little rounds. Flat like crepes, okay?" He handed her a pin. "About three-inch diameter. Lots of flour. Don't let them stick or they'll rip when we fill them."

"You sure you want me in your kitchen?"

"I want you in any room." He gave her a half smile. "Besides, I did these when I was seven. You'll be fine."

"Yeah, but you're supernaturally gifted."

"I didn't taste a single ghost till I was eleven. These my dad taught me."

She picked up the rolling pin, pushed it experimentally over a puff of dough.

"Did he cook a lot?"

"Whenever he wasn't working. He loved food. Was obsessed with the tastes of things."

"Reminds me of you."

MAURA ROLLED AND Konstantin mixed.

She took her time making a neat stack of thin, floury discs. When she pressed too hard, or ripped one lifting it off the counter, Kostya showed her how to mend it—pinch of new dough, sprinkle of water, press and roll until you close the tear.

"My dad used to say it should be thin enough that you can see through it, but not thin enough to fall apart."

"And here I thought you threw me a softball."

"You complaining in my kitchen?"

"No, Chef! Just trying to live up to your exacting dumpling standards."

"How dare you? These are *varenyky*."

"Potato, po-tah-to."

"Potato's pierogies." He shook his head. "Don't make me demote you to dishwasher."

THEY FILLED THE meat ones first.

He placed ground beef and pork into a bowl, streamed salt through his fingers, cracks of fresh pepper, made a well for the onion with the back of a spoon. She stopped rolling dough to watch him chop it, his knife slicing so quickly through, down, across, over, tapping it into perfect, tiny cubes—*tap-tap-tap-tap-tap*—that she applauded when he was done.

"I've never been so moved by an allium. I could cry."

"That's the champagne talking."

"No. Watching you in your element—it's something else."

SHE STARED AS he drained the ricotta, twisted the cheesecloth, and scooped fresh cheese into a bowl, a little salt, sugar, touch of honey.

"I'm sorry, so you just, like, *made* cheese? Like out of air?"

"No, like out of milk. You just need an acid to get it to curdle. No big deal." He turned pink, pleased despite himself. "Ricotta's pretty idiot-proof."

"If I ever tried to make ricotta I would poison us both."

———

HE DRAINED AND sugared the frozen cherries, put them on the stove over medium heat until their juice warmed, thick syrup, sweet-tart and perfectly balanced.

"That smells like Heaven."

"Taste it." He fished a spoonful of soft, warm fruit from the saucepan and fed it to her.

"Marry me."

"We gotta seal these first."

HE SET A bowl of water on the table and showed Maura how to cup the dough in the palm of her hand, how to spoon the fillings in, less than you think you need. How to trace the edges with a wet fingertip to make them stick. How to fold one side into the other and pinch both tight, crimping the seal. Their fingers slipped together over the dough, water and flour like glue, goopy by the end. There were dozens of *varenyky* when they finished, perfect little packages ready for a bath.

"Here," Kostya said, replacing her champagne flute with a glass of Cabernet. "Have some wine, and I'll boil these up. Should be ready to eat in ten."

"Heard, Chef!"

"Remind me to stop teaching you kitchen talk."

As if in agreement, the lights above them blinked.

"Was it something I said?" Maura laughed.

They stuttered out, casting the room in dark.

"Shit, not again!" Kostya fumbled in a drawer and found a match, a couple candles. "It's been happening all week. The wiring's like a million years old. Held together with paper clips and prayer. The breaker's in the basement, lemme just—"

"Actually? It's nice this way." Maura took the candles from him, set them on the table, lit the wicks. "Leave them off."

———

IT WAS SOME of the best food he'd ever made.

And sharing it with Maura, along with tidbits from his dad, felt like he was passing on a legacy. The way she closed her eyes; the small, appreciative sounds she made; her smile, *that* smile; the way she wouldn't let him take her plate until she'd savored every bite—it all made Kostya full in a way entirely divorced from food.

Maura inhaled the savory course, bathing the pelmeni in a spicy, creamy, soupy blend of mustard, vinegar, and sour cream.

She shook her head, ecstatic as she tasted the sweet ricotta variety, hot, pillowy dough smothered in butter, oozing sugar and light-as-air cheese into her mouth.

But when it came to dessert—the sour cherry *varenyky*, which Kostya served with hand-whipped cream—things fell flat. They were supposed to be the literal cherry on top, the flawless close to the meal. Maura was trying to be discreet about it, but he saw right away that it wasn't cutting it. She ate slowly. Nodded. Smiled. But there was none of that sheer joy in her eyes. No gleeful abandon. No moan.

"Okay, what's wrong with it?" Kostya asked, dubious.

"Huh? No! It's delicious."

He picked up his spoon. "Liar."

He tasted, waited for the turn, for the flavors to develop in his mouth, to deepen, for the tart cherries and sweet cream to make magic. They didn't.

"No. You're right. Something's off."

"It's a little too sweet, I think? Maybe?"

Kostya tried another spoonful. Cloying. Almost like the cherries had somehow fermented, turned, since he'd removed them from the stove.

"Yeah, that's no good. But I can fix it. Gimme a minute."

———

HE COMBED THROUGH his spice cabinet, fingertips strolling along grinders and shakers, vials and pouches, tiny tubes of ingredients you paid for by the ounce, until he came to the container he wanted, a palm-sized glass jar full of what looked like wet, grey sand.

"Open your mouth!" he called from the kitchen. "And close your eyes!"

When he came back to the table, seeing Maura in the candlelight, her eyes closed, a curious smile at the edges of her open mouth, a flutter went through him. He wondered if this was how he'd looked as a little kid, playing the tasting game with his dad. The absolute openness to any adventure that awaited. The flavors ready to transport him.

He tipped a small mound of *fleur de sel* into his palm and dusted her tongue with the world's finest salt.

"Don't rush it," he told her. "Just let it melt. Taste the salt's journey. The Atlantic, where it was born. The marshes, where it grew up. The things it met along the way. Fish. Eels. Snails. The channels it wound through. The sun that pulled all the water away, leaving just the salt behind."

Maura was nodding slowly, her eyes still closed.

The look on her face shifted, curiosity into wonder. As though, behind her eyelids, she was there, standing on the edge of a salt flat.

"I can taste it," she whispered. "I actually can."

"Can you see them?" he asked, feeding her more. "*Paludiers* in aprons? The same for hundreds of years. You know, they never let men do it? They didn't have the right touch. Only women, harvesting the salt, stooping in the water. See the way they skim the surface with their rakes? Can you hear the way the crust crumbles? The scrape and crush?"

Maura was so still he could barely hear her breathe.

He spooned whipped cream into her mouth, a cherry *varenyk*, another sprinkle of salt. He watched the flavors marry as she chewed, saw the smile, *that* smile, spread across her face.

He wanted to kiss her, to taste what she tasted.

"There it is," she whispered.

"*Fleur de sel*," he said, holding up the little jar.

"Flowers of salt." She opened her eyes. "That's beautiful."

"You're beautiful. It's just salt." He felt his face burn as soon as he said it. He wasn't good at this part. "And I, apparently, am mostly cheese."

"I like cheese." She pushed the crystals in his hand around with a fingertip. "And I like it when you get all culinary. Tell me more. How do you cook with it?"

"It's finishing salt. You just use a pinch at the end, to elevate the flavors. This stuff—you wouldn't believe the way it changes things. It brings food to life."

Maura stared at him, something different in her smile. Unexpected.

"Sorry"—he flushed again—"I'm rambling. It's just really special. Extraordinary."

"I've seen a lot of things, Stan," she said, reaching for his salt-covered hand. "Stuff you wouldn't believe. And I wouldn't call most of it extraordinary. But you?"

She lifted his hand to her mouth, watched him watching her.

"Your food? What you can do?" She ran her tongue across his palm, clearing a trail through the *fleur de sel*, sending a thrill all the way through him. "That's extraordinary. *You're* extraordinary. This?" She tasted it again, his heart hammering inside him. "It's just salt."

It was, suddenly, so much more than salt.

She licked it from the creases of his hand, from his life line, his love line, the crystals melting in her mouth, into his skin, *fleur de sel* blending with the minerals of his sweat.

So much more than salt.

He was dizzy with the things he wanted to feel. His whole body bent to her mouth, to how much he wanted to be inside of it.

More than anything.

More than salt.

He shivered as he pulled her close—nerves, he figured, or adrenaline. A rush of blood.

She got goose bumps when he kissed her, chills—a kiss *that* good, she thought, knee buckling.

Extraordinary.

Salt.

BUT IN FACT, the temperature in the room had dropped.

The whipped cream ceased melting in its bowl. The wine stopped opening, stopped breathing, its bloom stilled by chill. The silverware iced over, edges of cutlery and cusps of spoons overtaken by frost, their surfaces no longer reflecting the encounter at the table, or the new arrivals with their Hungry eyes, watching from above.

Shadowed faces pressed through the ceiling, hot knives through butter, hovering in obscurity, unseen by the Living at the table, too consumed, too insatiable, too absorbed in the pleasures of their mouths, to even register their presence.

!!!!!!!!

THERE ARE SO many souls in his Hell's Kitchen apartment.

Every spirit the Chef has ever raised.

A nun, a rock-climber, a little kid. Two teens—a guy and girl—brooding together. A ballerina. A wife. Someone's grandma. The Chef's own dad.

And now you.

You're all stuck. Scared. Becoming what you feared.

Hangry.

Because even though you've gotten closure, you're still trapped and can't move On.

The ones who've been here longest are already showing signs. Wild eyes. Rage that ebbs and flows. Cravings that they can't control. They're stronger now, can make things happen. Make themselves known. Make themselves seen.

The Hangrier they get, the more apparent they become. Their bodies limn in eerie light. Their forms cast shadows on the ground. They have an edge, a shape, a look-and-feel. Ghosts Hollywood would die to catch on film.

You cluster for comfort, an anxious swarm of souls. Your thoughts are a hive, no longer yours alone. You writhe and shiver and howl as one.

And in this collective state, pushing and pulling and thinking together, you notice it.

The veil—the one between worlds—isn't solid like you'd thought.

It's not a wall, rigid and hard.

It's more like skin. Film on hot milk. The membrane of an egg.

And while it doesn't yield to any one of you, when you work together, pool your strength, you find that you can make it stretch.

Thinner and thinner.

Translucent as dough.

The idea hits everyone at once—string lights on a fairy chain. If we can make it back to the Afterlife before the Hanger consumes us, then maybe we can still fix things. Stop the process. Save our souls. Find a way to finally move On.

All we need is more strength. More hands. For the Chef to raise more of us.

With a critical mass, we can tear the veil apart.

PART FOUR

Acids & Trips

*But being hungry is like being
in love: If you don't know, you're probably
not. Your body lets you know in no uncertain
terms when it wants food.*

*Mind hunger, on the other hand, is
endless, bottomless, erratic.*

Geneen Roth
Breaking Free From Emotional Eating

THE FIRST TIME *I died, it was an accident.*

It didn't last long. Four minutes, thirteen seconds on the hospital monitor, the flatline a horizon.

There was no otherworldly announcement when it happened. No choir. No gates. Just the sight of my own body, doctors and nurses swarming, everything tinted with haze like a smudged camera lens, the film that separates the Living from the Dead revealing itself only after I passed through it.

I watched the hospital staff try to bring me back—paddles, clear, shock, pump, breathe.

I willed myself to live.

I wasn't ready, yet, to go; I was twenty-one—a baby. It was Halloween. A year to the day of Everleigh's death. I'd been at a party, in the bathroom with some guy I didn't know, taking a mystery drug that was supposed to make me—his words—levitate.

That night, all I'd wanted was to forget. To not feel.

When Ev died, I couldn't handle it; I didn't know how. I should have been sadder. Bereft. Riddled with guilt, unable to untangle myself. Or crawling my way through those five stages of grief toward some halfhearted acceptance, a halcyon light. But I was young and stubborn and didn't want to sit with those feelings. I wanted to act like I was fine. Like Everleigh had chosen to leave me behind, so I had no problem leaving her, too.

Grief shows up in a lot of complicated ways, and mine was denial.

After her funeral, I decided I wasn't going to feel sad or angry or numb all the time. I just wanted to feel good again. To feel alive.

I started chasing thrills.

Ecstasy, adrenaline, spark—they beat the hell out of hurting.

It wasn't a particularly deep or self-reflective period in my life. You could call me a hedonist, if you were being charitable. A steaming dumpster fire if you weren't. A junkie. A pleasure-seeker. Attention whore. Party girl. I was all of the above.

The problem with living fast is you're never satisfied. After a while, running doesn't feel good anymore. You want to sprint. You want to fly. You seek out the next rush, and the next.

I looked for it everywhere. Anywhere. In tattoos, and piercings, and razor blades. In VIP, and secret clubs, and penthouse apartments. In drugs, and booze, and the bodies of strangers. In places I never should have gone.

And that night, finally, it all caught up to me.

An attending zipped around my body, barking commands. A nurse held a finger on my carotid. They backed away again, loaded another paddle, made me jerk.

I shimmered backward through the air, suddenly aware of this new way I moved—weightless. Bodyless. Then they were intubating, running thick, corrugated plastic down a throat, into a chest that used to be mine. I was seizing up, convulsing, something going wrong, and I didn't want to watch anymore.

I closed my eyes, pictured a happier place, a happier time. A happier Halloween.

We were sitting on the porch. Eating Reese's. Laughing. Everleigh and me.

It was one of those moments when we were entirely present. Charged by the magic of loving and being loved. Cemented by the flavor in our mouths. A taste, a memory, that brought my sister back to me.

And suddenly someone was saying my name.

M-Maura?

Ev's voice went through me like water. When I opened my eyes, saw her there—staring, stunned, beside a booth in a carbon copy of our local arcade— it felt like every piece of my soul had filtered to the floor.

She looked so different. Still young, still lanky, still wild faced and violet haired, but there was a wrongness to her now. Her eyes had lost their flickering light; her skin stretched tight over her bones. Her mouth hung open, desperate.

She looked so hungry. So haunted.

But I didn't care.

I threw my arms around her neck, and she hugged back, tight, and I felt her there, against my chest, spirit on spirit like solid flesh. Maybe it was worth it, I thought, dying, to feel this again.

Ev? *I gasped.* Everleigh? Are you all right?

She shook her head, her eyes wide and full of pain. Full of panic.

No, *she whispered.*

She wasn't okay.

It's the Hunger. *Her words came fast, like she was running out of time.* Maura, please—I need your help.

And I would have done anything for her then. Given anything.

I need you to let me—

BUT THE DOCTORS *around the crash cart succeeded, then, in bringing me back to Life.*

I woke to everyone cheering like they'd just performed a miracle.

I guess, technically, they had.

Don't get me wrong—I was glad to be alive. But I was also devastated.

It was loss and grief and pain all over again. Only this time, I had watched my sister suffer. Had heard her beg for help. She was reaching out; she needed me.

And I know someone more skeptical might have questioned what they'd seen. Chalked it up to hallucination. A drug-induced dream. But if there was even a chance it was real, I had to try.

When Ev took her life, I hadn't been able to do a damn thing to help her. But now that she was Dead? Maybe I could.

Gravy Train

IT WAS LATE September, the air honey crisp, leaves expiring in oranges and reds.

They were shooting in DUMBO, on a cobblestone street with a view of the bridge. The camera made another quick succession of clicks—*pow-pow-pow-pow-pow*—and Konstantin winced as if he were under fire. Which, now that he thought about it, might have been less painful.

He hadn't had a professional photo taken since the sixth grade—what was the point when they never had the money to buy school pictures?—and in the handful of candids of him from the last decade, caught absently at the weddings of friends and relations, men and women his age who had managed to follow life's recipe, find love, make a family, he'd looked sad and envious, and more than a little drunk.

Kostya thought of this as he sucked in beneath his new chef's coat, crisp white with his name in black thread, the sleeves rolled casually to the elbows, the way the stylist had pinned them. Instead of kitchen checks, she'd put him in navy chinos, which would've fared terribly during dinner service, but which he had to admit had looked pretty cool, especially since he'd dropped a few pounds.

He hadn't had a binge in months, not since the night Frankie died. Those waves of emptiness he used to stifle with endless bags of chips, rich-frosted donut holes, the entire contents of his cupboards, came few and far between now. Being with Maura, having someone to wake up to and fall asleep with, someone he could be himself around, who made him feel wanted, went a long way toward filling that void. Not to mention all the ancillary exercise he was getting, both at home—Maura was insatiable; they burned calories in just about every room—and at the restaurant, up and down the stairs a hundred times a day, reconfiguring tables and chairs into various dining room incarnations, hauling deliveries of ingredients and equipment in preparation for their fast-approaching preview week.

Kostya woke early each day, unable to sleep, excited for it to start. Every moment brought him closer to the opening, to what he'd privately begun thinking of as his new beginning. Even stupid moments, like this photo shoot.

"Move a step to the right; I wanna get the bridge in the frame. Okay, gimme sexy!" the photographer directed him.

His name was either Viper or Vapor, a '90s grunge leftover with long hair and sleeveless flannel.

Kostya squinted, wondering if brooding and sexy translated to the same thing on film. Viper (Vapor?) clicked.

"Beautiful, Kon-*stan*-teen!" he called encouragingly. "Now cross your arms over your chest. Just rotate your wrists—I wanna see those tats. Tilt your chin down—good! Look at me like you're not taking any bullshit."

Kostya blinked and scowled a little.

"Amazing. You're a natural. Jen, touch-up!"

The makeup girl appeared with a pot of putty and began re-tousling Kostya's hair.

THE PHOTO SHOOT—like the stylist, the new haircut, and the rugged scruff Kostya was growing over his cheeks and chin—had been Viktor's idea.

"We need have photos, for when press want interviews," he informed Kostya, who had never in his life imagined anyone wanting to interview him. "I know good photographer. I set up."

Everything with Viktor went that way—he was always one step ahead, had a solution ready before the problem even presented itself. He'd hired a publicist for the restaurant the day after the throwdown dinner, and she already had reviewers lined up—*chomping at the bit*, she'd said—for their soft opening in a couple of weeks. He had a connection at the MTA (*Old acquaintance, owes me favor*), who had agreed to plaster ads all over the major subway lines. There were enough contacts in Viktor's phone to build a city, and he had a team of workers lined up overnight, the demolition at Swingline beginning before the ink had even dried on the lease paperwork.

It had been three months, and Kostya was living the good life in the Musizchka Inner Circle. The benefits were real—not just money, but the savvy Viktor brought to the table. Kostya felt secure here; he felt guided. Mentored. Like he belonged.

Kostya's mother had tried (and kept trying) to put the fear of Musizchka in him, but as usual, she'd been quick to judge and doggedly wrongheaded. *You will see, Kostya!* she yelped from his voicemail. *People never change, and this is bandit, and you will say to me, Mama, you were right!*

But so far, the only unsavory thing Viktor had done was insist on a fairly stupid name. Kostya had sent him a list of ideas as long as his arm—Diner d'Esprits, The Haunt, Last Supper, The Other Kitchen—only to be met with stubborn persistence that they name the spot for him.

"*DUH!*" Viktor insisted. "For you, for *Duh*ovny! Is perfect, DUH. *Дух* mean spirit, and *Дух* mean you."

"But no one's gonna read it that way!" Kostya whined. "They'll read it as *duh*. As in, *duh*, why would we eat there?"

"Maybe we spell Russian way. *D-Y-X*?"

" . . . that's dicks."

Naming aside, Viktor cared about the project—of course he did; he was putting so much into it!—and he cared about Konstantin. As bits of information about the restaurant began leaking out—*a new place downtown, something to do with ghosts, a sort of food séance*—the interest in Kostya was piqued, and Viktor made sure that he was ready. A social media manager handled posts on platforms Kostya had never even heard of. A personal shopper had reorganized (read: burned) the clothes in his closet, replacing his ratty T-shirts and bargain-bin jeans with soft crewnecks and organic denim. There was even a speech consultant on hand to coach Kostya on interviews and talking points.

"You public figure now," Viktor reminded him that morning, as they walked through the restaurant space, choosing textiles. "You the face. For what we charging, you gotta look serious, or no one take you serious."

Kostya frowned from one napkin sample to another.

"Or maybe this?" Stella, the designer, pulled a third option from her bag, a charcoal linen with black stitching around the edge.

"Totally." Kostya nodded at her. "This one. And what do you mean," he added to Viktor, "for what we're charging? What *are* we charging?"

That had been a sticking point. The night of the penthouse throwdown, Viktor had seen the look on his guests' faces, and he'd seen dollar signs.

He wanted to charge five hundred bucks a head—to start!—for the Chef's Tasting. Kostya fired back that that was robbery, that no one would pay that much for a meal, that it went against the whole idea of helping people reconnect and get closure. Guests who could afford to drop that kind of dough on a single meal, he told Viktor, probably had other ways of coping with death. Like therapy. Or yachts. Spaceships they were building to colonize Mars.

"Rich bleed just like poor," Viktor informed him. "Plus they keep lights on."

"But it shouldn't just be for the one percent! Besides, prices like that—we'll be laughed out of town. Even in New York, there's not one other debut chef that would charge that much. It just isn't done."

"Eleven Madison charge four hundred a head, and they don't serve ghosts," Viktor shot back. "I hear they talking about not even doing meat no more."

"Eleven Madison is an institution! We're an unproven concept!"

"Concept is everything," Viktor told him, then turned to Stella, who was replacing the napkins with samples for curtains, upholstery for chairs. "What you pay, Stellachka, to know love one is safe?"

"To—to see my mom again?" She fingered a piece of grey velvet, its sheen like moonlight.

Kostya blinked at her, asking himself the same thing. What would he have paid, at eleven, if someone could snap their fingers and bring back his dad? Or the moment he'd gotten that phone call, to see Frankie again?

The whole settlement check from Saveur Fare. Everything he owned. Years of his life.

"Anything," Stella answered. "It's why I took this job."

"You see, Kostik?" Viktor exclaimed, triumphant. "You pay what it cost. I tell you what—we have troubles filling seats at this price, we can discuss change."

"*Fine*," Kostya moaned, grudging. "But we're paying everyone a living wage. Plus benefits. None of that *stage-for-free* shit here. Oh, and Stella? How about next Tuesday? Come by around noon."

She looked at Kostya like he had handed her a winning Powerball ticket.

"Oh my God." She had tears in her eyes. "*Thank you*. I'll be there."

"That reminds me." He turned back to Viktor. "I want a way to do more."

Viktor raised a skeptical eyebrow. "For example?"

"One night a month, I want to open for people who can't afford to spend rent on one meal. Twenty bucks a seat, to cover the ingredients."

He thought of his dad, his love of pizza parlors. He felt almost ready to see him, to bring him back. Once his restaurant was open, once he could show his father all he had become, he thought he might finally find the words.

"Every *other* month." Viktor frowned. "And I have my guys clear names on wait list, make sure no one causing trouble."

"Deal."

"Speak of guys—you hire kitchen?"

HILARIO TORRES HAD been Kostya's first call.

They met in Harlem, at the modest one-bedroom he shared with his wife, two cats, and an ancient parakeet, and over Rio's famous *café de olla* (the piss of actual angels) they caught up about Wolfpup (the insurance company still on their bullshit about suicide), Kostya's new look (*Look at those threads! You got some muscle on them bones, eh? And new ink! Good for you.*), and Rio's current gig (a guest chef stint at a chain of burrito places—an absolute waste of his talent).

"Well"—Rio took a long sip of his *café*—"while it's real good just to shoot the shit, I'm guessing that isn't why you called. What you got, Bones?"

Kostya took a breath. "Actually . . . I'm opening a restaurant."

"Yo, *órale*! That's what's up! Look at you, baby chef's all grown."

"Maybe. But I need help. You're the best I know—the way you brought Frankie up, taught him how to balance a menu, how to run the business end—I need that, Rio. I know it's not your own spot, and I can't offer you EC, but the pay—"

"I'm in."

"You—you are?"

"Hell yes. Mia's been overtime since the fire, and I've been picking up what I can, but we got bills—I need something steady. Besides, whatever went down, Frank's my brother. And he loved your dumb ass, so that makes us *familia*, too."

"How about the other guys? Anyone looking to start a new line?"

"I'll make some calls."

Kostya grinned. "This is gonna be great! The kitchen's almost built. Wait'll you see; it's a fucking Sistine Chapel. And I gotta figure out the menu, stuff people can order while they wait—"

"Wait for what?"

"So . . . there's something I should explain."

"Uh-oh." Rio crossed his arms. "We the kitchen for a show or something? One of them dinner theaters?"

"Not exactly. You superstitious at all?"

"I'm Mexicano. I spice in the form of a cross."

"Right. You might wanna sit down."

IT WAS EASY, telling Rio. He nodded, laughed, a sort of *if-you-say-so* expression on his face, as if Kostya were explaining some new way of roasting pork, plausible but unorthodox. Unlike Frankie, who had no trouble believing in aftertastes but no personal experience with ghosts, Rio had welcomed spirits back before; he did it every year. Early November, everyone he knew was all-in on Día de Muertos, prepping sugar skulls and mezcal and tamales and tortillas, *flores de cempasúchil* and copal, the whole family gathering, cooking, remembering, visiting together, the Living with the Dead.

While he'd never actually *seen* a ghost, Rio often felt the spirits of his loved ones.

"Don't act like you invented it," he told Kostya. "*Fantasmas* come back for my food, too."

"I just hope my cooking's as good as yours. If not, let's keep the place open till the checks clear."

When he told Rio the salary, his eyes went wide.

"Shit," he said. "That's for real. You sure it's cooking we're doing?"

"That's what they keep telling me."

II

THE SECOND TIME *I died, it was by choice.*

It took me months to find a safe way back.

Brink, the place was called. A death club.

Death clubs are maybe the city's best-kept secret. Fleeting as a dream. Just two or three in existence, though even that's impossible to confirm. They arrive in the dark, usually someplace dead or dying. Are gone again by morning. Never in the same place twice.

The night I went, Brink was in the Meatpacking, inside the corpse of a trendy Asian fusion spot. The elaborate décor—opulent settees, ornamental lanterns, spiral stairs, and painted silk screens—had all been co-opted, defaced, draped in shrouds and moss and black-flame candles until the space reanimated from an expired clubstaurant into some sort of deathless in-between. Not a party, exactly. More like the ghost of one.

Around midnight, palanquins appeared, carried by beautiful women and men. They were dressed like djinn—midnight scarves obscuring their mouths; thick, teardrop liner emphasizing their eyes. They really romanced the hell out of dying.

Psychopomps, *a stranger beside me whispered to another.*

They wound their way through the room like shadows, taking guests by the hand, leading them back to their deathbeds. When I was selected, I didn't feel fear or hesitation, only want, the draw to death like leaning in for a kiss.

The mattress smelled like velvet, the pillows like dust. My psychopomp rolled up my sleeve. I let her plunge a syringe into my vein without even asking what was in it.

Was anyone ever so naïve, so brazen? So sure they could die and come right back?

When the poison took hold, the room went still. Fog gathered at the edges of my eyes. The psychopomp leaned close and whispered in my ear, her breath a feather.

Follow the sound of my voice.

I'm coming, Ev, *I whispered back.*

Then she counted down from ten, and I died for the second time.

It was different than before. I didn't watch the life leave my eyes. I didn't wake to Everleigh's voice. I just passed over. Through.

The veil between the Living and the Dead drew me in, guided my spirit, deposited me before the welcoming glow of—I shit you not—an In-N-Out Burger.

Turns out the Afterlife? Where you go when you die? It's a Food Hall.

There were good things to eat in every direction. Spirits strolled the streets with the lazy haze of tourists. They ate crepes in waxed paper; they licked swirls of ice cream. They chewed translucent strips of prosciutto folded inside newsprint cones.

My stomach growled at the sights; it moaned at the smells. Garlic crisping in foaming slabs of butter. Crusty bread, still steaming from the oven. Glossy discs of chocolate melting over double boil.

In the Hall, it was impossible to think about anything but food. Everywhere I looked, something beckoned. And as I passed a storefront—a sweetshop, the candy arranged in the window like so many jewels—the cravings won.

Just one bite, I thought, and pulled open the door.

Inside, on a marble counter, a black box appeared. Nestled inside were four perfect confections—a sampler surprise. The aroma was decadent—thick and bittersweet. I didn't even think before shoving one into my mouth.

A gourmet peanut cup.

Dark chocolate. Crunchy nut interior. Hard, thick outer shell.

A bastardization, but enough to trigger a memory so strong I nearly dropped the box.

Reese's.

Everleigh.

Halloween.

The whole reason I was there.

It felt like being yanked out of a trance. I was supposed to be looking for her! She needed my help! She was in pain, and here I was, wasting time I didn't have.

I felt panic rise into my throat. I shivered.

And then the candy shop swam before my eyes, going liquid.

The Hall was gone.

Back at Brink, they'd administered the antidotes.

STRANGE MUSIC FLOODED *my ears as I awoke; a penlight dilated my* eyes.

How do you feel? *the psychopomp asked me.*

The answer toppled out before my brain knew what my mouth was saying.

Hungry.

That's normal. *She smiled.* Let's get you a snack.

But this Hunger, it turned out, wasn't normal.

It belonged to the Afterlife, to the Dead.

And it had followed me home.

If You Can't
Take the Heat

LINCOLN CENTER IN the evening—pink light hitting the white stone across the plaza, flickering across the fountain, anointing the theatergoers dressed in sequins and silks, in thick suits and the air of cultural condescension, their costumes as elaborate as the performers'—was like traveling back, witnessing a time that used to be. Another era that, if not entirely dead, was teetering dangerously in that valley between shadow and death.

Konstantin was teetering, too. Balanced on the edge of the fountain, waiting for Maura, drinking an extremely overpriced espresso and trying not to get his new suit (courtesy of Viktor's stylist) wet in the spray.

He'd planned a special night out, a big, fancy evening to sweep her off her feet. He'd gotten tickets to *Matsukaze* (standing room, and in Japanese, and he hated opera, but Maura had been dropping hints about the ghost sisters plot for close to a month), followed by drinks at The Smith (touristy, but part of the whole theater routine), and an evening stroll through Central Park (always a winner), the ideal place for a deep conversation, a romantic encounter, the perfect way—the evening softened by champagne and music and elegance—to finally tell her that he loved her.

He wasn't sure why this particular confession felt so difficult for him. Especially now that he'd announced his clairgustance—his closely guarded secret of twenty *years*—to the entire world. Not to mention that, compared to ghost tasting, loving someone was basic stuff. The kind of thing people experienced all the time! And still, the mere thought of saying those three words to Maura dredged Kostya in cold, sticky sweat.

Would she smile politely, then say something soul crushing in return, like *aww* or *thank you* or *that's so sweet*? Would she just rush in—*oh yeah, me too!*—without so much as a thought, a perfunctory exchange no more meaningful than adding fries with that? Would she go the opposite direction and tell him he was rushing things, his feelings completely out of sync with her own? Or, worst of all, would she say it back—*I love you, Konstantin*—in a way he'd believe, that felt real, but then not actually mean it?

Kostya didn't know if he could handle that kind of blow.

He was deeply in love with her. Truly. Madly. A kind of love he'd never dared fathom. It hadn't happened in an instant—a flash in the pan, quick sear, raw within—but over time, his initial wallop of attraction so thin and bland beside the concentrated feeling that consumed him now, this love that had simmered slowly, sauce marrying over long, low heat.

Maura with the tarot, shuffling his cards, dashing his dreams, telling him to quit in a way that only drove him to think about her: *the tartness of tomato, stewing over flame.*

Maura in the dark, pulling down his mask, kissing him in the stairwell of that strange immersion theater: *the heat of hot pepper flakes.*

Maura in his bed, in his T-shirt, eating grilled cheese in the middle of the night, feeding it to him, crumbs on the comforter, her fingers in his mouth: *the sweet emulsion of butter.*

Maura arguing with him, one hand on her hip, pissed the hell off: *basil, torn.*

Maura working through a problem, her forehead furrowed, eyes in such sharp focus: *the concentration of tomato paste.*

Maura walking into a room, the air shifting, his eyes finding hers: *garlic, caramelized.*

Maura when she said his name, when she whispered it, when she traced it into his shoulder, gasped it, screamed it, held it in her mouth like a secret: *pepper—red and black and white—grinding in a mill.*

Maura in the world, living with so much life, so much yearning, so much hunger, that all he ever wanted to do was feed her, satisfy her, love her, make her feel as full as she made him: *streams of salt and salt and salt.*

It had all stirred together inside him until there it was—love—and everything else he'd ever tried just fell away, tasteless.

Hence the opera and the uncomfortable shoes and the anxious scanning of the crowd to see if she'd arrived.

When he finally saw her, every other person in that plaza seemed to vanish, his gaze tunneling toward her, the way she looked getting out of the cab, pulling a stray strand of violet hair away from her face, crossing the sidewalk in this unbelievable dress. Having no idea how beautiful she looked.

She started up the ivory stairs—layers of pale lavender tulle floating around her, a long skirt she had gathered in front—like a living confection, a cotton candy dream. The crowd milled, smoking final cigarettes, taking selfies. He was grinning, and when she caught his gaze she beamed back, mouthed, *Hey, Chef.* A taxi honked and a dozen birds flew overhead. He was making his way toward her across the square, rounding the fountain, snaking past theatergoers. A wind kicked up in the courtyard, unseasonably cold, and as it ruffled the fabric of her dress he saw her stumble, not just her feet but all of her. His heart began to pound and he moved faster, something clearly not right, clearly very, very wrong. And then he saw it—the stutter in her eyes like they were going dark, the same way they had that first night in her bed.

He sprinted down the stairs to catch her as she crumbled.

Instead of a night at the opera, they spent the evening in the ER.

In a moment of adrenaline-sponsored heroism (or rash bravado, depending how you looked at it), he'd scooped her into his arms and sprinted three blocks south to Mount Sinai West, screaming at pedestrians to get out of his way.

"God, please," he panted as he ran. "Wake up, Maura! Wake up!"

She weighed barely anything, like a bird, all fluff and feather and frail bone beneath. She wouldn't open her eyes. He was terrified of letting her go, his whole body numb as they wheeled her into the ER and out of sight.

He worried a hole in the lining of his pocket, anxiety manifesting in his fingertips. He tried to get tea from a waiting area vending machine, his normally steady hands—hands that sliced things with sharp knives for a living—trembling so badly he spilled scalding water all over himself. He was reading and rereading the same sentence of a magazine, none of the words coherent, when a nurse came to inform him that Maura was conscious.

SEEING HER IN the hospital bed—a paper gown replacing her dress, an IV braceleting her wrist, the little oxygen tubes dipping into her nose—undid him.

"But what happened?" he asked her again and again. "What do you remember?"

She didn't have an answer.

The doctors said she had probably fainted. Her glucose levels had been low when he'd brought her in, and it was possible her blood pressure had dipped, and they'd said something about testing her inner ear for vertigo blah blah blah blah *blah*, but none of them had paid any attention to what Kostya had told them, what he'd shouted as they hovered around her, about the way her eyes had just blinked off, not unconscious but dead.

It had scared the hell out of him.

He held her hand on the thin hospital blanket, tracing his thumb over her fingers, along her wrist, over the old scar tissue there, one of the many things about Maura he still didn't know, had been too afraid to ask.

"Listen," he told her, "if there's something wrong—you can tell me, okay?"

She stiffened.

"I just fainted, Stan. It's embarrassing. But that's all it was."

"Yeah." He swallowed. "You said that. Except, I—" He frowned at her. "Maura, I've seen you do that before. That little—like a little death."

"*What*? When?"

He shrugged. "That first night at your place. A few other times we slept together. Your eyes just go . . . empty."

"Maybe you're just that good."

"Stop deflecting? Please?"

She looked away, at the hospital monitor, the peaks and valleys of her heart rate, the gentle drip of the saline bag.

"Maur?" he tried again. "I need you to tell me what's going on."

She shook her head, strained on a smile. "It's nothing. You don't have to worry, okay? I can handle it."

"Yeah?" He traced her wrist again, the puckered skin, the scars she'd put there. "Then tell me about these. A time when I'm guessing you couldn't handle it?"

She snatched her hand away. "Those are from a long time ago."

"No. Don't do that. Don't shut me out." He shifted closer to her, leaning in, as if he could bridge the gap between them all by himself. "I saw something happen to you tonight. I carried you into an emergency room thinking you might die in my arms. I watched a bunch of doctors take you through a swinging door, without any certainty that you were coming back. And I'm still here. I will *always* be here. But I deserve the truth."

Maura took a breath. Nodded.

"When this happened," she said at last, "all I wanted was to die. Things had gotten so out of hand that it felt like my only choice. But now? I'm not that person anymore. I want to live, Stan. I fight every day to make sure I do."

"What things? Fight *what*?"

She stared at the IV entering her vein, the way it bulged the scarred skin. Something had happened to her. Something that was maybe still happening.

"I don't want to talk about it."

"Fine," Kostya said, setting his jaw. "Then let's talk about the Reese's."

She looked up at him. Deer. Headlights. "The Reese's?"

He nodded. "I've been tasting them again. A lot. Even though I already brought Everleigh back."

She was breathing fast now, one of the little sensors attached to her beginning to beep.

"You never told me."

"Because when I raised her you were—I don't know—weird? Secretive? You didn't exactly jump at the chance when I first offered, and when you finally did come around, you sent me away." He could feel it all coming up, vomiting out of him. All these thoughts he'd had for weeks, had shoved down out of respect, a desire to wait till Maura was ready to share. But he couldn't wait anymore. "Which, okay, I get you needed privacy, but then you never brought it up again! You never told me what you talked about, or if you even got closure. I didn't want to pry, but—God, Maura, not a word? And you said she'd had issues. That she lived with *darkness*? And now I keep tasting her, which hasn't happened with *any* of the other ghosts, and you've got those scars, and mysterious *things* from your past, and there's all these moments when you're, what? Dead? Dying? Jesus, is she haunting you? Is she"—his voice broke—"*hurting* you? Whatever it is—let me help you. *Please*."

Something cold flashed in her eyes. Hard. A wall, slamming back in place.

"Look, Stan," she said slowly, "what happened is between me and Ev. No one else. That conversation—seeing her again—it's private. I haven't asked you—not once!—why you haven't brought your father back. Because I trust you to handle your grief. And I need you to trust me."

"But it's not the same thing! She's *doing* something to you!"

"No." Maura shook her head. "This isn't Everleigh."

"Then what is it?"

She gazed out the window, her eyes shining, face resigned, and shrugged. "You heard the doctors. It could be a lot of things."

"But you have no idea? None at all?"

She shook her head again.

And Kostya was about to press, to dig further, when he got his own answer. A puff of air in the back of his throat, the flavors warm and unwelcome as they flooded his mouth.

Chocolate and peanut butter, the edge of the cup dented. Like always.

Her sister, right there in the room. Restless. Hungry. Contradicting everything Maura had said.

III

THE THIRD TIME *I died was a mistake.*

I did it to find Everleigh, but also to feed the Hunger.

It didn't vanish after Brink. It stuck around and ruined my life.

I tried so many things to satisfy it. Anything you could binge. Video games and vampire novels. Pop albums. Trash TV. I strolled museums and gorged myself on art. I ran miles, inhaling runners' highs. I crawled the bars and filled myself with booze.

Oh, and the food! All over the city, I ate and ate and ate.

But none of it worked for long.

It took me over a year to understand what it was Hungry for. Why touching Ev's old things—her tarot decks, her spirit board, the stack of prescriptions hidden in her drawer—quieted the cravings. Why the moments I felt desperate—jogging the Manhattan Bridge, staring at the river, considering a leap—made it go still. Why I found myself drawn to sharp objects, dangerous places, walking at night.

The Hunger wanted Everleigh. To take me where she was.

It pulled me toward Death, a tether to that world. It was a connection between us, this sisterhood of empty stomachs. Sickness that we shared.

So I decided to go back. To find a way to feed it. To cure us both.

I wanted control this time. To do it on my terms.

I researched near-death experiences. Joined obscure Reddit forums. Went to Survivors' conventions. Other near-deathers were only too happy to recount every detail of how they'd died and lived to tell. Every step I'd have to replicate.

Some methods were so involved they required PhDs. Ingredients I couldn't get. Chem lab access.

But others were straightforward.

Electrocution.

Guided drowning.

Strategically slicing my wrists apart.

I thought it'd be easy. A razor blade—deep, but not lethal. A timed 911 call. And I'd find my sister, feed our Hunger, get this magical, Technicolor, happy ending.

Not so much.

I lost enough blood that it was almost a one-way trip. I roamed that fucking Food Hall calling Ev's name, but she never showed. Oh, and the best part? The cherry on top?

When I got back, the Hunger was worse.

Insatiable. Constant. No relief, not even from what worked before. Everything ached, not just my body, but my soul.

I didn't feel invincible anymore. Or lucky, like I'd felt after the overdose. Or motivated, like I'd felt entering Brink. Just scared. Lonely. So damn foolish.

I couldn't risk another trip, not even for Everleigh. Not unless I was okay with not coming back, and I wasn't. Nearly bleeding out was a wake-up call. Even as fraught and complicated as the Hunger made my life, I wanted to live it. To at least try. To do it right, the way I might have if Ev had never died.

So I swore to myself I'd stop fucking with things beyond my control. That I'd find some way to live with the Hunger. That nothing in the world would make me tangle with the Afterlife again.

And then, Stan, at that party, I met you.

Setting the Table

IN THE WEEKS before previews, Kostya hired bartenders and servers, runners and busboys, hosts and a maître d'. He trialed florists and laundries and cleaning services. He unpacked endless boxes of linens in every imaginable shade of black. He ran through dinner service on the line, Rio and Ale and Big Mike and a dozen others making dishes to Kostya's specifications, following his lead in the kitchen, calls of *Heard that!* and *Seven buff chix all day!* and *Dorade on the fly for Table Six!* music to his ears as the senior servers rapid-fired tickets for the rail. He finalized arrangements for the deliveries of food, single cases of hundreds of different ingredients, order sheets that drove Baldor and Rozzo and D'Artagnan crazy.

With all this going on, Kostya should have been laser-focused. Eating, sleeping, and breathing DUH. And he was, mostly. Whenever he wasn't obsessively worrying about Maura.

He'd be in the kitchen, showing someone how to plate a dish, and picture her passing out while crossing the street. He'd be going over inventory with Rio, and pause mid-sentence, imagining Everleigh just showing up, uninvited, fire and brimstone and ghostly wrath. He'd be looking at a table Stella had set, staring too long at an embroidered napkin, envisioning some sort of *Freaky Friday* scenario—Maura and Everleigh trading places, one sister possessing the other.

Maura hadn't had another episode since the hospital (at least, not that she'd admitted), but Kostya couldn't shake the feeling that she wasn't telling him everything. Each time he asked about it, she waved him off. Eye-rolled. Laughed. Like he was making a croquembouche out of a donut hole.

And maybe he was! Maybe he was freaking out for no reason!

Or *maybe* his instincts in that hospital room had been right and Everleigh *was* responsible, was somehow drawing Maura toward those freaky deathless deaths. Maybe she was dangerous. Lashing out. And maybe Maura was protecting her, or in denial about the whole thing.

All Kostya knew was that he didn't trust Everleigh, but that he had no idea what to do about it. Not that he had much time for ghostbusting even if he did.

After, he promised himself. Once DUH opened, once things were running smoothly, he'd revisit this thing with Maura and her sister. Hopefully, by then, she'd be ready to tell him the truth.

WITH TWO WEEKS to showtime, Kostya studied the etching on the entryway door—*DUH by Executive Chef Konstantin Duhovny*—and felt his hands shake. He traced the letters—of a name he didn't even like!—and had to take several steadying breaths. Seeing it there, written, he felt like he'd finally arrived, not just on the culinary scene, but at the doorway to his life.

With a week to go, he walked through the space that they'd built—that he'd built—feeling as though he'd been reborn. The kitchen was breathtaking, soaring, its deco arches doming over top-of-the-line ranges, a row of ovens, salamanders and sous vides, two enormous walk-ins, a lowboy at each station, a reach-in freezer, a blast chiller, every imaginable kind of gadget reflected in the row of antique windows, the 6 Train shooting past at regular intervals, dazzled by the gleam.

Upstairs, the entry hall—dark-mirrored floor; curtains the color of smoke; an enormous host stand shaped like vertebrae—led to a cocktail chamber—leather and bone; chrome; black glass; the double bar fanning out from a central column of stools, like a rib cage—where guests would wait to be taken either to the main dining room or to a private aftertasting chamber. There were ten of these in all, five along each wall, flanking the sleek black tables and skeletal seating of the main dining room. Each chamber was enclosed in mercury glass, the décor within dim and minimalist, the lighting sultry and low, the effect like walking through a rhodium mine.

What you couldn't see from the bar were the gaps in the mercury coating, places where light could bleed through the iridescent glass. When Kostya retrieved Stella's mom, the lights that heralded her return had given Stella the idea. She designed the rooms so that, as diners met their ghosts, their chambers would glow from within, a preview for the next guests waiting to be reunited. A paranormal light show.

"Like an aurora of souls," she'd whispered, showing him the sketch.

"It'll be incredible, if it works."

"*When*," Stella corrected him.

THE WORLD—THE CULINARY world, at least—seemed to agree.

It was only a matter of time. Chef Duhovny, heretofore unknown (not even a chef!), was being heralded. There were articles in *Time Out*, in *Epicurious*, in *Nosh* and *Foodie* and *Eats*, all speculating on what would actually go down at DUH, and whether it was worth the hefty price tag. Several chefs he'd never met, as well as—color Konstantin surprised—Michel Beauchêne had come out in support of the endeavor, with hot takes like how Kostya was resurrecting FiDi's culinary wasteland, bringing attention to worldwide traditions centering food and loss, reminding us how powerful the connection was between eating and mourning, and eating and memory.

They prerecorded a feature for *Good Morning Manhattan*, set to air the day before the opening, Kostya talking into a mic on a sound stage, bantering with the host as beauty shots of the restaurant aired on a screen between them:

"The space is just divine!" she gushed, grinning, her teeth blindingly white and square. "And speaking of divining—before we wrap, let's set the record straight. I've heard some rumors that a meal at DUH includes more than just food." She leaned in conspiratorially. "Are you really offering people the chance to resurrect a loved one? And you're saying you can do that through a meal?"

Kostya felt like someone was holding his hand to a hot burner, but he kept a calm smile plastered to his face.

"DUH means soul," he said, reciting what he'd practiced with his media trainer. "At our restaurant, the goal is to create a reunion of souls, through food." He wove the fingers of his hands together, cat's cradle. "To bring diners—especially those who have lost someone—closure, by helping them revisit their past through taste. And whether raising the Dead is part of the dining experience at DUH"—he gave her the mysterious smile he'd practiced in the mirror, the *come-find-out* variety—"I'll tell you that our food certainly offers a spiritual experience. Beyond that, you'll have to get on the wait list and see for yourself."

They'd been careful not to lead with the idea of ghosts in the press. To tiptoe around it, play it off like an intriguing mystery. The publicity team was adamant that mention of actual ghosts had a chance of blowing up in their faces, of making the whole thing into a joke. A gimmick. To make this work as a high-end, elevated restaurant, they had to sell people on the idea of the food first, and let the word of mouth—and there would absolutely be word of mouth—do the talking.

Which, it turned out, had been the right move.

When the reservation system went live, the available slots booked up in hours. By the end of the day, all the seatings—even unpopular ones, the early and late tables—were gone. Their week of previews, beginning in just a few days, had been filled way in advance; the publicist was actually turning media away, cherry-picking only the biggest outlets and most notorious critics.

"You better wow them next week," she warned Kostya. "Some of these guys—they'll make or break you."

THE LAST FEW days were a ticking clock. Kostya worked the kitchen hard, his own anxieties—worries about impressing the critics, and Maura's *thing*, and living up to the promise he was making every person who came to eat his food, a promise he wasn't certain he could always keep—worming their way into every dish he made.

He overcooked chicken and undersalted liver and tore the skin right off the cod during demos. It was amateur. The kind of thing that would get you fired off the line at Saveur Fare. Worse still, when his guys fumbled an execution, he couldn't explain what was wrong with their food, only that it didn't taste right. They needed to be a well-oiled machine, but the assembly instructions were only in his head, difficult to articulate. You couldn't "salt to taste" if you didn't know what it was supposed to taste *like*.

His cooks all felt it, the saucier and chef de partie and even the lettuce-green commis (the stones on him!) ragging on Kostya until Rio stepped in and shoved them back in line.

"Yo, ballbusters! We're days out and I don't got soigné from any one of your stations. You got time to run your mouths, your food better be on point. Miguel, you got four buffalo soups on the fly. Let's go, *papi chulo*! Stephanie, I want livers—seven. You gonna give me a look? Make it eight. Ricky Martin—three tuna rye. And I walk in that pantry it better fucking sparkle."

"Heard!"

"Yes, Chef!"

"On it, Chef!"

But privately, in Kostya's office, Rio told him to get his shit together.

"You're leading them into battle. You gotta show them you're in control. That you got this. That you got *them*. You do that, they'll follow you anywhere. But you fall, they fall. Feel me?"

THE NIGHT BEFORE previews, Kostya lingered in the restaurant long after his staff had gone home. He double- and triple-checked the dining room—Were the places properly set, the napkins folded, the silverware polished? Were there typos on the menus, nicks in the furniture, scuffs on the floor?—until it could have earned the approval of a stodgy English butler. He inventoried the pantry, the walk-in, the bar, running all sorts of scenarios and hypotheticals to make sure there'd be enough food. He turned all the lights in the place on and off, checking for dead bulbs, for short circuits, for fire risk—a painful snatch in his chest for Frankie as he tested the fire safety latch inside the walk-in—and then did the same with the sinks, the toilets, the water heaters, looking for leaks.

When he was done, Kostya stood in the dark in DUH, in *his* kitchen, and held a long breath. It was happening. The air felt thick with what he was about to do, this thing he was about to unleash, to usher into the world. There was something almost palpable in the room, like if he reached out just far enough, he could touch it.

He thought of his father, of how it would have felt to bring him here, cook him a meal, show him what he'd done. He would have been proud; he would have told him every single thing tasted delicious. He might still, when Kostya brought him back; next week, he'd promised himself. Once they opened.

He thought of Frankie, pain unfurling in his chest, a power blend of sorrow and guilt. It should have been him there instead, helming Manhattan's hot new culinary kingdom. Kostya owed it to Frankie to make this place matter. To keep his flame alive.

He thought of the ghosts. All the ones he'd returned to life, their spirits overflowing with gratitude. All the ones he'd failed to resurrect, the unfulfilled promises of Hell's Kitchen Supper Club. All the Living he'd helped and harmed, the diners who walked away floating and the ones who slunk back in grief, maybe more than before, because he'd given them hope that had never materialized. He didn't want to make anyone feel that again.

Just stay the course, he reminded himself. The aftertastes had led him this far. And they'd take him to the finish line.

The 6 Train blistered suddenly past the windows, casting the kitchen in thunderous sound and strobing light. Kostya watched it race, his face reflected in the panes of glass, hovering among the gleaming counters, the knives and pans and tools. His own expression surprised him. It was the face of someone at home. Easy. Relaxed. Happy.

And then the 6 was gone, its light slurped into the mouth of the tunnel, the whole event so brief that he hadn't even had time to look up, to lift his gaze just a few feet higher. If he had, he might've seen the other faces reflected in the windows' panes, all the ghosts casing his kitchen, gathering like a storm.

WHEN KOSTYA FINALLY crawled home it was close to 3:00 AM. He stumbled through his dark apartment, stripping clothes in a bread-crumb trail. He was exhausted, and he'd have to be back at DUH in just a few hours for prep, but sleeping felt impossible now. This time tomorrow, either he'd be reprising this walk, peeling off his chef's coat, his checks, his steel-toed kitchen shoes, in abject defeat, *or* he'd be across town, drinking heavily, hugging everybody, toasting his triumph with his entire staff.

He paused at his bedroom to pull off a sock and froze.

Maura's skin was so pale in the moonlight, her body so still it barely looked like she was breathing. She was curled in his bed, violet hair across his pillow, fast asleep.

He hadn't seen her all week—his schedule had been crazy, and they'd agreed he needed focus—but he'd missed her, more even than he realized, and seeing her there, waiting for him, sent warmth flooding through his chest. His heart felt full. Bursting.

She rolled over, blinked awake. "Honey, you're home." She gave him a sleepy smile.

"Honey, you're here." He sat down on the bed beside her.

"I wanted to be with you. Tomorrow's a big day."

"Yeah." He released a puff of air. "Real big."

"It'll be amazing." She scooted up, leaned against him.

"I hope."

"It will. Look at everything you've done."

He gave a queasy smile.

"Hey, I know it's hard, doing this without your dad. And Frankie. The people you love who—"

"You're right here," he whispered.

He felt it all welling inside him, joy in one hand, grief in the other. His jaw got tight. His eyes stung. His body ached, spent, but he was wide, wide awake.

"I—I love you, too," she whispered back.

He'd felt it for months, maybe from the first time he laid eyes on her, but it was new now. Tremendous.

"No." He shook his head.

"No?"

"No. I don't love you, Maura. Not just love." Her face was a question and the answers flowed out of him, things he didn't have the words for, feelings like flavors. "It's more. So much more." He was staring at the floor now, afraid to look at her. "I adore you. I worship you. I like everything about you. Every single thing. Even the things you hate. Even the ones that scare you. You drive me crazy; not just spring fever raging-hormone teenage boy crazy, but out of my mind, conquer the world, run away with me crazy. You make me want things. You make me try. You make me happy—like stupid happy. Like I can't imagine happiness without you. You make me feel alive. And I can't imagine living, Maura, not without you. You're my coffee. My wine. My—"

"Sugar?" She smiled indulgently at him, but he shook his head, hard.

"Salt." He looked up at her, daring, nodding, finding what he meant. "You bring out the best of everything—the sweet, the sour, the bitter. You're the reason to savor things. You're the first seasoning, and the last. You're the sea. You're the stars. Life is built on salt, and I—I want to build mine with you."

"Say it again," Maura whispered, and he thought for a moment she was teasing, but her eyes were glassy, wet.

"I love you like salt."

She blinked, and a tear streaked her face.

"I love you, too. Like that." God, the way she looked at him. "Like salt." She moved close, her breath against his face. "A circle of you keeps the bad stuff away."

He wrapped his arms around her, fingers looped behind her back. A ring of salt.

She pulled him closer, down into the sheets.

"Make salt to me."

IT WAS WINE, decanting in a glass. Breathing slowly, opening, releasing, transforming; growing full, and bodied, and smooth; their edges blurring, every sip softer, deeper, more complex and intense, dark fruit and terroir, tasting of all the places they had been, the barrels they'd aged in.

HE KEPT WAITING for her to vanish, for her eyes to empty, so brief he could almost convince himself he'd imagined it. But she didn't; she stayed. She stayed the whole time.

It was he who disappeared instead, tasting something.

Maura squeezed his hand and there it was, in the back of his throat. *Sweet grainy chocolate peanut.* The edible haunting he kept on swallowing.

A craving—her sister's—reaching for Maura, unwilling to let go.

THE SCARS ON *my wrists were still pink when you strolled into my tent and claimed you could taste the Dead. That if you cooked their food, they'd come back.*

Did I believe you, Stan? Would you have *believed you?*

But then you did taste it. The one thing that could've changed my mind. That Reese's was a message in a crimped paper cup: I'm still here, Maura. Don't you care?

I was terrified. Too freaked out to think clearly. I couldn't mess with Death again. Couldn't afford more mistakes. And you seemed clueless and reckless and determined to play with fire. So I warned you to stop. I scared you away.

Only, once you left, I read your cards. They said you were the real thing. And that we weren't through yet. I started thinking I'd been hasty. That there might be something to what you were doing, bringing spirits here instead of going there to find them. That maybe you could help me. That your food could help Everleigh. But by the time I swallowed my pride and rushed out to find you, you were gone.

I spent weeks tracking you down.

I posted on Missed Connections. Cold-called hundreds of numbers. And then on Instagram, this influencer posted something strange—food and ghosts.

A restaurant. I barely let myself believe, but there I was, messaging her for your address.

I took the train to Hell's Kitchen, thinking how to explain things without seeming totally unhinged. But when I got there, there was red tape everywhere. A Notice of Closure from the Health Department. And you, sitting on the stoop, staring at your phone. Sobbing.

I left that night to give you space, only now that I knew where you lived, I couldn't stay away. I kept coming back, looking for an opening. I followed you to Frankie's funeral. To the candlelight vigil. To the grocery store.

It wasn't pretty; I stalked you.

It's like that old Snickers ad. You're not yourself when you're Hungry? They have no idea.

And then you went to Last Rites. I know Cal—he did the art on my ribs—and I know that after a drink or two, he gets chatty. I took him out, got him to give me the appointment right after yours. I didn't know you'd have that reaction to the ink, but I was grateful you did. Reading your palm broke the ice.

And then we were walking through Soho, and you were nice, so much nicer than I deserved, and I kept trying to work up the nerve to tell you what I'd come there to say. To ask for your help. To explain about the Hunger, and my sister. To apologize for what a jerk I'd been.

But I got cold feet. I was too afraid you'd freak out and tell me to fuck off. And I couldn't risk that. You were my best chance to see Everleigh again. Maybe my only shot to stop the Hunger. And there was something else. Something more.

Being around you—it was the first time in months I didn't feel like I was starving. Talking to you, touching your hand—it fed something in me. And maybe it was just your proximity to Death that did it, but it felt like so much more. Like everything.

By the end of the night, I didn't fight it.

When I kissed you, the Hunger—it was like you smothered the flame. I felt a shiver of life again, like I could be more than a vampire, a zombie, this

Hungry, Hungry Ghost. I took you home because I didn't want to let that feeling go. And what happened when we slept together—it changed things.

I died in your arms.

One moment, your eyes were fixed on mine, intense as stars. The next, I was back in the Afterlife.

On a food tour.

The guide was gorgeous. Tall. Dark. With curly black hair and dimples that spelled trouble. He barely looked dead.

It took me a minute to recognize him from his funeral portrait. Frankie.

Spirits gathered round him, pressing closer, straining to hear.

No need to push, fam, he was saying. Plenty of room! If you're here about the tour—the Konstantin Duhovny Culinary Experience—gather round.

And there you were, Stan! An Afterlife experience in your honor, before you even—as far as I know—managed to die. Frankie was explaining about your food. How it was special, what it could do. How it could feed us like nothing else could.

You looking for Aftertastes? *He lowered his voice.* A way to see the folks who been holding you back? That's just what my guy does.

A ripple moved through the crowd. Through me, and every other spirit there. The Hunger, I realized. We all had it.

And I understood what Frankie was really promising.

A reunion. A cure.

What you can do, Stan? That closure you offer the Living? The Dead need it, too.

It's all connected, *Frankie was saying.* Our Hunger, their grief. Moving On, and letting go. Living and the Dead.

And you, Stan, your food, were the link between it all.

I hung on his every word, desperate to understand. I tried. But I was fading. Losing my grip.

Then I woke up beside you. Shivering. Laughing.

Asking for more.

At first, it was all I wanted.

To sleep with you again. To let your hands, your mouth, your body, take me to the other side. To die without worrying about the consequences.

I started thinking I didn't need you to raise Everleigh. That I could just go back and find her myself. That I could take that tour and feed my own Hunger.

I told myself it'd be easier that way. Cleaner. You wouldn't even have to know.

Except then I fell in love with you.

I had all those leftovers after Ev, so much love and no one to feed it to. And there you were, fork in hand. I never imagined what we would become. What you would mean to me. More than a friend, or a partner, or a lover.

Everything, Stan. You are everything.

And I'm so, so sorry for what I made you do.

Previews

THERE WERE WHISPER-THIN crepes spread with translucent smears of butter. There was *sinigang*, blistering hot and bracingly sour, tamarind and bilimbi and mangosteen lip puckering beneath fish sauce and prawn. There was tangy, creamy, homemade skyr, topped with good olive oil and flakes of hand-harvested salt, smoked sturgeon roe, garnished with dill. There was spicy chorizo on crisp, toasted bread, fennel sliced thin over top. There was a T-bone cooked medium-well (making everyone wince) but also seared octopus, deep caramel brown, its tentacles a Fibonacci dream, and olive-and-rosemary leg of lamb, and oysters Rockefeller, Ritz crackers subbed in for the crumb. There were charred vegetables, peppers and eggplant and whole heads of garlic spooned over grill-marked Halloumi. Eggplant another way, caponata, piled atop shallot-rubbed toast. Eggs, deviled with caramelized onions and just a kiss of mayonnaise, and Whampoa-style, creamy, with cornstarch and fish sauce, and scrambled in a bacon-egg-cheese-salt-pepper-ketchup on a hard roll. A bowl of Lucky Charms with all the marshmallows picked out, then added back in once the cereal got soggy. A peanut butter and pickle sandwich on white bread, the crusts cut badly, uneven, like a teenager'd done it.

And there was something else Kostya noticed now, his focus sharper than it had ever been. The way emotions hit his tongue—not just something that he witnessed between the Living and the Dead, but feelings he could taste right in his mouth. The unabashed joy of spaghetti carbonara. The absolute abandon of a triple-decker turkey club. The particular sadness of lemon cake. When the ghosts appeared, Kostya could see it in their faces—the sentiments he'd tasted, seasoning the memories that shepherded them back.

He wished he could watch forever, every reunion, every tearful or uproarious or tender goodbye, the way he'd been able at Hell's Kitchen. But he was booked solid. Previews were busy, seatings slamming them every hour from noon to four and again from five to eight, reviewers and VIPs whisked through DUH's black mirrored entry to an aperitif at the rib-cage bar (two if they were behind) before being escorted to their private chamber, a server waiting inside to explain the menu.

In the dining room, Kostya saw the effects of his talents for the first time, the light show as the spirits arrived eliciting gasps and awed applause. (Stella had totally nailed it.) Downstairs, there was a steady churn of chits, the ticket machine sputtering as diners sampled the regular menu (which expanded nightly to include the latest aftertastes) in preparation for their main event. The kitchen hummed, everyone cooking not only with technical skill but with care, their hearts clearly in it.

It wasn't like at Saveur Fare, where precision demanded silence and the tension was thick as Texas toast. At DUH, the noise and chaos mutated into a calm, easy focus. With the occasional dirty joke, because it *was* a kitchen, after all, but still, there was reverence here. The knowledge that what happened in these rooms was a miracle.

BY THE END of the first service, they'd worked out a rhythm.

Once he got an aftertaste, Kostya would return to the kitchen and hand out assignments—*Listen up, everybody: Room Three's got apple tart. I need someone mincing McIntoshes, and I mean mince, not dice—Tony, that's you.*

I need a pâte sucrée, *but the butter's gotta be by hand—Stephanie, go. And Mica, I know you just walked in, but I gotta send you out again—Bourbon Vanilla Extract; we only got the regular stuff.*

That was one liberty they'd taken with the Escoffier method of kitchen labor. Unlike restaurants that served off of a standard menu, they found it hard to stock everything they might need to get through their Chef's Tastings—the ghosts could, and quite often did, order *anything*—so Mica, the youngest guy on the line and the greenest, became their runner, on standby to get any ingredient they were missing, a map pinned to his station with the nearest bodegas, supermarkets, specialty stores and restaurants, and the fastest bike routes to each.

Once they got that going, aside from the usual kitchen shenanigans—servers getting antsy (*I need my apps out yesterday!*); someone slicing their hand open (*Yo, man, pass me that stack of towels! Now, now, now!*); or the occasional small fire or burnt dish (*Ain't no saving that. Do it again!*)—things were basically butter.

The aftertastes came in without hiccups, no missing pieces or lost connections. Kostya knew what to do now; he had learned. His movements were so assured in the kitchen, so intentional, that he overheard the *garde-manger* whispering to Rio, wondering if this could really be the same guy who'd been here just days before, messing up dishes.

He still got the occasional diners who couldn't generate an aftertaste, but that wasn't a problem, exactly. Kostya had agonized when it happened in Hell's Kitchen, but he saw it differently now. So did his patrons, once he explained. The realization had come from something Maura said: *Hungry Ghosts are the kind that come back.* The spirits who returned were ones without closure. The kind still searching for peace. The Living who couldn't feel their departed—it was because their Dead were full. Which, while disappointing for their dining experience, was a pretty good thing, generally. (Still, to soften the blow, Kostya threw in dessert on the house.)

Big picture, it was all much simpler than he'd built it up in his head to be.

Almost like the ghosts who wanted dinner had been there, waiting nearby for Kostya to open DUH's doors. Like they'd been in line, just itching to cross. Maybe he'd somehow made a reputation for himself on the other side. Maybe there was an otherworldly reservation system that tapped into his. Maybe, he flattered himself, his name was over there in lights, being hailed in ghost newspapers or whispered in phantom bars.

And (bonus points) since they'd opened, nothing bad had happened! No *darkness* had followed anyone across the border. No one was coming for anyone else. It was *Only Dana*, it turned out, *and no Zuul*. And Maura had been fine—perfectly conscious—this whole time. What a relief! Finally, *finally*, after all he'd been through, everything was going right.

FRIDAY WAS THEIR last service of the week, and the final preview seating before their official opening to the public on Saturday. It was nearing close, and they'd had a full house save one no-show (the nerve!). The kitchen was winding down, the dishwashers elbow deep in suds, Big Mike scrubbing down the sauté station. Kostya had notes for the team—new aftertastes he wanted to include in the standard rotation, a happy-dance-inducing pork belly *bao* bun and a fully loaded (with cornichons and anchovies and seared tuna and cheddar) baked potato that was like Niçoise salad's sexier cousin.

"Gather round, everybody!" he said. "We got updates. Opening night tomorrow. But first—I gotta tell you. You all kicked ass this week. Made me proud."

"Don't get soft, homie," Rio said, grinning, but Kostya could tell he felt the same way. Their kitchen had absolutely killed.

The crew assembled around *garde-manger*, Rio at his side with a notebook, a few of the guys still wiping their hands on towels, Steph honing a knife at the counter, the zip and clank of steel.

Kostya was in the middle of the ingredients list for the pork belly when

Allison, the hostess, sprinted down the steps, her face flushed, fear in her eyes.

"He's here!" she panted. "The no-show? It's the *Times*! Wants the full menu in thirty minutes." She turned to Kostya, mortified. "And he said to tell you he wants a word."

WHILE THE KITCHEN returned to a rolling boil, the language decidedly saltier than during the other seatings that week, Kostya buttoned a clean chef's coat and ascended the stairs.

Dan Evans, MFA, CWPC, FU Very Much, was an unflattering caricature of food critics. The kind of guy who had been known to make chefs cry, to fold restaurants over his knee for a spanking, to take them from toast of the town to just, well, toast. His bad reviews had doomed Angelique in Midtown, Meat Market in Bushwick, and the entire Duck Duck Goose chain (may their commoditized confit rest in peace). To top it all off, he was notoriously shitty to waitstaff, purposefully abusing them just to see if they'd stay polite, to make them, in his words (June 11, 2017, "Aria—More like Recitative") "sing for their supper without souring the notes."

Viktor's publicist had briefed Kostya on him, a whole half hour filled with headshaking and hand-wringing and you-better-nots.

"He will hit right where it hurts," she informed him. "Gird your loins."

When Kostya opened the door to Tasting Chamber No. 4, he recognized Dan from the grainy photo the publicist had slipped him. He wasn't supposed to know what the critics looked like—they were supposed to be anonymous, to dine just like everybody else—but this guy had become so notorious in food circles that people passed around stills to warn one another.

Beyond being generally loathed, he was aggressively unappetizing. Short, squat, his face wide and jowly, with bags beneath his eyes and thick folds in his forehead. Kostya was reminded (a little pang hit him) of Freddie

Mercury, his ex's Frenchie, only Dan Evans was far less cute and certainly less friendly. He surveyed Kostya with beady brown eyes, artificially magnified by expensive glasses, and cleared his throat.

"Good evening, sir," Kostya said carefully. "Our hostess said you wanted to speak with me?"

"You"—he frowned—"are the executive chef? Oh dear."

Michel wouldn't have taken that. Even Frankie, after a drink, might have offered him the door. Kostya only nodded.

"I take it you know who I am?" Dan asked.

Kostya nodded again.

"Then you're less of a dolt than half the people I review, at least." Dan removed his glasses, examined them in the dim light, then put them back on. "I don't like bullshit. You like bullshit?" He didn't wait for an answer. "So why don't we cut right through? This isn't going to be a rave, pal. No Disney movie happy ending where I eat your ratatouille with tears in my eyes. I despise gimmicks; you should know that. Consequently, I refuse to participate in the farce that is this restaurant. I'm here only because my editor insisted and I didn't feel like a fight tonight. So here is my proposal: I will order from your standard menu only. I will skip the Chef's Tasting—I'm not ingesting some parboiled dish you've got waiting in the wings, pretending it came from my great-aunt Mabel. And I will judge DUH by the same standards I use to judge every other establishment: on the merits of your food."

Kostya let this wave of disdain wash over him.

"We don't prepare any of the Chef's Tastings in advance," he said carefully. "Only made to order. Based on what the spirits feed me."

"Speaking of your menu," Dan continued as if Kostya hadn't spoken, "and I say that in the most elastic sense of that word, what sort of cuisine is this, would you say? Bastardized American?" He perused the sleek sheet of black vellum, the dishes printed there in silver. "Knock-off Japanese? Some sort of Mediterranean fusion, heaven forbid? I mean, pick a lane."

It took every ounce of Kostya's restraint not to break something.

"What we serve at DUH goes beyond any one culinary tradition. We help people say goodbye. That's the cuisine. Grief, and closure."

"Didn't I *just* say I don't appreciate bullshit?"

Kostya looked at Dan, at the meticulous white button-down that had been tailored to fit his proportions, at the fancy fountain pen laid neatly beside him, its nib already inked with venom, at the way his face arranged to form the nastiest version of himself. Something had hurt him. Someone. Kostya could see it.

"I'm sorry for your loss," he said slowly.

"What loss?"

"Patrons come to DUH because they've lost someone special to them. I only assumed the same was true for you, Mr. Evans."

"You assumed wrong. My old man died in May"—he barked out a laugh—"but quite frankly, good riddance."

Kostya looked at him differently now. For all his bluster, Dan was just like him. A kid without a dad. Lashing out.

"I see. When I lost my dad—it made me feel alone in the worst way. I'm very sorry."

"Like I said, it wasn't much of a loss," Dan countered. "Now what do you recommend for starters? Nothing seems to appeal."

And then Kostya tasted it.

Scorched. Bitter. Unpleasant. Just like its intended recipient. A once-flaky crust turned brittle with char. Inedible. The hint of cinnamon sugar not enough to resurrect this break-and-bake disaster.

"Thanks for your feedback," Kostya said. "I'll have the server bring you out some selections."

KOSTYA SPRINTED DOWN the stairs.

"Mica! I need a run! Pillsbury dough—the crescents. Get every kind they make. Go, go, go!" He turned to Rio. "Get all the ovens preheating. Four-fifty. We're gonna burn 'em." He stopped his lead server on the stairs. "And Mikey! Slow down service. Tell everybody. One dish at a time. *Crawl.* We have to keep him here until his aftertaste's ready."

DAN EVANS ATE exactly one bite of each dish he was served. A spoonful of Sister Stacy's buffalo chowder. A nibble of NamastayHigh's sardine tartine. A morsel each of mini-wieners with sautéed sauerkraut, and Peking duck ragout, and jammy strawberry bread. By the time he'd shoved aside the spaghetti with peas (not even a sniff), the crescent rolls were beginning to brown.

Kostya had doctored them—cinnamon, sugar, a brush of egg white—and set them in the oven to burn. He sampled a roll every few minutes to get just the right level of ruin. When they were finally blackened to order, he pried one from the sheet pan with a butter knife, and carried it to Dan himself.

"What, and I mean this sincerely, the actual fuck?" Dan asked, squinting at the plate.

"A burnt crescent roll. From your father, if I had to guess. He's knocking. It's up to you whether you open that door." Kostya turned to go, then added, "Oh, and for the record? I don't adjust the aftertastes to taste good. Sometimes, spirits are bitter. What they need to return, that's what I make. Down to the charred crust."

KOSTYA WATCHED FROM the dining room, Rio by his side. For a while, nothing happened. Other patrons departed—raving! thrilled!—leaving the last tasting chamber in shadow, Dan Evans deciding what he wanted to believe.

When the mercury glass encasing his room exploded with light—orange strobes setting the dining room aflame—Rio threw his arm around Kostya's neck.

"Well, I'll be damned," he said. "Can't nothing stop you now."

KOSTYA RODE THAT high through midnight, when he sat alone in his kitchen, the restaurant empty, the staff sent home to rest (who was he kidding; they were almost certainly at a bar) before their grand opening the next day. He took a long swig of champagne from one of the two fizzing glasses he'd set out, and opened the plastic bag beside them, a dozen packages of Reese's Peanut Butter Cups inside.

Maura was on her way to meet him.

"I want to give you a tour of the restaurant," he'd told her. "Just us. Before the insanity of opening to the public. I want to show you everything."

"Can't wait," she said. "We gonna eat in your fancy kitchen?"

"Absolutely. I want you to taste the whole menu. And I"—he said it before he could stop himself—"I might even have a surprise."

He'd decided it the night he'd come home to find Maura waiting for him. They had just experienced the euphoria of love, of confessing it and receiving it and making it, this incomparable feeling he had waited and hoped for, and then, right there in the room, practically climbing into bed with them, had been Everleigh.

Maura would never be free so long as her sister's ghost held on. He would never be free either. Never be certain that Maura was safe. That Death wasn't just around the corner, threatening their happiness. That they were truly alone together.

But he had the power to change that.

He was going to bring Everleigh back again. To give Maura and her sister another chance at closure. He wasn't sure it would work; some of the ghosts he'd resurrected had implied that these were one-time trips. But unlike those ghosts, Everleigh was still here. Still sending him aftertastes. And if that wasn't a sign of wanting more, he didn't know what was. So he'd made up his mind to try. He'd gathered the Reese's. He had everything he needed.

Everything except Maura's permission.

And knowing how she'd hesitated before bringing Everleigh back, how secretive she'd been, how unwilling to open up about it, she would probably take some convincing.

Kostya puttered nervously around the stations, trying to keep himself busy. He arranged and rearranged the food he planned to serve, moved things out of the pantry (and back in), added oil to the deep fryer, washed produce. He refilled (then drank more of) their glasses of champagne. He was in the middle of changing clothes (nervous sweat had soaked right through his button-down) when Maura texted that she was a block away.

"Stupid stylist. Stupid tiny buttons," he muttered, fumbling with the holes.

He wanted tonight to go right; he *needed* it to. If he could make it to opening night with Maura safe from ghosts and by his side, the culinary world at his feet, all those people he might help, both Living and Dead—it would be everything he'd ever wanted.

And then, at long last, he could do the other thing he'd been waiting for. The thing he'd been longing to do since that first ghost appeared in The Library of Spirits.

He could bring back his dad.

Here, Maura messaged him, and Kostya swallowed the flavor of chocolate in the back of his throat and rose to meet her.

FUCK, I HATE this part.

Deep breath. Okay.

I slept with you again. Every chance I got.

I visited the Afterlife.

I kept tabs on the Food Tour.

There were more spirits gathering. So many. The crowd restless, eager to begin. Sooner or later, I figured, Ev would show up there. Be on that tour when it left. Which seemed like a better way to find her than aimlessly searching the Afterlife.

But there were delays. Frankie kept stalling. He gave tours of your early aftertastes; he explained how you brought those spirits back. But no one new went through. Not yet.

He was waiting on you, he told us. On your restaurant for ghosts.

It didn't take me long to figure he meant DUH.

So I encouraged you. Pushed you toward Viktor even though he was a sleaze. Pushed you toward the Dead despite the risks. Pushed you into the kitchen because that was where I needed you. But it didn't work fast enough.

My Hunger took a turn.

When I wasn't around you, the cravings got worse. They were eating me *alive, reaching for Death, demanding it. I was scared to be alone, to go to sleep. The day I showed up with those pastries, I'd woken screaming, the Hunger pangs so sharp and strong I had to fight to wake at all. I was scared that, one day soon, I'd close my eyes and never open them again. That the Hunger would take me while I dreamed.*

I couldn't wait for the tour, or for your restaurant.

I had to do something. To make it stop.

So I begged you to bring Everleigh back.

I should have told you then. All the things Ev said when she returned.

How her Hunger had been my fault. How my Hunger had been hers. How when we don't let go, it starves the ones we love. How the Hunger pulls us toward each other because it craves a last goodbye. How that's what all your ghosts want, too.

She said that what we had to do to feed it was to let each other go.

So we did.

But once Ev disappeared, I still didn't feel full. Only empty. Only Hungry.

I wish I'd put it together then. I wish I'd guessed. That there was something off with what you were doing. But I just thought the flaw was me—all the times I'd died; all my bad decisions. I'd messed up everything else, so why not this?

I told myself I'd find some other way to feed it. That it could still be okay. That Everleigh was safe now. That most of all, I still had you.

And then, a few weeks later, I started slipping through the veil.

It happened without warning. Without my meaning to. In the middle of a card reading. Halfway through a video game. That night at the opera.

It was like the Hunger finished what it started in my sleep. Like it had found a way to drag me, briefly, through the veil.

And what I saw? Things were messed up in the Afterlife.

Food was burning in the Hall. Stalls were closed, or cooking things no one would eat. The souls on Frankie's tour were crazed, like any minute they might bolt.

There were signs on our side, too. Like a fungus, spreading from the Dead.

Cold spots in your apartment. Lights that glitched. The thermostat. Food rotting for no reason. Your fridge—it isn't broken, Stan; it's haunted.

In the hospital, when you said you tasted Everleigh? I started thinking that your closure wasn't really closure. That maybe you were tasting her again because she hadn't actually moved On. Only, if that was true, then where the hell was she? Back in the Afterlife? Somewhere else? Somewhere worse? Where, for that matter, were all the ghosts that you brought back?

This morning, I found out.

Here, Stan. They're still here.

They never left.

Perishables

MAURA ELIZABETH STRUK traced her trembling fingers over the lettering on the smooth black door. *DUH.* An unforgivably stupid name, and yet she could feel the energy in the etching, like a living frost. A restless soul, swirling within.

Or maybe it was her own pulse.

Her head spun. Dizzy. Hot. Every inch of her trembled. It felt exactly like it had on the Met steps, just before she fell. Hypoglycemic. Half-dead.

She was so fucking Hungry.

She pushed open the door and made her way into the foyer—dim, cool, a body cavity—to wait by the host stand, where Konstantin said he'd meet her. Her heels echoed across the floor, the pale silk of her skirt swirling like a phantom over all the shiny surfaces, her face reflected, ghostly, in the mirrored glass.

She drank in the space, feasting her eyes.

DUH was breathtaking, the stuff of designer dreams and architectural hard-ons. But Maura couldn't shake the feeling it gave her—the feeling it was intended to give—like she was surrounded by Death here. By spirits. By places so thin you could slip right through the barrier to the other side without even realizing you'd gone.

No, she warned herself. *Don't you dare.*

She chewed her lip, studied the gauzy curtains, the way they floated over her reflection, a corridor of apparitions.

A sea of ghosts.

Maura swallowed.

She was to blame for how out of hand this had gotten. She'd played it fast and loose with Konstantin. Had been negligent, willfully so. Had swallowed down every objection and hesitation and warning, for her own reasons at first, yes, but then because she was in love with him. And now it had caught up with her.

There was no other choice, not if she wanted to stop what was coming.

She had to tell him everything. Tonight.

It might already be too late.

"DON'T MOVE," KONSTANTIN'S voice drifted through the dark. "I want to remember exactly how you look, standing in my restaurant."

She felt the warm weight of his gaze and turned.

He was watching from a doorway. His white shirt glowed against the black velvet behind him. His eyes were wide, taking her in, his dark hair disheveled. He was in his element here. It was beautiful.

He beamed, and she felt her stomach flip, momentary relief from the Hunger clawing through her. The way he looked at her—it felt like things might wind up okay.

"So?" he said. "What do you think?"

"Stan, this place"—she spun around, gesturing—"is unreal."

"I was planning on being humble tonight, but fuck it. It's pretty sick, right?" He walked toward her, his giddy laugh echoing off the walls. "Welcome to DUH."

"Oh," she teased, "you pronounce the *H*?"

"Take it up with Viktor."

"I'd like to air my grievances directly to the chef, actually."

She scooted up in her heels and wrapped her arms around him, a tremor scaling her spine. When she kissed him, relief coursed through her, right down to her toes. The shiver in her hands, her arms, receded. Like antivenin.

The Hunger loved Konstantin.

His fingers curled around her waist. "You hungry?"

She put on her brightest voice to drown out the ache of pulling away, the stomach-sinking knowledge of what she was about to tell him.

"Always."

HE LED HER through the cocktail lounge and dining room, the clean, dark, Afterlife–meets–Apple Store aesthetic in full swing in each of the private dining chambers they passed. She was expecting something similar when he guided her down a flight of steps to the kitchen, but seeing it, she gasped.

"It's like going back in time." Her gaze swept the arched ceiling, the etched glass, the wall of antique windows.

"I know! I still can't believe it's mine. Did you catch my name on the door? Here—sit at this station."

He led her to a barstool at a stainless-steel prep counter, two slender glasses awaiting them, bubbles rising in bright champagne.

"To you, being here," he said, handing her one.

"To us." Maura raised her glass. "To being together."

They clinked. Sipped. Then began to speak at the exact same time.

"Speaking of being together—"

"I have to tell you something—"

He laughed, held up a hand.

"Can I go first? Please? I've been working up the courage and I'm afraid I'll lose my nerve."

Maura bit her lip, hard enough to focus through the Hunger. "Sure."

"Okay." He took a breath, his neck going pink beneath his collar. "Right.

I love you, Maura. And I want to share everything with you. My whole life. I asked you here tonight because I wanted to share DUH"—he swept his arm out toward the kitchen—"with you, too. And I said I had a surprise, but it's more of a question, really."

Maura's heart pounded. Did he want them to move in together? A wedding? A life? They were things she'd wanted one day, too, with him—with only him—but which seemed impossible now.

"And I know there's stuff in your past that you don't talk about," he continued, lifting a plastic shopping bag up onto the counter, "but it doesn't scare me. I've thought a lot about this. And I want to help. I want to get you the closure you need. To let go. To move on." He reached into the bag and removed a package of Reese's Cups. "To be free of Everleigh, and whatever her death has done to you. I think we should bring her back again. Tonight. Give up that ghost, once and for all. You in?"

Maura went pale. Whatever she'd imagined, it hadn't been this. Summoning Ev was the exact opposite of what they should be doing. The very thing that had gotten them into this mess.

"We can't," she gasped.

"Sure we can."

"Stan, you don't understand—"

"Hey," he said gently, "I get it. It's scary. But you can trust me. It'll be fine; I've really gotten the hang of—"

"It's not fine!" she shouted. "You have no idea how broken things are!"

"What are you talking about?"

"We messed up, Stan. You. And me. There are so many things I wish I could take back."

He came around the counter, slow, like he was afraid she'd startle away.

"Maura? You're freaking me out."

She blinked at him, her breath shallow. Coming hot and fast.

"There's something I need to tell you."

"Just the words every guy wants to hear."

"About the ghosts you raised. About the Afterlife. About a lot of things." She blinked, and a stream of thick, hot tears rolled down her face. She pushed them back with the heel of her hand. "It's a long story." Her voice was shaking. "You should sit down."

He pulled up the chair beside her. Sat.

"Um, okay?"

"I just need you to listen," she said. "Please."

"I'm not going anywhere."

"God, will you still say that when you know?" She shook her head, smeared more tears across her face. "No, it doesn't matter. Just let me get it out. All of it."

The 6 Train flashed past then, bathing them in ghostly light.

"The first time I died," she began, "it was an accident."

Hard to Swallow

MAURA TOLD HIM everything.

How she died. How she came back. How the first time had been an accident, and the second a choice, and the third a bad mistake. How she'd contracted a Hunger, and how nothing she tried would feed it.

She told him about Everleigh. And . . . a Food Hall? And—was she serious?—*Frankie* in the Afterlife. Running some tour for the Dead. A tour about *him*. Which, evidently, had something to do with DUH.

Kostya's head was spinning.

He listened, stunned, his lips parted as if there were words he wanted to say, his breath catching in his mouth when he couldn't bring himself to say them.

When she told him about Seyoncé, about Last Rites, about how and why she'd slept with him that first time, he pressed his lips together, tight, a cold, thin line.

The way he looked at her then—hurt, crushed, like he'd never seen her before, like he might never want to again—made it difficult for Maura to continue. She wanted to stop, to fall to her knees and beg him to forgive her, but there was no time. There were things in play now more important than her feelings. Bigger than the two of them.

When she reached the part about the opera—the way she'd tumbled through the veil, how she'd known something was wrong—he shook his head, eyes flashing with dangerous light.

Anger. Disbelief. Disgust.

By the time she arrived, finally, at that morning, she couldn't stop shaking.

"They're still here, Stan. They never left." She tried to keep the tremor from her voice. "In your kitchen—on your ceiling. Ghosts. Dozens of them. They're not just Hungry; they're next level. Something *else*. They've been trapped here. They can't get back to where they belong. And I think that all of them, gathering together—it's doing something to the veil. That's why it's barely there now. Why I've been slipping through."

She paused, recalling how she'd gazed into her coffee cup and seen them there, reflected, all those faces. How they'd shattered when she dropped the mug, smashing it to smithereens. How she had looked up and watched them writhe against that threadbare veil, pushing and pulling and gnawing at it—and known that her time was up. That she couldn't fix this on her own anymore.

"I need your help, Stan."

She looked at him, and he cast his eyes away.

"I know I don't deserve it," she said softly. "I should have been honest. Told you all this from the start. I was just too ashamed. Of the Hunger, and my sister, and the way things began with us. Of being so out of control I couldn't make a single good decision."

Her voice grew thinner with each word, fragile as glass.

"I was weak, Stan. And selfish. I fucked up so much, trying to—I don't even know? Handle things myself? Not ask for help? Be the big sister?"

Her voice cracked, half laugh, half sob. He still wouldn't look at her.

"And then we happened, and despite what came before, that was *real*. It *is* real. Like salt. And I just wanted you to be happy! To chase your dream. To get *here*."

She gazed around the kitchen, its light dimmer now, the air like ice, all its magic gone.

"Only now—" She shook her head. "You can't bring back any more ghosts. We've gotta fix the veil somehow. Send those spirits back where they belong. Get Frankie to stop that tour. *Please.*"

Overhead, the bulb lighting their station blinked.

Discomfort Food

IN THE KITCHEN of DUH, Konstantin was trying to remember to breathe.

He felt like he'd just been blast-chilled, every one of his extremities numb. Vibrating with exquisite pain.

"Stan?" Maura's face was blotchy, slick with tears. "Say something."

He shook his head.

This wasn't how the night was meant to go. They were supposed to be celebrating. He was supposed to bring Everleigh back, and give Maura closure, and fix what had been wrong. To have a romantic dinner in his kitchen and spend the rest of the night christening every last inch of his restaurant.

Instead, she'd torn his heart out and thrown it in a blender.

She reached for him, but he pulled away, fast, a reflex against a dangerous stove.

"Konstantin," she whispered, "I'm sorry. I'm so, so sorry. *Please* . . . just try to understand how it felt, how complicated—"

Something inside him burst. A flavor spread over his tongue, not aftertaste, but memory. Betrayal. Pine-Sol.

"Oh, I understand completely," he snapped. "You used me. Seduced me. Fucked me to get what you wanted. All these months, you made me think—God, I'm such an idiot!—you had me believing you actually loved me! And now you claim some shit went down with ghosts and a veil and you're blaming me for it? And—and Frankie? Who's dead, by the way, so I'm not exactly sure how he figures. That about sum it up?"

"That's not fair." She felt like she was falling. "Something did go down. I *saw* them. I *do* love you."

"Bullshit." He stood up, everything itching inside, that sick sensation like he was about to hurl. "You love not being Hungry. You love yourself. You love that you can hitch a ride to the Afterlife whenever you feel like taking off my pants."

"No! Konstantin, that isn't—that might be how it started, but it isn't how it stayed! I fell for you. It would have been so much easier if I hadn't."

"Glad we're just doing what's easy now."

He walked around the station, angry-clearing plates. The glasses of champagne. He needed to move. To keep busy. To not look at her.

Maura steadied herself on the edge of the counter, the steel a block of ice beneath her grip.

"It wasn't easy. Any of it. I'd give anything to take it back." It was hard to breathe; she couldn't get enough air. "The Hunger . . . it took so much from me—"

Konstantin slapped a wet kitchen towel down, the sound so loud it made her jump.

"Yeah? As much as tasting the Dead for a couple decades? Or thinking you're insane every time some mystery flavor appeared? And let's not even talk about my assorted paranoias and trust issues. But hey, you're the only one who's ever suffered, right? At least you know what you did to deserve it. My mouth just happened to me." He snatched the plastic bag of Reese's and dumped the whole thing into the trash. "You should go, Maura."

"Please." Her voice was a sliver. "I need you to believe me."

"I don't know what to believe anymore." He scrubbed angrily at the counter, scouring it, his blurred reflection staring back from its surface. "But I can't see you right now."

"What about the ghosts?"

"What *about* them?" A vein pulsed in his jaw. "I haven't seen an actual issue yet. So, uh, thanks for the tip; I'll figure it out when I get the time."

"You can't just *figure it out*. There's a hole in the veil! We have to do something."

"There's no *we*, Maura. And what *I* have to do is focus on my opening." He gestured toward the stairs. "Just go."

"Stan." She stood, wobbly on her heels. "I know you're mad. So mad you might never forgive me. But this is bigger than us. You can't open. You can't bring more ghosts back. Promise me."

"Wow." He gave a strangled little laugh. "Right. You wanna take this away, too? Cooking—raising them—it's the one thing that still has any meaning right now. The only thing that's real."

"I'm real!" Her voice cracked. "But you can't—"

"Don't tell me what I can and can't do."

The 6 thundered past them again, the train flickering the lights in the kitchen, making things look slow, stop-motion. Maura stared out at the platform, tears falling, diamonds in the strobing light. Suddenly, her expression changed.

"Did you see that?"

"See what?"

She pointed at the train, was racing across the kitchen toward it, rushing the row of windows to press her face against the panes.

"What're you—"

"These windows," she asked, breathless, "do they open?"

"I don't know? I don't think—"

But she was already jimmying a latch, prying it up, and with a snap it swung open. She held her hand out to him.

"Come on," she said. "If you don't believe me, believe your own eyes. I just saw Everleigh on the tracks."

Kostya didn't move.

Part of him—a small, annoying part that still loved Maura, that always would—wanted to cross the room and follow her. To pull her into his arms. To forgive her. To believe that she really did love him, and that it was true about the ghosts, all the things she'd said. That part just wanted things to be okay again.

But another part of him—the part that didn't want to be an idiot—wondered what kind of mess she was walking into. Like, how, exactly, had Everleigh gotten there? Was she dangerous, like he'd long suspected? Maura wasn't exactly the poster child for solid decision-making, and if something went down—if Everleigh hurt her—would he be responsible if he sent her off alone?

Because most of him—the part winning this internal argument—was still too numb, too raw, too angry to be in the same room as Maura, let alone follow her into some wild-ghost chase through the bowels of the MTA. She had lied to him! Used him. Preyed upon his deepest vulnerabilities, seen his desperate desire to be loved and dangled that carrot to her own ends. For all he knew, this was just another manipulation. Some ploy to get him to forgive her. He wouldn't let her fool him twice.

"Stan? Please?"

"I—"

But before Kostya could answer, his phone exploded with sound, making them both jump. A text. Viktor.

Kostik, where are you?

DUH kitchen, he shot back. **Why?**

Have urgent business. Viktor pinged him. **We coming down.**

Down? Were they already here?

"Viktor's on his way," he told Maura, his voice carefully detached. "To the kitchen."

"What? *Now?*"

"He says it's urgent."

"Well, tell him to wait! This is literally life-and-death."

Kostya looked at her, weighing the choice.

Maura or Viktor. Maura or DUH. Maura or clairgustance.

So many times, he'd chosen her. Over Frankie. Over himself. Always her. And she'd betrayed him.

"We open tomorrow. And my boss needs to see me."

She blinked at him, pain shivering across her face.

"You're really gonna open the restaurant? After everything I just told you?"

He didn't answer, just set his jaw.

She nodded once, resigned, then climbed through the window onto the platform.

He hesitated, then called after her, "Be careful, okay? With your sister."

But she didn't reply, the click of her heels already swallowed by the dark.

A MINUTE LATER, he heard a different pattern of steps.

A pair of Givenchy loafers—Viktor's—appeared on the stairs. These were followed by black leather sneakers—the workingman's shoe—and a pair of orange Air Jordans, both sets of feet moving slowly, gingerly, as if their owners were carrying a couch.

Once Viktor's head appeared, Kostya opened his mouth to ask him what, exactly, was so urgent, but he shut it again once he got a look at the package the other two were hauling in. A thick, black garbage bag, secured on either end with duct tape, the contents inside stiff and unwieldy. They flung it unceremoniously down atop one of the clean prep stations and looked to Viktor, who was taking a leisurely drag of a cigarette, for further instruction.

Kostya recognized them.

Black leather sneakers was The Comrade (real name: Stanislav Boroholshik), the bodyguard Kostya had met at Viktor's apartment, complete with navy track suit, large, round Rolex, and resting *I-kill-you-now* face.

Air Jordans was a tech guy Kostya had seen around the restaurant—Max, or maybe Mark—who'd installed the Wi-Fi, the security cameras, the alarm system, and who seemed to be busily disabling those features from his phone.

The whole thing was giving major Tarantino: high tension; high risk. Like any moment there might be blood. Kostya swallowed, the spit thick and unpleasant in his mouth.

"Gentlemen." He tried to sound casual. "What, uh, what's going on?"

Viktor stubbed his cigarette out on the counter.

"We have business tonight, in restaurant. Is good you here, Kostik. Good we can talk."

Viktor toyed with his lighter, flipping the cap open and clicking it closed.

Flip. Click.

Cold beads of sweat wound down Kostya's back. Something felt wrong. Very wrong. He squeezed his hands to stop the tremor in his fingertips.

"Talk?"

"About DUH. Very much riding on opening."

Flip. Click.

"Yes. Definitely. Big day tomorrow."

"Is big investment for me. And location—is *very* important location stay open."

Flip. Click.

"I understand. Of course. That's what I want, too. For this to work."

"Is more than want, Kostik. It *must* work. We lose location, then we have big problems."

Flip. Click.

"We're ready. I mean, it's not exactly Restaurant Row, but we'll try our absolute best to make it a success."

"Is no *try*," Viktor said flatly. "You stay open. My business"—he nodded at the station beside him, acknowledging the mystery package for the first time—"depending on it."

Kostya's eyes snapped to the bag. He couldn't look away, couldn't stop tracing its odd lumps and shapes. He thought horribly of all the warnings his mother had lobbed at him—*mobsters, drugs, dirty money, bad deals, bang bang.*

"What's in there?"

"Do not worry about this," Viktor said smoothly, selecting a fresh cigarette. "Stas and Max, they will come by kitchen sometimes, to move"—he placed it at the corner of his mouth and lit up, spoke around it—"*ingredients in and out.*"

"Ingredients."

"Yes." Viktor nodded. "And you will keep restaurant open so they can do this work."

"Is—is that coke? Or heroin? Is it money?" Kostya swallowed around a walnut-sized lump in his throat. "Is that a bo—"

Viktor chuckled. "Oy, Kostik! Better you not know. Plausible deniability."

"Fuck," he said softly, his eyes still glued to the bag.

"For you, is very simple." Viktor took a long drag of his cigarette. "You make smash tomorrow. So big that DUH stays open long, long time. Lots of press. Lots of ghosts. More is more." He blew smoke from the side of his mouth. "If not, then we have problems."

On cue, The Comrade's hand shifted at his hip, revealing the handgun tucked into the waistband of his pants.

"I don't want any problems," Kostya said quickly.

"Good." Viktor shut his lighter again. *Flip. Click.* As if that settled it. "What time you have?"

Kostya fumbled with his phone, swiping past the usual string of missed calls from his mother. "Eleven oh three."

Viktor nodded at his goons. "Two minutes. Time to go."

The Comrade and Air Jordans lumbered over and hoisted the package up again. They heaved it across the kitchen—whatever was in there decidedly heavy, odious, an association Kostya did not want—but instead of heading back up the stairs with it, they tugged it forward, toward the subway.

Kostya's blood seemed to curdle in his veins.

Was Maura still there? How much had she seen? Had she been able to escape through the other side of the tunnel, or was she on the platform now, witness to what was probably a crime, one exacted by a bunch of criminals who surely wouldn't blink twice before cutting a loose thread?

He scanned the windows, hoping she was far, far away, and nearly choked on his spit. There she was, at the end of the row, peeking out behind the glass. His head gave an infinitesimal shake. *Get-the-fuck-away.* She vanished out of sight, but not before he registered her face, the way all the light had left it. All the hope.

She must have seen the whole thing.

"Wait!" he shouted, trying to buy time. The goon squad turned to stare. "You—you can't just take that on the subway! There's cameras!"

Viktor waved him away. "Max take care of this."

"What about the conductor? The other passengers? Someone's gonna see you if you take—" Kostya fumbled for a word, "*that* onto a train."

"Next train our driver," Viktor said calmly. "Express to Brooklyn."

"But what about—"

"Move aside."

The Comrade shoved past him. He turned the handle on one of the panes of glass—like he'd done it before; like he'd been intimately familiar with this convenient feature of the architecture—and climbed through it to the platform. Air Jordans heaved the package over the ledge—it landed on the other side with a *thunk*—and climbed over, too.

For a moment, nothing happened, and then bright light washed over the kitchen, the 6 Train flooding the station, not speeding past like it usually did, but slowing down, the brake screeching to a halt. *Ding-dong*, the subway doors pealed as they opened. The goons hustled the package in. *Stand clear of the closing doors.* And away they went. As if they'd timed it.

And, Kostya realized with a start, Viktor had.

"Kostik," Viktor said then, "go home. Rest up. Like you said, tomorrow big day."

Kostya's eyes burned, liquid with fear. How had he not seen it, been so willfully blind? Viktor didn't care about him, or his food, or even the ghosts. He didn't care about restaurants, or Michelin stars, or reviews. He just needed the 6 Train. This abandoned station.

"The restaurant was a front," he said, numb.

"Of course." Viktor shrugged like it was obvious. "Original plan not so good as you, I confess. Was only going to be so-so Russian nightclub. Enough for cover. But then I meet you; you say I make killing, and I think to myself, 'I like cake, to have and to eat also.' More successful restaurant bring more money. Less suspicions. Longer lease. Win-win-win."

He exhaled smoke in a long, slow stream, the room so cold it hung there in the air.

"Until tomorrow." Viktor rose from his seat and patted a stunned Kostya on the cheek. "Remember: Many ghosts. No whammies."

He stood frozen, staring at his kitchen as Viktor walked up the steps and out of sight, as he listened to the creak of the floorboards overhead, as the heavy entry door gave a bang and Viktor exited the building.

In the morning, whether he wanted to or not, Kostya would come back here. To lead a team of cooks, people he actually cared about, in service of this man, this mobster—damn it, his mother had been right!—to raise enough Dead to keep them open for a year, which, according to Maura, would bring about some sort of ghostpocalypse.

Maura.

He darted to the windows and threw them open, shouting her name onto the platform. Angry or not, seeing her that close to danger had shaken him.

But only his voice echoed back.

Maura was gone.

Dear Stan,

I'm not big on letters, but there's some stuff I have to say and I don't expect you to listen any more tonight than you already have. So here. For whenever you're ready.

First—about us. I'm sorry we didn't start like you deserved. But my love isn't any less real because it's messy. Probably the opposite. Some salt gets mined out of the ground, every crystal perfect, its flavor so predictable it graces every kitchen. But other salt comes out of marshes, gets harvested by hand, tastes like the journey it took to find you, including the wrong turns. I love you more because of where I've been, and I'd stay Hungry forever if it would make you believe that loving you was never about not feeling empty. It was about the chance to feel this full.

Second—ghosts. Sorry I dropped that bomb on you. It's a lot. Too much. And I heard what Viktor said. That you have to raise a zillion ghosts—or else. He's a fucking movie villain, but I can't put you in danger, not when I pushed you at him. So do what he says. Try not to worry. On the tracks tonight (Ev says hi, btw) I think I figured out a solve. A way to fix things. And I can do it without you. So here I go again.

Stay safe in the meantime. Stay alive. And maybe someday, if I'm lucky, I'll be able to beg you to love me again.

Xx, M

Food Poisoning

KONSTANTIN CALLED. HE texted. He emailed and even—was it possible to hate himself more?—slid into her DMs. But Maura never replied.

He tried her apartment, too, but she wasn't there, the spare key she normally kept above the door gone, which he took as a sign that she really didn't want to see him. His best guess was that she'd watched him cave to Viktor, fold like the coward he was, promise to raise oodles of ghosts after she'd begged him not to. She was probably too pissed to talk.

Well. It wasn't like he'd be overjoyed to see her either. He was still angry. Still felt used. And lied to. Hurt. It was just that he also wanted to make sure she was okay. You know, alive. Breathing.

He finally slipped a note under her door—*Hey. Just wanted to make sure you made it out of the subway. LMK.*—and went home, a mix of emotions simmering inside him.

What a fucking night.

WHEN HE GOT to his apartment, he heard the faint sound of the TV behind the door and felt the tension in his chest unspool. Had Maura gone to his place? Was she inside right then, waiting to talk? He fumbled with his keys.

"Shit, you really had me—"

But instead of Maura, it was his mother seated on the couch, the blue light of the screen casting shadows on her face. She turned at the sound of him, her cheeks damp with tears.

"Mama? What're you—how did you get in?" he began, but stopped when he heard his own voice chuckle through the speaker. A fake laugh. A TV one.

She was watching his interview.

"Actually," the TV him was saying, "the DUH concept came out of my own experience with food, and with death. I lost my dad as a kid. And my best friend, Frankie—Chef Francis O'Shaughnessy, of Wolfpup—earlier this year."

He watched himself on-screen, in hair and makeup. Confident. Cool. Even a little handsome. The tattoos—visible from his elbows down, where the stylist had tucked his sleeves—an extension of him, no longer just an imitation of an actual chef. He was owning the room, this other Konstantin, this stranger who looked more together than he'd ever felt, certainly more together than he felt right now. But what he was saying was his truth, Kostya's own words. The one part of the interview unscripted by the media trainer. Unvetted by the publicist.

"Food is how I found my way back to them. Eating the food they loved, the things they cooked. Someone told me once that grief is like having leftovers, with no one to serve them to. So the things I still had to say, all the moments we never got to have, the love I never got to give them—I put it all into my kitchen. I used it to feed other people."

His mother paused the DVR. He waited for her to tell him he'd given a great interview. That she'd been moved to tears by the power of his words. That he'd looked good on-screen. To congratulate him on the opening, or maybe tell him he'd lost some weight. Instead—

"You trying give me stroke?"

"What?"

"Why you not answer phone? I call! I text! What you wanting, carrying pigeon? I'm so worried I come myself to make sure you alive!"

"Jeez. Okay, Mama. I'm alive." He pinched the bridge of his nose, trying to divert the oncoming headache. "Listen, I really have to get to bed; the opening's tomorrow and—"

"*Nyet.* I'm not leaving now! You just get here. You ignore me and ignore and ignore and now I see you opening restaurant with mafioso!"

A few days ago, he might have argued the point, but now, well. Touché.

"Yeah . . . I know he's not exactly a model citizen. Thank you for your concern. But I'll take care of it, okay? It'll be fine."

"*Nyet!*" She stomped her foot on the floor. "*Nyet,* you not taking care of nothing. You take my help this time."

And maybe it was just the culmination of an unbearable few hours—of feeling utterly betrayed by Maura, who was supposed to be the love of his life; of discovering Viktor's two faces, one of which was decidedly blood-thirsty and unhinged; of finding out that everything he had worked so hard to create was more than likely a Chekhov's gun with a kickback like Chuck Norris—but his mother, sitting in his living room, force-feeding him help of the wrong variety, trying to pretend she suddenly cared after two decades of judging and nagging and shipping him off to a psych ward, was absolutely the last straw.

"Are you *serious* right now?" He could hear the acid in his own voice.

"Yes. Very serious. I am here to help."

"In what possible reality"—he dripped venom—"do you think I'd ever want your help? After what you did?"

"What, Kostya!" she shouted back, hurt. "What I do? I care about you! I love you! I try and try to talk!"

"You abandoned me." He let himself go off. "In a lunatic asylum! I didn't even think they made those in the modern world, but let me tell you, that shit hasn't changed since the fifties. Sedatives. Restraints. No fucking socks! I trusted you, Mama. And you gave me up. *You.* You did that."

In all those years, he'd never let it out, a kettle boiling away, exploding now, under pressure. It hurt to tell her; it hurt to remember.

"And when I came home? When I finally managed to lie my way out of that fucking monstrosity? Papa was dead and it was like I didn't have a mother anymore either. I was *ten*, Mama! I couldn't even fry an egg! And I had to take care of me *and* you. My whole childhood, I had to be *your* parent. Figure out keeping food in the fridge, and the rent paid, and the heat on. Figure out how to make you happy—or at least make you not sad all the time. I had to be the adult because you were too fucking selfish to pull yourself out of your own grief and realize I was hurting, too."

The aftermath of the room was so still. She pressed her lips together.

"Kostya—I—"

"Save it." He swallowed the lump in his throat, tried to blink away the tears that had begun to form. He shoved his keys back into his pocket, turning to go. If she wouldn't leave, then he would. "I'm done. I don't need your help. And I don't need to tell you anything, okay? You don't get to be in my life. You never wanted me in yours."

"Kostya—stop!" His mother looked so small now. So much older. Grey salting her hair, her eyes pruning at the edges. It had been a long time since he'd looked at her, really looked, and time had not been kind. "You know where I was, when you staying with Natasha?"

"Who cares? You dumped me with her for a month! Every day, I thought Valerik was just going to leave me at the boardwalk pool and never come back. You weren't with me, Mama. Didn't even call once. I was a little kid! A baby! You left me to rot. To watch all the kids and their dads, all summer long. And right after Papa died."

"I—" she sobbed, burying her face in her hands, "I try dying, too, Kostya! I left you with Nata, and I try. Tamara find me, full of pills."

Something in him stopped. Her words weren't rendering. He didn't understand.

"Tamara? The neighbor?"

His mother nodded. "She take me to clinic where her son work."

"You didn't go to a hospital?"

She shook her head. "Tamara say they take you away, if I go."

"Who? Who's they?"

She shrugged. "America."

Kostya could feel pins coming into his fingers.

"So, what? You were suicidal and that makes it okay to institutionalize me? You wanted another couple weeks to yourself?"

She shook her head, no fight in her. "You tell me you taste Sergei, and I think that he trying to call you, too. That"—her voice broke—"you have same sickness I have. And you deserve real help, not dark Russian clinic without license."

"You—you thought I was suicidal?"

She nodded, tears rolling down her face.

"Wait," he said slowly. "What do you mean, *too*? Did you—could you taste something?"

She looked at him, stricken, her eyes asking if maybe they were both crazy. "In weeks after he die, when I think of him, I taste *pechonka*."

"Oh my God. *Mom*."

"The pills I take—while you with Natasha—I take to make it stop."

Kostya's eyes burned. He blinked and felt hot tears fall. Of all the people in the world who could actually understand what he'd gone through, who might relate to how it felt to have your most painful moments synesthetically, magically, impossibly punctuated, inescapable in their strangeness—his mother had known. But unlike him, she hadn't thought the tastes had come from his father; she'd been sure it was the distress of her own mind, the deterioration of her psyche, a nervous break at the loss she couldn't handle.

"Oh, Mama." He hugged her, a real hug, the kind he hadn't given her since before his dad died, no withdraw to it, no itch to move away. "Do you—can you still taste him?"

"No," she whispered. "Not since pills."

And Kostya seemed to understand. When his mother had tried to end the aftertastes by ending her life, his father had backed off. Had stopped trying to make her feel him. He'd moved on to Konstantin. And somehow, other spirits had followed.

"I'm sorry, Mama. And Papa—I'm sure he's sorry, too."

She gave a weary sigh.

"Sometimes the people you love hurt you. Sometimes they mean to. And sometimes they don't mean, but cannot help. It is you who must decide to keep loving them anyway."

Kostya thought about his father, the way he'd driven his mother almost to madness, right up to the edge of death, and she'd still forgiven him. Had kept loving him, all this time.

He wondered how much of his own pain he must have inflicted on her over the years. And she had kept loving him, too, had kept trying. No matter how caustic he had been.

He thought of Maura. Of what she'd put him through tonight. Of the way she'd hurt him, bone deep, but without meaning to. He wondered if he could forgive that.

His mother put a clammy hand over his. "You still tasting him?"

"Sometimes." Kostya shivered, a draft in the room like someone had left the fridge open. "The *pechonka*—the burnt one—it happens when I miss him most."

She nodded, and he knew she understood. And like he had been listening, had been waiting in the wings, Kostya's father materialized in his mouth.

Rich morsels of liver, the texture too firm, overcooked. Onion so sweet it melted between his teeth. Crystals of salt, crackling on his tongue. The bitter char in the back of his throat.

The liver had been burned the way Kostya burned now, itching to prepare this dish, to share it with his mom, to bring his dad back. He knew in his gut that this was the time, that if he made this dish now, it would absolutely work. All the components of the recipe were right here, in this room—his father, their shared grief, the best memory of his dad's life.

"They say on TV that you bringing back Dead with your food."

He looked at his mother, the subtle way her eyes grew wide. She believed it, believed in him. It was right there, everything he'd wanted. Everything he'd spent the last year working for, that had all come unraveled tonight. He wouldn't get the girl, or the dream, but maybe—*maybe*—he could still have this.

"I can bring Papa back, Mama," Kostya said softly. "Right now. We can say goodbye."

His mother looked at him for a long moment, tempted. Then she shook her head.

"*Nyet*, Kostya. That's only for us. Best thing for Papa is to let him rest."

"But—"

"It's twenty years. We holding him back long enough." Her eyes glazed with tears. "Now real love is to let him go."

She was right. Of course she was.

All the spirits ever wanted was to rest. To make peace. All this time he had been holding on, Kostya never once stopped to wonder whether he had been holding his dad back.

Was this what Maura had meant? Had she been telling the truth? That there were ghosts stuck in his apartment, tethered by their Living? By his food? Waiting to be let go? He still hadn't seen them for himself, but then, he knew better than anyone that he didn't have to see them to know they were there.

His mother suddenly laughed, breaking his train of thought. "You know, you so much like him. You looking like him now. Same expressions! And cooking; oh, how he love food! And," she teased, "leaving house in mess, for anyone to walk in!"

"What mess?"

"Coffee mug on floor! Glass all over, in kitchen. But don't worry. Cleaning girl pick up when she let me in."

"What cleaning girl?"

"With purple hair." His mother sniffed. "I normally don't like this color, but she is single? Maybe you ask out?"

"Shit. Mama, did she say anything?"

His mother frowned, thinking. "She leave you note, I think, in kitchen. And she take notepad. Say she needed borrow recipes."

KONSTANTIN TORE HIS kitchen apart, searching. Maura had taken his Saveur Fare order pad, all the recipes he'd recorded—a complete inventory of every aftertaste he'd ever made. Not that it mattered for the opening; every cook at DUH could make those dishes handcuffed and blindfolded. But what did Maura, who couldn't cook to save her life, plan to do with them?

Her note said she'd found a solution, one that didn't require him. But maybe it required his food. His instructions. His way of summoning the Dead.

He read and reread it.

Her words wore away at him, the things she said about her love, about her Hunger. They made him text her again, call, wish she'd call him back. She didn't.

He stayed up all night praying she wasn't doing anything foolish.

Dessert

The Konstantin Duhovny Culinary Experience

Y'ALL READY?

I know you been waiting, and I appreciate your patience! It's about to pay off.

DUH opens tonight!

And that means doors are about to open up for us now, too. I mean, just look at this place. Check out that kitchen. Peep that subway. You catch that dining room? Made for spirits. Our guy outdid himself!

So let's talk logistics. Doors open at seven, so let's post up here till then. We'll track who's going back, if your Living got reservations, how that first trip through the veil goes down—

Oh, hey, girl. Love the hair—what they call that, periwinkle?—it's a vibe. You got a question?

. . . .

Wait, wait, slow down. What you mean, danger?

Hunger Strike

KONSTANTIN STOOD IN the DUH kitchen, his chef's coat on, his name over the lapel, his big moment kneeling at his feet.

Upstairs, Viktor schmoozed patrons and press. The publicist escorted VIPs to premium tables. The room buzzed with life and death and craft cocktails.

It was opening night, Kostya's big culinary coming-out party, but he couldn't bring himself to care.

Maura still hadn't answered.

It had been almost twenty-four hours since he'd last seen her. Since she'd vanished on the subway platform. Since she'd broken his heart, and Viktor had broken his spirit, and he'd seen two men rest an unnerving mystery package right where his cooks were standing now, prepping Sister Stacy's soup.

In a moment, the cooks and servers and runners and busboys, the pruny dishwashers, the smug bartenders, the moody coat check chick and the gossipy hostess all expected him to deliver a rallying cry and lead them into glory. Instead, he had his back to them, was staring at his own troubled reflection in the windows.

He pulled out his phone and texted her again, the parade of unanswered messages so long it spanned several zip codes.

Just tell me you're okay.

Behind him, the kitchen hummed, reversed in the glass. Brushed stainless; warm wood. The line was ready, every station prepped, all the mises in place. The brigade was starting some of the appetizers, bracing for an influx of tickets as soon as the cocktail hour wound down. Rio was making rounds with a clipboard, checking final items off a long list with a Sharpie.

The plan was to let everyone order off the main menu first, give the kitchen time to shine, and then parade Kostya out like a dignitary for the ghost encounters in the tasting rooms.

Raising those ghosts was the last thing he wanted to do now. It felt like walking toward trouble while holding a grenade. Then again, so did not raising them.

Kostya gripped the windowpanes, his hands beginning to shake.

He was stuck, ground between a mortar and its pestle. The ghosts, looming, on one side, and Viktor and his band of bandits on the other.

"Yo, Huesos? You good?" He felt Rio's hand on his shoulder. "Opening-night jitters?"

"Something like that." Kostya took a breath.

"Here. Got something for that." Rio held up his hand, a scoop of salt cupped in his palm. "Frank and I, we did this at Wolfpup our very first night. And every big service after. Sort of a tradition." He threw a pinch over Kostya's shoulder. "May your fire always be hot." Another pinch, over the other one. "May your food always be seasoned." A third pinch, aimed straight at his balls, which made Kostya crack a reluctant smile. "And may you cook with your head as much as your heart. Go get 'em, Chef."

Kostya fought back tears as he pulled Rio into a hug.

He didn't know what he was leading them into tonight. Only that he had to protect his brigade. He needed to get his shit together. Perform. Bring back every ghost with a smile on his face. Not give Viktor any reason for retribution. Make the night a smashing success for profit and publicity. (He'd deal with any repercussions from the Afterlife later, he supposed.

Just sort of, like, corral the ghosts? Find a way to get them back in the box? *Fuck.* He really wished Maura would text him back.)

He was still hugging Rio, who cleared his throat.

"Okay. Well. I think they're all waiting for your word, Boss."

When Kostya turned, the staff was assembled before him—pristine, preservice, gathered around the stations and along the stairs, leaning against walls. Every one of them counting on him. They'd supported him, and followed him, and believed. Part of him had once believed, too. He took a breath and faked it.

"Hey, everybody." He gave a nervous little wave. "Here we are, huh? I'm not as good with words as I am with food, so this won't take long. I just . . . thanks. For being here. For believing"—the word was a bone in his throat—"in what we're doing. Because you have to have a little faith, right? When impossible things happen, it's got to be"—he tried not to choke— "because they're meant to. And we were meant to do this tonight. Because our kitchen" (the cooks gave a cheer), "is badass. So fucking special. And our front-of-house" (whooping from the stairs), "well, you guys are a pain in the ass" (laughter all around), "but we . . . we love you anyway. That's what it takes, to share a kitchen. To make food. To feed people. Love. I really mean that. And there's two things I'd never go up against without the people I love. The first are hungry New Yorkers." (More laughter.) "And the second is the Dead."

Pindrop silence, heavy in the room.

Kostya's eyes filled, stinging. He didn't want to tell them what he was about to say next, tried to suck back the words as they left his mouth.

"So let's—let's go raise some spirits, all right? Let's feed some Hungry Ghosts."

DINNER SERVICE WAS the stuff of restaurant dreams. The diners were dazzled. They oohed and aahed. They took selfies. They gasped as they were guided to their tables, the interior of DUH unlike any dining room they'd ever seen, the walk through its obsidian hall a journey *elsewhere*.

The staff worked an intricate choreography, hosts and servers and runners all twirling in a silent ballet, the black of their uniforms blending into the backdrop, making it so they were barely noticed by the patrons, living phantoms in a spectral place. The effect was that glasses of water and silverware and amuse-bouches seemed to just magically appear at tables. As if they'd been spirited from the other side.

The bar was busy, drink orders lining the rows of vertebrae as two bartenders shook and mixed and stirred, Spectral Sours glistening alongside dirty martinis and old-fashioneds, waitstaff whisking the frosted glasses away before they even had a chance to bead.

The kitchen was busy, too—knives stuttering across chopping blocks, the sizzle of blistering pans, the stream of water in the sink, plates clanging across the line, the ding of timers, the call of *Fire! Table Four!* and *Order! Two tartines for Six!* And *Yo, Miguel, you got dead dupes; pick it up!*, a sweet, final comfort to Kostya's ears.

As the servers paraded out the first round of apps, Kostya stood at the top of the stairs, hidden in shadow, watching. His heart thumped in his chest, adrenaline coursing through him, making him shiver.

Showtime.

In his pocket, his phone buzzed, and his heart did a pirouette as he pulled it out, praying for Maura, but it was only his mom.

Kostochka, good luck. Be safe.

He began typing a reply, but the lights flickered overhead, his signal, and he shoved the phone back into his pocket, the message half-written.

Konstantin walked slowly across the dining room. He could feel the weight of so many eyes on him, taking in his every move. The noise of revelry dwindled, wineglasses paused midair, the clink of flatware and cutlery stilled.

His reflection followed him along the high-gloss floor, across the mirrored panels sheathed in gauze. The room was so cold. Like a walk-in. Like a morgue.

He forced on a smile, turned the handle to Tasting Chamber No. 1, and pushed open the door.

THE FIRST GHOST ordered moussaka and fries.

Easy. A softball. The aftertaste blooming across his tongue as soon as he stepped into the room, as if the spirit had been waiting for him.

If every aspect of his world weren't circling an existential drain, this might have given Kostya more pause. But in his terrified-slash-furious-slash-panicked state, he worked on autopilot, making the dish in silent focus.

When it was ready, he garnished the plate (drizzle of olive oil; hand-torn parsley) and stared down at it with disgust.

He didn't want to serve it.

He didn't want to witness what would happen when this spirit came back. Didn't want to keep imagining Maura's face when she found out that he'd done it. Didn't want to feel the terrible, sinking feeling that kept whirling in his gut, like he was leaning over a ledge, the fall so far away he couldn't see the bottom.

He had half a mind to dump it directly into the trash when The Comrade shoved his way into the kitchen.

"Where is dish?" he barked. "Diners impatient. Viktor displeased."

Kostya braced himself.

"Right here."

IN TASTING CHAMBER No. 1, he set the plate onto the table and lifted the cloche with an unsteady hand. The aroma—meat, béchamel, fries—drifted into the room amid delicate tendrils of smoke. He could feel it in the air, a spirit stirring, like a vibration, an instrument being tuned.

And then, before his diners even had a chance to chew, there was a disturbance in the main dining room.

A cry. An exclamation of surprise. Delight.

Then another. And another.

Kostya could see it through the mercury glass of the chamber he was standing in.

Lights, overhead. Dim, but glowing.

A moment later, applause. Enthusiastic cheers. Whoops and hollers for someone—something—he hadn't brought back.

And then, a cascade of glass, the shatter of precious, delicate things. Not like a server had dropped a tray, but like the world had fractured apart.

Followed by a different kind of cry.

Screams.

First one person and then many more, their voices avalanching until the whole building shook from the sheer force of sound.

Kostya burst through the door and felt his heart stop.

Ghosts were *everywhere*.

Raining down from the ceiling; crowding in through the walls; rising up from the floor.

Their translucent bodies multiplied in the glass and mirrors and reflective surfaces until it was impossible to understand how many, exactly, there were, only that they were endless, that they were coming, that they wouldn't stop.

The diners who weren't in private rooms rushed the doors, skidding over broken plates, slipping on scattered forks and knives. There were cuts on their hands, across their faces, blood streaking their wounds, flecking the floor. The waitstaff were frozen, petrified, unsure if this was part of the plan or some horrible malfunction, not knowing whether to reassure their sections or run for their lives. Cooks and busboys vomited up from the kitchen, chased by more ghosts, their mouths—enormous, distorted, hungry mouths—all howling.

And, in a horrible moment where time congealed, Kostya recognized them.

The flap and flutter of Sister Stacy's habit, the nun transformed now, dead eyed, gaunt and grave and terrifying. The climbing bro whose sister had tanked Hell's Kitchen, mutated, murderous, his mouth a gaping hole. The teenager whose *abuelo* had come to find him, who had returned once Kostya tasted the ketchup soup of his own childhood, matured into something dangerous, bloodthirst in his gaze.

He had done this to them. His food. His aftertastes. His every bad decision.

Maura was right. He'd poisoned them.

As they crested the stairs, other spirits floated up behind them. Ghosts he'd never seen before. Ones he hadn't raised. Hungry Dead that had somehow crossed over. Uninvited. Unprevented.

The veil had been compromised.

Shouts and cries rose from the bowels of the kitchen, and Kostya fought against the crush of panicking people to get back to his line. Patrons shoved past him, pushing toward the exits, scattering around debris. A waiter slipped behind a thick velvet curtain only to be driven out by a cackling ghost, glee upon its face. The hostess was on all fours, seeking shelter beneath the dining room tables, a handful of diners crawling behind her.

Overhead, a swarm of spirits massed, gumming together in a terrifying cloud. It was chaos. The fear in the air was metallic on Kostya's tongue, aluminum, iron, so much like blood, and then, all at once, every bulb in the place shattered in unison, leaving the room in absolute dark.

Thin shards of glass rained down. Kostya felt them hit his face, slice through his eyebrow, across his cheek. He couldn't see a thing—every window had been blacked out to maximize the effect of the returning souls' light—but he could hear.

Shouts. Screeches. The slap of shoes against the floor. Gasps and painful yelps. Cries. The explosion of more glass as dishes and stemware and mirrored walls were smashed to smithereens. The distant rumble of the 6 Train in the restaurant's bowels.

Rectangles of light appeared as people ignited their phones, searching for ways out, finding ravenous ghosts blocking their paths. Kostya felt a patch of frosty air creep along his spine and turned, casting the light of his own phone into the dark to illuminate a spirit, close enough to touch.

Time stretched, taffy, as he looked at her.

This ghost—he felt a shiver of recognition—was gaunt and haggard, her skin mottled with patches of rot, her bones protruding in places. Like she was haunted. Or maybe cursed. Like touching her might turn him to stone, or at minimum give him a terrible rash.

She stared hard at him, her gaze a dull knife, something once sharp and precise and powerful rendered impotent, destroyed by lack of care. She'd been beautiful once, but all that was left of it now was a thicket of violet hair and the shadow of a smile, her mouth black with decay, the teeth small and pointed. She'd died so young he could almost read it in her face, all that unrealized potential.

Everything about her made Kostya cold except her eyes. They were so familiar that for a moment he couldn't breathe. Chocolate brown, flecked with gold. Wide set. Strange and beautiful and hungry. Just like her sister's.

"Everleigh?"

"Konstantin Duhovny." She inclined her head, her voice nothing like he expected, not gravel but velvet. "Just the guy I've been looking for."

He backed away, slow, broken glass crunching beneath him.

"Oh, um, yeah? Well, you found me." His back hit a wall, sitting duck confit. "Please don't hurt me." In a crisis, his inner hero really shone through.

"Hurt you?" Everleigh rolled her red-rimmed eyes. "You're the only one who can fix things. We need you."

"I—what?" He blinked at her.

"We need your help," she repeated.

"My *help*?" He gaped at her. "Aren't you, like, some evil spirit? You haunted your sister!"

"Wrong again. *She* haunted *me*."

"But all those Reese's, every time I tasted one—"

"—was because Maura was hurting," Everleigh supplied. "And starving me in the process. When the Living don't let go, the Dead go Hungry; we can't move On. Which is why I was looking for a way to see her again."

"But how did you—"

"Look, we don't have a lot of time. The short version? Your food brings spirits back, but it also tethers us to *you*, which basically traps us *here*. To rot. To go Hangry—which is like Hungry, except a whole lot worse. Only, the Hangrier we get, the stronger we get, too. Which is why you can see us now. Why we can move things. Why all the smashing and pillaging. And once we realized we had some power, a bunch of us figured we'd just"—she hand-waved—"pop a little hole in the veil. Sneak back through. Save ourselves. But it turns out—funny story—just going back doesn't do the trick. We broke through to the Afterlife last night, but we still couldn't move On. Which, I think, is because we're still attached to *you*. And now the veil's busted and there's a whole bunch of other spirits using the hole to pour out of the Afterlife, and the longer it stays open, the more Hell's gonna break loose, and—"

Just then, a chandelier crashed down, illustrating her point. The spirits in the dining room cheered, shrill laughter rising like steam.

"Slow down," Kostya said, trying to follow her panic attack. "Are we talking, like, *actual* Hell here, or more like a metaphorical Hell, or—"

"*Focus*, Konstantin! We don't want to keep going all poltergeist, but we don't have much choice. The Hanger's driving most of us now; it's chaos. You have to get everyone back to the Food Hall before it fully sets in. All the spirits here. You have to move us On."

"Yup. Okay. I can do that!" He was nodding. "How do I do that?"

"You brought the Dead here, to the Living world, so I'm betting you can do the same thing in reverse. Pied Piper us back with a meal."

"You mean the aftertastes."

She nodded.

"Only—you can't do it from this side. To pull us into the Afterlife, you'd have to be *in* the Afterlife."

"So . . . ?"

"So, if you want to help, you have to die."

"Wh-what?" He heard the startle in his own voice.

"I'm sorry." She looked it. "I wanted Maura to tell you; I warned her last night on the platform, when it was clear that the whole 'tear the veil' thing didn't work out. I thought you might help us, but she didn't want you involved."

The platform. Those last words he'd said to her, just before she went, about how there was no *we*. Her radio silence after. And the recipes she'd taken. Her note.

"*No.* No no no."

"Yeah." Everleigh nodded. "She said she was gonna try and fix this herself."

"We can't let her! It's *my* fuckup. Just tell me what to do," he said quickly, and Everleigh floated closer, whispered in his ear, her breath like ice around his neck as his dining room crashed down around them.

"Go," she said, pulling away. "Out the subway. Hurry."

And Kostya wove his way back in the dark, toward the staircase to the kitchen, his fingers sliding over broken glass, smashed mirrors, countless years of bad luck, the sheer curtains shredding beneath the palms of his hands, just like the veil between the Living and the Dead.

ON THE LANDING, he felt a rumble. Kostya stared down the steps, bracing himself for more ghosts, but instead, it was the kitchen crew—Rio and Big Mike and Miguel and Stephanie, Mica and Ale and Lin. They came rushing up the steps, armed with pots and pans, canisters of salt, wooden spoons tied into crosses with kitchen twine. They were coming to his defense—the loyalty hit Kostya right between the ribs—to fight for him.

He waved them back.

"No!" he shouted, shaking his head. "Go out the back. Through the subway! It's okay. It's—it's me they want."

Rio looked at him in horror. "Huesos, these are—these ain't house spirits. You need an exorcist."

Kostya shook his head, finally understanding.

"No. What I made them before—it wasn't any good. They're sending it back to the kitchen."

"The fuck that mean?"

"It means they're still hungry. And I gotta feed them."

IN THE KITCHEN, illuminated by emergency lights, Konstantin wrenched open the windows to the 6.

"Go!" he told his staff. "There's an exit on the platform. I'll be right behind you."

But then they heard footfalls, the angry stomp of expensive shoes, and Kostya looked up in time to see Viktor, purple with rage, descending the stairs.

"Where everybody going?" he barked, voice edged like a knife. "Dinner service still on."

He was trailed by The Comrade, who limped down, bleeding at the knee, a gun very visible in the hand not gripping the handrail. Viktor was dabbing his face with one of the DUH dinner napkins, blood flowing freely from a cut on his cheekbone, another on his chin.

"What are you *talking* about?" Kostya balked at him. "There is no service! There's no restaurant, not after this! It's done. It's"—he couldn't believe he was saying it—"it's over."

Viktor waved his bloody napkin in the air. "Get back to work!" He turned to the cooks. "All of you! We comping tonight's dinner. Telling everybody it part of the show. Ghosts terrifying when they hungry. We must feed quickly! We already giving this story to customers."

"No." Kostya stood his ground. "There are angry spirits still up there. It's dangerous. We're not serving anyone else. We're done."

Viktor nodded at The Comrade, who aimed his pistol in Konstantin's direction.

"Whoa!" Rio shouted, his hands thrown up.

"The fuck, man?" Big Mike was saying.

"Get back to work," Viktor said again. "Everybody. Stations."

Kostya could feel every set of eyes on him, waiting to see what he'd do. Adrenaline coursed through him, and hatred for Viktor, and anger at himself, the agony of knowing every moment wasted here was putting Maura in more danger, every subsequent second the one where she might finally leave him, leave this world.

"We're done, Viktor," he repeated. "I'm leaving."

He turned back to the windows, toward the platform, was starting toward them when he heard it. The unmistakable click of a gun being cocked.

"Think *very* carefully," Viktor warned him.

Kostya turned back around, heat rising inside him, radiating.

"You wanna shoot me? Go ahead. Maybe then I can finally do some good."

But before he could process what was happening, Rio stepped in front of him.

"And then you better shoot me, too, asshole."

"And me." Big Mike was nodding.

"All of us." This from Mica, who looked like he was trying not to cry.

"And smile for the camera while you do it," Stephanie added, her phone pointed at Viktor and The Comrade like a firearm, recording everything. "We're streaming live, bitches. Say hello to all my followers."

Viktor and The Comrade exchanged glances, The Comrade lifting one brow as if to ask, *What's the plan, Boss?*

"DUH's closed," Konstantin said clearly. "Out of respect for the Dead. Now get out of my kitchen."

And, with Kostya barely believing what was happening, that it had worked, Viktor stepped aside, a thick vein in his neck throbbing angrily, pulsing like it might pop.

OUT ON THE sidewalk, it felt like they could breathe.

"I can't believe that fucking worked," Rio pronounced.

"Have I mentioned I love Instagram?" Kostya panted, heart still racing.

"Little does he know, I've only got four followers!"

There was a strange, giddy camaraderie between them, the unity of having just survived a brush with death (two brushes, technically). They were laughing. That nervous, giggly, *can-you-believe-we-made-it* kind of laughter. Kostya knew it wasn't over, that Viktor would retaliate, that the police might need to get involved, but right then, he was hugging everyone, trying to hold on to this moment, this relief and joy and love.

And then the air hit the back of his neck, a breeze like a kiss.

The cool puff in the back of his throat.

A chill went through him, and his heart sped fast, faster, double espresso. He swallowed, and there it was, the faint, metallic tingle on his tongue.

Salt. The world's best. The minerals in it like the marshes of Guérande.

And knowing even then he might be too late, Konstantin began to run.

Secret Ingredients

HE WAS IN a cold sweat when he reached Maura's apartment. He banged on the door, shouted her name, threw his shoulder against it twice before he remembered the spare key.

It was there this time, above the frame. She'd put it back, as if she'd been expecting him. As if she'd wanted him to come.

Inside was the shrill buzz of silence.

Kostya shook, adrenaline and terror flooding his veins as he crossed the long hall toward her kitchen. The room drew him like an instinct, back to the first night they spent together, the first meal he made her, all the late nights they stood hunched over the counter, drinking coffee, or whiskey, or wine, and talking, all those conversations, every last kiss in the kitchen, every memory contained there a good one, except what he might be walking toward right now.

He could taste it still—or perhaps again—*fleur de sel* in the back of his throat, the bite of it. He could feel her absence in his bones. And when he saw her violet hair spilled on the floor, the way she lay, like she might only be asleep, his heart sank down into his gut, through the floor, to a place deep underground, from which it would never, never rise.

"No. *No.* Oh, God! Oh God oh God oh God."

He felt for a pulse, listened for breath, begged her to come back as if she hadn't just made the hideous choice to leave.

"Maur, please. *Please.* Wake up."

He'd seen her do that trick before, the life flooding back into her eyes.

Only this time, it didn't.

Trembling, he typed 9-1-1 into his phone, his finger hovering above the call button.

He pictured paramedics rushing in, seeing the scene, wheeling Maura away. He wondered if they'd take him, too. Lock him up, send him right back to a mental ward. Straitjackets. Tranquilizers. No socks. They'd have his old hospitalization records, plus word of what had happened back at DUH, form a narrative of him being unhinged, a history of psychosis. A tragedy. A crime.

Not that it mattered now.

He'd deserve what he got, after all the people he'd hurt, Living and Dead, without ever really considering the consequences. And now the woman he loved, growing cold on the floor beside him because he hadn't believed her, hadn't helped her even when she'd begged him to.

He didn't care what she'd done. He wasn't mad now, only desperately sorry. He just wanted her to come back. To return long enough to hear him say it.

"M-Maura." He sucked back tears, his snot salty and hot, the words jumbling. "Maur, I—I love you. I'm s-sorry. I *believe* you."

He leaned close to her face, touched her hair. He wept harder, his stomach a stone. Had she taken poison? A bottle of pills? He pressed the call button on his phone, waiting for the operator, wondering what to say when they picked up. Whether it might still be possible to save her.

But then the body on the floor gave a sudden jolt.

"Nine-One-One, what's your emergency?"

A huge gasp.

An intake of air.

And Maura Elizabeth Struk opened her eyes, her soul flooding back into her body after an Afterlife trip she hadn't planned to take.

"Wrong number," he stammered, and hung up.

She blinked at him. "Konstantin?"

And though the world was on fire, his restaurant in shambles, a portal to the Afterlife open in the Financial District and no real plan to stop it except some hunch from Maura's dead kid sister, Kostya pulled Maura into his arms and kissed her the kind of kiss you get once in a lifetime, maybe, if you're lucky.

It said everything.

I'm sorry, and *I was wrong, and an idiot*, and *Forgive me.*

Let's fix this, and *I love you*, and *There* is *a we, of course there is.*

I believe you, and *I trust you*, and *I'm sorry I doubted.*

I won't ever lose you again.

She kissed him back, held on, and it would have been so easy to lose themselves in it, to shut out everything they'd caused and stay wrapped up in each other's arms.

Instead, they pulled apart, the same thought hitting them at once.

"We really fucked up," Kostya said, pressing his forehead against hers.

"Told you so." Maura gave a weak smile.

And then she told him where she'd been.

SHE'D DIED AGAIN last night, after DUH. After she'd taken his recipes.

"It's stupid how easy it is to get what'll kill you," she explained. "Penicillin from an Urgent Care. A forged prescription for an EpiPen."

She'd had them prepped for weeks, since she first slipped through the veil without meaning to. She took the penicillin, all four pills, and waited for the allergic reaction, the anaphylaxis, the EpiPen needle already in her thigh, her thumb waiting until her very last moment of consciousness to administer the medication. The time it took the adrenaline to make it through her system—that was her window in the Afterlife.

Kostya scrubbed his face, trying not to think about what could have happened if she'd been a moment too late.

"What was your plan?" he asked.

"Ev said the ghosts were all tied to you because of the aftertastes, and that they needed to be tied to the Afterlife instead. That they could follow their food home. So I borrowed your recipes and went back to the tour. To another chef I know. One who's already dead."

Kostya blinked at her. "Frankie?"

Maura nodded. "He was at DUH with a crowd, waiting on the other side of the veil for you to open your doors. I told him everything, and he agreed to try to cook your food. See if we couldn't pull one of Ev's ghosts back through. But it didn't work. He couldn't get the dish right."

Kostya nodded grimly.

"Yeah. We tried it here, a bunch of times. The aftertastes have to be exact. Precise. He'd have to taste them himself to make them right. But—you stayed *that long* in the Afterlife? Long enough to watch him cook?"

"I almost didn't make it back," she whispered. "I heard you banging on the door as I was coming to. I held on to your voice."

"Fuck," he breathed, fighting the sting in his eyes. "And just now?"

"That was like the Met. I just . . . slipped through." She shook her head. "It's getting harder to stay alive. The Hunger—it wants to be *there*. As much as I don't. And it keeps winning." She bit her lip, remembering. "Things are bad in the Hall. Spirits starving. The restaurants falling apart. There's this gash, right in the central square. Spirits shoving one another out of the way to get through."

"The tear in the veil?"

"Had to be."

"I met your sister, by the way. She's nice. Could use a bath."

Maura smiled. "Plus some eternal rest."

"She, um"—Kostya traced Maura's face, steeled himself for what came next—"she told me what to do. To move them On."

"Yeah." Maura frowned. "She told me, too. But that can't be the only way. I can go again. Maybe Frankie could—"

"No," he said gently. "Everleigh's crew already tried tearing the veil. You tried luring them back with Frankie. It didn't work; it *won't* work. Because they're tethered to *me*. It has to be me, Maur. The spirits I trapped, and the ones that are here now because of the veil—only I can help them." He took a breath. "It was my choice to bring back the Dead. It's on me now, to let them go."

She searched his eyes for any hesitation. A doubt she could cling to. But he'd decided. Was sure.

"Okay," she agreed. "But while you're cooking up closure, someone's gotta seal the veil. Otherwise they'll just keep coming."

"Frankie can do it."

"*I'll* do it." She took his hand. Squeezed. "I made this bed, too. I need to help fix it. Something Ev said gave me an idea, and—"

"No. No way. I won't let you make a one-way trip. You just said your Hunger—"

"I can't let it control me anymore. I need to shake it off. Put it back where it came from." She cupped his face, her hands so cold. "I can do it now. I can let Ev go. As long as she moves On, my Hunger will, too."

"But what if—"

"I have no intention of staying Dead, Stan. I want to live when this is over. You and me." She stared hard into his eyes. "I trust you to get those spirits where they need to go. Can you trust me to help you?"

Kostya looked back at her. Finally, he nodded.

"I trust you." He let out a breath. "But I go first. Anything goes wrong, you abandon ship."

"Deal."

"And while we're on the topic—" He took her hands in his, tried to make them warm. "What's the least painful way to die?"

"In your sleep, probably." She smiled. "But we don't have to *die* die. We just have to *near* die."

"You make it sound so easy."

"Remember those conventions I went to? The near-deathers? Well, this guy told me a way once. Near painless, he said. I couldn't get the ingredients, but I bet you could."

"What do we need?"

KOSTYA MADE TWO calls. Both started the same way.

"Hey, it's Konstantin. Long time. I need a favor."

MICHEL BEAUCHÊNE TOOK a moment to consider the request.

"You just opened a restaurant," he said at last. "Why would you need my walk-in?"

By some miracle, news about the disaster at DUH hadn't reached him yet.

"You know I wouldn't ask if I had any other choice."

"Are you planning something illegal?"

"There's nothing illegal about cold storage," Kostya said evenly. "I'm just trying to keep something important on ice."

"What's your max time out?" Michel asked, businesslike, no doubt trying to guess what Konstantin was storing.

"Four hours. Five, tops," Kostya lied. "Please," he begged, "it won't fit in mine."

"And I don't get to know what it is?"

"Plausible deniability."

"Because you're doing something illegal."

"Because . . . in case."

Michel was quiet on the line. And just as Kostya grew sure he would say no, gloat, deliver a lecture on the importance of bridges, of loyalty, of hard work, he said this instead:

"Okay."

"Seriously?"

He could hear Michel smile. "You're one of us now. Exec at a buzzy New York restaurant. It's a small, lecherous little club, but we stick together. Heavy is the crown."

"Well, shit. Thank you."

"Just tell me one thing. The ghosts you claim to serve, those spiritual reunions—is it all true?"

The question surprised him. "What do you think?"

"I think you're a terrible liar, so it must be." He cleared his throat. "Maybe you can fit me in for a seat one night. At your house."

Kostya's eyes watered. This was everything he'd searched for in the kitchen—a connection, a way to help—coming too late.

"Anytime," he choked out, knowing he might never keep that promise. "It would be an honor, Chef."

Michel exhaled into the phone.

"Service door's unlocked. Anyone asks, you let yourself in. Don't do anything stupid."

YUME KUTSUKI TOOK more convincing.

"I can't," she said flat out. "I'll lose my license."

"Yume, *please*. It'll never get back to you."

"And when someone shows up dead? When your knife slips and game over?"

"I'm not serving it! I'm just experimenting. With a new technique."

"There are *rules*—a dozen exams you have to take before they let you anywhere near fugu."

"Which is why I'm coming to you," he said, then added, shamefully, "You had a feeling, didn't you? About the Hungry Ghosts? You left the kitchen when I served."

She didn't answer.

"You were right, Yume." He tried to keep his voice from breaking. "And I have to fix it. This is how."

He could hear it in the silence, her consideration.

She hesitated. She didn't want to get involved, tangled in whatever this might be. But she also wanted to put it to rest.

"Give me an hour."

THEY GOT TO Saveur Fare after midnight, Maura hauling a bag of supplies, and Konstantin lugging the cooler Kutsuki had dropped off, salt water sloshing inside.

He led the way through the service entrance, down the familiar subway-tiled hall, and into the alcove where three large walk-ins stood side by side, gleaming. They entered the last one, an ice-cream freezer, its temperature set to fifteen below, or, in technical terms, *fuck, it's cold.*

Cold enough to keep the poison from spreading too quickly through his veins.

Cold enough, once Kostya passed into the Afterlife, to keep his body preserved.

They stripped down to T-shirts—the colder they got, the better—and Maura lined the floor with butcher paper, stopping once or twice to breathe on her hands, her fingertips numb, the room so cold their breath hung like fog. Kostya set Kutsuki's cooler on the floor and unzipped the bag containing his knives.

"You ready?" he asked her.

"Are you?" she countered.

He nodded once and pulled the lid off the cooler. They both peered in, their fates contained in the rather ugly fish swimming around inside.

Kostya lifted it out, spearing his finger on one of its spines, and, cursing in pain, pinched its belly hard, right where Kutsuki had shown him. The puffer swelled with air. He set it carefully down onto the butcher paper, where it writhed and flopped as violently as if it knew what was coming.

Kostya picked up his knife. "This is it."

"Don't get scared now," Maura said softly.

"I didn't realize I was heading to the Afterlife with Kevin McCallister." She gave a weak smile.

Kostya held the fish down and sliced its belly apart, dark blood sluicing over the butcher paper and onto the floor. He gazed inside, at its ribs, and guts, and still-beating heart, and, ignoring Kutsuki's guidance completely, reached into the body cavity and removed its liver.

The single most poisonous part.

No known antidote.

No way to survive the toxins once they overran a body. But a way, maybe, to leverage them. If they could slow it down.

The plan was all about timing. He'd eat the liver in the walk-in, his blood flow and oxygen restricted by the cold. Hypothermia setting in alongside the poison. A one-two punch.

The moment he crossed to the Afterlife, Maura would set a timer. Five minutes in, she'd call an ambulance. That would give him ten, maybe fifteen minutes before help arrived. Long enough in the Afterlife, hopefully, to ferry the ghosts home. The paramedics would rush him to the hospital—another ten-minute ride—where they'd pump his stomach, get him on a respirator, replace his bodily functions until he metabolized the tetrodotoxin. In a few days, he should be home free.

You could survive it, the near-deather had told Maura, if you acted fast. He'd done it. Hundreds of people, all around the world. The key was medical attention in under an hour, and they'd keep it to forty-five minutes, to be safe. Plus the freezer would buy them more time.

And Maura would be right there, watching, just in case.

If all went to plan, she'd eat her portion of the liver right after she called for help, paramedics already on the way, and seal the veil before they even arrived. Everleigh had said it stretched like dough, so Maura thought it might patch like dough does, too. Like *varenyky*. The way Konstantin had taught her. She hoped she'd get the chance to try. But if things didn't go to plan, if something went wrong, they'd agreed she'd stay behind.

"Only if it's safe," Kostya made her swear.

"Relax, Dad." She'd grinned. "It's not my first rodeo."

But neither of them smiled now, as Kostya lifted the liver onto a plate, sliced it in half.

"Wait," Maura told him, and leaned in, pressed her frozen lips to his. "I love you, Stan. Be careful. I'll see you on the other side."

"I love you, too," he replied. "Meet you back here after for beer and burgers and the rest of our lives."

She nodded, trying to mask the worry on her face as Kostya wiped the puffer's blood from his hands and lifted the tiny morsel—pinkish grey, soft, like a smear of jelly—to his mouth.

IT WASN'T LOST on him, the poetry, the symmetry of this last bite.

Everything had begun with a taste of liver. Now it would end with one.

Kostya reached inside himself, to the place in his gut that felt inevitable, an entry point, its emptiness like a door. He reached for his dad. For Frankie. For the other side.

He could almost feel the hands of the Dead reaching out for him in turn.

He placed the pufferfish liver onto his tongue.

Wet, cold, slippery with blood.

Toxic, exotic, a once-in-a-lifetime taste.

He chewed hard, fast, before he lost his nerve.

Fatty, mineral, metallic, cream. Bitter, in the back of his throat.

Tears streamed down his face. Liquid fear.

Like salt, he told Maura, instead of goodbye, and swallowed.

PART FIVE

Salt & Earth

*A recipe has no soul. You, as
the cook, must bring soul to the recipe.*

Thomas Keller
The French Laundry Cookbook

His life doesn't flash before his eyes;

it skips across his tongue.

The things he savored.

The moments that soured him.

Memories that were sweet.

Others that repulsed him.

The morsels—places, people, passions—

that he wished he could keep tasting.

All the flavors that seasoned every thing,

in every season,

of his brief,

delicious life.

SAVORY

Miso
Shiitake
Papa making
breakfast while I
watch cartoons
Bone broth
Demi-glace
"You start
tomorrow."
Bacon
Soy sauce
Frankie at the bar
Nostalgia
Nutritional
yeast
Freddie Mercury
licking my face
Sardines
Seaweed
"Here's to us,
Bones."
Fish sauce
Parmesan
"Wanna get out
of here?"
Coconut Aminos
The last sparks
of life, twitching
over your tongue

SOUR

Buddha's Hand
Key Lime
Lemon Pine-Sol
Vomit
Cumquat
Frankie's grave
Cranberry
Passionfruit
"You're a waste
of fucking talent."
Cherry, Mont-
morency
Cherry, popped
Kefir
Cottage cheese
Boys with their
dads at the pool
while I burn
Sour cream
Yogurt
Rejection
Champagne
The smell in Van-
ya's van after a
long summer day
Maura, the life
leaving her eyes
Vinegar
Nerves
"There's been an
accident."
Wanting to live,
as my body dies

SWEET

Sugar
Acai
Your small, cold
hands
Honey
Moscato
Success, even brief
Corny jokes
Maple syrup
Moonlight in
Tompkins Square
Melons
Stevia
Flowers in a vase
Lychee
Snake fruit
Kissing you,
every single time
Manischewitz
Marshmallow
Dancing slow
Aspartame
Xylitol
My name in your
mouth
Carrots
Cola
Your name in
mine

BITTER

Coffee
Pith
Apricot pits
"What now,
Mama?"
Endive
Grapefruit
supremes
Baseball games
and little leagues
and father-son
anything
Radicchio
Radish
Certain days
of the year, no
matter how much
time goes by
Peppers
Poison
Losing a friend,
your best, your
brother
Onion, raw
Losing a parent,
the one that
understood
Burnt bread
Burnt sugar
Burnt liver
Burnt flesh
Being used by
the person you
trusted with love
Cheap spirits
(booze)
Hangry spirits
(ghosts)

SALTY

Table salt
Kosher salt
"Go to Hell"
Sea salt
Fleur de sel
Electrolytes
Maura in my arms
Blood
Sweat
Brine
IV drips
Tears
Anchovies
Expletives
Skin
Olives
Cum
Feta
Vegemite
How I love you;
how I'll always

Feast your Eyes

THE FOOD HALL is a feast.

For the eyes. For the tongue. For the mind.

It is vast as desire, an ocean of food. Its edges a horizon you could approach for all eternity and never actually reach.

It's also really freaking fun.

There are groves of sun-ripe fruit, air thick with the scent of peaches and plums, lemons and limes, deep-jungle soursop, grapes on the vine, pitaya and stink nut and green mangosteen, pomegranates descended from Persephone's own pips.

There are city-sized mazes of street meat, umami smoke rising in columns, the sizzle of griddles and grills caramelizing everything from *anticucho* to bún chả, lamb gyro to *pani câ mèusa*, dodo wing to Tyrannosaurus thigh.

There are islands of cheese—actual islands—afloat in whey, burrata barges shuttling souls through a paneer pass to an ivory *ibérico* coast, an isthmus of ricotta connecting it back to a Muenster mainland.

In the Food Hall, the world is an oyster! A Kushimoto white as sky, an undiscovered varietal untouched by human hands. A bowl of cherries!

Amarainier, Montmorello, cross-bred juices sluicing down your chin. A box of chocolates! Clustered coconut, stickjaw caramel, a heart-shaped Whitman Sampler Wonka Wonderball Surprise.

But amid all this magic, all the tastes and smells and flavors of fantasy available to the deceased, when Konstantin Duhovny arrived, when he squinted, blinking, into a band of unflattering fluorescent light, he found himself standing before a combination Pizza Hut and Taco Bell.

He was in the food court of a mall—was this Hell?—only impossibly large, so big he couldn't fathom where it ended or began.

His first and only thought was that he had to get cooking.

He started down the linoleum tile, passing two Starbucks, a Panda Express, a cupcake vending machine, a soda fountain (a real, working fountain spouting cola through its pump), a Fifty Shades of Gray's Papaya, a trio of breakfast joints, and an appetizing counter called Goldie's Lox, a dancing salmon flapping back and forth across its sign. These places might have had some rudimentary reheating capabilities (microwaves, toaster ovens, maybe a fryer), but he'd need a full kitchen, and real ingredients, if he was going to cook half the meals on his list.

He spotted an Exit door (small miracles!) and pushed through it to find himself in a sort of restaurant row, the chains and fast casuals giving way to an alley of Michelin stars, glamorous dining rooms flanking lamplit streets, linoleum swapped for cobblestone. This was more like it.

Kostya stopped before a window to gape at a knock-off Saveur Fare, the likeness so uncanny he half expected to see Michel excoriating a busboy. He went inside, looking for a waiter, a hostess, *someone* to lead him back because here, surely, was a kitchen! But the restaurant was unmanned, the dining room deserted. Kostya made his way through the space, trying every door he saw, but instead of a kitchen, he only found shortcuts, pathways to *other* places in the Hall, *more* ways to eat. Almost like the kitchen didn't want to be found.

Finally, he chose a door, stepping through into a tent at dusk, a lively night market sprouting up before him like a cluster of chanterelles.

"Kitchen?" he asked at a *Khanom Bueang* stall, the crepe shells folding themselves up in response.

"*Kitchen?*" he begged pots of boiling ramen, water hissing as unmanned chopsticks scooped noodles into bowls.

"*Kitchen?!*" he tried at the *kaitenzushi*, the conveyor zipping a little plate over to him with a placard reading: *No soup for you, Rulebreaker.*

The Afterlife, apparently, had his number.

Everleigh had said it would be easy. That there were stalls and restaurants all over the Hall that he could cook in; that getting ingredients was just a matter of thinking of them. But she, apparently, wasn't on the naughty list.

Okay, he thought mutinously. *Fine.*

If the Hall wouldn't help him, he'd help himself. Eating was kind of the point of this place. There was food everywhere! He'd just steal some ingredients and make it work.

He pushed through a beaded curtain and into bright, Marrakech daylight, the smells of *kefta* tagine and raisin-studded couscous, spicy harissa and skewers of lamb, saffron-stranded *b'stilla* streaked with cinnamon sugar all beckoning him forward, mouthwatering.

At a spice stall, he ran his fingers through sacks of coriander, cumin, and clove. He palmed a handful of cinnamon, but as soon as he stepped back from the stall it vanished. He tried again with turmeric. Gone. Black pepper, ditto.

"Oh, come on!" he shouted. "What do I have to do, huh?" He kicked the wooden table, the spices gasping in a rainbow cloud. "What's it gonna take?!"

He kicked it again, one of the sacks toppling over in a puff of red.

He opened his mouth to shout something else, but a hand on his shoulder silenced him.

"Bones," a voice whispered, the syllable tempering Konstantin like chocolate. "Keep it down, bro. You're Public Enemy Number One. Keep drawing attention and it's over before it even starts."

EVEN DEAD, FRANCIS K. O'Shaunessey looked like about a billion dollars.

"Frankie!" Kostya threw himself at him.

"I missed your dumb ass too." Frankie laughed, hugging him back. "And I do mean dumb. Come on."

Worry flicked across his face as he turned and started zipping through the marketplace, Kostya in tow.

"Fucking with the Dead, bringing people back—we messed up, man."

Frankie turned down a street lined with bread stalls, then cut through an alley of—were those bricks of *compound butter*?

"*I* messed up," Kostya corrected. "*You* didn't do anything."

"That's . . . not exactly true. Did my fair share over on this side, too."

"But you wouldn't even be here if it weren't for me! It's my fault you're . . ." Kostya slowed, the word like wet cement. "Dead. You should be *alive*, Frankie. Fuck. Was it the ghost? That girl at Wolfpup? I'm so fucking sorry."

"Wait, *what*? No. That ain't on you, Bones."

Frankie waved him forward, barely pausing.

"Of course it's on me! I brought her back."

Kostya shimmied between the bricks, the lane narrowing around them, the butter softening, greasing his arms.

"Wasn't the ghost that killed me"—Frankie shook his head—"it was the hustle."

"I—what?"

"It's a fucking stupid story. I'm embarrassed to tell it."

"Well, swallow your pride. Not knowing is killing me."

"Just don't judge, alright?" Frankie sighed, stepping through an archway toward a stand of unusual fruit. "Round that time, I had a hundred balls in the air, remember? There was Keller calling. Delia all up on me to commit. And Wolfpup. James Beard noms. My mama pushing me to settle down. Student loans. Nights out. You and the Supper Club. I was burning it at every end."

"That's just what you do when you're young and hungry."

They passed an arrangement of square watermelons, blue raspberries, electric plums.

"Maybe, but none of it felt good enough. Not after I saw what you got up to."

"Me?"

"You were doing the real thing, man. Food that meant something. Special. Least that's how it felt at the time. Hindsight's a bitch."

Frankie squeezed past a cart of sour grapes, stopping at the entrance to a fish mart.

"Sure is," Kostya agreed, following. "I'm sorry I dragged you into this."

"Way I remember it, Bones, *I* dragged *you*. You were 'bout ready to do the smart thing and give up. But me? I dragged you to Wolfpup to experiment. Dragged you to Saveur for that job. Dragged you—"

"—what? *No!* You *encouraged* me."

"—out of bed to start Hell's Kitchen," Frankie continued. "And it wasn't just 'cause we were friends. I wanted fame. Glory. So bad I didn't care if I had to ride your coattails to get it. My priorities were that twisted. Right up till the night I died."

They passed a table of rainbow trout, their gills fanned in prismatic color. A display of lobsters—red, green, blue. A tray of *uni*, their insides like fire.

"What do you mean?"

Frankie exhaled. "I was hustling, trying to get my own spot open. I'd been up so many nights that I lost count. And there I was at Wolfpup, testing menus after hours."

"I remember."

"Well, I poured myself a drink to mellow out, and started prep. But the booze made me woozy, so I took some of Ale's uppers. Started feeling good then—*too* good—so good that when I was done tweaking recipes, thought I'd keep it going. Stay and experiment. I thought"—he looked over at Kostya, an apology on his face—"I ain't proud of this, Bones, but I thought that what you had going on, with the ghosts? That I could do it, too. Maybe even do it better. Steal some thunder for myself."

"What are you talking about?"

Frankie wove through an aisle of oysters—shells of every imaginable color and size—and took a hard right turn into another large tent, this one crammed with sacks of rice.

"You'd been complaining how you couldn't get it right. Couldn't figure how to bring those spirits back. And I was a cocky motherfucker, so after half a bottle of Barcelo and two more pills, I decided I would bring back your pops. Do what you couldn't. Liver, I figured—how hard could it be? Well. I put it on the stove, but the uppers and the rum and no sleep were a nasty combo, and I passed out on the line. When I came to, kitchen was full of smoke. And I was so loaded I didn't know which way was up. Climbed in the walk-in thinking it was a way out. By then, it was so thick in there I couldn't see straight. Or breathe. So I stayed put, hoping help would come." He shrugged one shoulder. "Came too late."

Kostya gaped at him.

"*Fuck*, man." It was the saddest thing he'd ever heard. "Dying like that, when you had the best life of, like, anyone I ever met."

"That really how you think it was?" Frankie zigged and zagged around the bags of grain. "It looked good from the outside, but none of it was deep. Just surface. The parties, the crew. They were good to fuck up a Saturday night, but that's all it was. You and Rio were the only ones who actually cared."

"That's not true! Women loved you! You had more game than an arcade."

"Game," Frankie repeated, bitter. "I was young. I looked good. The women—I got lucky. I had some fun nights. And days. And mornings." He cracked a small smile, remembering, then wiped it away. "That's all it was, though. Nothing real. I was so caught up in myself and my spot that I never let anyone in. I never loved anybody. Not like you."

"Please. What did I know about love?"

"Plenty! When I died—I felt you. Right here." Frankie tapped his chest. "Holding on. So tight I couldn't set one foot out the Hall."

"*Fuck*, Frankie, if I made you Hungry—"

"You didn't." Frankie cocked his head. "Least not for long. When you met your girl, that grip you had on me? It let go."

"Leftovers," Kostya whispered.

"But being Hungry," Frankie continued, "even for a little, made me see how bad others were hurting."

"So you started the tour."

Frankie nodded.

"I'd seen you do your thing, so I thought, hey, I can help folks. Give you a little help from the other side. Make those aftertastes easier to come by. Finally get that chance to make my name, too. Get famous for the good I did." They came to the end of the tent, and Frankie shoved through it into the freckled light of a grove of trees, their sweet, fermented smell hanging in the air. Apples. "Joke's on me, huh?"

He strode through the orchard, Kostya jogging to keep up.

"I tried reaching out so we could sync up, but you kept your word, Bones. Let me stay Dead. Which, in retrospect, was damn lucky. Kept me from going Hangry."

"Shit." Kostya panted, realizing. "You were waiting on DUH because there was no other way to get in touch. You didn't know the spirits I brought back were getting stuck."

"Wouldn't have done any of this if I had. *Definitely* wouldn't have brought the whole tour to your big opening night. I just thought I was serving closure. Same as you. We wanted to believe it so bad, man. Both of us. That we were the good guys."

"I wanted to make things better." Kostya kicked hard at an apple on the ground, sent it flying. "Turned out like always."

"Well, there's still time. C'mon. We got an Afterlife to fix."

Frankie sped along the row of trees, through a garden gate, and toward a fork in the road, evaluating the options before heading down a path Kostya hadn't even seen—an aisle of Granny Smiths.

"I don't see how. I can't get within ten feet of an ingredient. And I bet the kitchen's gonna be uphill, too."

"The Hall can really hold a grudge. But I know a spot you can cook. And the ingredients—won't be easy, but there's a work-around."

"Okay?"

"See, most of the food here?" Frankie picked an apple off a tree, took a bite. "It's just for show." He tossed it to Kostya, who startled at the strange *nothing* beneath its skin. Air, where there should have been flesh, pith, seeds. "It's just there to make you hungry. Sights. Smells. Hocus-pocus. For food you can eat—it's made to order. From your memories."

"The food here eats memories?"

"The food here *is* memories."

Kostya stopped walking. It made sense, like something he'd known way down in his bones. Every aftertaste he'd ever cooked had been like that— a shorthand for something else, each dish a memory shared by the Living and Dead.

"So then, can memories *be* food? Like—like raw ingredients?"

"That's how the Hall cooks." Frankie nodded. "It translates memories into meals, so we can process. But the hard stuff, like aftertastes—it doesn't always have the chops. And you're a *real* chef, a better one. You channel the Dead and you *feel* what they felt. Taste it. Pour your soul into every dish you make. The Food Hall can't do that. So if anyone can cook with memory, my money's on you."

Kostya gave a half smile, despite himself. "I bet you say that to all the cooks."

"Only the ones worth their salt."

"But if the food is memory, then when you eat it, what? It's just . . . gone?"

Frankie shook his head. "Forgetting's not the same as closure. You remember; you just . . . don't crave it anymore. At least"—he gave Kostya a meaningful look—"that's how it works when they're your own memories."

"I don't follow."

"The spirits you're tryna help, Bones," he said gently, "they're not in the Hall now. You can't use *their* memories as ingredients."

"But then how do I—"

"I think"—he looked unspeakably sorry—"you gotta use yours."

Kostya swallowed, his mouth dry. "And when they eat *my* food? My—*my memories*—what happens to me?"

"I dunno. Not for sure. But if I had to guess? You'll forget."

It hit Kostya like a bag of ice. What he stood to lose. All the things that could vanish. All the people. He thought of Maura, waiting for him on the other side. Of his mother. Of Rio, and his kitchen staff. He thought of the memories it would take, every moment of the life he'd finally begun to live.

He didn't want to give it up.

But he had done this. Had caused these spirits harm. He owed them.

"There's no other way?" he choked out.

"Not unless the Hall decides to forgive and forget. And from what I've seen, it's a petty little bi—"

As if it'd heard, the ground beneath began to quake.

"Watch what you say!" Kostya yelped, trying to keep his balance.

"That wasn't me!" Frankie grabbed the trunk of a nearby tree. "The Hall's been out of whack since the veil burst. That's why it's so pissed at you." As soon as the tremor went still, Frankie hustled Kostya through the grove and toward a wall of rock candy, a tunnel visible in its face as they drew near. "I been keeping us moving, but we gotta set things right while it's still standing. It falls apart, the whole Afterlife goes Hungry."

"It's that bad?"

"Yep. And long as the veil's open, Hungry Ghosts will keep pouring into Manhattan. Looking for closure, blood, or both."

"Maura." Kostya suddenly remembered the pufferfish, Saveur Fare, his body in another world. "She was gonna come through and try to close it."

"She'll need help. Hangry spirits will put up a fight."

"*Fuck.*"

"But one thing at a time." The tunnel led to a half-rusted door, and Frankie wrenched it open, revealing steps. "We need to get you cooking."

"What's even the point?" Kostya whined, making his way down. "The Afterlife's fucked, and the Living are fucked, and the Dead are fucked, and the Food Hall couldn't help even if it wanted to because it's fucked, and it's all fucked because of me, so what's the point of going anywhere and doing anything? I'm the King Midas of fuckery. Everything I touch turns to fucks."

Frankie laughed, his voice bouncing through the dark. "You ever oversalt a dish? Overcook spaghetti? Make something that tasted *bad*?"

Konstantin thought horribly of Christmas at Saveur Fare, that ill-fated holiday party and badly sauced cavatappi.

"Hasn't everyone?"

"What separates the good chefs from the bad is whether you can take that mistake and make lemonade."

"How do you make lemonade out of fucks?"

"I really gotta spell it out? Right now, the Food Hall's just your dining room. You're the pantry. The stations. The fucking *Chef.* Make those ghosts a meal they can't resist, and meanwhile, we'll seal the veil. Maura have a plan?"

"Something about dough."

"I knew I liked her."

They came to the bottom of the stairs, and Frankie stopped before a subway turnstile, the entrance to the 6.

"Wait," Kostya said slowly. "Where are we going?"

"To your kitchen. At DUH," Frankie said. *"Duh."*

———

DUH IN THE Hereafter was, down to the bathroom tile, the same as DUH in the Heretofore, except for two things. It was missing its people, and it was missing its food.

This had a strange effect. As though the restaurant itself were on the brink of death, the soul that had given it life abandoning its body.

Kostya gathered supplies at his station—knives and cutting boards, pans and pots and kitchen towels—and took a deep breath, trying to exhale his nerves. He needed ingredients now. Would have to make them. Find them in himself. Frankie had explained this part to him (twice), but Kostya still wasn't entirely sure how it worked—*if* it would.

"Remember," Frankie reminded him.

Kostya nodded, trying to look braver than he felt. Death was one thing. Forgetting was another.

"I better get started. While I still know what I'm doing here."

"Shit, Bones." Frankie pulled him into a hug.

"Frankie, if—" The words caught in his mouth. "If, in the end, I'm not all there, I just want you to know: you were the best friend I ever had. Thanks for pushing me into the kitchen."

"Thank me again when this works."

They pulled apart, Kostya's hands still clutching Frankie's shirt.

"Come back, okay? Soon as you find Maura. And close that fucking veil."

"You got it, Bones. I'll see you soon."

"But seriously? Hurry."

"SERIOUSLY, HURRY!" MAURA had shouted into the phone, and left it there, dangling down the wall, knowing the dispatcher would trace the landline to Saveur Fare's address.

She was trying to remember if she'd given them enough detail—pufferfish, toxin, respirator, dying—as she raced back down the steps to the kitchen, down the hall to where the walk-in was, where Konstantin's body had betrayed him.

Something had gone wrong.

The poison had hit him faster than expected—she'd started the timer on her phone once he stopped responding to her voice—but barely two minutes into his death, he'd begun convulsing. Vomiting. Foaming at the mouth.

He was ice-cold to touch. Impossible to wake.

She'd sprinted up the stairs to call an ambulance, far earlier than they'd planned, and she was supposed to wait for the paramedics now. To abandon her trip back. They'd agreed: only if it was safe. But looking at Konstantin, the edges of his lips turning blue, his fingers, the frost forming in the pool of sick at his feet, she couldn't do the safe thing.

She had to find him. To save him.

For the real thing, you hold on, she thought as she swallowed the other half of the pufferfish liver.

THE KITCHEN WAS still as Kostya closed his eyes.

He began at the beginning, with the first spirit he'd ever raised.

Cava, he thought at the Food Hall. *Gin. Lemon juice. Luxardo cherry.*

He repeated the names of the ingredients over and over, the words stretching thin, until the syllables barely made sense.

Nothing.

What had Frankie told him? That every memory carried a particular flavor. A taste. That the Food Hall just needed to know what to serve him.

He tried again.

Cava, he thought. *I need Cava. Bubbly. Dry. Slight tang. Acidic, but with a sweet resolution. Warm in the throat.*

And this time, he felt it, a voice like honey, coming from somewhere inside him. *What does that feel like?*

Kostya hesitated for only a moment before offering it up; he hadn't thought of it in years.

The time he'd gone into Olympia Diner to steal sugar and half-and-half, had been stuffing packets into his backpack when a waitress caught him, a girl he knew, Demi Papadakis, who'd switched schools in sixth grade but remembered him, and instead of kicking him out she'd given him a burger on the house, said sorry about his dad, told him she'd lost her mom that spring.

The Food Hall took it—he could almost feel the way it left his mind, like being sucked through a straw—and a moment later, a bottle of Cava appeared, its bubbles so delicate, impossibly fine. *Sweet resolution. Slight tang. Warm in the throat.*

The gin took a night he spent camping with his dad, mosquitoes biting through his sleeping bag.

Lemon was when Alexis dumped him, standing there in the threshold, the way she'd yanked Freddie Mercury's leash from Kostya's hand.

Luxardo cherry was the first time he had sex.

The patchouli oil was harder, difficult to match until he remembered his first fatherless birthday, the bouquet that arrived—that his dad had scheduled—the way his mother had thrown it in the trash, but the scent still lingered, the smell of decay.

WHEN ANNA APPEARED, it wasn't in a shower of sparks. Her light was dim now, cast in shadow. Her face hollow. Like there was barely anything left in her to save.

"Please," Kostya begged, "forgive me."

He handed her the glass.

Her sips were tentative at first, but with each one, light flooded back into her face. Halfway through, her cheekbones softened, grew less sharp. Her face filled out, to the way it had looked the first time she'd appeared, a ghost in The Library of Spirits. By the time she finished, she was beautiful, aglow, all emerald green, and as she set her glass down at his station, he watched his kitchen flood with brilliant, golden light.

It was coming from the windows. A train.

Not the 6, but something else.

Kostya watched her board the gleaming car, ride away through the tunnel. On to her next journey. Her next life.

Then he got to work.

ONE BY ONE, he brought the spirits back.

There were hundreds of ingredients, each a little piece of him.

An angry outburst at his mother traded for Tabasco sauce.

His first day stocking the bodega shelves became saltines.

The lie he'd told Maura—that he'd stopped with the ghosts, one and done—a greasy tin of smoked sardines, marinated in the time his classmates saw him dumpster dive for food.

He was frugal with his ingredients. Saved lemon halves to use again. Pinches of salt. Pats of butter. He tried to keep himself whole for as long as he could. But even so, after a dozen spirits moved along, he felt an emptiness press in, a dim ring haloing the edges of his mind, and knew that it was time. Ready or not. No more delays.

There was one dish he'd avoided out of nerves and insecurities, but it, more than any other, needed him coherent. Comprehending. *There.*

Because it wasn't just closure for the spirit; it was Kostya's closure, too.

When he summoned the ingredients of his father's dish—his own death, and winning Viktor's competition, lying in the grass with his dad when he was six, and how it felt at DUH, hearing Maura tell her truth—his breath caught in his throat. He didn't know if he could face his dad now. If he could handle seeing what his grief, his refusal to let go, had done. Would he be angry? Hangry? A shell of a man, consumed by the Hunger Kostya had unleashed? Did he still carry scars, all these years later, from the words Kostya shouted as he left the house?

He cooked in silence, braced himself as he sprinkled on the dill.

But when Sergei Duhovny materialized before his son, he was smiling, pride shining through him like a beam.

The lines were deeper in his face now; Hunger lingered in his eyes, dulling their flame. The memories had dimmed in Kostya's mind, so many precious moments with his father sacrificed for savory, for sweet, flavors he couldn't access any other way. Still, he knew him. Recognized him. His heart did. His soul.

"Kostochka," Sergei whispered, his name the sweetest in his father's mouth.

"*Papa.*"

Sergei mussed his hair, held Kostya's face in his penumbral hands.

"My son," he said, tears welling in his sunken eyes. "My cherrystone. I knew you'd come. To play our game. To find my final taste."

And Kostya broke down then, this answer too much, the key to all his doors.

He had held so tightly to his grief, had stoked his guilt for all those years, had prayed for his father's forgiveness and yet had never seen his aftertastes for what they were. The answer he had needed. Not forgiveness, but acceptance. Proof that his father had seen him. Had understood. Not a gift, or a curse, but a game. *Their* game. Transformed by Death and sent him by his dad so they might meet again. Play one last round.

"*Pechonka,*" Kostya stammered through his tears. "Your taste."

"*Nyet!*" his dad choked out, face streaked, too, with salt. "Love."

It passed between them in a glance—the guilt and the apologies, mistakes they'd made, this love that had held fast through time, and space, and death. A hook. A tether. An unbreakable chain. A bond that would be something else now, leading Sergei to his future life.

"*Кушай*," Kostya told his dad at last, handing him the plate of food, ready, after all this time, to let him go. "Eat."

HE RESCUED EVERLEIGH, who hugged him tight, told him he'd better be good to her sister or she'd haunt him into the next life. He returned Baba Fira, who insisted that he try her borscht, a babushka until the end. He righted Dan Evans's father. Stella's mom.

Countless others that he didn't know by name.

More than Kostya had anticipated.

Swarms of Hungry Ghosts had flooded through the tear, and Frankie tried to track them all now, keep them away from Maura as she fought to patch the veil.

"Like herding cats, man. But worse," he told Kostya. "She'd better hurry."

Kostya rushed to make their dishes, trying to staunch the bleed, these sharp new aftertastes assaulting him like chits on a Saturday night—overwhelming, relentless, no end in sight.

He cooked fried chicken. And congee. Schnitzel, and vegan Bolognese. Khasiko Bhutan. Salmon *en croûte*. *Sawagani*. Paella. *Ptitim*. So many dishes, so many ingredients, so many spirits waiting for his aid that he lost track of what he'd used. How little he had left. How few memories remained.

He was making birthday cake—an agony of ingredients, taking so much from him that he shuddered as he stirred—when he realized he'd forgotten his own name.

How strange, he thought, to have lost himself but still know *this*, how to cook, how to feed. Was there some dish, he wondered, somewhere, that might bring him back? A morsel to remind him? Perhaps on the other side, where he had come from.

The Living, after all, ate mostly to remember. They marked their lives in food.

In birthday cakes, and champagne toasts. In bowls of ketchup soup and Michelin-starred menus. In cups of coffee. In Happy Meals. In sides of fries. In Sunday dinners with Gigi or Yaya or Năi Nai or Ba.

To eat was to celebrate. Food was living, after all; food was love. It was how the Living coped. How they kept going. Shorthand for their entire lives.

But the Dead? This place? The Dead ate to forget.

To let go.

To taste, for one last time, that vivid spark of Life before they left it all behind. There was no *more* for the Dead, no second helping. Only a record that they might leave. A recipe.

A recipe could tell you who someone had been, what they had loved, the things that sustained them. It was a way for others to carry them along, to bring them back, to keep them close once they had gone. A way to never really die.

He could feel them now, the spirits yearning for his food. And he obliged, nourished them with dishes even as their preparation ate his memories away.

He gave so much to feed them. Everything.

He lost the wonder of his childhood, the years his father was alive.

The devastation of his death.

The pain of high school, its acrid humiliations, its bitter defeats.

Every small triumph—his first kiss, first job, first apartment.

Those years of driving Vanya's truck (though maybe that was for the best).

The last months of his life—his happiest—when he discovered all that he could do.

He lost Frankie, painfully, his final memory the first time they met—to discuss living together after Kostya replied to that Craigslist ad—at an East Village café with pornographic wallpaper, where Frankie'd given Konstantin his name—Bones—once he learned what *Kostya* meant.

He lost Maura, her love like salt, though he tried desperately to hold on, to save her for the very last, to stretch the time until she made it back, until he could see her. Until he could save her. But most of the dishes he made required the flavor of her memories, not bitter or acid, which he had in spades, but kinder tastes, addictive ones, heat and salt, sweetness, umami, and he'd already sacrificed his dad, and Frankie, the greatest moments of his life, as seasonings.

He lost himself.

Loses.

Making the aftertastes takes everything out of him.

AND THEN, THERE'S just one memory left.

A last tendril to life, delicate as silk.

A memory he both clings to and aches to cast away, a moment of shame, of pain, in early morning light. *Papa . . . give me a taste!* and *There's never a later!* and *Go to the Devil!*

He doesn't know what will happen if he lets it go. If he empties himself. Becomes a vessel instead of an urn.

He licks his lips, gazes around the kitchen, at its gleaming surfaces, the bits of food dotting the counter, a mess someone has made. This place feels important, meaningful, though he no longer knows why, can't fathom what he's doing there. There's a knife on the counter like the tattoo on his arm, but he isn't sure why, in another life, he would have chosen it.

He reaches for the answer, screws his eyes tight, wills himself to remember, but it doesn't come. It is painful to forget. A wound that won't close. Emotional. Mental. An ache in his head, pounding.

Clap-clap-clap.

So loud he can almost hear it.

Clap-clap-clap.

There it is again.

Not in his head but against the window. Tapping.

"Stan! Are you in there?"

The voice goes through him like water, comes back again, louder. Closer. "Konstantin!"

And she sweeps over the sill, violet haired, wide-eyed, breathless.

The most beautiful woman he's ever seen. She throws herself into his arms, clutches him like they know each other. Like they'd been something, once.

"We did it," she says into his shirt. "The veil—what you taught me about dough, Frankie and I—it's closed! It was just like *varenyky*, pinching and crimping; you have to see—"

She looks up into his eyes, the world there, in her smile, and he watches it wither as he gazes back, his face a question, a blank plate.

"No. *No.* Oh, Stan."

"Do I know you?" He wants to, very much. Wishes that he did.

She presses her lips together like it hurts. "What do you—how much do you have left?"

"Just . . ."—he shakes his head, not knowing how she knows—"just one last thing."

She takes his face into her hands. They're so warm he almost shuts his eyes.

"Don't let it go," she whispers. "Hold it tight. Stay with me. We—" Her voice is breaking. "We're going to be okay. Please, just stay. I'll figure it out. Get you back somehow. All of you. I love you, Konstantin. I love you like salt. And I'm going to fix this."

Salt.

More than salt.

Morton's. Himalayan.

Sweat. Blood. Capers. Roe.

Maura.

So much more than salt.

Something shakes loose inside of him. An instinct to feed her.

He only has one memory left, enough for a single ingredient. Something salty—he was salty in it—all attitude. But with an undertone of regret, a dash of guilt. A longing for affection.

He recalls it—*the kitchen, the refrigerator door, the way the cold air felt along his skin*—lets it travel along his tongue—*his father and that awful tie, the kids and all of their unkindness, his own fear and shame and loneliness*—rolls it like a marble inside his mouth—*the anger that exploded from his chest, his dad's defeat, his own terrible regret*—and feels it harden, rough and textured, crystalline, saline, its nooks and crannies and hand-harvested flakes seasoned to taste, flavored by this memory—*the ache for attention, for connection, for love.*

It's a subtle salt. Delicate.

Fleur de sel.

And for one brief, brilliant moment, in the time it takes to taste, he remembers.

Understands.

Decides.

He knows he can't return. His body is poisoned now; his memories gone. And even if he could, he's needed here. For other souls who need release. Those many Hungry spirits that the Food Hall cannot feed. But he can. So he'll stay. He'll help.

And maybe one day, in return, he'll get to see her again.

Because Maura can still live now.

Without Hunger. Without Everleigh. Without the constant draw of Death.

He can't let her follow him, not when most of him is gone, will vanish again in a moment's time. Not when he knows she isn't done being alive. Isn't done playing, and finding, and feasting.

All he wants now is to let her.

To send her back.

To love her enough to let her go.

———

THE *FLEUR DE SEL* is melting in his mouth, vanishing fast, and he reaches for her—*I've seen a lot of crazy things*—presses his parted lips to hers—*you're extraordinary*—kisses her with abandon—*more than salt*—tongues the taste, their aftertaste, his final memory, into her mouth—*so much more than salt.*

This—this salt, this kiss, this love—is the greatest thing that either of them has ever tasted, and in this moment, it reminds her. Takes her back. Hitches her to Life.

"I love you," he whispers now, "like salt."

She gasps as silver mist begins rising from her skin, as she glows, as she feels the pull back to her body. Back to Life. Her eyes search his, fill with fluorescent tears.

"What did you do?"

And he wants to tell her, to explain, but the words are falling away, beyond his reach. She takes his hand into her evanescing palm.

"Wait for me, Stan," she pleads. "Don't forget. *Please* don't forget."

She kisses him again, a kiss goodbye, the kind of kiss he should remember, except he has already forgotten.

It's on the tip of his tongue, who she is, who she might be, what she means to him, but he cannot recall, can no longer taste, and it doesn't come back even as she vanishes in a twist of light, dissolves like salt in water, travels out of sight.

LAST BITES

Petits Fours

Please one more
kiss in the kitchen
before we turn the lights off

W. S. Merwin
"Wish"

Salé

MAURA ELIZABETH STRUK—no longer haunted by Hunger—wakes in the walk-in of Saveur Fare, between exquisite trays of house-made custard and the frozen body of the man she loves. She trembles, both from cold and from the toxins in her blood. Her breath comes in ragged puffs, tracing cirrus clouds through freezer air. Her tears freeze solid to her lashes. She isn't ready yet to leave this place, to leave him behind, and either way, she's paralyzed, so she stays staring at his face, committing it to memory, recalling the taste of Konstantin's last kiss.

In time, the steel door of the walk-in swings open, and strangers rush in, all doctors' bags and sterile tools.

"Pufferfish?" they balk, examining Konstantin, trying to help what can't be saved, and she only blinks once, very slowly, to confirm. *Pufferfish*, they write on his death certificate, though it was so much more than that, really.

One of the paramedics gives her a look. Frowns.

"Hope it was worth it," he says, venomous as the fish, as he moves her to a gurney.

She tries to be.

———

SHE GOES BACK to school. Gets her degree. Codes a dozen games.

There's one about the Food Hall, a mission where you help a Chef remember. It wins awards, sells out its copies, but she's proudest of the way the gameplay screens for suicide, the many lives it's saved.

She lives in Tokyo awhile. In Melbourne. In Tangiers.

She learns to cook.

She eats. A lot.

She loves but never falls in love again, although this doesn't feel like loss. Only like waiting.

Mostly, though, she remembers. She takes him along.

Salt reminds her. She tastes it in everything, minuscule pyramids of Maldon, coarse grains of Kosher, perfect pink granules of Himalayan Sea, black flecks of Kala Namak, plain old crystals of iodized Morton's, the little yellow salt girl on the label. Her favorite is always *fleur de sel*, its delicate flakes like petals, and as they melt across her tongue she can feel him, their bond unbroken even in death, and in her mouth he lives again, is right there, his aftertaste.

He isn't here, she knows.

But he's not gone.

Frais

VERA DUHOVNY IS upstate, living in a small, brown, featureless farm-house on an orchard—cherry, not apple—that she tends with motherly love. She resembles Kostya as she works, not in feature so much as expression, the fold of concentration in her forehead, the way her eyes close as she tastes, how her brows reveal surprise.

One tree has pushed its fruit out early, outpacing all the others, the cherries that it bears bright red, their skin so delicate, the first bite almost achingly tart, so sour it draws tears from her eyes. *Vishnya*. She'd gone back to Ukraine to get it. To the village Sergei's grandmother once lived. She dotes upon it like a child, this family tree she's saved.

In the kitchen, she sucks another cherry clean, and spits its pale stone into her palm. The same way Kostya used to. The rest she washes, pits, and jars, makes preserves to send away. To the people who knew him. Who loved him. Rio. Frankie's mother. Maura, who eats them with a spoon.

The recipe's unorthodox. Unexpected. One that Sergei taught her. A way to keep them all together, memories sun-sweet in her mouth. The tartness of life's cherries tempered not by sugar, but by salt.

Glaces

FRANCIS K. O'SHAUNESSEY no longer answers to Frankie, or Frank, or Kosh, or Handsome, though old habits die hard on that last one. In his kitchen, where he spends every hour of every cloudless day, every moment of each starry night, feeding one lucky spirit at a time, he answers only—ecstatically—to Chef.

Last Supper is not merely located in the trendy part of the Food Hall; it *is* the trendy part of the Food Hall. There are no reservations, the queue always out the door. There is only one seat, a bare barstool at a simple wooden counter. The menu does not exist. No one who goes in to eat ever comes back out.

The meal, it is universally agreed, is worth waiting for.

The Chef watches proudly as his patrons eat their fill. As the flavors of their memories dance and twirl across their tongues. As they vanish, beaming, in a gleam of sparks. He's making good on his promise to help them find closure. He's doing it right this time. When they return from their visits, satisfied, they move right On. To the next course in the infinite feast of the soul.

His Sous-Chef watches, too.

An unassuming guy, the Sous does all the cooking. It takes him time to learn technique; his mind is scrambled as an egg. But aftertasting comes so naturally to him, a skill that can't be taught. Rare enough that the Hall was convinced to let him stay.

He's got great instincts, a natural flair for seasoning the memories he plates.

Though, it must be said, he's prone to oversalting.

Still, the Chef thinks one day soon, he'll pass the ladle of Last Supper on to his successor.

He'll board his own train On, and leave his Sous in charge.

Deguises

THE SOUS LOVES the kitchen.

He loves the food. He loves the diners. He loves the Chef.

He loves watching spirits vanish in a burst of blinding light.

He loves, most of all, that he has been allowed to stay.

When the Sous awoke it was sans memory, no recollection left to tie him back to where he'd been. A clean plate; a clean slate. He should have moved straight On.

Yet here he still is, inexplicably, working in Last Supper. Still cooking. Still serving. Still turning memories into food.

Something happens, each time he serves a meal.

Ingredients get left behind.

He finds them as he clears the plates—a crumb of bread; a flake of pepper; a stray tomato seed.

Keep 'em, the Chef says. *You earned it. Maybe one day, you'll make your own last meal.*

So the Sous collects them in glass vials, labels them with tape, stores them in a drawer. It will take a lifetime to amass enough to cook with, but he's in no rush. There's something he is waiting for.

Someone.

It is an instinct, subconscious. A feeling in his gut just like intuiting a meal. One that makes him stay, tells him she'll come, that he should feed her when she does.

IN THE END, he doesn't know her by sight, or touch, or sound. Only by taste.

The flavor of her kiss a craving, its quality like coming home.

The best thing he has ever tried. Will ever. Ever could.

A special kind of salt.

Acknowledgments

THE NUMBER OF people who helped make this book possible could fill a busy brunch at Balthazar. It's an honor and a privilege to raise my glass to you all.

To the incomparable Lucy Carson—when writers describe their dream agents, even their wildest imaginings don't come anywhere close to the magic of working with you; thank you for believing in this story from the very first pages, and for every single thing since. A thousand pages wouldn't be enough to thank you for all you've done.

Thank you to everyone working at, and in partnership with, The Friedrich Agency, to bring this book about death to vivid life—Sylvie Rabineau at WME, a dream-maker who helped me realize mine with such kindness and care; Caspian Dennis at Abner Stein, whose early enthusiasm for this book helped it make waves across the pond; Molly Friedrich, who welcomed me so completely and enthusiastically; Marin Takikawa, whose keen insights made the earliest drafts shine (and ensured I didn't misspell "shiitake"); Hannah Brattesani, who helped make *Aftertaste* a reality in so many countries and languages; and Heather Carr, whose patience and guidance are the cherry on top.

All of the champagne and roses go to my brilliant editors, Carina Guiterman at Simon & Schuster and Alexis Kirschbaum at Bloomsbury. I am absurdly blessed to have had your keen eyes, sharp minds, and stunning support on this book, and doubly blessed to have had the benefit of your partnership. Carina—I knew from the very first conversation that working with you would be special; your kindness, wit, and collaboration are the things author dreams are made of. Thank you for every conversation, every margin note, every ounce of guidance and wisdom and patience. Alexis—you were the very first to want to make this manuscript into a published book, and your enthusiasm, insights, and attention have made my publishing process into an absolute fantasy; thank you for catching every wobbly piece of world-logic, and for working so patiently with me to make them rock solid. Thank you both, most of all, for choosing this book, for loving it, for making it shine; you've changed my life, and I will never be the same.

Thank you a thousand times to Stephanie Rathbone for your deep reading and even deeper thinking about this novel; your excitement, care, and questions made this book so much better, and I am forever grateful.

My deepest thanks, absolute adoration, and truckloads of Reese's go to the brilliant marketing and publicity teams that helped *Aftertaste* find its readers—Danielle Prielipp, Emily Farebrother, Maggie Southard, and Nawal Qadir at S&S, and Ros Ellis, Amy Donegan, Fran Owen, and Cristiana Caserini at Bloomsbury. Truly, no one would ever have found this book (and so many others!) without your enthusiasm, championship, and creative strategies; you are magicians, and I am so lucky to have launched *Aftertaste* with your enchantments.

Thank you to everyone working behind the scenes to acquire, steward, copyedit, design, produce, print, sell, distribute, and publish this book; some of you I haven't yet met at the time of this writing, but please know you have my enduring gratitude. For those I do know: Tim O'Connell—your excitement and support for this book meant (and continue to mean) the world; Sophia Benz—thank you for answering my million questions; Anna Hauser—thank you for making the production process smoother than French butter; Yvette Grant—thank you for your sharp copyedits, production expertise, and kind collaboration; Greg Heinimann—thank you for this absolutely stunning, whimsical cover, and for all of your vision, care, and patience in creating it; Wendy Blum—thank you for this gorgeous interior layout; Caroline Baptista—thank you for the stunning author photo; Wendy Sheanin, Joe Roche, Sarah McLean, Carrie Pitt, and all the sales teams who worked to bring *Aftertaste* to market in the US and UK—I am so, so grateful to you for getting this to readers' hands.

So many people read bits of this book along the way, encouraged me to keep going, and gave me suggestions on how to make it better. To the sparkling Sash Bischoff, Blair Hurley, Laura Hankin, and Lovell Holder—our writing group is so much more than a workshop; your endless encouragement, keen observations, and, above all, friendship mean everything to me. Thank you for talking me off the ledge every time Maura was giving me trouble, and for being cheerleaders, sounding boards, therapists, and fierce friends. Sara Knudson, Jesse Karlan, David Hura, and Alex Deguise—thank you for being early and enthusiastic readers, and for the Zoom workshops that kept me writing throughout the pandemic. Joan Silber—thank you for the novel-writing course where Kostya and Frankie began their journeys, and for every kindness since. David Hollander—the first person to make me feel like a real, capital-letter "Writer"—thank you for being a mentor, an advisor, and for pushing this book to better, always. Julia Phillips—one of the most generous artists I know, and a treasure of a person, thank you for your enthusiasm, encouragement, and incredible insight into plotting as I tried to wrestle this bear. Peter Kang—thank you for reading this early, and for your vision about all it could be. Renee Harleston and Veronica Vega—thank you for helping me fine-tune Frankie's voice and for your keen notes on his experience. Paulina Soberon—thank you for your help with Spanish, and for educating me about Mexican flora!

Thank you to my family and friends, who never wavered in their encouragement as I pursued this dream. To my parents, Vlad and Jane, who introduced me to cooking, to food, and to literature, and whose love of all three things made me who I am—all the delicious parts of *Aftertaste* are thanks to you. To Max, my very first reader, the world's best brother—thank you for combing this book's Russian-language sections, and for being the light that led me onto my path as a writer. To my in-laws, Ann and Jerry, for being so excited and enthusiastic about every step of this journey; your support, encouragement, and bowls of pasta kept me going to the finish line. To my aunts, uncles, cousins, and extended family—I am extremely lucky to have a family as excited and supportive as you are; I'd be nowhere without you. Special thanks to Freddy, who fact-checked my restaurant scenes against his many years of chef experience; to Marina, who read early and often; and to Brittany, who always asked how it was going, and always wanted to read what I wrote next. Thank you to Logan, Sabrina, and Darren, for always offering me a break and for being excited for Mommy's book news; making you proud is the biggest reason I write. And thank you, most of all, to James—it's impossible to list out everything you've done and continue to do to make our life more magical than Kostya's mouth; your support for my writing and this book are astonishing, and I love you more than there is salt in the sea.

Sincerest thanks to every food service worker I've ever encountered—from the lunch ladies in my elementary school cafeteria to the baristas at my favorite coffee shops to the delivery folks that make it easy to try something new on a Tuesday, all the way up to the Michelin-recognized chefs whose food I've been lucky enough to eat in this lifetime. A little piece of every bite I've ever taken is in these pages.

My eternal gratitude, love, and salt goes to all of my dearly departed. I know you're with me, guiding my hands as they make worlds out of words. I will never forget it.

Finally, to all the readers who've connected with *Aftertaste*—with Kostya, or Maura, or Frankie, or Everleigh (anyone except Kevin, really)—*thank you*. Stories are how we connect with the world, and how we can process some of its most beautiful—and most difficult—moments. If you or someone you know is struggling and needs help, please visit Samaritans at https://www.samaritans.org for a range of resources, or dial the National Suicide Prevention Helpline at 0800 587 0800.